LEGEND OF THE FIVE RINGS

The realm of Rokugan is a land of samurai, courtiers, and mystics, dragons, magic, and divine beings – a world where honor is stronger than steel.

The Seven Great Clans have defended and served the Emperor of the Emerald Empire for a thousand years, in battle and at the imperial court. While conflict and political intrigue divide the clans, the true threat awaits in the darkness of the Shadowlands, behind the vast Kaiu Wall. There, in the twisted wastelands, an evil corruption endlessly seeks the downfall of the empire.

The rules of Rokugani society are strict. Uphold your honor, lest you lose everything in pursuit of glory.

BY THE SAME AUTHOR

ARKHAM HORROR
Wrath of N'kai

WATCH DOGS LEGION
Day Zero (with James Swallow)

ADVENTURES OF THE ROYAL OCCULTIST
The Whitechapel Demon
The Jade Suit of Death
The Infernal Express

EXECUTIONER (as Don Pendleton)
Border Offensive
Arctic Kill
Murder Island
Final Assault

JIM ANTHONY, SUPER DETECTIVE
The Mark of Terror
The Vril Agenda

WARHAMMER 40,000
Deathstorm
Primogenitor
Clonelord
Lukas the Trickster
Apocalypse
Manflayer

THE HORUS HERESY
The Palatine Phoenix

WARHAMMER FANTASY
Knight of the Blazing Sun
Neferata
Road of Skulls
Master of Death
The Serpent Queen
Return of Nagash
Lord of the End Times

WARHAMMER: AGE OF SIGMAR
Skaven Pestilens
The Black Rift
Fury of Gork
The Undying King
Plague Garden
Spear of Shadows
Soul Wars
The Mirrored City
Black Pyramid
Dark Harvest

NECROMUNDA
Sinner's Bounty

Wake the Dead
Dracula Lives!

POISON RIVER

A Daidoji Shin Mystery

JOSH REYNOLDS

First published by Aconyte Books in 2020

ISBN 978 1 83908 019 7

Ebook ISBN 978 1 83908 020 3

Cover art by John Anthony di Giovanni

Rokugan map by Francesca Baerald

Distributed in North America by Simon & Schuster Inc, New York, USA

Printed in the United States of America

9 8 7 6 5 4 3 2 1

ACONYTE BOOKS

An imprint of Asmodee Entertainment Ltd

Mercury House, Shipstones Business Centre

North Gate, Nottingham NG7 7FN, UK

aconytebooks.com // twitter.com/aconytebooks

For Lottie, without whom this book would not be half as good. And for Erik, without whom I would never have attempted to write this book in the first place.

Dragon Lands
Unicorn Lands
CITY OF THE RICH FROG
Rokugan
Lion Lands

CHAPTER ONE
Daidoji Shin

"Cheater!"

A fist came down, punctuating the accusation. Dice rattled on the table.

Daidoji Shin looked up from the game board, his expression mild. "Yes," he said. "I most humbly agree with your assessment."

His accuser paused in shock. The man had the rough-edged look of a sailor; perhaps one of those who plied the harsh waters of the Drowned Merchant River. But the way he handled the gaming tiles spoke to a secondary profession – that of gambler. It took quick hands and a keen mind to make a living that way. Sadly, he appeared to possess the one quality but possibly not the other. "You… admit it?" he grunted.

Shin, in contrast to his accuser, was tall and willowy. His robes were of no particular color and bore no insignia. His white hair had been daubed in oil and ashes, so as to look black in the dim light. The disguise was more for tradition's sake than anything else.

Those of the Crane were expected to make some small effort to hide their origins when they frequented places such as this. It made the lower orders more comfortable if they could pretend they were dicing with a fellow commoner, rather than a scion of one of the Great Clans. Though he was somewhat estranged at the moment. A little matter of an illicit rendezvous, soon to be cleared up he was certain. And if not, well, there were worse fates than being estranged.

He studied his accuser. "That you are a cheater? I do not see how one can deny it. But I thought it rude to say anything, seeing as how I am a newcomer to this fine establishment. I assumed it was a – a test of sorts. Bit of a joke on the new player." He looked around the gambling den, as if to assure himself of this supposition.

It was an ugly little knot of a place, as such houses of vice often were. In Shin's opinion, the uglier the better. Pretty facades were for tradesmen. For one such as himself, gilt and glamour were little more than distractions for the senses. He longed for a spot of discordance in his otherwise orderly existence.

It consisted of a single room, built around a central fire-pit. The air was thick with smoke, the stink of spilled sake and the odor of rotting fish. The slap of water against the wharfs could be heard in the occasional lull of voices and music. Tables and benches were crowded with gamblers and hangers-on. Dice rattled and tiles clacked.

Shin's accuser hesitated, parsing the sudden flow of words. "I'm not the cheater here. You are." His hand dropped meaningfully to the knife sheathed at his side. Shin's serene gaze flicked to the blade, and then back. His expression did not change.

"A meritless accusation. And somewhat unfair, given that I am merely playing by the rules you established. Perhaps you wish to reconsider?" Shin smiled. "Come, I will even buy you a drink. In fact, drinks all around!" There was a murmur of appreciation from around the room at this show of generosity. The other men at the table nodded.

"No. I don't drink with cheaters."

"Then you'll be drinking alone, for we're all equally guilty I fear." Shin looked around speculatively, but none of the other players met his gaze. He nodded in satisfaction. "As I thought." He looked back at his accuser. "You see? Now sit. We will continue, and may the most cunning cheat win."

His accuser stared at him. Shin could read the other man's face as easily as a scribe might read a book. There was anger there, but mostly consternation. This was not going how his accuser had foreseen. Shin suspected that this scene had almost certainly occurred with regularity in this establishment – accuse the newcomer, demand compensation and send them packing before they realized what had happened. A good game, and profitable.

But Shin was not interested in that sort of game tonight. He felt a tremor of obstreperousness deep within himself. It was a familiar sensation – an urge to be contrary. It was an affliction of the mind and soul that had gripped him since his youth, putting him ever at odds with his family, and it showed no signs of lessening with age.

He studied his accuser and allowed himself a smile. It was the sort of smile that a foolish man could not help but see as provocation. His accuser reacted as he expected. The hand on the knife clenched and the blade came free with a savage whisper. The gambling den fell silent in an instant.

Shin rose. His accuser halted, uncertain. Shin spread his hands to show that he carried no blade. A man with a sword was more likely to get into trouble than a man without, to Shin's way of thinking. He hadn't even brought his wakizashi. "Think carefully now," he said. "Is spilling my guts really what you want to do?"

The attack was clumsy, untrained. The gambler was a brawler, skills honed in back-alley skirmishes. Shin, however, had been trained by some of the finest warriors in Rokugan – when it had suited him to pay attention to their lessons. He stepped back, caught his seat up without looking and whipped it around between them. The knife lodged deep in the wood, and it was a simple matter to send both chair and blade crashing out of reach with a flick of his wrists. The gambler hesitated, eyes widening.

That moment of reflection was his undoing. Shin slapped him on the nose, not hard, but firmly. The way one might discipline an unruly animal. The gambler stumbled back, clutching at his face. Shin did not pursue. "Let that be an end to it," he said, loudly. "Else I might begin to take offense."

All eyes were on the confrontation now. Some more hostile than others. Benches and stools scraped back across the dirt floor, and men rose. Five of them. They were rough-looking and well-armed for their surroundings, with knives, axes and one spear.

Shin frowned. The odds were no longer in his favor. It was time to make a rapid, yet elegant, retreat – something he'd done more than once over the years. As the men advanced on him, he shoved aside one of his fellow players, snatched up the man's chair and slung it towards the approaching thugs. Then he turned and ran. He heard a crash and shouts, but didn't look back. He went out the door, sliding in the muck of the street as he fought for balance.

Dogs barked and someone cried out from a nearby doorway as he raced down the narrow alley towards the river. This part of the city was a warren of crooked streets and stalls, the last vestige of the humble fishing village it had once been. It was early morning, and even the river birds were still asleep.

He turned a tight corner onto a side-street, following the sound of water, and slid to a stop. A figure waited for him at the other end, illuminated by the lanterns strung across the mouth of the street. She was clad in lacquered armor the color of stormy skies and bore two blades sheathed at her side – katana and wakizashi. Her face was uncovered, and her hair bound atop her head. Her expression was, as ever, disapproving.

"You are an idiot," she said, sternly.

Shin smiled. "Hello, Kasami. I thought you were sleeping."

Her expression became thunderous. Hiramori Kasami had been born in the Uebe marshes, daughter of a vassal family. But the Crane were not ones to let a simple accident of birth obfuscate potential. She was now a blade of the clan, honed to a killing edge. A fact that was evident even to the most foolish of men. She was also his bodyguard, something that no doubt pained her to no end. "Is that why you chose to sneak out without alerting me?" she demanded.

Shin shrugged. "Well, that, and I knew you'd try and stop me."

She made a sound low in her throat, somewhere between a sigh and a growl. "How can I protect you if you insist on leaving me behind?"

"Did it ever occur to you that might be the point of these excursions?" Shin turned at the sound of running footsteps. "Either way, you'll be happy to know I've reconsidered. You may resume your duties now."

Kasami's reply was lost in the blistering torrent of curses that heralded the arrival of the gambler and his associates. The newcomers slid to an undignified halt as Kasami drew her katana and fell into a ready stance. The sight of the blade silenced them.

The gambler pushed his way to the fore and stopped, a perplexed look on his face. He looked from Shin to Kasami in growing realization. That someone like her was here now implied that Shin was no mere mark for the taking, but someone of substance. Someone who had seen his face, and those of his comrades. Shin watched the look of calculation on the man's face become one of fear. He went pale, and took a half-step back. Kasami's gaze fell on him with predatory focus, and he froze.

"I did warn you," Shin said. "But some men's ears are closed, even to the whisper of fortune." He smiled thinly. "Kill… three of them. That will serve as an object lesson, I think."

She glanced at him. "No."

"Very well. Kill all of them."

She stepped back and sheathed her sword without flourish. "If you want them dead, do it yourself. I'm not here to clean up after you."

"But you are here to keep me alive. And they do intend to murder me."

"Looks to me like you provoked them."

Shin frowned. "I am your lord, you know."

"No. Your grandfather is my lord. You are my burden."

Shin's expression became one of injured innocence. "Well that's just hurtful, Kasami. And after all my efforts to show you a good time since we arrived..."

She snorted and leaned back against the wall of the street, her hand resting atop the hilt of her blade. She looked at the gambler and gestured. "Well? Have at it."

The gambler and his associates had been watching this interaction with bemusement. Now they looked at one another, uncertain as to how to proceed. Sympathetic to their situation, Shin decided to lend his counsel. "She won't interfere, of that you may be certain. She's quite serious about all of this, more's the pity." He held up a finger in warning. "But, should something untoward happen to my person, she may well take offense."

Kasami nodded. "It would be my duty – as well as my pleasure – to avenge you." Her smile was as sharp and as cold as a sword's edge.

Shin spread his hands. "There. You see?"

The gambler licked his lips, considering the matter. But, once again, he proved himself a fool. "There's only two of them. Kill them both. Then we're in the clear."

Shin glanced at Kasami. She sighed and stepped away from the wall, loosening her blade in its scabbard. He turned, and the gambler came for him in a rush. Shin sidestepped and drove the stiffened edge of his hand into the back of the man's neck. The gambler fell in a heap, the knife clattering from his grip. Shin scooped it up and whirled – but there was no need for haste. Kasami, as ever, had the matter well in hand.

She twitched her blade, freeing it of blood. Four of the gambler's associates were dead in as many moments. The fifth, merely injured. But from the look of him, he would not last the night. He sat against the wall, face waxen, arms tight about a belly threatening to spill its contents onto the filthy street. Shin sighed. "I thought you weren't going to kill them."

"I had little choice." She turned and looked down at the gambler. "What about him?"

Shin tossed aside the knife. "I think he's learned his lesson." He crouched beside the other man and prodded him with a finger. "Haven't you?"

The gambler whimpered. Shin poked him again. "What's your name?"

"K- Kitano," the gambler stuttered. He stared at the remains of his associates, already attracting flies. "Don't… don't kill me, my lord, please."

"I wouldn't dream of it, Kitano. But Kasami is quite adamant on the subject of leaving witnesses." Shin leaned close. "That said, one might be able to make an exception if an individual were to, say, make himself of use. Do you understand?"

Kitano swallowed and nodded. "Y- yes."

"Good man. A word of warning – I wouldn't make yourself difficult to locate, when next I come calling. Kasami might lose patience and you wouldn't want that…" Shin gave the bodies a meaningful glance. Kitano nodded jerkily. Shin rose to his feet.

"Enjoy the rest of your night. And my thanks for a most entertaining evening."

CHAPTER TWO
Deliveries and Demands

The teahouse had no name. It sat alone on a narrow, stinking street opposite the Unicorn docks, and catered to a very small clientele. To find it, you had to know where it was. To know where it was, you had to be invited by the owner.

Captain Lun had received an invitation years ago, though she'd rarely had the inclination to visit. She preferred stronger spirits. She studied the teahouse with her good eye from across the street. The sun was a pale pink streak along the edge of the rooftops and the evening mist receded, stripping the streets bare. She could hear the sounds of the city waking up – or, in some cases, going to sleep.

The merchant had asked her to come the morning after delivery for the rest of her payment, and she was impatient to collect it and be away. A boat was no good to anyone in its berth. It was only profitable in motion. Much like its crew, and its captain.

Lun dressed like a common sailor, despite her rank – bare

feet, bare arms, and her hair cropped short. She'd learned early on that advertising rank was a bad idea. She touched her patch, her fingers trailing down to the scars that marked her cheek like cracks in porcelain. The eye was lesson enough. She'd had no desire to lose anything else.

"I hate this place," her bosun, Torun, muttered. Torun was a short man, and round like a statue of Hotei, the Fortune of Contentment. Despite his appearance, Torun was not especially jolly or friendly. But he got the best out of the crew of trash she was forced to ride the river with.

"But you like being paid," Lun said, without looking at him. She scratched the inside of her wrist where a faded tattoo of a crane's feather marked her sun-browned skin. Like her eye, it was a memento of a simpler time.

Torun grunted. "There is that." He leaned over and spat onto the street. "You should have gone out with us last night."

"I like to keep my money close, not gamble it away."

"Some pretty bird from one of the clans showed his face. Nearly got it stomped in, too. Shame, as he was winning up until then."

"What happened to him?"

"No clue. Probably dead in an alley, somewhere. Or floating in the river."

"Good." Lun pushed away from the wall where she'd been leaning. "Wait here."

"Are you certain?"

She glanced at him. "Worried about me, or the money?"

Torun grinned. "Why not both?"

Lun snorted and shook her head. "Stay here, Torun. Keep an eye on the street."

"Aye, Captain."

She made her way across the street, bare feet splashing heedlessly through puddles. She kept one hand on her sword as she ducked through the curtain and went inside. The sharkskin hilt was a comfort. The blade was solid. Reliable. A marine's blade, meant for bloody work in close quarters.

Lun had been a marine, once. A soldier. She had thought there was nothing better than to serve her masters. To fight in their name, for the glory of the Crane. But experience had cured her of that particular foolishness. She'd learned that it wasn't the samurai who went hungry, who stumbled barefoot through snowy passes and along rainy roads. It wasn't samurai who were left screaming on the deck of a burning ship, an arrow jutting from their head. It wasn't samurai who died, and died, and died.

There were better ways to make a living than dying for a piece of blue cloth.

The teahouse was all but empty this early – or this late. The proprietor, a fat little man with half a nose and a kimono that looked as if it should have been buried rather than worn, barely acknowledged her. She returned the favor by ignoring him and striding to the back. The wooden floors creaked under her feet as she made her way down a tight corridor to what would normally have been a supply room.

The merchant, Saiga, was waiting for her in his office. It was a small room, and cramped. Crates and sacks of what she knew to be illicitly obtained cargo were piled along the patched and tattered walls.

Saiga's desk sat opposite the door, in front of low shelves burdened with ledgers and papers. The desk was the nicest thing in the room, Saiga included. He was short and bulky, with a soldier's build under homespun robes that didn't quite fit him. His face was round, like a sling bullet, solid and smooth but not soft. Nothing about Saiga was soft.

He knelt before his desk, a ledger open before him. He'd been making notes when she entered. "Ah, Captain. As punctual as ever. Sit, please. Tea?" He gestured to the tea set beside his elbow, but she shook her head.

"No tea."

Saiga nodded. "Just the money, then?"

Lun sat, but didn't reply. Saiga sighed and reached into his robes. He produced a pouch and began extracting coins. "That's why I like you, Lun. Right to business. None of this false courtesy."

"Courtesy is for samurai."

Saiga laughed. "How right you are." He stacked coins on his desk. "No problems, then? With the delivery, I mean." Saiga had hired her vessel to deliver a load of rice to the Lion docks the previous morning. It had likely been stolen from another shipment, but Lun didn't worry about such niceties. She hadn't stolen it, and knew nothing other than what the paperwork said.

"The usual. The Lion are on edge."

Saiga chuckled. "The Lion are always on edge."

"They like to complain, the Lion. Said the shipment was short."

Saiga frowned and paused. "I hope you showed them the papers. They got what they paid for, not a grain more or less."

"I did."

"And?" Saiga asked, as he resumed his stacking.

"They still complained."

He sighed. "Of course they did." He smiled ingratiatingly as he pushed the coins towards her. "A most adequate job, Captain. You exceeded my expectations."

"You hired me to deliver rice, Saiga. Let's not make it something other than what it was." Lun reached out and scooped the coins into her own pouch. She fixed him with her good eye. "That said, if you should wish to hire us again, I'm at your service."

Saiga sat back. His smile didn't waver. "I may well require your services in the future. But for the moment, enjoy your largesse." He paused. "You are berthed at the Unicorn docks?"

"For the moment."

"I ask only on the off chance I should need you."

Lun considered this. She didn't trust Saiga. He was oily, even for a merchant. But he was no cheat. He'd always dealt fairly with her, which made him practically a saint in her eyes. "Willow Quay," she said, flatly. "You know it?"

Saiga arched an eyebrow. Lun laughed and stood. "Yeah, I figured you knew it. That's where I'll be. If you decide you require my services, you can find me there."

"Good to know," he said. He made to continue when the sound of a floorboard creaking made him pause. "Did someone come with you?"

"No," Lun's hand fell to her sword. "A raid?"

"I'm all paid up for the season," Saiga said. "Who's out there?" he called.

"Me," a male voice replied. "I need to speak to you."

Saiga grimaced. He looked at Lun. "I can trust you to keep your mouth shut, yes?"

She stared at him without replying. He snorted. "Stupid

question. My apologies." He pushed himself to his feet. "Come in, I'm just concluding some business."

The man who entered looked nervous. He shied away as Lun made for the door. "Who's she?" the newcomer demanded.

"No one," Saiga said. "Lun, close the door behind you."

Lun did, weighing the coin pouch on her palm as she did so. She paused in the corridor, tempted to eavesdrop. Saiga had been tense, and the other man had seemed downright afraid. She shook her head and kept walking.

Whatever was going on, it was no business of hers.

Eito Saiga relaxed when he heard the creak of the boards signaling Lun's departure. He sat back and looked at his guest. "You are a fool," he said, bluntly. The noise from the teahouse was muted back here in his rundown little office. Crates and sacks of unclaimed or newly purchased cargo were stacked against the walls, further muffling the sounds from elsewhere in the building. The office was small, but it had served him well enough for a number of years. It was close to the wharfs where most of his business originated, and well hidden from prying eyes.

"Watch how you speak to me, merchant," the other man said. He was tall and dressed like a rich man's idea of a poor man, meaning he looked like a rather prosperous merchant. Saiga, in contrast, looked like a poor merchant in rough homespun.

For all intents and purposes, a poor merchant was what he was. A known buyer and seller of black market goods. A thief and a fence. That was the mask that he presented to the world, and sometimes he thought it was who he would always be.

But in his quieter moments, he hoped not. He hoped,

someday, that his loyalty would be rewarded and he would be allowed to serve his clan in the open. Even if it wasn't the likely end for a man like him.

"I will speak to you how I wish, given the situation you have put us in," Saiga snapped, annoyed by his guest's tone. He knocked a fist against the surface of the small writing desk set before him. "How did she find you?"

"I was hoping you could tell me."

"And how would I know that?"

"She only came looking for me because you refused to pay her!"

Saiga paused. "Ah." That put a new light on things. "She said that?"

"Not directly, no. She left a note pinned to my desk where anyone might have seen it."

"No need to raise your voice. I understand that this is upsetting."

"Why did you not pay her?" His guest was becoming more agitated. He was not used to this, and it showed. If Saiga did not placate him, his nerves might well get the best of him.

Saiga frowned. "I intended to. But she decided to be foolish. She wanted more money than such a task was worth. I assumed we were haggling. It appears I was mistaken." He shook his head, annoyed at himself. He'd known better, but the shinobi's manner had irritated him, and he'd allowed himself to act spitefully – and foolishly. "I warned you about hiring such a person. There are people in the city who would have done it for less… Chobei, for instance. He and his cadre could have undertaken this task with no difficulty…"

His guest frowned. "The whole point was to hire someone

with no ties to the city, and a pressing reason to be elsewhere soon after the deed was done. Which, you assured me, she was."

Saiga sighed. As far as he'd been aware the shinobi had been perfect for the task at hand. Over his years of service he had developed a number of contacts, experienced in determining such things on his behalf. One of them had recommended a renegade daughter of the Cat – Nekoma Okuni. Saiga had not delved into the whys and wherefores of her exile, or the circumstances that had brought her to such a state, but had duly extended an offer through the appropriate channels.

Even so, he had been against hiring the shinobi from the start, but his guest had been adamant. They'd insisted that it was a necessary component of their scheme. A scheme that Saiga privately found to be overly intricate and far too complex for its result. Then, that was the danger of dealing with an amateur. Especially one who thought himself a strategist.

"What do you intend to do?" he asked, finally.

"She wants to meet. At dusk."

Saiga frowned. "Well, you certainly can't do that."

"I don't see that I have any choice."

"You could not go. That is a choice."

"And what if she tells someone? Our whole plan will come unraveled." There was a hint of fear in his voice.

"Your plan," Saiga said.

"You helped me!"

"A fact that I am starting to regret." Saiga looked away. "I was a fool, and I allowed you to exploit my foolishness…"

"Your loyalty, you mean." A pause. "Or was I mistaken?"

Saiga's gaze snapped around and his guest shrank back. "I am loyal. But not to you. To the clan. Do not forget that."

"And you should not forget what is at stake," his guest said, rallying slightly. He straightened, chin up and chest out, trying for a bravado he obviously didn't feel. "You agreed with me that this was a necessary thing – the best thing – for the clan. If our deception should be discovered, we will come to ruin and our efforts will be for naught."

Saiga bit back a sharp reply. The other man was right, of course. And it was something he had planned for. But there was no reason to tell his guest that. "Where are you meeting her?"

"Three Duck Street, wherever that is."

"Near the Foxfire Theater," Saiga said, idly. Which made sense, given their shinobi's double-life. He shook his head. Another needless complication, in his opinion. "Are you to meet her alone?"

"Of course. No one will recognize me there of all places." The way he said it made clear his feelings on both the theater and those who patronized it.

"Yes, well, I urge you again not to do so. Let me handle it."

"I left you to handle it, and you bungled it. So, I must do it myself. I will see what she wants, and then confer with you." His guest rose, face set in a grimace of determination. "Do nothing until you hear from me. Is that understood?"

Saiga hesitated. "Yes."

"Good. Now, I must get back. Is there a way out of here without being seen?"

"The way you came in." Saiga smiled at the expression on his guest's face. "I assure you, no one is paying attention to you. They know better."

His guest frowned in distaste. "Even so, I will be glad when this is over and I can pretend that we have never met."

"As will I." Saiga watched the other man go and silently cursed the day he'd made the fellow's acquaintance. Despite himself, he'd found that he agreed with his reluctant partner on a number of subjects – including those related to the current political quagmire that grasped the city.

It was time for a change. Sudden or gradual, it didn't matter – so long as the change brought benefit to Saiga's masters. But he was starting to see that they'd made a mistake. Ambition had blinded him to the real consequences of this scheme.

He'd thought to upset the balance of the city, but never considered that his own was just as vulnerable. His identity – the life he'd made for himself – was all at risk because of a single, wayward shinobi.

He sat back on his cushion and tried to shake the sudden sense of weariness that gripped him. Then he picked up a new sheet of paper and a bottle of ink. There was no choice now. He had to let his master know what had happened – and accept the consequences. Whatever they might be.

His hand was shaking as he started to write.

CHAPTER THREE
An Afternoon's Entertainment

"What were you thinking?" Kasami growled. Her voice echoed through the private box and nearby patrons of the Foxfire Theater turned, startled by the sudden noise. Shin sighed and readied himself for the tirade to come. It wasn't the first he had endured today, and it almost certainly wouldn't be the last.

If he were being honest with himself, he found that he enjoyed it. It was rare that anyone bothered to take him to task, especially these days. The novelty of Kasami's opprobrium had yet to wear thin, especially when her fury overrode her diction and her accent roughened ever so slightly. He knew she was truly angry when certain rural invectives, common to the Uebe Marshes, crept into her speech.

Idly, he smoothed his kimono. After returning home he had bathed and slept, but only for a few hours. He needed no more than that; he'd found that too much dulled his perceptions. Awakening refreshed, he'd dressed for the day's entertainment. His kimono was of the finest blue silk, and emblazoned with a pattern designed to draw the eye. His white hair was drawn back from his narrow features. He cut a handsome figure, he thought, though modesty prevented him from saying as much.

"I asked you a question." Kasami made a slicing gesture, cutting off his reply even as he opened his mouth. "No. The answer is – you weren't." She pointed an accusing finger at him. "Or rather, you were thinking only of your own pleasure, as always."

"Not entirely," Shin said. He waved his fan apologetically at their neighbors as he spoke. She wasn't speaking loudly enough to be heard, but one could not help but notice her gesticulations. "I thought you might enjoy a night free of your burden. Was I wrong in that?"

"Your generosity is appreciated. But next time you will do me the courtesy of letting me know. Or better yet – not going to some back-alley gambling den at all. Are you that much of a fool? Have you learned nothing since the last time?"

"I have, as a matter of fact. I'm much better at dice, for one thing. And in any event, that was a year ago, and in another city. We are here now and I intend to enjoy myself to the fullest extent of this city's hospitality."

"By which you mean gambling, drinking, whoring and making a spectacle of yourself," Kasami said, bluntly. "The very things that got you – and me – in this mess in the first place."

"This mess, as you call it, is a great opportunity for both of us," Shin said. "The City of the Rich Frog is far from the prying eyes of the Crane, or the politicking of the Winter Court. We can both relax here, serene in the knowledge that our responsibilities are minimal and no one cares about us in the least."

As he spoke, he let his eyes roam the playhouse. It was a sturdy affair, small in the way of such places, and tucked into an out of the way street just off the main thoroughfare leading from the docks. Orange lanterns lit the exterior, advertising the performance. Inside, it looked like a hundred other playhouses he'd patronized in his time.

The stage occupied the majority of the space, stretching across the far wall and jutting pugnaciously into the audience. The flower path extended through the ground floor benches, bisecting the space at intervals. From this walkway the actors would strut and preen amongst the audience, or else make a dramatic exit.

There were three levels of seating. The lowest level, on the ground floor, was for the poorest patrons. They were closer to the stage, but had only rough benches to sit on, if that. Slightly above this was a level of public boxes, set aside for well-to-do tradesmen and merchants. And above them were the private boxes of the nobility. Shin had rented one such box for himself and Kasami. It was a somewhat cramped affair, but the benches were cushioned and one could recline however slightly.

The air was stultifying, however. The playhouse was too warm, even for spring. There was condensation on the beams and sweat beaded on his forehead. But such discomforts were a minor price to pay for entertainment. A bit of sweat never hurt anyone, after all. And it was well worth it.

Kabuki was another of his passions. Nowhere else could one find such a diverse crowd gathered under one roof, united in their enjoyment. It was a place to see and be seen, and he spied a number of notable faces in the boxes opposite his, including Iuchi Konomi, daughter of the Unicorn representative Iuchi

Shichiro, and Kaeru Azuma, one of the more highly ranked ronin in Governor Tetsua's service.

He saw others like himself as well – representatives of clans that had no claim on the city, but an interest in trade regardless. One box even held a group of masked and veiled Scorpion dignitaries. Shin raised his fan in polite greeting, and received not so much as a nod in return. Then, the Scorpion had a peculiar notion of courtesy.

Shin snapped his fan open and attempted to stir the stuffy air of the box. The outer spokes of it were made from sharpened steel, and it could be employed as a weapon should it become necessary.

He preferred the war-fan to the sword, even going so far as to learn the iron fan technique from a courtier of his acquaintance. She herself had supposedly learned that art, among others, from a tengu in the Shinomen Forest, though Shin wasn't sure he believed that particular claim.

He fancied he was reasonably skilled with the fan, though he doubted he could match a trained swordsman in open combat. Still, that was what he had Kasami for. And, failing that, he was something of a swordsman himself – though he much preferred to humble his opponents with discourse rather than decapitation.

"I don't see why you have to be so… so…" Kasami groped for the correct invective.

"Charming?" Shin offered. "Interesting? Entertaining?"

"Frustrating," she said, with a glare.

Shin hid his smile behind his fan. "I am what I wish to be."

"And that is selfish." She sat back, arms folded. "You are selfish." She plucked at her kimono as she spoke, clearly uncomfortable – though whether that was due to her clothing or the accusation, he could not say. Shin watched her fidget for a moment. It was rare to see her dressed in anything less than full armor. She faced each day as if preparing for war.

Despite his amusement, he chose his next words carefully. "Why deny myself the pleasures of life in order to please those who give me no thought at all, save when I might be of use to them?"

"You're talking about your grandfather."

"Among others."

Kasami looked at him. "You should show him more respect."

"I tried that once. Neither of us enjoyed the experience." Shin snapped his fan closed. "He thinks I am an embarrassment. That suits me just fine."

Kasami started to speak, and then fell silent and looked away. Shin hid a frown. Despite everything, he was fond of Kasami. She was loyal, if somewhat stodgy, and lethal when provoked. An excellent companion for someone like himself, though he had no doubt that she wished it were otherwise.

That was one of the reasons he allowed her such leeway. It was a sign of respect, though she might not recognize it as such. He liked to think that she did, even if she would never admit it. Kasami kept him honest with the world – and with himself most of all. An invaluable service, and one he could not afford to dispense with.

He sighed and turned his attentions back to the stage. The traditional kabuki performance combined many aspects into one cohesive whole. It was like watching some ornate mechanism, comprised of several dozen moving parts. This particular play was set during the Battle of White Stag, though it featured little in the way of stage combat, focusing more on the immensely awkward romantic entanglements of a young samurai and a gaijin. It was almost a comedy of errors – if one ignored the tragic conclusion.

It was also several hours long, which made for a full afternoon. Kasami had yet to make it through a performance awake. Shin, who had more stamina, found it somewhat short by his standards. A play was at its best when it had room to breathe – anything less than five hours made for terse storytelling.

Kasami looked at him. "Why did you have me spare that fool last night? He tried to murder you."

"And now he owes me his life. A man like that has many uses."

"You mean he can sniff out more depravity for you to indulge in."

"Among other things." Shin gestured languidly. "He was a sailor – perhaps still is. Sailors are useful sorts of fellows, especially when one lives alongside a river."

"How do you know he was a sailor?"

"His dress, his walk, his knife, the curses he employed so liberally, all speak to a life lived on the water. His fellows were sailors as well, I suspect. No doubt some captain is now lamenting the disappearance of a substantial portion of his crew."

"You're the one who told me to kill them," she said, stung.

"I was bluffing, obviously."

"I don't bluff," she replied. "Daidoji do not bluff."

"Oh of course we do, and frequently," he said, dismissively. "We bluff our enemies, we bluff our friends, we'd bluff the gods themselves if there was some gain in it for the Crane. There was no gain in their deaths for me."

"Other than preserving your life, you mean."

"Other than that, yes. In any event, he may come in handy. Commoners are not deaf, dumb and blind you know. Despite what some samurai might think." He gave her a pointed look. "They gossip as much as any courtier, and often know things that their betters are not privy to."

"Does that mean you're actually going to take your responsibilities here seriously?"

Shin turned back to the stage. "Time will tell. Now be quiet. The performance is beginning, and I do not wish to miss a moment of it."

Kasami immediately tuned out the performance in order to imagine herself anywhere else. It would last most of the day, and she settled in for a long haul. She had always thought that a samurai should be above such base entertainments. Let the lower orders waste their coin on the stamping and yelling of itinerant actors. There were greater joys to be had in contemplating the correct fold of an origami shape than in listening to some pompous fool belt out a soliloquy. Shin did not agree, however.

Despite her boredom, she did not let her guard slip. More than one nobleman had met his end in the comfort of a private box. Shin would not be one of them. She glanced at him and frowned. She had been so proud at first. Her family had served the Daidoji for centuries, and to be chosen as a bodyguard for one of their sons was a high honor.

Then she had met Shin.

He was quick of wit, but licentious and lazy. He parceled out his honor in gambling dens and sake houses, racking up debts and making enemies. He seemed to have no ambition beyond wasting as much money as possible. He could be kind, in his way, and was less concerned about propriety than most, but taken together with everything else it made him seem a hapless fool. A wastrel, of no note or importance save in his name.

Or such was his intent. After more than a year in his company, she had come to realize that there was some flicker of potential in him. If anything, it only made matters worse. It was as if he were deliberately wasting his talents. Maybe it was nothing more than adolescent truculence carrying over into adulthood. Some men were like that.

She glanced at the stage. A swirl of garish costumes and shouting performers filled the space, engaged in a largely senseless plot involving mistaken identities, star-crossed lovers and a giant skeleton. Shin had attempted to explain the intricacies of kabuki to her on several occasions, but she had little interest in such things.

He leaned forward suddenly, eyes narrowed. "Hmm. That's odd."

She looked at him. "What?"

"I've seen this performance twice now. Both times the role of the young samurai was played by Nekoma Okuni." He pointed at the stage with his fan. "But this time, it's someone else. Curious."

"Is it?"

"Yes. No announcement was made. Therefore, it must have been a last-minute substitution. I wonder what's wrong."

"Why would you think something is wrong?"

"Because otherwise she would be on stage." He sat back, frowning.

"Why does it matter?"

Shin didn't look at her. "It doesn't. I was merely curious."

Kasami eyed him knowingly. She was all too familiar with Shin's preferences when it came to female companionship. He liked women of a certain character – or lack thereof. "Merely curious," she repeated.

Shin continued not to look at her. "Are you implying something?"

"No."

"Good."

"Maybe she took ill."

"Maybe," he said, but his tone was doubtful.

There was a soft knock on the door. Kasami glanced at Shin. Without turning from the stage, he twitched a finger, and she rose to answer it. She slid the door open, and a kneeling servant offered up a scroll in silence. Kasami took it and gestured for the man to depart before closing the door. "Message," she said, tossing it to Shin.

He caught it deftly and examined the wax seal, even giving it a cursory sniff before slicing it open with one of the steel blades hidden in his fan. He gave a soft grunt of surprise. "Well. Isn't that interesting? I've been invited to Saibanshoki at my earliest convenience. Governor Tetsua wishes to speak to me."

"The governor – why would he want to see you?"

"I have no idea." He smiled widely. "But I am most interested to find out."

"Does that mean we get to leave early?"

"Sadly, yes. But before we go, I will need you to deliver an invitation to the master of the troupe."

Kasami perked up. "What? Why?"

"I wish to properly thank him for the quality of the performance."

Kasami looked at him in disbelief. After enduring her baleful stare for a few moments he sighed, and added, "Fine. I am curious as to Okuni's whereabouts. I wish to ask him what happened to her."

"I knew it."

"It is harmless curiosity, I assure you," he protested. "Nothing more."

She shook her head and bit back a sulphurous reply.

"Does that mean you'll do it?" he pressed.

"Yes," she said through gritted teeth.

Shin smiled cheerfully and turned back to the performance. "Why thank you, Kasami. It is a comfort to know that I can always count on you."

CHAPTER FOUR
An Actor's Life

Backstage, Wada Sanemon, master of the Three Flower Troupe, gnawed his cuticles in frustration. The audience had noticed. Of course they'd noticed. Okuni was the draw, she always had been. Without her, the troupe faltered. They tried their best, but she was the heart of every performance, and she damn well knew it. But some things were more important, according to her.

He growled softly into his fists. Nekoma Okuni was good at acting, but a bad actress. "Why me?" he muttered. "What did I ever do to deserve this?"

"Would you like a list, or a brief summation?" a voice inquired. Sanemon glanced over to see one of his actors, Nao. Tall and effete, Nao could pass easily for either a man or a woman, depending on his mood.

"What do you want, Nao?"

"Is she not back yet?" Nao asked, in amused tones. "How unexpectedly rude of her."

Sanemon glared at the actor. Nao was wearing Okuni's costume, and doing so with admirable grace. He often played multiple parts in plays, and had achieved some renown for his ability to shift from one role to the next in full view of the audience, as well as to transition seamlessly from the more popular bombastic style of acting to a gentler, more realistic performance. Transformation dances were all the rage this season, and Nao was adept at making the awkward business of turning a double-sided kimono inside out look magical.

"No. She is not back yet."

Nao quirked an eyebrow and came to stand beside him. "This isn't the first time our kitty cat has gone astray, Master."

"Nor will it be the last," Sanemon said. "Shouldn't you be on stage?"

"Not quite. Do you think anyone has noticed?"

"Yes."

"Of course they have," Nao said. "I'm much prettier than her. And a better actor."

Sanemon looked at him. "Is there something you need, Nao? Or are you just trying to get under my skin?"

"The others are worried. They have asked me to speak for them."

Sanemon snorted. "More like you took it upon yourself, but go on."

Nao frowned. "Unusual as it may be, I am being serious. It's not like her to miss a performance. Something has gone wrong."

"Of course it has. This is kabuki, Nao. Something always goes wrong. But we persevere, because it is our calling."

Nao rolled his eyes. "This is different and you know it. She's done something foolish, and now it's biting all our tails."

Sanemon scrubbed his cheeks with his palms. "And what am I supposed to do about it exactly?" He closed his eyes and pinched the bridge of his nose. The incipient headache he'd felt brewing earlier had arrived in force. The noise from the stage wasn't helping. Nao was right, of course. Nao was always right.

"Find her, before she gets us into more trouble. Remember what happened in Tsuma?"

Sanemon winced. "This isn't Tsuma."

"No. It's a larger city, and therefore more dangerous." Nao swatted him affectionately with the folded fan. "You're a good master, Sanemon. I'd hate to abandon you."

"But you will."

Nao laughed. "In a heartbeat. An actor of my caliber cannot afford to be seen with riffraff." He paused. "Also, I would like very much not to die. At least, not in a squalid river port such as this."

"This is one of the most important trade hubs in Rokugan."

"That doesn't mean it's attractive. Oh – there's my cue." Nao swatted Sanemon with the fan again and strode off. "Time to make my second big entrance of the night."

Sanemon watched the actor go, and briefly imagined tipping a load of scenery onto his head. But the idle pleasure of that daydream was soon replaced by an all too familiar anxiety. It happened every time Okuni left on one of her errands. One day, he knew, she might not come back. And what then? Back to the gutter where she'd found him?

He looked down at his hands, battered and scarred as they were. The hands of a cutthroat and a peasant, not the master of a performing troupe. It had been a long time since he'd held any blade heavier than a carving knife, but he thought he still remembered how to use a spear well enough. Ashigaru were always needed – experienced soldiers even more so.

His hands curled into fists. No. Better the gutter than that. Running backwards never got anyone anywhere, and Sanemon desperately wanted to be somewhere.

He lowered his hands and deliberately smoothed his kimono. Shabby as it was, it was a sign of his status. A status he had fought for, bled for, and would keep. He was master of this troupe and nothing would change that. Not even his debt to Nekoma Okuni.

The performance went by with treacly slowness. Sanemon distracted himself by standing just off stage and exhorting his actors to greater heights of emotion with gestures and silently mouthed obscenities. It did little to calm him, but it gave him something to focus on besides Okuni's absence.

When that no longer proved engaging, he turned his attentions to ensuring that a steady supply of food and drink was brought in from the teahouses near the theater. It was best to keep the audience well-fed and lubricated, especially in this heat.

The teahouses were only too happy to provide refreshments. He paid them enough, after all. He ran a hand over his shaved pate, trying not to think about cost. It was more expensive to put on a proper performance than most people realized. You had to rent a theater, pay off the local gangs, provide food – and that wasn't even taking into account paying the members of your troupe, most of whom drank like fish and made it a point to cause as much trouble as possible when not on stage.

It was enough to make a man think about tossing himself into the river.

As the afternoon wore on his worry grew. It wasn't like Okuni to be gone this long, not without sending a message. Something had happened. He went back to gnawing on his fingernails, trying not to think the worst.

The performance, at least, was going well. A few hiccups; some broken props, a few missed lines and a slightly off-key song, but nothing the audience would notice. He retreated backstage to find something to occupy his mind.

He slid open doors and bellowed at the stagehands to cease their gambling and get ready to work. Repairs needed to be made to both costumes and props, and the trickwork of the stage required checking before the next scene. There was nothing more embarrassing than a trapdoor that wouldn't open – or worse yet, refused to close.

Behind him, someone cleared their throat and he whirled, diatribe brewing. The words died in his throat when he saw who it was. The woman was short and stocky, but clad in a richly appointed kimono the color of a summer sky. She wore it uneasily, as if used to something heavier, and her hand rested on the hilt of her wakizashi.

Sanemon swallowed. He knew a samurai when he saw one. "Are you in need of something, my lady?" he asked, tremulously.

She fixed him with a cold eye. "Direct me to the troupe-master."

"I- I am he, my lady. Wada Sanemon, at your service." He bowed as low as his substantial girth allowed. She peered down her nose at him, and he felt the urge to flee. "How might I be of assistance to one such as yourself?"

"I have a message from my lord, Daidoji Shin. He wishes to invite you to his residence, before your next performance two days from now. Will you attend?" The way she said it implied that she, herself, was not interested in his response, but that he had best make it quickly.

"He… does?" Sanemon blinked. "I- I am honored, of course, but might I ask why?" A hundred possibilities flew through his head in an instant.

The woman gave an unladylike grunt. "That is for him to say. I have delivered the message. Come, or not, as you wish." The implication was that he'd show up, if he knew what was good for him. That she had not provided directions was of no consequence, Sanemon was expected to know how to get there. He bowed again.

"I will be there, yes, of course. Convey my most humble thanks." Even as he said it, he wondered what Okuni would think when she returned. If she returned. He watched the samurai walk away, back ramrod straight, and let out a breath he hadn't realized he'd been holding.

"Who was that?"

Sanemon froze, and his heart convulsed in his chest. He spun and glared at the young woman standing behind him. He hadn't heard her approach. He never did. "Where have you been?" he snarled. "Nao had to take over for you!"

"Did anyone notice?"

"No."

"Good. It wouldn't do to let Nao get any ideas about upstaging me." Nekoma Okuni smiled thinly. At the moment, she was utterly ordinary in appearance. Only her poise gave her away. She wore a simple smock and trousers, such as a peasant might wear, and had artfully smudged her features. "As to where I've been – well, rest assured it was important."

Sanemon frowned. "I assume it had something to do with your… other profession?"

She reached up and patted his cheek. "Probably best if you don't know."

He stepped back. "Tell me."

Okuni frowned. "They wanted to cheat me, so I have made sure that they know how bad an idea that is."

Sanemon closed his eyes. "What have you done now, woman?"

"Nothing that will come back to you, Sanemon. Not that it matters, of course. It's not as if this is your troupe – remember?"

He grimaced. "You don't have to remind me."

"Are you certain?" She poked him in the chest. "I found you in the gutter, Sanemon. And I can put you right back there if you outlive your usefulness to me."

He glared at her. "You're not that good an actress, you know," he said after a moment. "And you don't have to threaten me, anyway. I know what I owe you."

Okuni stepped back. "Good. I'll be out tonight. Don't wait up for me."

"I will."

"I know," she said. She turned away. "Now, if you'll excuse me, I need to get my costume back from Nao. I don't want to miss the climax." She paused. "Don't worry, Sanemon. I have it under control."

"That's what you said last time," he called out after her.

Nekoma Okuni slid the door to her dressing room shut. Only

then did she allow herself to relax. A soft sigh escaped her as she sank down onto a cushion and stripped off the wrappings around her legs. She began to knead her calves, trying to ease the persistent ache that came with roof-running. Sore muscles were common in her profession.

Both professions, in fact.

She had only herself to blame, really. She had done her best to excel in both paths. Even when that meant going against the wishes of her clan and striking out on her own.

She dismissed the thought, and the sudden pang of regret that accompanied it. Once, her troupe had been her family. Cousins, siblings … parents.

Now, her fellow actors were all castoffs and strays of the acting community – of the twelve, half were drunks, one or two were mad and the others were spiteful misanthropes. Few ever stayed with the Three Flower Troupe long, seeking greener pastures elsewhere. The money she earned as a shinobi was the only thing keeping them afloat most months.

Sometimes she wondered why she bothered. Why she'd chosen so difficult a path. But no answer was forthcoming. Maybe she just enjoyed the stage too much to give it up. Maybe she was simply too stubborn, as her mother had often complained.

If she went back to her family now, would they forgive her? Even as the question occurred to her, she pushed it aside. She would not abase herself, whatever the cost. For better or worse, this was the path she had chosen, and she would not veer from it now.

She stretched. Something in her back realigned itself and she groaned softly. Too much time spent crouching on rooftops and in doorways, eavesdropping on people trying to cheat her.

She crossed her legs, placed her palms flat on the floor, and pushed herself up. She held herself suspended for several moments, and then slowly lowered herself back to the cushion. Her muscles and joints complained but she ignored them. Refusing to stretch after prolonged exertion led to aches and pains, as well as stiffness.

As she stretched, she considered the problem before her. She'd followed Saiga's partner to the teahouse, hoping to confirm what she suspected. Saiga was clever, and too well-protected to approach unawares. The teahouse was more than it seemed – nightingale floors and reinforced partitions were the least of its surprises. The roof had been rigged as well, with slippery slates and loose thatch.

Luckily, she'd been prepared for such tricks. Once she'd identified them, avoiding them had been child's play for someone as well-trained as herself. She had spent much of her childhood learning how to spot unpleasant surprises – and how to deal with those she couldn't avoid. She'd managed to hear most of what was said in Saiga's office – enough, at least, to know that Saiga's partner intended to do as she had requested.

The thought brought some satisfaction. Saiga had tried to haggle – an insult. The best punishment was to force him to pay what was owed. That she'd had to threaten his partner was an unfortunate complication, but a necessary one.

Loosing a light breath, she rolled forward and stood on her head, stretching her toes towards the ceiling. Something cracked in the small of her back and she grunted in relief. An old injury, one of many. Her skin was a map of scars.

For a shinobi, every scar was a lesson learned. That was

what she had been taught as a child. Whatever didn't kill you made you stronger. Smarter. At least in theory. A shinobi had to be smart – pragmatic. To know when a thing could not be accomplished was as important as succeeding in your task.

Knowing when to admit defeat was considered a virtue by her clan, but it was not one Okuni indulged in with any regularity. There was always more than one way to accomplish a goal. One just had to be willing to seize the opportunities when they presented themselves.

The door slipped open, and a blue-clad figure stepped in. Okuni bent until her toes touched the floor and righted herself. "Get out of my dressing room, Nao."

Nao pulled off the wig he was wearing. "Oh. You're back. How wonderful. I just came in to check my makeup."

Okuni smiled mockingly. "You're improving. I almost felt the sincerity that time. My wig, please." Nao tossed the wig at her, and she snatched it out of the air. "I'll need you to fill in for me this evening, as well. After the intermission."

"Oh?" Nao frowned in puzzlement. "Something wrong?"

"No. Why do you ask?"

"This is a small room and you reek of tension."

"Is that your way of telling me I need a bath?" Okuni gave herself a discrete sniff. She smelled of sweat and the city.

"Or better perfume." Nao waved his fan in front of his face. "What's got you all coiled up this time?"

She looked at him. "None of your concern. Take off my kimono please."

He sighed and slipped out of the kimono. "We should really trade roles. Blue doesn't suit you at all."

"I quite like blue," Okuni said. "Speaking of which, why was there a Crane samurai sneaking around backstage?"

"Sneaking? More like stomping." Nao finished undressing and handed Okuni the kimono. "And I have no idea. One of the crew mentioned a Crane nobleman in the audience. Maybe she belonged to him. Maybe she was passing on his regards."

"Maybe she was complaining about your performance." Okuni settled herself on a cushion in front of her mirror. It was one of her most prized possessions, purchased at no little expense from an Ide trader. Nao coveted it, and borrowed it at every opportunity. Nao coveted a great many things of hers, including her position. If he were anyone else she might have encouraged him to find a new troupe. But good actors were hard to come by.

"Cruel girl," Nao said.

"Cats have claws," she reminded him.

"I am well aware. And you ought to think before you unsheathe yours." He raised his fan as if to swat her on the head, but thought better of it and retreated. "Remember Tsuma? You drew your pretty knives and nearly lost your head."

Okuni frowned. "I remember." She began to clean her face with a damp rag, resting atop a stone bowl nearby. Normally, the rag was used to wipe away greasepaint, but it worked on dirt as well.

"Are you certain?" Nao gestured with his fan. "Because I am starting to see similarities in that incident and our current situation."

"You are mistaken," Okuni said. Despite her words, when she'd spied the bushi talking to Sanemon, she'd felt a momentary flicker of panic. The Crane weren't the sort to forgive and forget but, as far as she knew, she hadn't angered the Daidoji.

"Mmm." Nao crossed his arms over his bare chest and studied her. "It's not like you to miss a performance. Even for your hobby."

"My hobby, as you call it, is what pays our bills." She turned to look at him. "And that is what I was doing – making sure we could pay our bills."

"For which we are eternally grateful, I assure you. Down to the meanest stagehand. But you cannot spend money if you are dead."

"If you are scared, Nao, you should feel free to find employment elsewhere."

Nao met her glare coolly. "Just make sure we have plenty of warning when it all goes wrong this time. I was forced to abandon a perfectly delightful wardrobe in Tsuma. I'd hate to lose anything else."

"Speaking of which, perhaps you should go get dressed. We're on stage in a bit." Okuni turned to the mirror and pulled on her wig. She watched Nao's reflection depart and then took a deep breath.

It was time to take off one mask, and put on another.

CHAPTER FIVE
The House of the Frog

Rokugan was a land of wonders. Generations of scholars had attested to this fact. As a consequence, Shin thought that his countrymen were prone to make much of little. A mountain was a mountain, and a river was a river.

But even Shin, jaded as he was, had to admit that Saibanshoki was not just a willow tree. Or, rather, it was the epitome of a willow tree. It was a vast presence that dominated the intersection of the two rivers, and the shade of its branches reached the edges of either shore. A quintet of imperial docks nestled among the great tree's roots, emerging from the base like the spokes of some immense wheel. The tree's trunk was more than twenty yards across, and decorated with strange carvings.

If one listened to those who knew about such things, the carvings were centuries old and had greeted the first fishermen to take up residence along the shore. Shin longed to study them, if for no other reason than to satisfy his own curiosity, but doubted the governor would look kindly on such a delay. So he kept his eyes and hands on himself as he climbed out of the flatboat and onto the dock.

Kasami followed, her keen gaze fixed on the faces of their escort. The Kaeru soldiers were technically ronin – masterless mercenaries, loyal only to the coin. But their years of service to the imperial governor had earned them a family name of sorts, as well as some small amount of influence in the affairs of the city.

"Stop glaring at them," Shin murmured from behind his fan. "They might take it amiss and react accordingly."

"Let them," she said.

As if he'd heard, one of their escorts glanced at them, eyes narrowed. Kasami met his gaze challengingly. Shin pretended not to notice, confident she knew better than to start something here. Instead, he scrutinized the manor house that hung over the river. It was a beautiful structure, crafted so as to blend in with the boughs of the tree. In the light of late afternoon the pale wood was painted in shades of pink and orange.

At the base of the structure was a small, intimate courtroom, and the offices of the governor's agents were just above. On a series of small balconies, men and women used signal flags to communicate with parties on the other side of the river. Shin watched them as he and Kasami were escorted up the steps that ascended the tree's massive trunk, idly trying to translate the messages flying back and forth.

They stopped on a broad landing midway up the tree. One of the Kaeru held up a hand. "Wait here, my lord," he said, respectfully but firmly. Shin nodded agreeably and turned to face the river.

"What do you think the governor wants?" Kasami asked, watching the remaining ronin. They, in turn, studiously ignored her.

"Be patient. We shall soon find out," Shin said. Below them, the river was blanketed in a wide variety of craft; everything, from small skiffs to large grain ships, crowded the wharfs on either side of the two rivers. Some carried passengers, most simply cargo. There were fishing boats as well, often all but hidden by the larger vessels. The two rivers were densely populated at this time of year, between the cold grasp of winter and the unbearable heat of summer. Every major clan, and many of the minor ones, sailed these waters.

Officially, the City of the Rich Frog was a tripartite assemblage. Three clans claimed mastery of it, and had divided it between themselves. The western bank of the Three Sides River belonged to the Unicorn. The Lion claimed the eastern bank, as well as everything south of the Drowned Merchant River.

In contrast, the Dragon appeared to have no interest in trade at all. Instead, they'd ceded their claim to a minor clan – the Dragonfly – and contented themselves with the island-shrines that rose at the junction of the two rivers. The Unicorn and the Lion were more than happy to leave them to it. So was Shin, for that matter. The Crane had no claim on the city, and no interest in forcing the issue.

He fanned himself, listening to the raucous sounds of the afternoon traffic – jeers and catcalls, orders, curses, shouts and songs. Hundreds of voices, all competing against themselves and the steady roar of the flowing waters. He spied the Crane vessels among all the confusion easily enough. Most of them were smaller vessels, bearing the lightest of cargos – paper.

While many cities had their own paper makers, the quality of Crane paper was incomparable. It went for high prices wherever there was a substantial population of bureaucrats or priests. The City of the Rich Frog had plenty of both. Technically, that was his whole reason for being here – to oversee the trade in paper. But most of that was handled by other, more experienced individuals.

In truth, Shin was nothing more than a figurehead. A pretty face to see and be seen, to reassure the other clans that the Crane were present and accounted for. It was supposed to be a punishment. An unimportant post for a wayward fledgling, meant to teach him a lesson. So far, all he had learned was the locations of the better sort of gambling dens.

Kasami nudged him, and he turned. The ronin had returned, accompanied by a familiar face – Kaeru Azuma, one of Governor Tetsua's closest advisors. The latter nodded politely to Shin and said, "I will escort them to the governor. The rest of you are dismissed."

The ronin trooped away, leaving Shin, Kasami and Azuma alone. Azuma joined Shin at the edge of the landing. "The governor will see you in a moment, my lord. He thanks you for coming so quickly."

"I wasn't aware I was allowed to do otherwise." He glanced at Azuma. "I'm sorry you're missing the performance."

Azuma frowned in apparent confusion. "The play, my lord," Shin clarified. "The Foxfire Theater. I noticed you there earlier."

"Ah. Yes." Azuma looked nonplussed and turned away. Shin realized that he was embarrassed, and decided to change the subject.

"Tell me – why does our illustrious governor wish to see me?"

"A matter of importance," Azuma said, not looking at him. "That is all I know."

Shin doubted that, but did not argue. He took stock of the man beside him. Azuma was tall and whip-thin, with hard features and hair that was going silver. He stood like a swordsman in his imperial livery, balanced on the balls of his feet even with no enemy in sight. Ready to move at a moment's notice.

It was said that Azuma had been adopted into the Kaeru at a young age, after proving himself against a certain band of pirates infamous at the time. Looking at him, Shin could imagine him leading a charge across a blood-soaked deck, sword in hand.

"Well, I am honored either way."

"Good. That is as it should be." Azuma looked at him. Shin knew the man was taking his measure. He wondered if he would be found wanting. He hoped so. It was always best to be underestimated by a man like Azuma. Otherwise he might well be dangerous. Abruptly, as if he'd come to a decision, Azuma turned towards the door. "You may go in now. Your companion must stay outside."

For a wonder, Kasami didn't protest. Perhaps she realized that her presence was tolerated only as a courtesy. Azuma slid the door back and Shin entered.

The receiving room was small and sparsely decorated. The only notable item of furniture was a small, low table set in the center of the room. Atop the table was an intricately carved Go board, complete with two sets of stones – one group white, the other black – in their kitani bowls. A man in dark robes knelt before it, studying the bare board intently, as if preparing a strategy for a game to come. He was innocuous in appearance and bearing, and might have been a scribe or priest – but he was anything but.

"You are Daidoji Shin," he said, without looking up.

"And you are Governor Miya Tetsua," Shin said, bowing respectfully. "I am honored to meet you, my lord."

"I should hope so," Tetsua said, smiling slightly. He gestured to the mat on the other side of the Go table. "Please – sit."

Shin sat. There were no servants in evidence. Tetsua obviously wished for their meeting to have no witnesses. He gave the board a cursory glance. "I wasn't sure whether to bring a gift or not. Etiquette is vague on the matter – does this count as a home?"

Tetsua dismissed the question with a gesture. "It is of no matter. Do you play?" It was a simple question, on the surface. Even so, Shin paused before replying.

"A bit, my lord."

Tetsua gestured to the stones. "White or black?"

"Are we playing a game then?"

"I find it helps facilitate honest conversation."

Shin made to answer that, then stopped himself. "White, please."

"Black goes first."

"White," Shin repeated, tapping the bowl. Tetsua nodded and took the bowl containing the black stones for himself.

"A defensive player, then."

"Cautious," Shin corrected mildly, as he arranged his pieces. He was careful to keep connections between them, preventing an early defeat. Tetsua watched him carefully, even as he saw to his own pieces with the alacrity of an experienced player.

"I have not seen you since you first arrived," he said. "That was almost four months ago. The height of winter, as I recall. There was ice on the river."

"I am afraid that I have been most busy," Shin said, apologetically. Tetsua nodded.

"So I am given to understand. Since your first night, you have availed yourself of the city's entertainments. Occasionally not without consequence."

Shin hesitated. "Ah," he said, finally.

Tetsua looked at him steadily. "Yes. There is a saying I am fond of… do not confuse the slack of the rope for true freedom."

Again, Shin hesitated. "That is a strangely familiar saying."

Tetsua smiled thinly. It was the expression of a man used to getting what he wanted. Shin deployed his own smile in reply. They faced one another like that for several moments. Then, as if satisfied, the governor looked down at the board and made the first move.

"I count your grandfather among my friends."

Shin ignored the board, and kept his eyes on the man. "I'm certain that he reciprocates that consideration."

Tetsua chuckled. "Doubtful."

"Have you spoken to him of late?"

"Not since the death of your predecessor."

Shin met Tetsua's gaze and did not look away. "He asked you not to investigate."

"Death by misadventure does not require investigation."

"Is that what you believe – or what he told you?"

Tetsua frowned. "He told me nothing. I am the imperial governor. And this city does not belong to the Crane."

Shin bowed his head, accepting the implied chastisement. He moved a stone, cutting two of Tetsua's groups apart. "Indeed, it does not. My apologies, I spoke without thought."

"A common ailment." Tetsua looked at the board and stroked his wispy beard in consideration. He made a move, and balance was restored. "Do you believe I was in error?"

"It is not for me to say."

"If you will not, who will?"

White and black stones slid across the board in a stately dance. For a time, there was only silence. "This city was just a village, once," Tetsua said, eventually. "A bare handful of rude homes, scattered along the banks of the junction. Then came the Great Clans, and they raised up a city from the mud. Not a great city, but an important one. A vital one."

"I would not disagree."

"Then you would also agree that it is fragile. For years, the Lion controlled this port. And when the Unicorn returned, they also laid claim – though, some said, only at the instigation of the Crane."

Shin winced, well aware of his clan's history with the Unicorn. The Crane had been responsible for the Unicorn's admission into the Emerald Empire and, later, for civilizing them. Or, rather, attempting to do so. The bonds between the two clans ran deep. Though he had never heard a rumor like the one Tetsua had mentioned, he could well believe it. Many of the Unicorn's actions over the years had come at the counsel of the Crane.

"Only the command of the Emperor – and the intervention of the Dragon – stopped the fighting. And only his authority – through me – maintains peace here. But authority is a tenuous thing. It only has the power it is given. Defiance weakens it." He tapped a stone with his finger. Shin's gaze flicked to the stone and he clucked his tongue. Tetsua glanced at him. "A mistake?"

"That depends entirely on whether or not you are playing to win."

Again, Tetsua unsheathed his smile. Shin parried with a frown. He sat back and took in the silence of the room. He could not even hear the breathing of the guards outside. He looked at the board more closely. "You're not, are you?" he said, after a moment.

"No. I am playing for time." The governor paused. "What do you know of this city, Crane? Truly know, I mean. Not its history. Not what you might have heard, or been told. What have you observed for yourself?"

Shin's frown deepened. "Even at its most peaceful, the city is a powder keg. The Lion are belligerent, the Unicorn ambitious, and the Dragon inscrutable."

"And the Dragonfly?"

"Incidental."

Tetsua nodded. "A good summary. But any urchin could tell me the same."

Stung, Shin leaned forward. "I admit, I have made little study of the matter. People interest me. Politics, not so much." He looked at Tetsua. "Why am I here, Governor? What do you wish of me?"

"A bit more respect, for starters." Tetsua's tone was mild, but his words held the bite of authority. "Remember who I am, Crane."

Shin ducked his head. "My apologies. My impatience got the better of me."

Tetsua gestured dismissively. "I was once impatient as well. My time as governor has taught me better. But you are right. I have been remiss. You are here because of rice."

Shin blinked. "Rice?"

"A shipment of rice, specifically. Meant for the storehouses of the Lion."

"And what is so special about this shipment? Did it fail to arrive, perhaps?"

"No. Not quite." Tetsua reached down to the floor, retrieved a small teak box, opened it and extracted something. Shin started in shock and then stared.

"Is that a rat?"

"Obviously."

Shin studied the carcass, noting the unusual bloating and the contorted limbs. Ignoring the smell as best he could, he leaned forward to examine it more closely. "Poison," he said, after a moment. "And not one I'm immediately familiar with."

Tetsua nodded. "Even so."

"Someone poisoned the shipment."

"Indeed."

"Who?"

"That is why I asked you here, Daidoji Shin. I want you to find out."

CHAPTER SIX
Investigative Technique

Shin was silent for a moment. Then, unable to stop himself, he laughed out loud. It was a ridiculous request – impossible. And he said as much. "Surely this is a jest of some sort," he protested. "You are having fun at my expense."

"I assure you that I am not." Tetsua swept the rat back into its box. "The Lion are ready to go to war over this." He fixed Shin with a steady gaze. "Sadly, the Unicorn seem only too happy to oblige. Violence has long simmered beneath the surface here. I will not be able to stop it when it surges up at last."

"And you think I can? What exactly do you expect of me, my lord?"

"Exactly as I said. Investigate the matter. Uncover the truth."

"You have investigators of your own – why me?"

"My investigators will get nowhere – this act serves the purposes of both the Lion and the Unicorn. Neither is truly interested in the truth, and both will claim I am biased on behalf of the other."

"And what about the Dragon?"

Tetsua hesitated. Shin paused, and then nodded. "Ah. I see."

Tetsua frowned. "What do you think you see?"

Shin sat back. "Your weekly visits with Tonbo Kuma," he said. It was an open secret. Tetsua had begun paying regular social calls to the enigmatic shugenja of the Dragonfly Clan, though no one quite knew why. Having never met the esteemed shugenja himself, Shin was not inclined to speculate.

Tetsua nodded and looked away, as if ashamed. "Yes. Perhaps I have erred in choosing my… friends." Shin felt a pang of sympathy for the other man. He could only imagine the sheer drudgery of Tetsua's day-to-day existence. An able administrator who spent most of his time dealing with the, no-doubt tedious, difficulties posed by the clans who squabbled over control of the city. No surprise, then, that he had found solace in the company of someone like Tonbo Kuma.

In contrast to Tetsua, Shin knew nothing about Kuma. They were a cipher as far as the Crane were concerned, and Shin had made no effort to investigate further. But he'd heard stories regardless. Supposedly, it was Kuma who had taught Tetsua how to play Go. And there had supposedly been some trouble involving a young woman, Iuchi Shichiro's daughter Konomi, if popular rumor was to be believed.

"I don't think so," Shin said, finally. "But it is clear to me that someone counted on that friendship. The other clans will view your judgement as compromised."

Tetsua looked at him. "Yes. But the Crane are impartial in this matter. You have nothing to gain from any one clan becoming ascendant. That is why you are the perfect one to explore the matter."

Shin looked at the board and the scattered stones.

"Conducting an investigation of this sort will require politesse," he said, diplomatically. "The clans may not welcome my presence, neutrality or not." He paused. "In fact, I am certain that they won't, the Lion especially, if they are as intent on war as you claim."

"They may not welcome you, but they will speak with you. You speak with my voice in this matter, and to ignore you is to ignore me." Tetsua clasped his hands behind his back. "In fact, I have already made it clear to the representative of the Lion, Akodo Minami, that you are to be extended every courtesy."

"And what did she say about that?"

Tetsua hesitated. "She has yet to reply," he admitted with some chagrin.

Shin hid a smile behind his fan. "Nonetheless, I feel I should visit the Lion first. It might go towards assuaging their hostility somewhat."

"Probably wise."

"Iuchi Shichiro is a family friend, though we have not spoken since I was a boy. I will impose upon our prior relationship and see if he will speak to me."

"A family friend," Tetsua repeated. "A friend of your grandfather's you mean?"

Shin's smile was strained. "Yes. Though that might be rather a strong word for their relationship. They did not part on the best of terms, I'm told."

Tetsua frowned. "He may hold that against you."

Shin gestured airily. "We'll see. What about Tonbo Kuma, the Dragonfly representative? I'm told they rarely see anyone at all – except for yourself, of course."

Tetsua's frown deepened. "I have sent word to them. I expect that they will see you in their own time. Though I must say that I do not believe them to be involved in this matter."

"No? They could easily stand to profit if the Lion and the Unicorn go to war."

"No one profits if it comes to war," Tetsua said sharply. He recovered quickly. "Forgive me. My temper is… frayed of late."

"No apologies necessary, my lord. You are under a great deal of strain." Shin snapped his fan shut and tapped his lips. "What about the others? The Scorpion, the Mantis – both have trade representatives in the city."

"The Scorpion have already assured me that they were not involved, as have the Mantis. And neither would profit from this action, at least not in any way that I can see. They have no claim to the city, and their interests are limited to the purchase of rice and grain from the Lion."

"Rice," Shin said. "That brings up another question – this rice… why are the Lion importing something that they regularly sell?"

Tetsua smiled faintly. "You don't know much about trade, do you?"

"My interests have always veered somewhat to the left of the commercial, I fear."

The governor nodded, as if he had expected that answer. "Demand often outstrips supply these days. As such, the Lion have often found it necessary to buy and sell certain goods, including quantities of rice."

Shin pursed his lips, considering this information. "That means that the tainted rice wasn't meant for the Lion at all – they would have simply sold it on had they not discovered that it was tainted."

Tetsua nodded. "Yes. It is a complicated matter. You see now why I require an investigator."

"Indeed. How interesting." Shin tapped his chin with his fan.

"I thought you might it find it to be so." Tetsua turned away. "I can trust you to remain discrete, of course."

"Discretion is one of my few virtues." Shin bowed low. "I will have the answers you seek within a few days."

"So quickly then?"

"It appears to me that time is our enemy in this matter. Best it was handled quickly."

"Then I leave it in your capable hands." Tetsua gestured and Shin, realizing the audience was at an end, rose smoothly to his feet and bowed low.

"As you say, my lord." With that, he turned and departed.

Kasami was waiting for him outside, trading appraising glances with Azuma. When Shin exited, the Kaeru turned and entered without so much as a farewell. Shin looked after him for a moment, and then turned to Kasami. "Shall we?"

When they reached the wharf, she looked at him. "Well? What did he want?"

"Apparently, we are to investigate a case of sabotage and head off an incipient war."

Kasami began to laugh.

"Yes, that was my reaction as well. But it is no joke." Shin frowned. "It's my grandfather's hand pulling the strings, of course. The old bastard is determined to keep me from enjoying myself in my exile."

"Some might say that is the point of an exile."

"Some should keep their opinions to themselves." He tapped

his lips with his fan. "Still, I wonder what his interest in the matter is. It's not like him to interfere."

"You're overlooking the obvious."

"Am I? Illuminate me, oh sage." Shin smiled indulgently at her.

"War here serves no one – especially not the Crane. Any violence in this city risks spreading beyond its walls, as well as damaging long-term trading interests." Kasami poked him in the chest. "This is your duty, like it or not. Maintaining the balance of things for the good of the clan, and everyone else. That is why the Daidoji Trading Council sent you here."

Shin made a rude noise. "How boring." He looked up. The sky was sliding from orange to purple as night came on. The days seemed to pass more quickly in springtime. Perhaps because there was inevitably more to do.

Kasami shook her head. "Despite having a man's body, you are truly a child."

"Possibly. I will not deny a certain childish glee at the opportunity. Of late I have become fascinated by a form of investigative technique developed by Agasha Kitsuki." He snapped open his fan and gave the air an exploratory swipe.

"And how did you find out about this… technique?"

"A… friend of mine told me." He smiled, lost for a moment in pleasant memories. "Lovely young woman. Keen mind. Quite adept at sadane."

"A friend." Kasami snorted. "What was her name?"

"None of your concern. At any rate, I believe that by combining it with a more structured form of ratiocination, as devised by myself, I can perfect the art of investigation."

Kasami stared at him. "You… devised a form of what?"

"A process of educated reasoning," Shin explained, airily. "Quite superior to the mere observational method touted by the Kitsuki, in my humble opinion." He gestured. "Observation alone is not enough. One must align the observed elements correctly in order to assemble the true narrative of the deed. The why is as important as the how. Without the one, the other is impossible to determine."

Kasami rubbed her face as if suddenly struck by fatigue. "Spent a lot of time thinking of this, have you?"

"Not long, no. In my idle hours, really."

"Of which you have so many," she said through gritted teeth.

"Fewer now." Shin looked at her. "You will help me, of course."

"Of course."

"It might be dangerous."

"Good. I was getting bored. Where do we start?"

"With the scene of the crime. Unfortunately, that means waiting for the Lion to decide whether they wish to eat us first – or afterwards." Shin paused. They had come to the docks, and he looked out over the water towards the city. Lanterns were being lit all along the wharfs, casting fireflies of light across the water's surface.

For better or worse, it was his home now. The thought of it being torn apart by internecine conflict was not a pleasant one. Even so, a small pulse of excitement burgeoned within him. Here was something interesting at last.

He snapped his fan closed and looked at Kasami.

"Hopefully they will decide quickly."

Evening fell without grace. The city at night was no lovelier than during the day. Despite this, Nekoma Okuni felt a certain fondness for it. She had always felt more at home in cities. There was something vital about them – an urgency she found invigorating.

Three Duck Street was well named, she thought. It was as much a street as it was a duck. Rather, it was a trash-strewn stretch of alley between two buildings. It was also the halfway point between the Unicorn docks and the Foxfire Theater.

Abandoned crates and pallets crowded the alley, forming natural bulwarks against casual observation. Boarded up windows and doorways lined either side. Light drizzled down from the few open windows, and from a pathetic string of lanterns at the far end of the alley, closest to the theater.

As she waited, Okuni found herself wondering what her mother would say if she could see her now. Nothing good, she suspected. The Nekoma did not often lower themselves to poisoning and blackmail. They were spies and body-doubles, wielding stagecraft the way a samurai might wield a blade. Mostly, Okuni kept to those traditions where she could. But in lean times she found herself taking on whatever jobs came her way.

That Saiga had even found her was proof that she had fallen far from her family's ideal. A shinobi whose identity was known was often a dead shinobi. But she had to eat, and that meant dealing with individuals of dubious reputation. Sometimes they were even foolish enough to try and cheat her. But never more than once.

A splash at that end of the alley alerted her to the arrival of Saiga's partner. From her place of concealment she watched him approach. He cursed softly as dirty water splashed the hem of his robe. "Where are you?" he hissed. He sounded nervous.

She could understand why. Meeting an unknown person in a darkened alley at dusk was enough to test the resolve of any man not used to skulduggery.

On the whole, she preferred her clients to be nervous. It made negotiations much easier to conduct. She decided to let him stew for a moment, and gave no reply. Instead, she settled back noiselessly and watched him fumble about in the dark.

When she'd judged that he'd waited long enough, she retrieved one of a handful of loose stones piled up near her foot and tossed it over his head. It rattled against the street and he spun with a curse, peering into the darkness.

"Behind you," she said, throwing her voice expertly. He whirled back around, hand clutching convulsively at the hilt of his wakizashi. He was no swordsman though, and did not unsheathe his blade. Instead, he looked around nervously, seeking some sign of her.

She was not anywhere close to where he was looking, of course. She was to his left, huddled in a doorway, where she had a good view of both him and the alley. The spot he now stood on was illuminated by the light from a nearby window, and she studied him intently. He'd taken the precaution of wearing a disguise of sorts – a rough cloak and the rude garments of a sailor – but left his face uncovered.

"This is highly irregular," he said, and she almost laughed. He obviously knew nothing about how this sort of business was conducted.

"Is it? And are you an expert in such matters?"

"What do you want?" he demanded.

"I am owed a fee."

"Saiga was to have paid you."

"He has not."

He hesitated at this. "I gave him the money. It was all arranged."

"The arrangement has fallen through. A common occurrence, sadly."

"Then why not demand it of him?" he asked. "Why am I here? For that matter, how did you even find me?"

"If I were not skilled, you would not have had Saiga hire me. As to your other question, I find that in these situations it is always best to go to the source. Dealing with go-betweens is a tedious business, and I have little patience for it." She watched his face as she spoke. His expression flickered rapidly from haughty disgruntlement to worry and then, finally, to fear. He had not prepared for this. An amateur, then, as she'd suspected.

She felt a flicker of pity for the fool. She wondered if he truly understood what he'd set in motion – and, if so, what he hoped to gain. She dismissed the thought even as it occurred. It did not matter what his intentions were, or what happened next.

He grunted and tapped the hilt of his wakizashi. His thoughts might as well have been stamped on his features. He was considering killing her. She sighed. They always did. Most of them thought better of it, but he was an amateur.

But instead he said, "I can get you the money."

She paused. "A wise decision. When?"

"A week from now."

"I am due to leave the city in four days." The Three Flower Troupe's run at the Foxfire Theater would be ended by then, and they would be seeking a new audience.

"Four days, then." He took a deep breath and turned. She realized that he'd finally caught on to her deception. He knew she was hiding close by, but he hadn't spotted her yet. He was cleverer than she'd thought. "And how can I be sure you will not come again, seeking more, now that you know who I am?"

Okuni was startled. "Do you think it wise to insult me?" she asked, annoyed. "I am a professional. I take only what I am owed – no more, no less."

He laughed. "Do your sort have honor, then?"

Annoyance turned to anger. That she had been forced to take such a job was bad enough. Now, to be insulted for it? That was a step too far. She picked up another stone and flicked it at him. It bounced off his arm with stinging force, and he yelped. "Next time," she said, "it will be something sharp."

Rubbing his arm, he nodded jerkily. "I- I apologize. I meant no disrespect."

"You did, or you would not have spoken so freely." She paused, calming herself. "But it is of no importance. You have one day. Bring my payment here tomorrow, at this time."

"Here?"

"Would you prefer I came to your place of business?" she asked, archly.

"No! No." He swallowed. "I will be here."

But even as he spoke, she heard the distinctive shuffle of feet on the thatch of the roof above. It was a familiar sound to one who spent as much time on rooftops as she did. A moment later, this was followed by the shivery hum of thrown metal. She leapt aside as something small and sharp embedded itself in a doorpost to her left.

A shuriken. The exposed edges gleamed with an oily residue. Poisoned.

She hesitated, and it almost cost her. Another shuriken sank into a nearby barrel, causing the rainwater inside to spurt out. She ran. As she did, she reached into her robes, fingers seeking the knives sheathed against her stomach. The blades were long and flat, and each was made from a single piece of steel. The hilts were wrapped in silk, and the pommels were weighted rings, allowing for her to draw them at the same time. Instead of unsheathing them, she extracted a small pouch of smoke powder. She'd made a habit of carrying one in her youth – smoke and shadows were a shinobi's best friend.

But even as she extracted it, she felt something bite her side. She shouted in pain and spun, hurling the pouch against the far wall. It burst on impact and smoke billowed, filling the alleyway.

Okuni staggered back against the wall and looked down. Blood soaked through her robes, and she could feel something sharp in her side. She clawed for it, but found nothing. It was buried too deep in the wound for her to reach with trembling fingers. If it was poisoned as well… but she had no time to try and extract it. She looked back and saw vague shapes moving through the smoke. She didn't know who they were, but their intent was obvious.

She had to get away. But she couldn't just run back to the theater, not without risking the others. That left only one option.

She turned and ran for the river, one hand pressed to the wound in her side.

CHAPTER SEVEN
The First Move

"A fine report, Master Ito," Shin said, tapping the bundled stack of parchment before him. "As thorough and detailed as ever." He stifled a yawn behind his fan, and his guest politely pretended not to notice. Trying to cover his momentary inattention, he looked around the receiving room, with its carved columns and beams depicting scenes from the Crane's storied history. This room, more than any other in the manor, was meant to remind guests of the might and majesty of the Crane.

His residence lay on the edge of the violet-roofed noble district, closer to the heart of the commerce. There was no compelling reason for him to reside in the district proper – the Crane had no real influence in the city, despite their myriad business interests. Square and tall, the house was separated from the noise of the street by a thick masonry wall around the perimeter. Screened windows overlooked a tidy garden. The privacy of it suited Shin.

"Thank you, my lord." Ito bowed low, nearly banging his bald head against the floor. Shin resisted the urge to sigh at the merchant's obsequious display. Ito was good at making money. If that meant putting up with a bit of ostentatious sycophancy, it was his duty to smile and bear it.

Smiling was, in fact, the whole of his duty. Ostensibly, Shin was a representative of the Daidoji Trading Council. In reality, he had neither the authority nor the ambition to make anything of his position. He existed solely to deliver the orders of the council to the merchants who made up his minuscule fiefdom.

There were three of them, of whom Ito was the most successful and the only one he saw with any regularity. Of the others, one was a dealer exclusively in fish, and the other a purveyor of iron, he thought, though he was not certain. Neither was especially interesting, and they required little oversight. Ito, on the other hand, dealt in paper, which was interesting but only because of what it could be made into.

All three paid a portion of their profits to the Crane in return for protection. They were not family but were considered vassals, and therefore an insult to them was an insult to the clan. This gave them some advantages when it came to import fees, annual tithes and the like. And, of course, they could come to him in the event something went wrong.

Thus far, none of them, not even Ito, had bothered him with their troubles, for which he was grateful. It gave him more time to enjoy himself. Though Ito did insist on making these periodic reports in person. He was a dutiful sort.

Shin liked the merchant, despite his embarrassing behavior. He suspected Ito was a spy for his grandfather. Whether the man was keeping an eye on Shin or the city, or both, Shin wasn't sure. But Ito was entirely too ridiculous to be believed. He bowed like weights were attached to his ears, and fumbled for words.

But he also compiled detailed and precise reports about the flow of trade through the city. Shin rarely did more than skim them, but his meeting with Tetsua had stoked the embers of his interest. If he was going to investigate anything, it might be wise to first know the lay of the land. Who sold what, where, and to who. Potentially vital information when one was attempting to untangle a mystery such as the one before him.

Shin allowed the merchant's performance to continue for a few moments, and then gestured with his fan. "Enough, please, Master Ito. You humble me with this display of gratitude. Especially when it is I who should be thanking you. Your efforts on behalf of the Crane in this city have been positively heroic." As he spoke, Kasami slid the door open a fraction of an inch and made a meaningful gesture. Someone had come to call. He felt a sudden bristle of anticipation.

Ito gabbled profuse inanities, and made to resume his servile posturing. Shin stopped him before he could get started. "My apologies, Master Ito, but I have other matters demanding my attention. Kasami will show you out. But know that you go with the most heartfelt thanks of the Daidoji, and the Crane."

Ito bobbed and bowed even as he retreated to Kasami's side. Shin watched him leave with some amusement. Their conversation had returned more than once to Shin's visit with the governor, though Ito had been careful not to ask any direct questions.

Moments later, there was a rap at the frame and Kasami slid the door open again. She gestured, and he recognized the symbol for 'Lion'. He twirled his finger, indicating that he wanted to keep them waiting. She rolled her eyes and nodded, closing the door. Shin smiled.

It was petty, perhaps, but a little pettiness never hurt when it came to these matters. He began to count the moments silently, and kept time by plucking the strings of the battered biwa he lifted from beside his cushion.

The instrument was a coarse thing, made from driftwood and catgut. While most Daidoji favored the shakuhachi – the bamboo flute – Shin was fond of the biwa despite its ugliness, or perhaps because of it. He'd won it in a dice game – his first dice game, as a matter of fact. He'd taught himself how to play, though he was by no means skilled. Music was not among his gifts, though his tutors had tried their best. Or so he'd led them to believe.

It was an old game, and one Shin had always excelled at, even as a boy. A true courtier was always in control of the impression they made; how one dressed, the tone of voice used, even the food one chose to eat in public… all brushstrokes on the canvas. A flash of temper at the right time could swing an argument in your favor, if you were willing.

Shin had spent years painting the portrait of himself he wished others to see. The louche layabout, feckless and useless – but not disloyal. It had not been difficult. There were so many rules, more than one man could break in his lifetime.

The life he had thus crafted for himself was a satisfying one, free of responsibility and the burden of duty. Unfortunately, it was also somewhat boring, more so than he had anticipated. His mind rebelled at stagnation and sought new avenues of inquiry – he had taught himself many things that no proper samurai ought to know. He could shoe a horse and till a field. He could identify birds by their song and hoist a sail.

All useless. But now he was being given the opportunity to put some of what he'd learned into practice. To truly test himself, in a manner he found acceptable.

He paused, stilling the strings with the flat of his palm. That was enough stalling. He loudly cleared his throat and set his biwa aside. Kasami slid the door open again. "A messenger, my lord," she said, as another figure all but pushed past her into the room.

"Ah, do come in," Shin said, as Kasami closed the door behind the newcomer.

The man was broad and well built, a warrior. He wore armor, and was armed as if riding to battle. He looked about himself disdainfully, and the curve of his lip spoke to a barely suppressed sneer. He looked down his nose at Shin expectantly.

Shin did not rise to meet him. Instead, he remained seated, eventually forcing the impatient messenger to do the same. A small victory, but a victory nonetheless. "I bring a message from my lady, Akodo Minami," he said, as he removed his sword and set it to his left – a sign of distrust, if not hostility. Shin made no comment on this insult. If the Lion wished to provoke him, they would have to try harder than that.

Shin hid a smile. "By all means, share it."

The messenger frowned. "You are welcome at our gates this afternoon at sunset. That welcome will be rescinded should you not appear in a timely fashion." The tone was clipped, the words blunt, just shy of insulting.

Shin nodded politely. Sunset wasn't far away. He'd spent most of the day waiting for the Lion representative to show up. Minami had deliberately left little time, likely hoping that he would be unable – or unwilling – to come. He waited a few moments before responding. "That will be satisfactory, I suppose. Inform Lady Minami that I look forward to our meeting."

The messenger grunted and levered himself to his feet. "You may leave now," Shin said, and dismissed him with a casual gesture. He was rewarded by a flash of anger in the other man's eyes. Another point scored, though he likely hadn't endeared himself to either the messenger or his mistress.

Kasami returned after showing the man out. "Impolite," she said.

"Him or me?"

"Him. The Lion lack courtesy."

"Some might say the same of you." Shin rose to his feet, Ito's reports in his hand, and wandered about the room. He knew the basics, but Ito had provided a detailed economic breakdown of the city's three districts.

The Lion mostly traded in foodstuffs and textiles. They were on a perpetual war footing, scraping the fields of their peasants clean in order to buy raw materials that could be put towards construction or the forging of arms. The Unicorn, on the other hand, were more interested in lumber and coal. And the Dragonfly bought a little of everything.

The noble districts were the spokes of the wheel, and the city revolved around them. Traffic flowed in steady streams to and from the docks and warehouses. It was a city of tradesmen, and the most common sound was the clink of coins exchanging hands.

Officially, business in the city was conducted by clan

merchants, and cargoes were delivered by clan vessels, but there was an extensive, if largely unacknowledged, network of private entrepreneurs beneath the concealing shroud of officialdom. Free wharfs of varying sizes clung to either bank, and warehouses of dubious merit sprung up like mushrooms. Merchants of all sorts infested the city, looking to profit from the labor of others.

Shin looked up from the pages. Facts turned in his mind like cogwheels. He heard Kasami approach. "We shall soon enter the Lion's den," he said, without turning. "Keep your sword close, and a tight rein on your tongue."

"It's not my tongue I'm worried about."

Shin decided not to laugh. It would only encourage her.

Okuni surfaced slowly, carefully. Water streamed from her shivering limbs as she hauled herself onto the stone floor of the river shrine. The shrine was one of several on the western riverbank. They were built into the bank below the water level and out of sight of anyone who didn't know what to look for. She'd used it before, when setting out to intercept the rice shipment. It was largely forgotten and, as far as she knew, she was the first person to visit it in years.

She clambered across the rough floor, agony dancing through her with every inch. She'd torn one of her sleeves off and used it to fashion a crude bandage for the wound in her side, but she'd lost a great deal of blood in the interim. And the swimming hadn't helped.

At least her luck was holding. The sliver hadn't carried any poison with it. If it had, she'd have already been dead, rather than in pain. She rolled onto her back and took several deep breaths, trying to control the spasms that ran through her. As a child, she'd been taught how to regulate her involuntary reactions. To control her heart rate and breathing, to force herself past the limits of the flesh. A shinobi had to be able to sit motionless for hours, swim like a fish and endure temperatures that would crack the reserve of anyone else.

That she'd managed to do so with a wound in her side would no doubt impress her old teachers. She closed her eyes, and fought back the sudden swell of exhaustion that threatened to send her tumbling into oblivion. She had snatched rest where she could, but it wasn't enough. She needed somewhere to hide, and for the moment the shrine was it.

Okuni had always been good at hiding. Even as a child, she had been adept at concealing her presence from those around her. Later, she found that her talents extended to hiding in plain sight – or in playing a role. She could sing and dance, and play a variety of instruments with acceptable, if not great, skill. Becoming an actress had seemed only natural. And it was amusing to pretend to be someone who themselves pretended to be other people. It was like wearing two masks at once.

She wished dearly that she were on stage now, instead of here. She rolled back onto her stomach and levered herself carefully upright, one hand pressed protectively to her wound. Her pursuers were dogged hunters. They knew the city better than she did and had anticipated her every move till she'd taken to the river. Wherever she went they were there, or close enough. She had no doubt that they would find this place as well, but hopefully not for a few hours.

She staggered to the rear of the shrine, where a statue of a frog observed her plight with stony serenity. She left bloodstains on its round eyes as she slid to the ground behind it. The shrine could only be reached from the river. She would wait for night and slip back into the water. If she was right, she was close to safety – just a bit longer.

She closed her eyes. When she opened them, the light on the river was dull and ochre. It was afternoon. And she was not alone. A form crouched between her and the water, softly jostling the chain of a kusari-gama. It was an ugly thing, a sickle blade on one end of the chain, and a heavy weight on the other.

He was not wearing a mask this time. Perhaps he felt no need, having cornered her. He was a hard-faced man, one eye rendered a milky white in some long-ago struggle, his hair the color of steel. "I thought it best to let you sleep," he said.

"Thank you." She slid her hand into her robes, and hooked the pommel of one of her knives. "How long?"

"You were snoring when I arrived an hour ago."

"It is tiring, being hunted."

"So I have heard." He paused. "You are quick," he said. He let the chain swing back and forth as he spoke. "But predictable. I expected better from a Nekoma."

"I am sorry to disappoint you." She wanted to ask how he knew her name. Perhaps they'd been watching her for longer than she'd thought. Or maybe Saiga had told them. Either way, it didn't bode well.

He shrugged. "No apologies are necessary. Such is the nature of life." He swung the chain in a lazy arc, not looking at her. "It took us most of the day to find this place."

"I see only one of you."

He nodded. "We are not many. The others are waiting in

other places, just in case. It was my good luck to stumble upon you."

"I am happy for you."

"You led us a merry chase. A few times, I thought you might give us the slip. But here you are." He looked at the statue. "Sad that these things are forgotten. The memories of men are short, and they are ungrateful."

"A lesson all shinobi must learn," Okuni said. He nodded again.

"If they wish to prosper."

"How can you be sure you will not share my fate?"

"Because I was not so foolish as to mistake the servant for the master," he said. He changed the direction of the chain's spinning, making her feel vaguely nauseous. "You are an outsider, my lady – a stranger. But I was born here. I know whose hand feeds me, and when not to bite."

"Who hired you?" Okuni asked, gathering her legs beneath her. She still felt weak, but she had regained something of her strength. Not much, but hopefully enough. She would only have one chance to get past him. She gripped her knife more tightly.

He smiled. "You know I cannot tell you that."

"Then tell me your name."

"Chobei."

"Your cadre?"

He shrugged again. "We have no name. We do not need one." He slowly rose to his feet and began to swing the chain's weighted end. "Afterwards, I will return your body to your clan – as a show of respect."

"You are too kind," Okuni said. Pain-lights danced across her vision as she readied herself. He snapped his wrist forward, and the weighted end of the chain arced towards her. She lunged to her feet, knife in hand. She deflected the weight and drove the tip of the blade towards his face. As she'd hoped, he jerked back, leaving the path to the river open.

She ran, but not swiftly enough. She felt the chain snag her ankle even as she reached the water. She fell forward, her knife skittering from her grip. Pain lanced through her as she fell heavily on her injured side.

Okuni rolled over just in time to catch the descending blade of Chobei's knife between her palms. He snarled in consternation and leaned forward, trying to force the blade down. She felt the edges biting into her hands as she fought to keep it from piercing her chest. She forced the blade aside with a desperate heave, driving an elbow into his chin in the same motion. He fell back, dazed, and she scrambled for the water, leg still tangled in the chain.

She snatched up her knife and dove in, cutting the surface of the shallows cleanly. It was hard to see, thanks to the silt that billowed with every stroke, but she started swimming, knowing that to stop meant death.

She knew only that she had to get to safety. She had to get home.

CHAPTER EIGHT
The Jaws of the Lion

Kasami impatiently knocked a fist against her own bench. Their boat was a low, square thing – barely more than a raft – but sturdy, and the pilot was skilled at navigating between the larger vessels that crowded the river at this time of day.

Even so, it had taken almost an hour to procure transport. The Crane had no private wharf of their own, which made matters difficult. The rivermen commanded exorbitant fees to conduct passengers from one bank to the other, but it was still cheaper and faster than crossing the toll-bridges that connected the shallows.

"We are late," she said, glaring up at the sky. She tried to center herself, to push her anger and frustration over the delays down. She took a deep breath, closed her eyes, opened them. Even after all the time she'd spent in cities, she was not used to their routine of hurry up and wait. Things were simpler in the marshes. There was less noise, less confusion. Less of everything that took one away from oneself.

"We are not late," Shin said, unconcerned. He reclined on his bench, fanning himself. Despite the hour, the air was still muggy, and she could taste a hint of rain on the sluggish breeze. "Still," he continued, "one would think that Tetsua would provide us with transport, seeing as how we are about his business."

She looked at him. "We are late. The sun has set."

"The sun is setting. There is a difference."

"Do you think they will care?"

"As a matter of fact, yes. Calm yourself. Our feathers must remain unruffled, else we might miss something important."

"Like what?"

"Any number of things. A tone of voice, a meaningful glance… a lie."

"And how does any of that help us?" she asked in exasperation. Sweat trickled down her neck and beneath her armor. She had decided to wear it over Shin's protestations. She wanted to be ready, just in case something happened. It wouldn't be the first time the Lion had snapped their jaws shut on a foolish Crane's neck.

Any Daidoji worth their steel knew that the Lion could only be trusted to devour all those before them. And Cranes were among their favorite prey. The two clans had gone to war more times than she could recall, and while relations between them were largely peaceful at the moment, it would only take one mistake – one foolish comment – to set them at each other's throats once more. She prayed Shin would not be the one to make that mistake.

Shin sighed. "The key to any investigation is context – who, why and how. Three simple points. Who stands to gain? Why choose this method? And how was the deed accomplished?

Answer those three questions, and you have your solution. That is what I intend to do."

Kasami rolled her eyes. "And how is this going to help?" she asked, kicking the satchel he'd insisted she bring. It was waterproof and covered in straps and buckles. Inside were various glass jars and instruments of metal and wood, none of which had any purpose she could determine.

"That is my equipment. Jars for samples, measuring rods and other tools. According to Agasha, all necessary for a professional investigator." He paused. "Though some of it seems a bit useless, I admit."

"So toys, then."

He sighed. "If you like." He paused, tapping his chin with his fan. "Regardless, we'll start with the scene of the crime, and follow the trail backwards from there. All will be revealed in time."

"You hope."

"I am confident," Shin said. He looked at the water, and his expression went flat for a moment. Kasami, who'd seen that look before, knew what he was thinking. His predecessor, Daidoji Aika, had been found in these waters, floating face down. A robbery gone wrong. A tragedy, but not an uncommon one. Or so it had been declared by those of greater authority than Kasami.

And yet, she found herself questioning it on occasions like this. There were whispers, of course. There were always whispers and rumors. Gossip. The servants talked when they thought she was out of earshot. Nor were they the only ones. For a time, Aika's death had been the talk of the city. Much had been made of the circumstances – the absence of her bodyguard, for instance – but no answers had been forthcoming.

She pushed the thought aside. Aika was not important. Shin was. And right now, Shin was walking them into the jaws of a hungry beast. Her hand tightened about the hilt of her sword as she watched the opposite bank of the river draw near.

Rather than wharfs, a defensive wall rose along the length of the eastern bank. The wall dated from a more violent period in the city's history, and still bore the scars of that time. The heavy palisade of wood and stone was inset with half a dozen canal gates, each of which led into a network of canals that reputedly extended far inland, past the limits of the city, to the riverside storage complexes of the Lion.

Kasami's skin prickled as she took in the armed warriors who patrolled the top of the wall. Keen-eyed archers gazed down at the river, ready to repulse any unwelcome vessel. The shallows around the gates were littered with the sunken remnants of blackened wreckages – reminders of past failed efforts to breach the Lion's defenses.

The gates were open, but already bells were ringing, signaling that they would soon be closed for the night. Kasami felt another flicker of annoyance as she considered how slowly they were moving. "Can you speed up?" she snapped, looking at the pilot. He bowed his head beneath the weight of her glare and redoubled his efforts to pole the flatboat across the water.

"Growling at him isn't going to make us go any faster," Shin chided. Kasami ignored him. Among his other failings, Shin was entirely too lenient on his inferiors. And contrary to his assertion, they reached the closest canal gate even as the assemblage of levers and pulleys that controlled it clattered into motion.

Another bell began to ring as the flatboat drifted through the gate. A minuscule quay of smooth stone emerged from the side of the canal, and the pilot made for it. Beyond the quay was a forecourt where ashigaru performed evening exercises.

Kasami studied them keenly. The Lion maintained a large standing army, and their peasant-soldiers drilled constantly, even when there was no need. It was different in Crane lands. In a Crane fortress, there would be no ashigaru save in time of war; only trusted retainers, whose families had served the clan for several generations.

When the boat thumped against the quay, a group of these armored ashigaru were waiting for them. Spears were leveled, forcing the pilot to keep his distance. Shin rose languidly from his seat. "I believe we are expected."

"You are late," a woman's voice said. A woman who could only be Akodo Minami stalked towards them along the canal, trailed by several bushi, all armed and armored as if for war. Minami was taller than Kasami, but not by much, and with a similar sturdy build hidden beneath her armor. They were of an age as well, though that was where the similarities ended as far as Kasami was concerned.

Shin made a show of looking up at the gradually darkening sky. "The sun has not yet set. Not quite, anyway. And if you would kindly ask your soldiers to lower their spears, we might yet arrive on time."

Minami glared at them, and Kasami could see that she was weighing Shin's request. Finally, she barked an order, the ashigaru lowered their spears and retreated up the steps. The pilot of the flatboat gave an audible sigh of relief and guided his craft more firmly up against the quay. Kasami hopped out, and then assisted Shin. As she turned, she saw that the soldiers hadn't gone far. Neither had the samurai.

Minami's companions eyed the newcomers with barely concealed anger. They were young, and they reeked of ambition and belligerence. Kasami found herself meeting their gazes one by one in silent challenge. If they wished to fight, she would be more than happy to oblige them, one after the next.

Shin had plastered on his friendliest smile. But before he could speak, Minami said, "You are here by the grace of the imperial governor, and for no other reason. We do not require the council of the Crane in this matter." She spoke firmly, and the set of her jaw told Kasami that her mind had already been made up. She glanced at Shin, hoping he would not take the bait. Minami was looking for a reason to send them away.

Shin sighed softly. "I do not come to offer council, or commiseration for that matter. In fact, I have little interest in you at all."

Kasami hid a wince. Nothing angered a Lion more than being told they were inconsequential. Minami's eyes flashed with anger, but her expression did not change. Kasami revised her estimation of the other woman ever so slightly. Minami was wiser than she appeared. "Then why did you request this meeting, Crane?"

"I did not. The governor did."

She dismissed this with a sharp gesture. "Answer my question."

"I wish to examine the scene of the crime."

"What?"

"The warehouse containing the rice. I wish to see it."

"Why?"

"To determine whether the rice was poisoned before or after it reached you."

"Before, obviously."

"Is it, though? Obvious, I mean. How do you know?"

"How would you be able to tell?" she snapped. Her companions stiffened at her tone, and the ashigaru shifted nervously. Kasami tensed. There were too many weapons in close proximity for her liking. One wrong word and things might well end badly. Shin, as ever, did not appear concerned.

"Oh, there are ways," he said. "I'm sure you would be bored to tears by the explanation. Suffice to say it involves rats."

"Rats?"

"Well, their droppings, mostly." Shin smiled beatifically. "If you'd like to accompany me, I would be happy to explain my methodology in full. It is so rare that I get to expound at length on such academic matters."

Minami's lip curled. "That will not be necessary. You are an agent of the governor. Your trustworthiness is… assured. I will see that you are escorted to the storage facility." She made to turn away, but Shin stopped her with a polite cough. "You wish something else?"

"Merely to ask who you think might have done it."

She looked at him as if he were a fool. "The answer is obvious. The Unicorn."

"Why?"

Kasami stared at him. He was being deliberately provocative, asking such questions openly. Thankfully, the tactic seemed to work.

Minami paused, clearly unsettled by his brazenness. "What do you mean?"

"What would they have to gain by such a clumsy attempt at sabotage? The Unicorn are known for many things, but clumsiness is not one of them."

"Are you here to defend them, then?" she said, softly. Her words bore an undercurrent of menace and Kasami silently pled with Shin to be quiet. As ever, he ignored her. "Is that why you were sent, Crane? To exonerate the savages?" She snorted. "Or maybe you have simply made up your mind already."

Shin's reply was mild. "Are you accusing me of bias?"

"It is not an accusation. It is a fact." Minami fixed him with a hard stare. "The Lion and the Crane are not friends. We never have been."

"No, you are correct. Relations between our clans have long been fraught. But we do not have to be adversaries, my lady. The Crane have only minimal interest in this city – and that only in regards to trade. We – I – do not care who rules here. Only that said rule is peaceful, and that trade is not disrupted."

"Then you will find in our favor," she said, bluntly.

"I did not say that. I intend to find the truth of the matter. If the Unicorn are responsible, I will inform the governor."

"And what will he do?" she said bitterly. "Nothing." She spat into the canal. "It is well known that Tetsua favors the Dragonfly above all others. He is besotted with the shugenja, Kuma."

"And you are greedy for glory," Shin said, sharply. Kasami had been with Shin long enough to recognize that the rebuke was calculated – precise. And it had its intended effect.

Minami flushed, visibly angry. "Watch your tongue, courtier. I will not brook insult from such as you. Speak such words again and we will meet on the field."

Kasami's hand fell to her sword instinctively, and she heard the Lion bushi make to draw their own blades. For a moment, it all hung on a knife edge. Kasami wondered if she could get Shin to the river before the first blow landed.

But, to his credit, Shin did not flinch. He ignored the bushi, and kept his eyes on Minami. "It is only an insult if it is a lie. Else it is simply fact. Unpleasant, perhaps, but facts often are." He parried Minami's attempt at a reply and pressed on smoothly. "You have made your feelings clear, and I can do no less. I do not think you are a fool, nor do I mean to play you false. I have been given a duty and I mean to discharge it to the best of my meager ability." He flicked open his fan with studied nonchalance. "If that means I must risk your wrath, so be it."

He paused, and Kasami was forced to admit that it was a masterful stroke. Minami had clearly hoped for a duel and Shin had given her one – just not the sort she'd imagined. Better, he'd proven himself her superior, at least for the moment.

Shin struck the killing blow after a suitable pause. "Now, may I examine the scene – or not?" Throughout it all, his placid smile never wavered.

Minami glared at him for long moments. Then, finally, she nodded. Kasami exhaled softly, quietly relieved. Perhaps she wasn't going to die today.

"Very well," Minami said. "Come. Let us go examine your… rats."

Sanemon paced back and forth across the stage. His big hands clenched and relaxed, his knuckles popping with every flex of the scarred flesh. Okuni had not yet returned. He had a bad feeling about this one.

Like any actor, Sanemon was superstitious. He knew the

world was deeper than it seemed. The shadows were darker, and the spirits closer than any save a shugenja might perceive. There were omens everywhere, if one but had the eyes to see.

"The sky was red last night," he said.

"The sky is red every night," Nao replied lazily. The actor lounged nearby, clad in a loose kimono, his face surprisingly clear of makeup. The stage was empty, and the theater lifeless save for the distant thunk of the backstage crew hard at their labors. The actors were elsewhere, relaxing in the baths or reciting lines in the privacy of the dressing rooms. There were a few hours yet until the performance, but the first trickles of the audience would soon begin to arrive.

"It isn't. Something is wrong."

"Then perhaps we should cut our tour of this fine city short and depart."

Sanemon stopped and turned. "You mean abandon her?"

"She would abandon us in a heartbeat."

"Even you don't believe that."

Nao's placid expression momentarily collapsed into something more human. "No," he said, softly. "No, you're right, I don't. So, what do we do?"

"I don't know. What about the others?"

"They're used to her leaving at odd hours and not returning. So far you're the only one panicking."

"I'm not panicking." Sanemon stopped. "I saw a Lion bushi challenge a Unicorn in the street today. Something about rice." He shook his head. "There's something going on. The city feels tense. As if everyone is waiting for something."

"What happened? With the samurai, I mean."

"How should I know? I didn't stick around to watch. When

samurai fight, the best place to be is elsewhere. This is her fault – I know it."

"And ours by extension," Nao said. He fanned himself lazily. "We are accomplices, after all. Not knowledgeable ones, I admit, but I don't think a magistrate would concern themselves with that distinction."

Sanemon hunched forward. Nao was right, of course. They were accomplices. Okuni was a shinobi – she committed crimes professionally. If she were ever caught or killed, that would be the end of the troupe. Sanemon had tasted samurai justice before, when he'd been nothing more than a peasant carrying a spear, and he had no intention of doing so again. "You're right. We have to leave."

"Or…"

Sanemon turned. "Or what?"

Nao pointed at him with his fan. "What about that invitation of yours? That Crane lordling who wanted to speak to you before today's performance."

Sanemon frowned. "What about it?"

Nao swatted him with the fan. "Think, you great oaf. There's only one reason a personage of such status deigns to extend an invitation to one such as you…"

Sanemon realized what he was driving at. "He might wish to become our patron."

Nao shrugged. "It is possible. And a wealthy patron – a Crane at that – might be able to protect us from whatever trouble Okuni has brought our way."

Sanemon nodded absently, his thoughts already turning back to the actress. "It isn't like her not to send word."

Nao huffed impatiently. "It is extremely like her." He paused.

"But I admit, you are right. Something about this feels wrong. Do you know where she was going?"

"Yes, an alleyway near the house she rented for us." He grimaced slightly as he spoke. "I told her it was too close."

"Have you been?"

Sanemon nodded. He'd seen nothing unexpected. No sign of her. No sign of anyone. Though he'd been unable to shake the feeling that he'd been observed as he poked through the refuse, looking for some clue as to her whereabouts. He shivered. "Wherever she is, I hope she's safe."

"Wherever she is, I hope she's keeping her mouth shut," Nao said. He rose. "I must get ready. Don't do anything foolish, Sanemon."

"When have I ever done anything foolish?"

"Ask me tomorrow," Nao said.

He left Sanemon standing on stage, staring out at the empty theater.

CHAPTER NINE
Rats and Rice

The storehouses of the Lion were farther inland than Shin had suspected. It took more than an hour on foot to reach the first of them, at the farthest edge of the city limits. No vessels larger than a skiff were allowed past the well-guarded cargo quays just inside the canal gates. Instead, the canal network had been designed to make best use of the river's current. Cargo was floated down to the massive storage complexes that straddled the river intermittently through the district, or else carried by wagon alongside the canals if it was too fragile to risk being floated.

Like the canals themselves, the storehouses were cleverly designed. They were built to rest over the river, so that cargo could be plucked from the water and drawn up into the belly of the structure. Improvised breakwaters of bamboo and rope were dropped into the canal in order to intercept the cargo, allowing the workers to hook the bales and haul them up where they could be unloaded in the shade.

"An ingenious operation," Shin said, as he and Kasami were escorted into the noisy confines of the storehouse. Workers labored in the shaded interior of the building, calling out to one another, shouting, laughing. "I see I have much to learn about such things."

Minami did not seem to appreciate his enthusiasm. "Keep your thoughts to yourself and your eyes where they belong, Crane. This is not a social occasion."

"Alas, no, you are correct. This is the warehouse, then?"

"We would not be here if it were not."

"Merely making certain," Shin said. "I like to be thorough about these things. Don't want to make any mistakes or upset anyone."

"You are too late for that," Minami said.

Shin chuckled politely. "Then I simply must make it up to you, my lady. Perhaps one evening, when this affair is settled?"

Minami stopped. "Do you think I would lower myself to consort with an individual such as you?" She gave a sharp laugh. "Like all Crane, you think too highly of yourself." It was a blunt accusation, as well as provocative.

Shin swallowed the insult with a smile. "Perhaps. But I'm certain that, once you get to know me, you'll think the same."

She turned away with a wordless growl. Kasami nudged Shin and gave him a pointed look of warning. He ignored her loftily and resumed his study of their surroundings.

While the exterior of the storehouse was sheathed in clay, the interior was mostly stone, including the roof. The proximity of the river kept everything admirably cool, and windows set at regular intervals in the walls allowed for the circulation of air and light. Even so, it was incredibly dim inside, and hanging lanterns wrought in the shape of rearing lions were strung throughout in order to provide light for the workers.

Shin could feel the vibration of the river through the wooden floor. At set points, great trapdoors marked the floorspace, and heavy pallets of cargo – including several hundred barrels of rice – awaited transport to their final destination. For iron and other raw materials, that meant being loaded onto the heavy wagons that waited outside the storehouse. For textiles and foodstuffs, it meant being moved to crude planks of shelving that lined the walls, or the open lofts above.

From Ito's reports, Shin knew that ore and wood were transported further downriver, deeper into Lion territory. But textiles and foods – two things the Lion had in abundance – were often bought cheaply in bulk and sold at cost.

After all, why go to the trouble of transporting rice upriver when they could just buy it for a pittance nearer to the city and turn a profit? Those who paid good money for Lion rice rarely asked its provenance – indeed, they were often only too happy to get it.

This was due to the fact that much of Rokugan was not particularly suited to agriculture, and what there was of arable farmland was valuable enough to wage wars over. Indeed, both the Lion and the Crane had done so on several occasions.

Minami and her bushi led Shin and Kasami through the storehouse and up a set of rough-cut plank steps to the lofts above. The air was full of noise and dust, even up here. Workers toiled, moving sacks and bales beneath the watchful gaze of overseers. The storehouse was well-guarded, Shin noted. Armored ashigaru were stationed at every access point, and overseers patrolled the stores diligently.

"You take few chances," Shin said.

"It is my duty to see that nothing impedes or endangers the flow of trade," Minami said without looking at him.

"And yet, somehow, a shipment of rice was poisoned."

"Sack."

"Eh?"

She snorted. "Not a shipment. A sack."

Shin raised an eyebrow, somewhat surprised. From the uproar, he'd thought an entire shipment had been tainted. But a sack – that was barely sabotage. "That is… interesting."

"Is it?" Kasami muttered. Shin nodded.

"Yes." Then, to Minami, "How can you be certain?"

"Certain of what?"

"That only one sack was poisoned."

Minami stopped again. She looked at him, but said only, "There." She pointed to where several men stood guard over a pallet of rice sacks. They moved aside at her gesture. Shin glanced at Kasami and then went to the pallet. One of the sacks was torn open – gnawed, perhaps. He looked back at Minami.

"Are vermin a common problem in your storehouses?"

"No," she said, flatly.

Shin didn't bother to reply. He adjusted his kimono and sank into a crouch. "Kasami, bring my equipment." There were a number of dead rats scattered about. Not many, but enough to tell the story. He examined the torn area of the sack. "Look here," he murmured. "This wasn't gnawed, at least not fully. Someone sliced it."

"Why would they do that?" Kasami asked, crouching beside him.

Shin looked at the rats. "The only explanation I can think of is that they wanted to draw vermin." He scooped a handful of rice from the sack and gave it a cursory sniff. He could detect nothing untoward, but that didn't mean it wasn't there. "Is that why they used a sack?" he murmured to himself. Typically, rice was transported in barrels. But on occasion sacks were employed, usually in small shipments. This seemed too large a delivery for that, however. One more curious thing to add to the list.

He unrolled his tool kit, selecting various items and making a show of employing them. He took various measurements, including the volume of the rice and the distance traveled by the rats before they died, as well as the length and angle of the blow that had sliced open the sack. It had been small, just opening enough to attract the vermin, but not as much to alert anyone handling it.

He was conscious of eyes on them as he worked. Minami did not trust them. He didn't blame her. In her place, he might well have done the same. Kasami was not so forgiving, however. She eyed the nearby guards warily, and kept her hand close to the hilt of her katana. Not so close as to deliver open insult, but close enough to annoy their hosts. Shin did not chastise her. It was bad form to do so in public, and, well, disrespect was its own form of currency, if one knew how to spend it correctly.

Instead, he bent a finger, summoning her close. "You seem tense," he murmured as he continued to sift through the rice. He found a scrap of cloth – dark silk – caught among the grains. Not deep, but close to the rip in the sack. An accident, perhaps. But during the loading – or the sabotage?

He rubbed the material between his fingers. Expensive. Not the sort of thing a laborer would wear. Maybe it had been planted, though that seemed altogether too subtle for whatever this was. He folded it and put it into his kimono. He glanced at Kasami. "I believe I asked you a question," he prodded.

"We are standing in the jaws of the Lion," she whispered back, from the corner of her mouth. Her gaze was never still, constantly flicking back and forth, taking in everything.

"We are standing in a storehouse. And we are here on the authority of the governor. We are in no danger." As he spoke, Shin glanced at their escort. Minami and the others stood well back, out of earshot. But they were watching closely.

"So you say."

Shin shook his head. "Minami is not a fool. Even if the Lion are behind this, she would not dare kill us. There are too many eyes on the situation as it stands."

"She does not strike me as being the pragmatic type."

Shin snorted. "No. But the Lion do not hand over command of vital ports to complete idiots. Or so I am told." He turned to look at Minami and called out, "Where was this shipment intended for?"

"Why do you need to know that?"

"To know who the intended target might have been."

"Us, obviously."

"But you intended to sell this rice on, correct?"

Minami frowned. "Yes. But it had no buyer yet."

"Did you have one in mind?"

"No."

Shin nodded absently. He believed her, though something about her account rang false. He sat back on his heels, trying to form an image in his mind of how the deed might have been accomplished. The cut in the sack was the obvious answer, but if that was the case, it would imply the poisoning had occurred at some point during transit. Otherwise the crew of the ship would have surely noticed, unless someone had paid them not to. "Where did you buy it? And who from?"

"What does it matter?" she replied.

"It might not. But, then again, it might."

"A merchant," she said after a moment. "I don't know his name."

She was lying. Shin let no sign of his realization show on his face. He wondered why. Spite, perhaps. But, more likely, she was hiding something. "Would there be someone available who might?"

She frowned and signaled an overseer. The man came over and bowed low. Minami murmured something to him, and he retreated. Shin waited for an explanation, but none was forthcoming. Finally, he turned back to the rice.

"I told you they weren't going to be any help," Kasami said.

Shin ignored her and continued to take his measurements. The distance of the rats from the rice indicated a quick acting poison. They'd eaten their fill and died almost immediately. But what might kill a rat would not necessarily do the same to a man. And, depending on the poison, cooking might reduce its potency even further.

Shin let a handful of rice grains slip through his fingers. "Only one bag has been opened," he said, after a moment. "But that doesn't mean the others in the shipment aren't similarly tainted. We'll take samples of each."

"Why?" Kasami asked.

"So I can test them, of course."

She grunted and opened the satchel, retrieving several glass vials. At his direction, she collected a few grains of rice from each sack, and placed them in separate vials. "This is foolish. What does it matter whether the other bags are tainted?"

"Context." He rose as Minami approached, a young woman in tow. The woman was clad in plain robes, and looked unhappy to be there. Frightened, even. She rubbed her arms and averted her gaze as Shin sought to look her in the eyes.

"This is the customs agent you wished to speak to," Minami said.

Shin ignored Minami and focused his attentions on the young woman. "Your name?"

"Ichime Mei," she said, lifting her chin. She attempted a scowl, but it fell flat. "My lord," she added, after a moment. Shin smiled.

"Good evening, Mei. I am Daidoji Shin. You accepted delivery of the shipment?"

The young woman nodded and cast a nervous glance back at Minami, who scowled thunderously. "I- I did." There was a faint familial resemblance between them. That was no surprise. Lesser cousins were often given positions within the lower hierarchy – family could only trust family, after all.

"Tell me about it."

Again, she glanced at Minami. "What… what do you wish to know?"

"Anything you can recall, however insignificant it might seem. Including the name of the seller, if possible."

Her recall of the incident was imperfect, but Shin had long ago become accustomed to the fact that his memory was sharper than that of most people. Of her recollections, only two facts stood out – the captain of the vessel had been a woman with one eye, and that nothing had seemed out of order.

The delivery had occurred early in the day, just after dawn. The ship had been a battered sloop, with patched sails and a hull that had met rocks more than once. Then, any number of disreputable vessels of similar description prowled the rivers. Free heimin captains, owing no allegiance to any clan or family, were often willing to carry cargoes others were not, and for less money.

The rice had been a late addition to the expected deliveries. A shipment had become available for cheap, and the Lion had pounced. Even so, Mei wasn't certain of its origin. As she made the claim, she looked at her mistress as if for permission – and received a terse shake of the head. That they were hiding something was obvious.

"And the name of the merchant who sold it to you?" he asked, when she'd finished.

Another look, another request for permission – and another slight shake of the head. Shin frowned. Something told him that pressing the issue would not be well received by Minami. She might even decide to take it as an insult.

"I- I don't remember," Mei said, not meeting his gaze.

Shin nodded. "Very well. Thank you, Ichime Mei. You may go now."

Minami dismissed the woman and said, "Are you satisfied, Crane? Have you seen all you needed to see?"

"For the moment."

"I hope so, because this is the only time you will be allowed in these storehouses."

"Then I'm glad I took samples," Shin said. He was baiting her now, despite his earlier intentions. He glanced at Kasami and saw a knowing look on her face. He straightened and said, "You have been most courteous, my lady. I shall speak highly of you the next time I speak to Governor Tetsua."

Minami looked at her waiting warriors and then back at Shin. "And what will you tell him about this matter?" she asked.

"That there is still much we do not know." Shin turned back to the rice. "From what I've seen, any tampering with the rice would have been impossible in the warehouse itself. There are too many safeguards and checkpoints between here and the river. But it is not likely it occurred elsewhere, as someone would have noticed…"

"What are you implying?" Minami demanded. Her voice cut the air like a blade. Shin turned, startled. "I knew you believed us to be responsible for this," she continued, before he could reply, her eyes bright with righteous anger. She was speaking loudly, as if for the benefit of her followers. People stopped what they were doing to watch.

"I did not say that," Shin protested.

"Then what are you saying?"

"Nothing at all. I am merely stating the facts as I see them."

"Your facts."

"Facts are facts," Shin said, fighting to retain his composure. Any show of anger could result in a challenge – or worse. There was no doubt she was trying to provoke him, and had been from the moment of their first meeting. The reason was obvious – a challenge would compromise his neutrality, and end the investigation even before it had begun. But was she doing it because she had something to hide – or simply because he was a Crane?

"What possible reason could we have for committing such an act?"

"Justification," Shin said. "But you knew that already." He looked past her, at her bushi. Young men, eager for war. Eager to prove themselves. She followed his gaze, and her scowl attested to the accuracy of his statement.

"It is time for you to go," she said. "We have indulged you long enough."

"I have more questions."

"That is of no interest to me."

"You think the Unicorn are to blame – why?" he asked swiftly. She had been about to turn away, but paused. She looked at him. "You never answered me earlier," he added. "Why do you assume it was them and not the Dragon?"

"Perhaps they hoped to provoke us," Minami said, flatly.

"And why would they do that?"

"Ask Iuchi Shichiro," she said. "We are done here." She gestured to the spearmen. "Escort them back to the canal gate. Do not let them go anywhere else."

"Wait," Shin insisted. "One more question. Where is the vessel?"

Minami paused. "What?"

"The vessel that delivered the grain? Surely you looked for it? Where is it now?"

"Where else? The docks of the Unicorn." But she didn't sound certain at all. She was putting on a confident mask for her followers, but she was just guessing. "Do not come back here, Crane," she added as she turned away. "You are not welcome in the Lion district." As she spoke, the spearmen closed in, making further interrogation impossible.

Shin looked at Kasami. "I think it's time we left, don't you?"

CHAPTER TEN
Chobei

"What do mean, gone?" Saiga asked, without looking up from his ledgers. Morning light filtered through the shuttered windows set high in the walls of his office. Outside, the city sounded much as it always did. He took comfort in that.

Chobei sighed. "Just that. She has gone to ground somewhere. It will take time to root her out, if she's still in the city."

"Which you do not think she is," Saiga supplied. He looked at the gray-haired shinobi, trying to see past the inoffensive facade. Chobei was a fisherman when he wasn't slitting throats. He looked mild and humble, despite the scars. He folded in on himself, making his frame seem stooped and small. In reality, he was a tall man and well-built. Strong. And smart – that was the important bit, as far as Saiga was concerned.

He had worked with Chobei's cadre for many years. They specialized in sabotage, and made a good living on the river. There were perhaps a dozen of them, all part of Chobei's extended family – cousins, nieces and nephews. Chobei himself had no children that Saiga was aware of. He could not imagine any woman finding Chobei the least bit interesting. There was more human feeling in a piece of driftwood.

"She would be foolish to remain. A wise shinobi knows when a task cannot be completed. Risk is for samurai. A shinobi's only armor is shadow and forethought."

"Poetic. What would you do, if you were her?"

Chobei's expression didn't change. "I would leave the city. Not by boat – over land. One of the Ide caravans, perhaps. Most shinobi function as part of a cadre. She does not. She has no allies, no resources. No options then, save to cut her losses and flee."

Saiga nodded. "Very sensible, and exactly what I have come to expect from you. And it would make my life easier if she did that very thing. Unfortunately for both of us, she is not you. She is brazen and determined. A bad combination."

"Then why did you hire her?" There was a hint of an edge to Chobei's question. Saiga wondered if he was insulted. It was hard to tell with Chobei. His face was like a mask, revealing little.

He and his cadre had been employed early on to sabotage certain shipments and Lion cargos, in order to create a trail for the Lion to follow when they inevitably started looking for culprits. But Saiga's partner had insisted on an outsider for the final thrust, to better cover their own tracks.

Another mistake. An amateur's mistake. And now it might well cost them dearly.

"As I have explained, it was not my choice." Saiga closed his ledger and placed his hands flat upon it. Despite his trade, they were rough and scarred. The hands of a fighter or so he liked to tell himself. They might just as easily have been the hands of a common laborer. He curled them into fists and looked at Chobei. "I have given you all the information I have on her. It is up to you to deal with her now."

Chobei nodded. "We will."

Saiga sighed. It was clear he'd insulted Chobei without intending to. "I know you to be competent, Chobei. And if you say you cannot find her, then she cannot be found. Besides, we have other matters to discuss." Saiga paused, gathering his thoughts. The last few days had been fraught. His message had been received and a reply had come almost immediately.

He was to do everything in his power to erase every part of the trail that linked his partner to the poisoned rice. To that end, he had contacted Chobei through the usual methods. His cadre were mercenaries, with no loyalties save to the one who paid them. They could be counted on to act professionally – especially when it came to murder.

The thought sent a thrill of repulsion through Saiga. Theft, sabotage, spying – all these were crimes he had committed, and gladly. But murder, even at a remove, was something else. He felt as if he stood at a precipice, and behind him, a tiger was approaching. The only choice was to jump, but having jumped one could not choose where one landed. It was all uncertain, and Saiga was not a man for uncertainty.

As a trader, he had learned to predict outcomes. Even his roughest guesses were often on the mark. But he could not see what end awaited him now, and it unsettled him. And not just him. Rumor swept through the city's mercantile quarters like wildfire – gossip was its own currency, and traders dealt in it as well as silks and rice.

The Lion were showing their teeth, their anger palpable. The Unicorn held firm, ready to meet whatever came. Both sides were gathering strength and testing the waters. Soon, one or the other would make a move and then the conflict would boil over into the streets.

"What matters?" Chobei prompted. Saiga cleared his throat.

"The governor has engaged the services of an investigator. A Crane. Daidoji Shin."

Chobei frowned. "They sent another?"

"Did you think they wouldn't? The Daidoji have been trying to worm their way into the dealings of this city for years." Saiga rubbed his face, tiredly. "This Shin is supposedly a fool – but even a fool finds the truth once in a while. That means we need to move quickly."

"We could kill him."

Saiga paused. "No. Not after the last time." He looked at Chobei. "One dead Crane is an unfortunate occurrence. Two is enemy action. The Daidoji Trading Council has already taken a strong interest in the city. If this one dies, and they suspect anything, they'll come in force. And I don't know about you, but the thought of a troop of Iron Cranes stomping around my wharfs looking for assassins does not fill me with joy." He shook his head. "No. No, the balance in this city is already tenuous enough. And I have made too many mistakes of late. I won't add another one to the pile."

Chobei nodded, but said nothing. Saiga drummed his fingers on his desk, thinking. Finally, he said, "Lun. The captain of the vessel that made the delivery. Is her boat still docked here?"

"No. They left yesterday."

Saiga frowned. "Then they'll be berthed at Willow Quay. Find the boat and sink it."

"And the crew?"

"Sink them as well, if they get in the way." Saiga hesitated. "Kill Lun. Make it look like a drunken brawl – or better yet, simply make her vanish. I want no connection between us. No trail for anyone, Crane or otherwise, to follow."

Chobei nodded and made to rise. Saiga stopped him with a gesture. "When you do it, be quick," he said, softly. "She is not at fault, and she has always been honest in her dealings with me."

Chobei nodded again. "It will be as quick as we can make it. What of the other – the Nekoma? Should we continue to hunt for her?"

Saiga paused again. But only for a moment.

"No. She will come to us."

Chobei stepped out of the teahouse and swept the street with a surreptitious gaze. It was being watched, of course. The Unicorn had long known of Saiga's involvement in the black market and kept a close eye on him, as well as those who came to see him.

He could not say whether Saiga himself was aware of this. He had never mentioned it, and Chobei was not in the habit of volunteering such information for free. For all that their relationship was an amiable one, it was still professional.

But when the watchers looked at him, they saw only a humble fisherman, and an old man at that. No threat, and not of interest.

Chobei was indeed old, as men in his profession judged such

things. Too old to be out and about, too old to be meeting with men like Saiga. But he had never liked sitting back and sending others out to do what he was not prepared to do himself. That was why he had taken on this contract personally, despite the risk.

His cadre was small, barely there at all. A dozen shinobi, who'd learned their arts from the masters before them. They'd come to the city from the mountains long before Chobei's time, looking to profit from the conflict between Lion and Unicorn. They'd stayed, afterwards. As the city had grown, so too had opportunities for the practice of their art.

Between contracts, they were fishermen. Chobei enjoyed it – weaving nets, the feel of the line in his hands. Sometimes he wished a fisherman was all that he was.

He felt uneasy about the situation. That they had felt the need to hire an outsider was an insult, but a minor one and easily overlooked. His cadre was not the only one in the city, after all, and this did not even take into account those who were affiliated with the Great Clans.

But the task itself – it was designed to upset the balance. To throw the city into chaos. Saiga had obviously thought better of it, but it might well be too late to stop what was coming. War was like an avalanche. Once it began, all you could do was try and get out of the way. That it might well prove profitable for his cadre had crossed his mind. But with greater profit came greater risk.

Saiga hoped that by eliminating certain links, the chain of his mistake would sunder and sink, forgotten. But a chain was still a chain, even when broken. And links could be repaired. Chobei wondered how long before Saiga's master decided that

Saiga himself was a link in need of cutting – and whether Saiga himself had already considered that outcome.

He dismissed these thoughts even as they occurred to him. It was not a shinobi's place to question the decisions of his masters – merely to enact their will to the best of his ability. As he crossed the narrow street a woman fell into step with him. His lookout was young, and dressed in the tattered raiment of a fishwife. An infant was slung across her chest in a loose wrap, supported by her arm.

"Three men," she murmured. "One at either end of the street. One in the teahouse."

"I saw them, Yui, thank you." He hadn't noticed the one in the teahouse, but saw no reason to tell her that. Yui was among the most talented of his students. Someday, when he was gone, she might well replace him as leader of the cadre.

"They are Unicorn, I think." Yui shifted her son from one arm to the other without disturbing him. "The same ones who've been sneaking about for some time."

"I expect so." Chobei leaned close and gave the infant a kiss on the fuzzy crown of his head. "How is he?" he asked.

"Either very loud or very quiet." Yui looked at him. "Well?"

"He is worried, though he won't say it."

"He should have hired us. Then he wouldn't be."

Chobei sighed. "We have had much business off him of late. That is enough to earn some charity on our part, I think." Despite his words, he agreed with her. Saiga – and his unnamed partner – had made a mistake.

Until the outsider had arrived, Chobei and his cadre had conducted a discreet – and profitable – campaign of sabotage against the Lion. Nothing too big or too difficult; damaged boats, stolen cargo and the like. All pointing to the Unicorn, if the Lion bothered to investigate. Chobei had not questioned it. Saiga had been orchestrating such minor campaigns for years, first against one clan and then the other, as if to make sure that the balance between them was maintained. Now, it seemed as if all of that had been wasted effort.

"What now?" Yui asked.

"Someone needs to go to Willow Quay and find a boat. You have been there before." It wasn't a question. Yui nodded, smiling slightly. "Take Kino and Riku," he added.

"Are we going after the pirate?"

"Yes." He paused. "Who told you she was a pirate?"

"One hears things at the well. She employs a good number of men who would not otherwise be working. They come home with money and drink most of it up. But they only deliver cargo every few weeks."

Chobei grunted. Trust Saiga to employ a pirate as a courier. "You are to sink the boat. Make it look like an accident."

"Of course. The crew?"

Chobei considered it. "If they interfere. Make sure Lun dies."

"An accident as well?"

"Yes. Be quick, and quiet if possible."

"If it's not?" Yui asked, as she soothed her son. The infant gurgled and clutched at his mother's face with chubby fingers. Chobei smiled and tickled the child beneath his chin, eliciting a coo of amusement.

"Quick will do." He looked at her. "Strike when they are ready to leave. Not before. Even if it takes a few days. We want no questions." He squinted up at the sky. "You have someone to watch the child?"

"Are you volunteering, Master?" She saw his look and added, quickly, "My mother will be glad to take him. She is lonely."

Chobei hesitated. "She is… well, otherwise?"

"She would be better if someone would visit," Yui said, meaningfully.

Chobei looked away. "Perhaps. Afterwards."

Yui smiled. "And what about the renegade?"

"Saiga believes she will return for her money."

"Is she that foolish, Master?"

"Determined," Chobei corrected. "And dangerous. We must take her next time." He watched her son shift in his wrappings, gurgling softly. In a few years, it would be time for him to take his place in the cadre. To learn the way of shadow and smoke, even as Yui had. He looked at her.

"For if we fail, we may not get a third chance."

CHAPTER ELEVEN
Beeswax and Poison

Kasami took the tray of tea from the servant. The young woman bowed solemnly. She was one of three, employed to look after the house. The families of all three had served the Daidoji for at least four generations. Even so, she was fairly certain that one of them was a spy for someone other than Shin's grandfather. She wasn't certain as to which one, and regarded them all with appropriate suspicion.

Her family had made do without servants. It seemed unwise to her to allow others to prepare your food and drink. But Shin had insisted, stating that certain standards were to be maintained. Privately, she suspected that he was aware of the spy – or spies – and was watching them even as they watched him.

Kasami carried the tray upstairs and knocked politely. "Enter," Shin called out. She slid the door open and found him kneeling before a low table, examining the evidence they'd gathered the previous evening. The door to the balcony was open, allowing in the sun. She could hear the soft, silvery tinkle of the chimes hanging in the tree branches below as she shoved aside a stack of papers and set the tray down.

Shin's room was a mess. He did not allow the servants past the door as far as she knew. Clothes and books occupied every available surface. Among his other vices, he was a voracious reader of pillow books. The more lurid the better. She picked up one and tossed it over her shoulder with a snort.

Shin peered closely at strands of sacking material. It glistened slightly, and he released a soft chuff of satisfaction. "As I suspected." He sat back and stretched.

"What is it?" Kasami asked, as she poured them both a cup of tea. It was decidedly aromatic. A special blend from the Dragon lands, imported at high tariff. Shin spent as much money on tea as he did on his clothes.

"Strands I collected from the sacking. Look here – see this residue? It's beeswax. It was used to seal the slit made in the sack. The rats ate it." He looked at her. "Someone slit the sack open, poisoned the rice and then carefully resealed it with beeswax to hide what they had done. But beeswax wouldn't last long… varying temperatures and the attentions of hungry vermin would soon disperse it. So that gives us a very definite window of opportunity for the poison to be administered. It could only have been done while it was in transit."

"You mean while it was on the river?" She frowned. "The crew, then?"

"No. I think not. Any rational captain would balk at such a scheme – they'd risk losing everything. And while greed can make a person do many things, I have a somewhat more realistic theory."

"A shinobi," Kasami said, anticipating him. While shinobi were hardly common, certain mercenary clans did exist on the fringes of society. Spying, sabotage, assassinations – these were their stock in trade. And while few samurai would admit to employing such individuals, they nonetheless somehow found an abundance of work.

Shin nodded. "They might have stowed away, done the deed and then slipped over the side just before the cargo reached its destination." He held up a shred of silk – another sample, she thought. He squinted at it, as if it were a puzzle he had not yet solved. He set it aside and went back to the sacking.

"Why not just remain on the boat?"

Shin shook his head. "The Lion are assiduous about security. They routinely search each boat that enters their territory for contraband. While I have no doubt that a talented shinobi might avoid detection, why risk it?"

"They'd have to be a strong swimmer."

"Or have a boat waiting."

Kasami grunted, unimpressed by the suggestion. "I like my theory better. Greed is simple, and the average heimin captain is stupid. Show them enough coin and most of them would cheerfully ground their vessels and burn the cargo." She paused when she saw that he was no longer listening. "What are you doing now?"

Shin set out the samples of rice. "Preparing to test the rice for poison."

"We know it was poisoned." She shook her head, annoyed by his obstinance. He seemed determined to make this affair into something more complex than it really was.

"But we do not know what type."

"Why is that important?" What sort of fool cared about such inanities? Poison was poison. Its presence was more important than its name.

"Context," Shin said. "The type of poison may point to the culprit, or at least give us a clearer idea as to the moment when the shipment was tainted." He went to his shelves and collected several texts on poisons and medical herbology. Kasami frowned at the sight of them. He'd purchased them at no little expense several years before, for reasons that escaped her. Most of the volumes on his shelves were like that – purchased at a whim, and left to collect dust once he'd satiated his momentary curiosity.

"But you just said you already knew!"

"I do not know for certain. And the timing of the thing is as important as the nature of the poison. It all helps paint the picture."

Kasami shook her head. "What picture? None of this helps us find who did it."

"Oh, but it does. Think – this was not a matter of letting a few drops of night milk run down a wire into a sleeping man's ear. It would require precise timing and preparation."

Kasami took a sip of tea and shook her head. "We should be tracking down that boat. Then we'll get answers." To her way of thinking, the obvious answer was usually the correct one. Overly complicated schemes only happened in pillow books and bad theater.

"And we will. That is why I am paying a visit to Iuchi Shichiro tomorrow morning. It is the earliest he will see me. If the boat is on the Unicorn docks, he will know where it is."

"What if he decides not to tell you?"

"Then we will have our second suspect."

Kasami frowned. "Who's our first?"

"Why, Akodo Minami." Shin nodded at her exclamation of disbelief. "Is that so unthinkable? Minami is ambitious – driven. This may well provide her the opportunity. And remember her outburst – did that not seem somewhat telling to you?"

"No true samurai would do such a thing." Kasami had not cared for Minami's attitude, but she balked at accusing her of such behavior. It was all but inconceivable that a samurai might lower themselves so. There was a right way to pick a fight and that was not it. If Minami had wanted a war, she could have gotten one easily enough.

"No. And whatever else, she is that." He closed the book before him. "It's not fire biter, or night milk. That leaves some form of noxious poison. It is odorless and tasteless, else the rats would not have sampled it." His expression sharpened. "Inheritance powder," he murmured. "That has to be it."

"I've never heard of it. What is it?"

"Deadly," Shin said. He went to another shelf and selected a wooden box. He set it down on his writing desk and opened it, raising up a wooden shelf lined with stoppered vials and other alchemical accoutrements.

"Is that a poisoner's box?" Kasami said, somewhat accusingly. Such boxes were banned in most regions, though not technically illegal. They contained various chemical paraphernalia that could be used to craft or detect poisons. That Shin had one didn't surprise her, though she couldn't help but wonder when he'd acquired it.

She often questioned the servants as to what Shin spent money on, mostly to make sure that he didn't spend too much.

His allowance was finite, and she had no intention of missing a meal because he wanted to buy some dusty text that was of no practical value. But no one had told her of this. And if they didn't know, that meant Shin had snuck out to purchase it himself – which was even more worrisome.

Shin shrugged. "That depends entirely on how you feel about such things. Now, as I was saying… inheritance powder is meant to be doled out over days and weeks, a few drops at a time, mixed with food or drink. The victim becomes weak and ill, and eventually perishes. But the poison leaves few traces, visible only to those who know what to look for." Carefully, he unstopped a vial. A stink like that of rotten eggs filled the room.

Gagging slightly, Shin dipped a wire into the vial and then shook a single drop of gleaming liquid into the mashed rice. She didn't recognize the liquid, but then such things were of little concern to a samurai. A normal samurai, at any rate. As soon as the liquid touched the rice, a yellow froth formed on the surface. But only the rice taken from the tainted bag. The others showed no reaction at all that she could detect. Shin sighed and put the vial away. "I was right."

Kasami stared at the vile colored froth. "What does it mean?"

"It means that whoever did this was not looking to kill. The amount of this poison required to render even a sack of rice deadly would be massive. If it had remained undiscovered, it would have made the recipients sick, but nothing more."

"What if the object was simply to taint the supply?"

Shin shook his head. "It would require a far greater expenditure of effort if that were the case. Not bags, but boatloads. No, whoever did this wanted it to be found before it left the storehouse. The question is – why? Who benefits, besides the Lion?"

Kasami frowned. "Then why do the Lion think the Unicorn are to blame?"

"That is a very good question, and one I shall put to Iuchi Shichiro tomorrow morning when I meet him. In the meantime, I think we deserve a bit of entertainment, eh?" He rubbed his hands together. "A meal out, perchance? Maybe a bit of fun afterwards?"

"And what would your guest think?"

Shin paused. "My guest?"

"The fat man from the theater, remember? You invited him."

"Did I?" Shin looked surprised. "Why did I do that?"

Kasami shook her head and fought back the urge to smile. It was rare she got to remind Shin of his responsibilities so pointedly, and she was thoroughly enjoying it. "I'm sure I have no idea. You asked him to come before the next performance. That means he will be here soon – if he comes."

"Perhaps he won't?" Shin said, almost hopefully.

"You think a man like that would refuse such an invitation?"

"No. You are right." Shin looked around the room and sighed. "I will be on the balcony. Let me know when he arrives."

Biwa in hand, Shin strolled onto the balcony of his room. The balcony overlooked the streets below. He'd insisted on it, despite Kasami's protests. It wasn't large – a little more than a shelf of wood, protected from the weather by screens on either side and at the top. A bench stretched across its width, and he took a seat with a sigh. The bench was raised slightly, allowing him a good view of the surrounding streets.

He sat and played, letting his gaze sweep across the street below. As he did so, he turned over what he had learned in his mind. The order of events seemed certain. The rice had been purchased, and delivered. At some point during the delivery, it had been poisoned. The sabotage had been discovered, the Lion had roared and now – what?

He paused. The discovery was the key. If the bag had not been damaged, if the rats had not gotten at the rice, the act would have remained undetected. Someone would have gotten sick, perhaps even died if they were of weak enough constitution, but while that might have embarrassed the Lion, it would not lead to the same result.

Namely, war. Or conflict, at least. Perhaps not open, but a contest of influence as the Lion attempted to bully concessions out of Tetsua and the Unicorn. Then, the Lion chafed at such things – they preferred open battle to the games of courtiers. So, war.

Had that, then, been the goal? The bag had not torn by accident. The cut had been too regular, too neat. Someone had ensured that the sabotage was discovered. Someone had desired this outcome, that seemed undeniable.

But war served no one. Not really. The river trade was too important to the empire as a whole. Whoever instigated such a conflict would suffer repercussions, if not immediately then eventually. A moment of glory was not worth a lifetime of censure. Not even the Lion would think that a fair trade.

Then, perhaps, provocation had been the point. An insult that the Lion would pounce upon and use as justification. The Unicorn would have no choice but to respond. But why the Unicorn? Shin frowned and stilled his biwa. He recalled

Minami's reaction to the question. There was something there. Something they had not told him.

Maybe Shichiro could spread some light on the matter. If not, he would have to risk the Lion's wrath and visit Minami again. Someone was at fault, and the quicker he found them, the quicker the whole matter could be settled.

There was a tap at the door. He turned. Kasami slid it open and nodded. Shin sighed and rose. "Very well," he said. "Bring him to the receiving room. And have one of the servants brew a fresh pot of Silver Needle as well, please."

He set aside his biwa, annoyed with himself. Inviting the troupe-master – Sanemon – had been a momentary whim, and one he was regretting. Still, he was curious about the missing actress' whereabouts, and solving a little mystery might be just the taster he needed to help him with the larger one.

Sanemon was already waiting for him downstairs when he arrived. Sanemon was not his real name, of course. It was possibly the name of the person who had founded the troupe, or the one who had taught Sanemon.

Stage names were passed through the generations, from teacher to student, parent to child. Such names held great honor and importance among the brotherhood of actors. To take up such a name was to embody the spirit of those who'd held it before.

However, the current owner of the name of Sanemon was a somewhat sad specimen. He was a small, portly man, with a deep chest and a deeper voice. The characters he occasionally portrayed on stage were often great, booming presences – much in contrast to the man behind the mask. Shin was somewhat disappointed to realize that the actor wore lifts in his sandals, in order to give himself height comparative to his voice.

Even so, he was an interesting fellow. The faint scars on his hands spoke to his life before the stage. A sailor perhaps, or a soldier. The way he walked inclined Shin towards the latter. Sailors often had a peculiar rolling gait that Sanemon lacked. He walked as if he were expecting a shower of arrows to descend at any moment.

Shin sat in meditative silence until the tea arrived, brought by one of the servants. It steamed between them, filling the air with its strong aroma. When the tea had fully steeped, Shin poured two cups and passed one to Sanemon. He huddled over it, as if afraid that someone was going to take it from him. His eyes darted about the receiving room nervously.

Without speaking, Shin took a sip of his own cup. The tea was sweet and fragrant. Finally, he said, "Thank you for accepting my invitation. It is rare of late that I get to speak with an artist such as yourself."

Sanemon perked up slightly at this. "The honor is all mine, my lord. But I am curious as to the nature of the invitation…?" The question held a hint of anticipation. Many samurai took it upon themselves to act as patrons for artists of various stripes. Sanemon might suspect that such was the case here. If so, he was going to be disappointed. While Shin had often considered doing so, it was simply out of the question at the moment.

"I wished to ask you a question," Shin said. Sanemon leaned forward, head cocked theatrically. "Your lead actress – I noticed she was not in evidence during the last performance. Nothing is amiss, I hope?"

Sanemon's expression crumbled comically. "You – you noticed?"

"How could I not? Is she ill, perhaps? If so, I would be willing to offer the services of my personal physician."

Sanemon looked away. "She is – she is unwell, yes."

"As I said, I am happy to provide a physician…"

"No!" Sanemon flushed. "No. That is not necessary, my lord. Just a touch of something. She will be back on stage in a few days, I assure you…" He was babbling, desperate. Had he been on stage, Shin might have accused him of overacting. But the look on Sanemon's face was real enough. Fear – and worry. Not for himself.

"You are lying," Shin said, and took a sip of his tea. "Why?"

Sanemon's torrent of excuses slowed to a trickle. "I assure you, my lord, I am not – I mean, that is to say–"

Shin cut him off with a sharp gesture. "I am not some provincial lord or magistrate, eager to prove his authority. I will not take your head for having the temerity to tell a falsehood. Just explain."

Sanemon swallowed. "She's gone."

"Gone? Where?"

"I – we – don't know." He hesitated. "She's missing."

"How long?"

Another hesitation. "A day. Almost two, now."

"Have you informed anyone?"

Sanemon looked down. "Who would we inform, my lord? We have no patron, and there is no evidence of wrongdoing. She is simply… gone." He set his cup down. "Thank you for your hospitality, my lord. I must be going."

"Sit," Shin said, softly. Sanemon jolted, but did not rise. He kept his eyes downcast and said nothing. Shin sighed and set his cup aside. "Why are you frightened?"

Sanemon said nothing. Shin frowned, wondering how best to approach the situation. He decided that being direct was best. "I wish to help you. But I cannot if you do not tell me what is wrong. Has someone taken her against her will?"

The other man cleared his throat. He was silent for a few moments, as if trying to think of what to say. Shin waited patiently. Despite being an actor, Sanemon appeared to be a terrible liar. Finally, he said, "She was … meeting someone."

"An admirer?" Shin asked, feeling a flash of irritation. He should have realized that a woman such as Okuni had admirers. Was he not one himself?

"I do not know," Sanemon said. He sighed, and there was no melodrama in the sound. Only a sort of paternal resignation. "All I know is that she was to meet someone, and she did not return from that meeting."

"And you fear that she has come to harm?" Shin asked. Sanemon was not lying; nor was he telling the entire truth. He was hiding something. The thought intrigued Shin.

Sanemon looked away. "Not all admirers are welcome, my lord. Many an actress, and not a few actors, have come to bad ends because of a patron's unwarranted and unreciprocated obsession."

Shin sat back. He'd heard similar stories. The life of a traveling kabuki player could be dangerous, and not simply for the reasons one might expect. He made a decision. "Do you know where this meeting was taking place?"

"I do, my lord." Sanemon looked at him, a hopeful glint in his eyes. "An alleyway near the theater. Do you think that you can find her, my lord?"

"I think that I can make the attempt." Shin stood and

Sanemon scrambled to his feet. "And I will begin tomorrow – after an errand or two."

"I- I don't know what to say, my lord. I cannot – we cannot repay you for this kindness…" Sanemon began, hesitantly.

Shin shook his head. "If anything, it is I who owe you. You have provided me with much entertainment. If I can help in some small fashion then I am bound to do so. Kasami will show you out." As he spoke, Kasami slid the door open and glared at him. From her expression, he knew that she'd been eavesdropping and that he would hear all about it once Sanemon was safely out of earshot. That was a problem for later, however.

In the meantime, there was a cup of tea to finish.

CHAPTER TWELVE
The Unicorn

The following morning was cool and quiet, save for the creaking of docked vessels and the cries of river birds. Lady Sun rose high in a gray-blue sky, momentarily casting aside the clouds that threatened to burst at any moment. The air held the promise of rain.

Guards clad in the livery of the Unicorn escorted Shin onto the covered uppermost platform of the watch tower where his host awaited him. Beneath its violet roof, the platform was open to the elements. A low table had been set up at the center of the platform, and the guards who manned it had been dismissed. Two stools had been set to either side of the table, and one of them was occupied by the representative of the Unicorn.

Shichiro was breaking his fast when Shin arrived. The old man hunkered over a bowl of aromatic rice, mixed with something that smelled decidedly of beef. Shin wrinkled his nose. Red meat was considered unclean by most right-thinking people. The Unicorn, however, were only a few generations removed from barbarism and had no such strictures. The old man looked up, mouth full, and said, "Ah, Daidoji Shin. You made it. May I provide you some refreshment? Some plum wine perhaps? I know you Crane favor it…"

"No, thank you. Tea will be sufficient."

Shichiro signaled to one of the waiting servants, and a tray of tea was brought up. Shin realized that the old man had had it waiting. "Forgive an old man his eccentricities," Shichiro said, after one last mouthful. He jabbed his chopsticks into the remainder of the rice and set the bowl aside. "I prefer to breakfast here, when the opportunity arises." His wrinkled features were brown from the sun and wind, and his body bent by a lifetime in the saddle. "Walls interfere with my digestion."

Shin nodded agreeably. "I am honored that you agreed to speak with me." The servant set the tray down on the table and poured the tea. It had an acrid aroma that put Shin in mind of harsh winds and empty plains.

"But not surprised."

"No."

Shichiro smiled widely. "And even if you were, you wouldn't admit it. You Crane are good at hiding what you think. I hear you teach your babes to cry only when no one can hear. Is that true?"

Shin returned the old man's smile. "I can only speak for myself, but I cried often and at volume. Or so my mother insists."

Shichiro laughed and slapped his knee. "That's good. Children should be loud. All of mine were at that age. Loud and strong." He looked out over the river. "Of course, there's such a thing as being too loud."

Shin followed his gaze and saw that he was looking at the

defensive wall that marked the Lion district. "Lions roar. It is what they do," Shin said. Shichiro grunted.

"I don't worry when they roar. I worry when they stop." He looked at Shin. "It wasn't us. I swear it."

Shin hesitated. He hadn't expected such a blunt declaration, but it didn't surprise him. The Unicorn were odd, in that way. Their idea of honor was less rigid, more personal, but no less potent than that of the other clans. "You will forgive me if I cannot take you at your word," he said, choosing his own with care.

Shichiro frowned. "My word has always been good enough for Tetsua."

"Ordinarily, I would agree. But I have been tasked with making an investigation of the matter, and I intend to do so."

Shichiro snorted. "What is there to investigate? Someone sabotaged a batch of rice. It happens all the time. We cannot wage war in the open, so we do so in the shadows. We sink boats, burn warehouses and set pirates on one another. How is this any different?"

Again, his bluntness caused Shin to hesitate. Even Kasami wasn't so plain-spoken. "Poison is not fire or even pirates. It is deliberate – one cannot pretend it was an accident. The Lion insist that it is an act of war."

Shichiro shook his head. "Of course they do."

"You think they poisoned their own shipment?"

"It is the simplest explanation." He studied Shin. "Then, it doesn't really matter, does it? They want war – they always have. They chafe in times of peace."

"And you do not?"

"I am an old man," Shichiro said. "I have held this post for twenty years – good years, most of them. But my time is coming to an end." He turned, looking away from the river, out towards the far horizon. His expression became wistful. "I have one last great ride in me, I think. One day soon I will take it, and leave this duty to one of my sons."

"Which one?"

"I have not decided." Shichiro gestured, vaguely. "There's seven of them. One of them is bound to be suitable."

Shin paused, and then asked his next question. "And what about your daughter?"

Shichiro stiffened. Then he chuckled. "You heard about that, then?"

"The whole city has heard about it. I wasn't sure there was any truth to it."

"Some." Shichiro sighed. "I'd hoped to make alliance with the Dragonfly. Strengthen our claim to the city, and ensure peace between our clans. Fate had other ideas." He gestured sharply. "I do not wish to speak of it. It has nothing to do with your investigation."

"Some might regard it as just provocation."

"The affair in question had nothing to do with the Lion."

"True. But a canny man might see an opportunity to provoke an enemy into a rash action. Such an act might also serve to humiliate the imperial governor."

Shichiro grunted and looked away. "It would take a more crooked mind than mine to think of a scheme like that." He sighed and shook his head. "No one was at fault, whatever the gossipmongers claim. A misunderstanding is all. And already forgotten."

"Tell me." Shin leaned forward. Gossip was as good as gold among the nobility. That Shichiro denied it so strongly meant it was almost certainly worth knowing.

Shichiro didn't look at him. "My daughter, Konomi, is promised to Tonbo Kuma. But she was seen in the company of Miya Tetsua. I do not know by who, though I can think of a few who might profit from such a scandal."

"Was it? A scandal, I mean."

"She swears nothing untoward occurred, and I trust her. And the governor is an honorable man – he would do nothing to jeopardize his position, or the peace. But word spread, and in spreading was blown out of proportion." Shichiro shrugged. "As these things inevitably are. As far as I am concerned, the engagement is still planned."

Shin wasn't surprised. A marriage proposal was a thing of infinite complexity. Once an engagement had been made, it required great effort – or great shame – to break it. "What does she claim happened?"

"Why does that matter?"

"Context," Shin said.

Shichiro was silent for a moment. "My daughter has nothing to do with this. If you press the matter, I may become angry." He spoke calmly, but there was undercurrent of heat to his words. The incident was clearly still a sore point for him. The potential for embarrassment was great, and it could not have been easy for a man like Shichiro to ignore the gossip, especially when it might have concerned his daughter's morals or suitability.

Shin decided to change tack. "The Lion claim that the vessel that delivered the tainted shipment came from your docks."

Shichiro nodded reluctantly. "It's possible. Do you know the name of the captain?"

Shin frowned. "Regrettably, the Lion were not forthcoming. I was hoping you might be able to point me in the right direction."

Shichiro grunted. "I bet they weren't. Stubborn bastards. I can have a look. Our captains keep records of every transaction. We like to know what they sold and to who."

"Wise."

"We learned it from you," Shichiro said, smiling crookedly. "The Crane do much the same, last I heard. You even keep records of what everyone else is selling."

Shin shrugged. "Information is currency."

Shichiro nodded. "So I've been told. I prefer steel, myself. It never loses its value." He paused. "Why are you looking for it? The boat, I mean."

"I need to know when the rice was poisoned. If it was onboard the vessel, the captain might well be a conspirator." Shin waited, but Shichiro did not protest as he expected. Instead, the old man sat back and stroked his chin, as if deep in thought.

"That is an unfortunate possibility." He sat forward. "How much do you know about how the river trade works?"

Shin hesitated. "Not as much as I might like," he said. It was always best to appear ignorant, that way someone was bound to come along and educate you – and in doing so, perhaps tell you more than they intended.

Shichiro chortled and slapped his knee. "As I thought. Most of the captains on this part of the river own their vessels. They hire their own crews, pursue their own contracts. They rent berths from us, or the Dragonfly, to offload their cargoes. We have no more control over them than we have over the pirates and smugglers who infest these waters."

"You mean, you might not be able to direct me to the captain in question," Shin said.

"The Lion deal almost exclusively with private captains – that is to say, either those already in their employ, or those who owe no particular allegiance to any clan. They don't trust us, or the Dragonfly. Why would they trust our captains to deliver supplies?"

"Ah." Shin made a show of pinching the bridge of his nose. He'd already assumed as much, but having Shichiro confirm it was something, albeit not particularly helpful.

"I am still happy to make inquiries, of course. But there is a very good chance that they will come to nothing. The vessel you seek is likely already gone – or at the bottom of the river. That's what I would do. Why risk a wagging tongue? Promise them the moon, and then give them the blade. At the end of the day, such men are expendable."

"And that is where we part ways, my lord," Shin said. "I have never considered other people expendable. I am told it is a flaw in my character."

Shichiro smiled. It was not a mocking expression, but genuine in its warmth. "Funny words from a Daidoji in this day and age, but perhaps not surprising. And I bet I know who told you that. Your grandfather and I clashed often in our younger days."

Shin bowed his head. "He will be pleased you remember him."

"I doubt that. He was an obstreperous sort, even then. I cannot imagine that the years since have improved his character."

Shin allowed himself a smile. "I would not know, my lord."

Shichiro snorted and looked out over the river. "He was one of the ones who arbitrated our current arrangement, you know. The Crane ever pursue peace, especially when it profits them. That is what my mother said, and I have always found it to be true."

Shin, who hadn't been aware of that fact, raised an eyebrow. "I must confess, my lord – my grandfather and I rarely speak to one another. Intermediaries are our preferred method of communication and have been since the death of my father."

Shichiro looked away. "Best way to deal with him, I always thought. I might have married your grandmother, you know. There was a time when I vied with him for her hand. Such an arrangement would have bound our families together. Instead, her father chose the wealthier suitor." He smiled. "I cannot say that was the wrong choice."

Shin was growing uncomfortable with this line of conversation. His grandfather was not someone he wished to discuss, especially here and now. He decided to change the subject. "What will you do?"

"If they decide to pounce, you mean?" Shichiro chuckled. "Let them. There's a river between us, and a boat is as good as a parapet for my archers. We'll beat them back across the water, bloody and chastened."

"You sound as if you almost look forward to the prospect."

Shichiro shook his head. "As I said, I am old. I have spent the better portion of my life here, serving ably and quietly. Facing the warriors of the Lion would be a good end to my story, I think."

"Especially if you were victorious."

Shichiro smiled. "Ah. There's the Crane guile. You think, maybe, we sent a bag of poisoned rice to the Lion to start a war. Like waving a hank of raw meat in front of a starving cur's snout, eh?"

"It did occur to me."

Shichiro picked up his bowl and took another bite of rice. "You remind me of your grandfather quite a bit, actually. He was a suspicious bastard too."

Shin was momentarily taken aback. "I meant no insult."

"Oh of course you did. You Crane always mean your insults. It's your compliments you make in ignorance." Shichiro pointed his chopsticks at Shin, an insult in and of itself, but one Shin decided to ignore, given the circumstances. "I can see the only way to prove our innocence in this matter will be to find that ship. If the captain is one of ours, I will find him and offer him up to you. And if not… I wish you luck."

Shin bowed his head gratefully. "I will take all the luck I can get, my lord."

Shichiro gestured again with his chopsticks. "Go and let me finish my breakfast in peace. I'm sure you have other people to bother today."

Shin stood and bowed respectfully. "Thank you, my lord." The guards were waiting at the steps for him, and he allowed them to escort him down the tower.

As they descended, however, they met another party coming the opposite way. Two sets of guards momentarily faced off, as the newcomers made way for Shin's escort. Shin paused. The newcomers were escorting a young woman of means and her ladies-in-waiting – a young woman he recognized easily.

"My Lady Konomi," he said in greeting, and bowed his head.

"My Lord Shin," she replied. "I believe I saw you at the play the night before last." Her voice was soft, but her words were calculated and her gaze was keen. She was a tall woman, and sturdy. A woman made to ride the plains and beat wolves to death with her bare fists. She looked somewhat ill at ease in her kimono, with her hair artfully arranged and her face powdered, surrounded by simpering maids.

"Yes. Did you enjoy it?" He studied her curiously. Konomi was one of the great mysteries of the city – she was the youngest of Shichiro's children, but the one most often seen in his company. Rumor had it that she had taken on the role of advisor to the old man. Perhaps that was why he was so eager to marry her off.

"Not as much as I hoped. The lead actress…"

Shin nodded. "Yes. A last minute replacement, I'm told."

"Oh? Are you on good terms with them, then?" She smiled thinly. "It is a rare man of quality who admits to knowing such individuals."

"I am told that I am one of a kind," Shin said. He paused. "My sympathies for your current… difficulties." The words were chosen with care, so as to apportion neither blame nor pity. But he wanted to see how she reacted.

"Thank you." She smiled, as if nothing were amiss. "You had a meeting with my father this morning."

"Yes."

"About the difficulties with the Lion?"

Shin paused. "Yes. You know about it?"

"Not much. Enough to know he is worried."

"He did not give that impression."

She hid a smile behind her fan. "No, I expect that he did not. And you? Are you worried? The Lion and the Crane are not on the best of terms of late – or so I have heard."

"I rarely worry myself with such matters, my lady. Politics is of little interest to me."

"And commerce?"

"Even less, I am afraid." He smiled openly and her eyes sparked with humor. She wanted to tell him something, he could feel it. "Though I am aware that the Lion rarely sell the products of their own fields."

"They blame us for this of course, for after our return the lands they had held in stewardship were reclaimed. It represented a substantial loss of fertile land, or so I'm told."

"The Lion have a great many grievances," Shin said. "Some of which are baseless. Let us hope this matter is among them." He paused. "I do wonder, however, why the blame fell upon the Unicorn. They insist that the rice came from your docks."

"Maybe it did." She paused, and then went on. "We lost a shipment of rice not long ago. Stolen off the wharf by persons unknown."

"An entire shipment?" Shin asked, incredulously.

"It wasn't large, as shipments go," Konomi said, defensively. "It was loaded onto a wagon – not one of ours – and vanished into the city. Likely it was stolen by someone looking to sell it on somewhere else."

"Like an unscrupulous merchant, perhaps?"

"Perhaps. If I were you, I might ask whether that stolen rice somehow wound up on a ship bound for the Lion wharfs – and if so, who put it there."

Shin bowed his head. "A fine question, my lady. And one I shall try to answer."

CHAPTER THIRTEEN
Thus Far

"So, you learned nothing then?" Kasami said, as she and Shin took lunch in the garden. It was lovely this time of year. Fragrant blossoms of all shapes and hues hung from nodding stems, filling the air with a mélange of pleasing odors. Fat trunked trees cast comforting shadows, in which one might escape the heat of midday.

Carved gourds, filled with seeds and grain, hung among the branches overhead, attracting the appreciative attentions of a variety of songbirds. Shin gently strummed his biwa, keeping time with their song. "Quite the opposite. Shichiro confirmed what I already suspected – Minami was being frugal with the truth. The ship had no connection to the Unicorn whatsoever. But the rice… ah, the rice. That is where things become interesting."

"This stolen shipment you mentioned," Kasami said, plucking a grain of rice out of her bowl and eyeing it suspiciously.

"Indeed. Someone stole the rice and sold it on to the Lion.

The Lion somehow knew this, and attributed the poison to deliberate sabotage."

"You mean, they think that the Unicorn allowed the rice to be stolen, in order to embarrass the Lion," Kasami said, frowning in puzzlement. "That seems… unlikely."

"Unlikely, but not impossible. Especially if the goal was simply to provoke the Lion into some rash action." Shin set his biwa aside and retrieved his own bowl. "Which it has done." He took a bite and paused. "On that note, I've sent a message to Lady Minami, letting her know of my findings."

"Are you mad?" Kasami spat. Her exclamation startled the songbirds and sent them into flight. Shin frowned and watched them circle the garden in agitated loops.

"No, and keep your voice down, please. The birds are sensitive."

"You sent a message accusing her of stealing a shipment of rice!"

"No. I sent a message accusing her of buying a shipment of stolen rice. A different thing entirely. If we are lucky, it will provoke a swift response."

"Like a length of steel in your gut."

"No. Like an honest conversation."

Kasami shook her head. "It's as if you want to die."

"Death is the furthest thing from my mind at the moment, I assure you. And I'm sure killing me has not even occurred to Lady Minami."

"She's met you, hasn't she?"

Shin raised an eyebrow. "You can be hurtful at times."

Kasami took a large mouthful of rice and chewed noisily. Shin took a more sedate bite. Kasami wasn't wrong. He and Minami had done their best to provoke one another, albeit for different reasons. He'd hoped she'd let something slip; she'd obviously been hoping to goad him into a duel. But Kasami either didn't see that – or didn't want to.

"Do you recall my last face to face meeting with my grandfather?" he asked.

She paused and looked at him. She swallowed and said, "Yes."

Shin reached down beside him, where his wakizashi lay in the grass. "He gave me his blade, as a reward for passing my gempuku. Do you remember what he said to me?"

She shook her head. "No."

Shin smiled. "He said, 'always remember the length of your steel'. He wanted me to remember that, often, only a few inches of metal separates one dead man from another. Rest assured that I know the length of my steel, Kasami – just as I know the length of hers." He took a bite and when he'd finished chewing, he added, "The question now is – where is the boat, and where is the merchant?"

"Shichiro was probably right – the boat is gone, or sunk."

Shin considered this. "Possible. Still, we must find it."

"That should be easy enough. How many boats are there in this city?"

"Your sarcasm is noted. But my point stands. And we'll have to hurry. I doubt we are the only ones to come to this conclusion. Shichiro may not be interested, but the Lion, at least, will be on the hunt – if only to prevent word of their black market dealings from getting out. Another reason for my letter. It will distract Minami from her own hunt for a few hours, while she tries to determine what I know, giving us time to begin our own search."

"And how do you suggest we do that?"

Shin smiled. "I need you to locate our friend, Kitano."

She stared at him blankly. "Who?"

"The gambler. Remember him? You killed his friends a few nights ago."

She frowned. "I remember. Why?"

"I require his services. And he owes me his life, so no doubt he will be only too happy to accommodate us. Find him – but don't kill him."

Kasami frowned, but nodded. "I can do that."

"Of course. I have every confidence in you."

"And what will you be doing while I'm doing that?"

"I will be at the theater. After a stop off in a certain alleyway."

Kasami stared at him, her mouthful of rice forgotten. After a moment, she swallowed and said, "You're not serious?"

"I made a promise, I intend to make good. You should be pleased. You're the one who reminded me of my responsibilities after all. Besides, how hard can it be to find a missing actress?"

After what felt like hours, Nekoma Okuni opened her eyes. She hurt all over, a litany of aches and pains that dyed the edges of her vision red. The chill of the river still gripped her, though she'd done her best to dry off. The bleeding had stopped, but the wound in her side needed attention. And she needed rest and food.

She looked up and around. It was early afternoon, as far as she could tell. The heat of the day was growing oppressive, driving everyone who didn't have business on the street back inside. She would have preferred to wait for night, but she didn't think she'd last that long. The pain in her side was getting worse, and she was flagging from hunger and blood loss. She needed a safe place to rest, and that meant taking a risk.

She got to her feet slowly. She'd been moving from doorway to doorway all night and most of the morning, doing her best to look like a beggar – of no importance and worthy of no attention. It was easy to do, filthy as she was and reeking of the river. She'd used mud on her face and limbs to further mask her appearance. She fancied even her own mother wouldn't recognize her.

There was no sign of her pursuers. Then, there wouldn't be. They were professionals, just like her. Perhaps even better than her, though her pride rebelled at the thought. They had dogged her trail, haunting the wharfs and all but stepping on her shadow. That she had managed to finally lose them was something of a miracle.

Unless she hadn't.

Maybe they were waiting to see where she went to ground. The thought gave her pause. It was what she would do – and had done, on more than one occasion. If so, she was leading them right to Sanemon and the others.

A shiver ran through her, and the street blurred. She leaned against the wall of the alleyway, trying to keep her balance. She would have to risk it. She wasn't going to last much longer without rest. She detached herself from the shadows and staggered towards the window at the other end of the alleyway.

She'd rented the house when they'd arrived in the city. It was small and close to the theater, but private, which was the important thing. It made it easier to come and go as she pleased. The rear window looked out over the alleyway. She tapped at the shutters, and then again. She hoped someone was listening.

The shutter was jerked upwards almost immediately. Okuni didn't wait for an invitation. She tumbled through the window and into an untidy heap on the floor. Thankfully, it wasn't far to fall. "Close the shutter," she said, her voice a hoarse rasp. "Quickly!"

"You're back?" Sanemon exclaimed. He stood looking down at her, his florid features twisted into an expression of surprise and disbelief. He looked as if he hadn't been sleeping well. Then, he always looked like that.

"What does it look like?" she snapped. Blood leaked between her fingers as she awkwardly tried to haul herself up. "Don't just stand there gawping, fool – help me."

Sanemon leapt to obey. "What happened?" he demanded. "Where were you?"

"Trying not to die," she said, as he helped her to a sleeping mat. She collapsed onto it and probed her wound. Pain flared through her. Pain was good. It meant she was still alive. "My kit, Sanemon – quickly!"

Sanemon hurried to obey. The frightened faces of her fellow actors and the stage crew peered through the open doorway. She heard the murmur of questions and twitched her head towards the door. Sanemon slid it shut as he brought her what she'd asked for, as well as a bowl of water and bandages.

"How bad is it?" he asked, as he gave her the roll of leather that contained her tools. She undid the thongs and unrolled it, selecting a sharp blade. She cut away her improvised bandages. Blood welled.

"Bad," she grunted. Sanemon hissed and snatched the knife from her weakening grip.

"Stay still. What am I looking for?"

"A shard of metal. I can feel it lodged near the muscle. You'll need to – ah! – cut it out." She convulsed as he pressed her back against the mat and began to operate. Sanemon was a dab hand with a knife, better than anyone might imagine. He'd been an ashigaru in another life – a throat-slitter with pretensions to art.

She'd never asked him why he'd decided to become an actor. At the time, she'd assumed he was an idiot, if a useful one. It was only later that she'd realized that, while he was a poor actor himself, he was an expert at herding them.

He sat back and held up a sliver of steel. "Is this it?"

She probed the wound and let out a groan of relief. "I think so." She peered at it. It was a dart, likely fired from a blowgun. Not poisoned, thankfully.

Sanemon tossed the offending object into the bowl of water and began to clean the wound. "What happened?" he asked again. "When you didn't come back, I became worried."

"I was ambushed."

Sanemon paused. "The client?"

"Maybe. Or maybe someone else." She lay back and let him work. It wasn't the first time she'd been hurt, but it had come close to being the last. "It doesn't matter."

"I disagree. We should leave now. I'll make arrangements once I'm done here."

"No," she said, eyes closed.

"What?"

She opened her eyes. "I am owed a fee."

"I think the chance to collect it has passed," he said. "We should go now, before whoever injured you comes back to finish the job." He glanced nervously at the window as he spoke.

"Not without my payment," Okuni said, stubbornly. "It is a matter of professional pride. And we need it. We have bills to pay, food to buy..."

"And how do you intend to get it?" Sanemon demanded. He shook his head. "I knew this was a bad idea. Nothing good comes of provoking the Great Clans."

"I do not recall asking your opinion," Okuni said. She yelped as Sanemon dug a knuckle into the edge of her wound and her eyes flew open. "Watch what you're doing!"

"Sorry," he said, unapologetically.

"What is going on in here?" Nao demanded from the doorway. He slid it shut behind him when he saw Okuni. "Oh, look what the cat dragged in."

"I'm not in the mood, Nao."

"No, you look dead," the actor said. He pushed Sanemon aside. "Go get some more water – and boil it. I'll see to cleaning the wound properly."

"I know how to do it, Nao," Sanemon protested.

Nao did not look up. "Yes, but she's not an ashigaru lying in a ditch. A more tender hand is required. Boiling water, please." He began to work, probing the wound. "I can stitch it, but you'll need to be careful or you'll just start bleeding all over everything again."

Okuni grunted as he went to work. Nao was more skilled than Sanemon. She'd never asked him where he'd learned such things, though she'd often taken advantage of it. "I'm always careful."

Nao gave a sharp laugh. "That's what you said last time."

She glared at him. Grateful as she was for his expertise, she had little patience for his wit. "Are you implying something?"

"Oh no, mistress. I would never imply that your pride has blinded you to the grim reality of your situation – and by extension, that of this entire troupe."

"It sounds like you are." She paused. "You heard, then?"

"Everyone heard. And you are mistaken. I would never show such disrespect for the one who rescued my struggling fortunes from the gutter. All of our fortunes, in fact."

"Good. See that you don't."

"I will, however, say that this is not the wisest course of action you could have undertaken. Then, we both know wisdom is not your forte."

Okuni grimaced. "If it was, you might still be performing in a rundown theater in a backwater marsh-town. And Sanemon would have drunk himself to death."

"A strong possibility, yes. You decided that a troupe of actors made for a useful mask. Especially a troupe that you owned." He wet the rag and began to clean around the wound. She twitched in pain. "You bought out debts and the name of a forgotten troupe, and filled it with the dregs of other troupes. The drunks and troublemakers, the addicts and the mad."

"That sounds like every actor," she said through gritted teeth.

Nao ignored her. "A wise shinobi might have abandoned such a mask at the first sign it was becoming burdensome. And yet here you are, worried about our funds – and us. Else you'd have returned at the first opportunity, rather than trying to lose your pursuers first." He peered at her. "That is what you were doing, isn't it?"

Sanemon returned before she could formulate a response. Nao finished cleaning the wound, and began to stitch it with brisk efficiency. Okuni bit down on a piece of willow bark as he worked, and almost passed out again. Somehow, the stitching hurt worse than the initial wounding had. As he worked, he said, "Has Sanemon told you yet?"

"About what?" she asked.

"About your secret admirer."

She looked at Sanemon. "What is he babbling about?"

Sanemon hesitated. "I may have made a mistake..."

Okuni paused. "What did you do?"

"I panicked. You didn't come back..."

"What did you do?" She grabbed his arm and he winced.

"Someone... someone offered to help. I- I didn't know what to do, so I... I went to him." He smiled weakly. "I might have engaged his services."

"Who?" she demanded.

"A- a nobleman."

"A Crane," Nao supplied. "Daidoji Shin."

Okuni stared at him for a moment, processing this new information. She recalled the name, and wondered at the coincidence. She looked back at Sanemon. "What do you mean 'his services'?"

"He claims to be an investigator of sorts, though he seemed more like a wastrel to me. Then I found out that he's been employed by the governor himself to ferret out whoever is behind the poisoned rice that's got the Lion snapping at the world." He gave her an apologetic look. "I didn't realize... if I had, I certainly wouldn't have put him on your trail."

Okuni wanted to shout, to rail at him. Instead, she closed her eyes once more. One could only yell at fate so many times. "No matter. Tomorrow night, I will have my payment and we will be gone soon after."

"Tomorrow night?" Nao shook his head. "You need to rest."

"And I will. Afterwards."

"And if he's not there – or worse, he doesn't come alone?"

"Then I will come back – or not." She looked at him. "If I do not return…"

"You will," Sanemon said, sternly. "You always do."

She heard him say something else, but moments later, she was asleep.

CHAPTER FOURTEEN
Three Duck Street

"Well," Shin murmured as he looked around. "Perhaps a touch more difficult than I anticipated." Three Duck Street was a filthy mess, full of rotting fish, torn sacking and other wharf debris. Lanterns were necessary, despite the fact it was only just late afternoon, for the shadows cast by the overhanging roofs were thick and impenetrable. He could hear rats skittering just out of sight. At least, he hoped they were rats.

He turned in place, letting his gaze stray across the alleyway, searching for any sign as to what might have taken place on the night in question. Thankfully, it hadn't rained since then. Drawing his wakizashi, he used the blade to clear away debris, revealing footprints in the muck. A man's sandals and something else – a padded slipper of some sort. Whoever had worn it had left a light tread. A woman, perhaps. Okuni?

"No way to tell," he said to himself. He turned, following her tracks with his eyes. He followed the trail, careful not to accidentally erase the prints. There was no telling how many people passed through this particular alleyway on a given day, but something about these prints had struck him as noteworthy, besides the fact that they'd survived undisturbed. Whatever sort of footwear they were, it was not the sort of thing worn by a heimin fisherman or merchant. Nor was it the footwear of a noble.

Whatever it proved to be, he followed the trail out of the alleyway and down another, where the tracks became deeper and more frenetic. "Signs of a struggle," he muttered. He caught sight of something embedded in a nearby doorframe.

He swept his sword out, dislodging the errant bit of metal with the tip of his scabbard. It fell into his waiting palm a moment later. It was a shuriken, or what was left of one. A dried patina of something smeared the edges. A shinobi's weapon, for times when a death was more important than its manner of occurrence. He paused as the implications sank in.

To the heimin, shinobi were little more than legends. As a nobleman, Shin knew better. They were all too real, but they were taboo – forbidden and forgotten. Every clan employed their services, but to admit such would be almost as great a crime as utilizing them in the first place. If shinobi were involved in this, it meant things were decidedly more complex than he'd first assumed.

He frowned and paced along the narrow alleyway, following the footprints. There were dark stains on the wall – handprints, he realized. He placed his hand over them, noting the size difference. Definitely a woman, and injured.

"She was leaving. Perhaps her business was concluded," he said, softly. "Moving down the alleyway, when she was attacked. Perhaps they were waiting for her to leave…" He stopped. "Or for someone else to leave. Her contact?" He started moving again. "So why isn't she dead?" There was only one answer that fit – she had fled. But where?

He looked up and saw the wharf. "Ah," he said. It was a shabby stretch of bank, clustered with rotting jetties and small boats. Fishermen, mostly, looking to sell their catches at the smaller heimin markets that shadowed the larger trading quarters of the city. People hastily averted their gazes as Shin prowled towards the water. The blood trail was faint here – a superficial wound, or else she'd managed to bandage it on the run.

He stopped at the edge of the wharf and peered down. There was blood on the wooden steps that led down beneath the jetty. He paused and turned back the way he'd come. For a moment, he'd felt as if someone were observing him. He swept the street with his gaze, hoping to spot a familiar face, but saw no one. Frowning, he started down.

The steps were roughly made and set deep into the soil of the riverbank. They carried him down into the shallows below the wharf, where a large section of the bank had been carved away in order to make room for support pylons and secondary jetties. Similar spots littered the length of the river. Some were simply shrines, forgotten by all but a few fishermen and mudlarks.

The others were used for any number of illicit purposes. Shadows clustered thick in the forest of pylons and stone foundations, and in some places there was room enough for a small boat to navigate the swirling eddies of the shallows.

Reeds rose from the water in dense patches, and frog-song was omnipresent, nearly drowning out the cries of dockworkers and the splash of oars. An abbreviated quay of roughhewn stone and rotting wood sat atop the water. Mooring posts ringed it, and a statue of a frog maintained a lonely vigil from its perch atop a cracked plinth.

Shin genuflected to the statue instinctively. It might only have been a small kami, but it was a kami nonetheless and worthy of respect. He turned and spied more blood on a nearby pylon. She had been making for the water. A long run for someone injured, especially an actress. He knew trained bushi who wouldn't have made it this far.

"Desperation – or skill?" A glint caught his attention, and he awkwardly shuffled across a length of rotting wood to the next pylon. Using his fingers, he pried a small metal disk from the pylon. Like the other, it had a sharpened edge that was stained a curious color, and he was careful to keep his fingers away from it. Another shuriken – and something else… a strip of bedraggled silk that had been pinned to the pylon by the shuriken.

He sheathed his wakizashi and stretched it between his fingers to study it. It was the same material and color as the scrap he'd found in the rice, he was certain of it. It wasn't the sort of thing laborers or sailors would wear. Nor an actress, come to that.

But a shinobi, possibly.

"Ha," he said, softly. "That is interesting, isn't it?"

This Okuni was definitely not the woman he'd imagined her to be. She was more interesting, for one thing. His desire to speak to her had only increased.

It was a striking coincidence, and Shin did not believe in coincidences, at least not in regards to matters of this sort. Still on his heels, he turned, studying the water. He had no way of telling whether she'd made it or not – only a feeling. If she had, there was a good chance that she was still alive. And if she was still alive, that meant – what?

Wood squeaked. He rose to his feet, smiling to himself.

There were two of them. Ronin, clad in Kaeru-gray and armored. "Good day, gentlemen. How might I help you today?"

"You can answer a few questions, Crane." The voice came from behind them. A third figure descended the steps – Kaeru Azuma. "Like why are you here, rather than investigating as the governor requested?"

"Who says I'm not?" Shin said. He cocked his head. "Are you spying on me?"

"Do not play the fool, Crane. It insults both of us. The governor dispatched me to collect a report on your progress." Azuma looked around. "So tell me."

"The Lion insist the Unicorn are guilty, but refuse to elaborate. The Unicorn deny any knowledge of the crime, but have no proof of their innocence."

"And the Dragonfly?"

"I have not spoken to them yet."

"Why?"

"I have not yet received an invitation."

Azuma grunted. He was silent for a moment. "I was against your involvement."

"I was against it as well," Shin said, agreeably. "But here we are."

"Yes."

Azuma fell silent. Shin waited for a few moments, and then asked, "What do you think about it all?"

"What do you mean?"

"The rice. Do you have a theory?"

Azuma shook his head. "No."

Shin heard the lie in his voice. Azuma had a suspicion, but didn't want to share it. "That is a shame, for I find myself in need of one. I cannot see a reason for it, you see… why provoke war, when it serves no purpose?"

"There is a reason," Azuma said. "Honor."

"Honor is not a reason," Shin said.

"Honor is the best reason – and the worst." Azuma looked at him. "How much do you know about this city's history?"

Shin frowned. "Not as much as I should, I admit. Military history has never been an interest of mine."

Azuma sniffed. "And you a Daidoji. A generation of Iron Cranes are wailing in shame in the afterlife."

"Oh, I suspect they were wailing long before now," Shin said. "But continue, my lord. I am always eager to be educated."

Azuma gave him a steady look. "The more we speak, the better I begin to understand your reputation." He dismissed Shin's reply with a wave and continued. "This city once belonged to the Unicorn. It was among those holdings given over to the Lion to hold in trust until the clan's return. When the Unicorn came back, the Lion were expected to turn it – as well as much of the surrounding region – over to its original owners."

"Let me guess, the Lion disagreed with this."

"Most strenuously, in fact. So much so, that they schemed to reclaim the city, at least. And they did, annexing it unopposed."

"I can't imagine that," Shin said.

"At the time, the Unicorn had little interest in the city. But the annexation changed that." Azuma paused. "Eventually, at high cost, order was restored and an imperial governor was installed – not to stop the fighting, but to ensure that it does not begin once more."

"So Tetsua implied," Shin said. "So far, the truce seems to be holding, however. And I'm sure there have been other incidents – possibly worse ones. Why should this one tip over the plum cart?" He paused. Azuma hadn't come all this way just to give him a history lesson. He wanted something. Perhaps to deliver a warning. "What's different this time?"

Azuma said nothing. Shin followed his gaze, back to the distant shrines. "Kuma," he said, in realization. "Tetsua admitted that both the Lion and the Unicorn felt his judgement to be… biased."

"That is a polite way of putting it," Azuma said. "Tetsua is a good man. A good governor, despite what some claim. This incident puts all that he has worked for at risk." Azuma looked at him. "You ask what is different? Tetsua is weak now. His reputation suffers – and will suffer further, if things get worse."

Shin blinked. "You think this was done to hurt his position. To weaken him in the eyes of the clans. To what end?" The question was an obvious one. He well knew the reasons, but he wanted Azuma's opinion on the matter.

Azuma snorted. "You think the Great Clans are the only ones who can play politics? The Hantei have their own games, and they play to win."

Shin frowned. The political one-upmanship of the imperial families was not unknown to him. There were more of them than there were posts to be filled at times, and that made competition fierce. Tetsua's position was one of great influence – influence he had chosen so far not to wield. But someone else might not be so discerning. "Do you have any proof?"

"Proof? No. Merely a feeling. Tetsua has too many enemies and not enough friends. I wager that when the culprit is discovered, the trail will lead back to some third cousin twice removed, looking to secure himself a position as governor at Tetsua's expense."

"There are simpler ways of having a governor recalled," Shin said.

Azuma shrugged. "Perhaps. But you asked for my opinion and I have given it."

Shin nodded. "So I did. And I consider myself illuminated." He paused. "I trust you are conducting your own investigation?"

Azuma hesitated. "If I am?"

"Then I have done you a disservice. Popular opinion has it that the Kaeru are nothing more than ill-bred ronin, incapable of loyalty save to the coin." He paused, and then hastily added, "I never believed it of course. But it is good to have my opinion confirmed."

Azuma grimaced. "We are not a family in the normal sense, it is true. We are a collection of orphans – men and women without masters or homes, looking to make something from nothing." He met Shin's gaze. "Do you know what Kaeru means?"

"Frog," Shin said. "I thought it was a joke."

"No more than your own clan name is a joke." Azuma looked at the statue of the kami on its plinth. "This place is our home now. It is the city of the frog. It is as much our holding as it is the Lion's, or the Unicorn's. And we will defend it – and its ruler – to the last drop of Kaeru blood."

Taken aback by this declaration, Shin could only nod. Azuma turned back to him. "I will leave you to your investigation, Lord Shin. And I wish you luck."

CHAPTER FIFTEEN
Actor and Gambler

"A satisfactory day, my lord?" Sanemon asked, as he and Shin stood in the wings of the stage, watching as the stage crew began to make ready for the evening's performance. As Kasami had not yet returned, Shin had decided to pay a visit to the theater in the hopes of finding out more about the mysterious Okuni.

"Not as such, Master Sanemon," Shin said, watching the controlled chaos from what he hoped was a safe distance. It was fascinating to see such preparations up close. There was an odd rhythm to it all, almost like a secret performance, seen only by a select few. "In fact, it has been quite the opposite." He was still pondering what Azuma had told him earlier, and how it might relate to his own investigation. He had a surplus of questions, but answers were in short supply.

"My apologies, my lord."

"It is no fault of yours, Master Sanemon. I only wish that I had better news for you. She has not returned, then?"

Sanemon frowned and shook his head. "No, my lord." Shin noted a slight hesitation. As if Sanemon had wanted to say something else – and changed his mind.

"Would she come back here at all, if she were hurt?"

Again, Sanemon noticeably hesitated before answering. "I don't see why not, my lord. Is she – do you think she's, I mean, is she … ?" He trailed off, clearly flustered.

Shin looked away. "I do not think so. But something happened in that alleyway."

"Perhaps one of the other actors … ?" Sanemon began.

"I took the liberty of speaking to most of them earlier when I arrived. I thought it best to talk to both them and the stage crew before they became preoccupied with preparing for tomorrow's performance." In fact, Shin had spent an enjoyable hour questioning actors and actresses, and then a less enjoyable one putting the same questions to the stage crew.

The latter were a surly lot of drunks and lotus-eaters, culled from nearby sake houses and gambling dens to pull ropes and shift scenery. The troupe followed the usual tradition of hiring locals to perform the more tedious tasks associated with the theater. They had little of worth to share, and seemed altogether too eager to escape his gaze.

In contrast, the dozen or so actors of the troupe were a motley assortment of artistic temperaments, status-seekers and stage-mercenaries willing to play any part for the right price. Most, like the stagehands, had little in the way of useful information about Okuni. They claimed not to even know her family name, though he thought this a lie. He wasn't sure however, as they were, by and large, decent actors. And those that weren't seemed to know nothing at all.

"And they were not helpful?" Sanemon said. He did not seem surprised.

"Not as such." Shin looked at him, hoping for some hint as to what the man was hiding. What they were all hiding. There was a secret here, and one they were all desperate to keep. "Are you certain that you do not know what she was doing in that alleyway?"

Sanemon shook his head convulsively. "She told me nothing."

Shin frowned. A neat sidestep, and not quite an answer. Conversation was a game of skill, full of feints and parries and counterthrusts. To witness two masters of the art discuss something so innocuous as the weather was a thing of fierce beauty.

Sanemon was no master, though he had some natural talent. His feints were clumsy – instinctive. But effective. An outright lie could have tripped him up. So he avoided them with the desperation of an ashigaru caught in open ground.

Shin decided to change tactics. "Is there anyone else I might speak with?"

Sanemon looked away. "Have you spoken to Nao yet? Our lead actor?"

Shin paused. "No. He seems to have made himself unavailable."

"Nao does that. Come."

Sanemon led him backstage into the small warren of spaces that served as the actors' dressing rooms. Most of the actors made do with curtained off sections of hallway or tents set up out back, but a few got rooms to themselves. Small rooms to be sure, but private nonetheless. He'd visited Okuni's room earlier, and found it distressingly empty of anything resembling a clue. It appeared unused. He suspected someone had cleaned it after her disappearance, but had yet to broach the question to Sanemon.

His thoughts were interrupted as Sanemon stopped and rapped politely at the frame of a door. "Enter," a voice called out from within. Sanemon slid the door open and gestured for Shin to enter ahead of him.

"After you, my lord."

"And who is this you have brought me, Sanemon?" the room's occupant said. "An admirer, perhaps? Come to wish me well as I carry tomorrow's performance on my shoulders?" The actor was tall and slim, and sat before a polished mirror of brass, set atop a table. He primped and preened as he spoke, not turning around. He wore a stylized white wig, and his features were powdered and marked by lines of ash. From the wig, Shin thought he was supposed to be the founder of the Daidoji, Doji Hayaku – one of the principle characters of tomorrow's performance.

Like Sanemon, his name was a traditional identity for an actor of certain talents. Nao could play a man or a woman, and was highly skilled at acrobatic feats. A utilitarian, but one of quality, probably able to command a high fee. Shin wondered why a man of his talent was working for such a small troupe. Then, he'd wondered the same about Okuni as well.

Sanemon cleared his throat. "This is Lord Shin. He has come to ask you about Okuni." He paused, and then, almost pleadingly, "Please be respectful."

"I am always respectful," Nao said. He turned and looked Shin up and down with a considering gaze. Then, slowly he rose and bowed humbly. "My lord, you honor me with your presence. I am told you are a regular attendee of our little dramas."

"It would be better to say that I am enthralled by them," Shin said. "I caught the show a few days ago. Your performance as Doji Hayaku was sublime."

Nao straightened and smoothed his kimono. "You are obviously a man of taste. I thank you for the compliment." He sat. "If you will excuse me, I must continue to get ready as we speak."

"Please, by all means," Shin said. "Though – isn't it a bit early?"

"Practice makes perfect. Even as you must occasionally hone that blade you carry, I must sharpen my skills with the powder brush. Speed and accuracy are of equal importance to samurai and actor alike."

Shin considered this for a moment, wondering if it was simply an excuse for Nao avoiding him earlier. Dismissing the thought as unimportant, he said, "What do you know of Nekoma Okuni?"

"She was a mystery," Nao murmured breathily.

"Was?"

"Is," Sanemon said.

"Oh, she's obviously dead in an alley somewhere," Nao said. "Let's not put on a brave face for his lordship."

Sanemon glared at the actor, and Nao turned. They looked at one another for a moment and then Sanemon said, "I have things to take care of before the performance. My lord . . . ?"

Shin gestured. There was clearly something going on, but he'd decided that patience was the best course. Things would unravel as they would, and he would seize on whatever opportunities presented themselves. "Thank you, Master Sanemon. I can see myself back to my box once I am done here." Sanemon hesitated, and then backed out of the room, bobbing his head obsequiously. He shut the door behind him.

Nao turned back to his mirror. After a few moments, he said, "Is he gone?"

Shin glanced at the door. There was no shadow on it, no sound of someone on the other side. "Sanemon, you mean? Yes. Why?"

Nao smirked. "No reason." He turned. "So, what do you think?" He stood and turned. "A good likeness? Be honest."

"Good, if a bit flamboyant."

"It's kabuki," Nao said. "Flamboyance is expected by the audience. Bright colors and loud songs are what they pay for."

Shin could not argue with that. "Then it is a good likeness indeed."

Nao sat. "You flatter me, my lord." He paused. "So what do you know?"

"About?"

"Our missing kitty-cat, my lord. Nekoma Okuni." Nao peered at him. "You know something. I saw your face when Sanemon was asking me about her – and his, as well."

"I did wonder about that. A warning?"

"Mmm. Let me guess… you've learned precious little about her from the others."

"It seems she is something of a cipher."

"All good actors are. But you suspect something."

"Is there something to suspect?"

"Oh, always, my lord. We are actors, after all. Dissembling is our rice." Nao fiddled with his makeup, peering into the polished surface of the metal. "But some of us are better at it than others."

"Okuni, you mean."

"Mmm."

Shin was silent for a moment, watching the actor finish his makeup. It was clear that Nao wanted to tell him something, but he wasn't planning on doing so freely. Shin decided on a bold feint. "She is not just an actress, is she?" The question was leading and guileless.

Nao smiled. "I didn't tell you that."

Shin smiled as well. Nao wasn't so easy to lure in. "If anyone asks, I will tell them you are blameless. Innocent as a babe."

"Not that innocent, I assure you, my lord." Nao turned. "Better?"

"Perfect."

"Thank you, my lord." Nao frowned. "I do not know why she was in that alleyway. I know only that it had to do with her… other profession."

"This other profession," Shin said. Now they were getting somewhere. "How much do you know about it?"

"I know that this troupe only exists because of it. We make precious little money, despite my considerable talent, and most of that vanishes as soon as it appears. And yet we persist." Nao looked back at his mirror. "We are a mask."

Shin digested this. "Then Sanemon is not truly master here."

Nao laughed out loud. "No. Though he does put on a good performance. He used to be a soldier, you know. And then some fool taught him how to read and write and forever inflicted him upon us all."

"And is he a bad master, then?"

"Not in the least. For all his foibles, he's better than most. Terrible actor, but an adequate manager." Nao paused. "If he asked you for help, as I have heard, then he is truly worried."

"He did – but you are not," Shin said. "You believe she is dead."

"That, or she's abandoned us." Nao stood. "I will not say things will be better without her. She was a tolerable actress. Sanemon will be devastated, of course."

"But not you."

"The show must go on, my lord."

"Why tell me all of this?"

Nao looked at him. "I am no fool, my lord. I keep my ears open, and I have heard that the governor has entrusted you with ferreting out the person or persons behind this poisoned shipment that has the city all a-flutter."

Shin did not let his surprise show on his face. He knew that word traveled fast in a city, but that his name was already on people's lips came as something of a shock. Things were moving faster than he'd anticipated. "And you believe she was responsible." It wasn't a question. He could read the certainty on Nao's face.

"I do not know that," Nao denied. "But I do know the wheels of justice can grind the innocent as well as the guilty, and I have no wish to be made into grist for something I had no hand in. It is my hope that you will remember that, when the time comes to apportion blame." Nao gestured languidly. "Now, if you would be so kind, I must disrobe and start all over. Practice, practice, practice, you know."

"Of course," Shin said. "Thank you for speaking with me. This was a most illuminating conversation."

"I always have time for a gentleman of quality, my lord. Do come and see me again, before we depart."

Shin paused at the door. "When were you meant to leave?"

"The day after tomorrow is to be our last performance. We were due on a river barge heading north the following morning. Though whether that is still the case, I cannot say. Sanemon will know."

"Two days, then." Shin nodded. "Thank you. I wish you a good performance tomorrow, Master Nao."

"I have yet to have a bad one, my lord," Nao called out as Shin departed. "And do enjoy your evening."

"You can come out now," Nao said, as he took off his wig.

Okuni slid open a panel on the opposite side of the room and stepped inside. All of the dressing rooms were connected by similar sliding panels, some concealed, some not. Every venue had its secrets and the Foxfire Theater was no different. Okuni had ferreted most of them out within a day of arriving. It always paid to know your territory, however temporary. "So that was him," she said.

"In the flesh."

"He's observant." The Crane had seemed at ease while he'd spoken to Nao, but he'd been far more alert than Okuni liked. He was no wastrel, whatever Sanemon thought. Handsome, as well, in that effete sort of way. In another life, he might have made a passable actor, she thought. He had presence, at least.

"He's a Crane," Nao said. "He was probably subconsciously judging the décor even as we chatted." He looked around. "Not that I blame him."

"He's clever. That's unfortunate." She winced as a spike of

pain dug through her, and she sat heavily on a cushion. She chewed on a strip of willow bark as she spoke. It helped give her something to concentrate on, other than the pain. "He talked to everyone?"

"And everyone stayed quiet."

"Except for you." She looked at him. "You're playing a dangerous game, Nao." The others, even Sanemon didn't worry her. They knew better than to talk, but Nao… Nao knew better, but wasn't able to resist. He had to poke and prod. She suspected that was part of the reason why she'd found him where she had, performing folk plays for food and lodging.

"And so are you," Nao said. He turned to look at her. "He might be able to help, you know. He's clever, as you say. And a clever Crane is a good thing to have on your side."

"As if you would know."

"There is much about me that you don't know," Nao said, pointedly. "We all have our own stories, Okuni. You make it a point not to ask." He turned back to the mirror – her mirror – and began to clean the makeup from his face. "Is that because it is easier to abandon us, if you do not know us – or is it because you are afraid that we might abandon you, if we knew the true you?"

Okuni took her willow bark from her mouth and pointed it at him. "Are you a mediocre philosopher now, as well as a mediocre actor?"

"Very funny. Careful you don't split your stitches laughing at your own joke."

Okuni smiled and leaned back against the wall. Annoying Nao was one of her great pleasures in life. "It's neither, you know."

"What?"

"I don't ask because I don't think to ask. I don't have to ask. I observe, like our Crane friend. For instance, I know that Juba –" she said, referring to one of the other actors, "– is particular to a certain variety of shōchū fermented from sweet potatoes. Or that Hisa is in love with her cousin, whom she writes to at every available opportunity."

"Hisa isn't subtle about her feelings, and Juba stinks of alcohol even when he's sober," Nao countered. "It hardly requires a trained observer to notice such things."

"I know that you were a soldier, just like Sanemon."

Nao fell silent. Okuni studied him. "No," she corrected, "not like Sanemon. I misspoke. You are bushi, Nao… when we fight on stage, you hold your sword as someone trained to it. Someone born to it."

Nao turned away. "Who I was is of no importance to who I am."

Okuni's smile faded. "I am sorry."

"You almost sound as if you mean that." He shook his head. "Never mind. As I said, it is of no importance." He looked at her in the mirror. "What about the Crane?"

Okuni shrugged. "What about him? There's nothing to be done without increasing my own risk. Best to avoid his attentions, if at all possible."

"Do you think he knows about Tsuma?"

"If he did, he hasn't shown any interest in asking about it. Then, he is a Daidoji. It might not be of any concern to him, even if he knows." Okuni adjusted her position, trying to ease the ache in her side as she chewed on her willow bark. "It's only two days more. I can avoid him that long."

"Then you've forgiven Sanemon?"

"There's nothing to forgive, really. He did what he thought was best. That is why I keep him around."

"And why do you keep me?"

"I need someone who makes me look good." She pushed herself to her feet. "I'll have the money tonight. After that, it's just a matter of not dying. Easy enough."

"You say that with such confidence," Nao murmured. "One might almost believe you, if one didn't know better." He leaned close to the mirror. "When you die, can I have the mirror? I'd hate to think of it going to waste."

"If I die, it doesn't matter does it?" Okuni didn't wait for his reply. She had her own preparations to make. She stepped out into the corridor, and found Sanemon waiting. "Is he gone?" she asked, without preamble.

"Yes," he said, not asking who she meant. "But he'll be back. What do we do then?" It was clear that the Crane's presence had unsettled him. He was looking for reassurance, rather than answers.

"I'm sure you'll think of something," she said. She paused and probed her wound. The stitches were holding, and she'd prepared an ointment to dull the pain. It was a special salve, known only to her clan, and made from ingredients found only on a small, uninhabited island off the Phoenix coast.

Sanemon glanced at her wound. "Perhaps I should go with you."

She bit back a laugh. "And how would that help me?" she said, as gently as possible. Sanemon flushed.

"I only meant..." He trailed off. "Never mind. Do as you will. Get caught, what do I care?" He threw up his hands in an attitude of resignation. "All I meant was, what do we do if you don't come back this time?"

"Leave the city, as we planned." She had secured them passage on a vessel heading upriver, into Unicorn lands. There, they could lay low for a few months, performing in small villages and towns. She paused. "In my things, there's a letter. It will have instructions…"

"On how to alert your family, yes, I know." Sanemon looked at her. "This isn't the first time you've told me about it, you know."

"I just thought I should remind you." Okuni hesitated. "Thank you."

"For what?"

"Being concerned enough to risk adding to our troubles." She smiled. "It was a foolish thing to do, but appreciated nonetheless."

He was silent for a moment. Then, he said, "Do you remember what you said to me, the day we met?"

Okuni paused. "No."

"No, I don't expect you do. You said we all wear masks, but some of us wear more than one. It took me a while to figure out what you meant. To see the mask beneath the mask." He looked at her. "Is this really about the money – or is it because you feel responsible for us?"

Okuni was silent. "I thought so," Sanemon said. "What do we do now?"

After a moment, Okuni replied, "You must prepare for tomorrow's performance. And I must prepare for tonight's."

CHAPTER SIXTEEN
Lion Comes Calling

Shin was in the garden when Kasami returned. It was peaceful at dusk, with only the sound of insects and frogs to accompany one's mediations. The nearby teahouses had not yet opened. Shin held his biwa, occasionally plucking a string as he waited. Beside him lay a missive with the seal of the Akodo family. Minami had finally responded to his provocation. Only time would tell whether it would prove of any use.

He heard the bells over the service entrance clatter, but did not rise from his bench. "You found him?" he asked, without turning.

Someone groaned piteously. Shin raised an eyebrow and turned as Kasami shoved Kitano to his knees. "Stop complaining," Kasami growled, twisting the gambler's hand behind his back. "It was only a finger."

"What was only a finger?" Shin asked as he looked down at the man. He spied a blood soaked rag wrapped about Kitano's hand and sighed. "Was that necessary?"

"He needed a reminder of his debt," she said. "He tried to knife me. You're both lucky I didn't just take his head."

Shin clucked his tongue and studied the whimpering gambler. "I thought you might have learned wisdom after our last encounter, Kitano." He grabbed Kitano's injured hand in order to examine it. He unwound the bandage and studied the wound. "A clean cut. You sheared the finger off just below the joint."

"I was aiming for his wrist."

"Even so." Shin carefully rewrapped the bandage. "Calm down, Kitano. You won't die. Not unless infection sets in. We have some time to talk." Kitano jerked his hand back and whimpered curses. "Stop whining. She could have cut off more than that." Shin leaned close to the gambler. "She still might, unless you pay attention."

Kitano focused on him with a teary gaze. He swallowed. "What do you want?" Kasami swatted the back of his head and he added a hasty "My lord," to the question.

"Nothing too onerous, I assure you. I need you to find someone for me."

"Who?"

"I don't know."

Kitano grimaced. He looked blearily around the garden. "Then why am I here?" Kasami swatted him again, and he yelped as the blow took him on the ear.

"Because you strike me as a man with his finger on the pulse of the city. I suspect that very little happens on the wharfs that you aren't aware of – or that you can't find out."

Kitano's grimace thinned into a speculative frown. "Maybe. Maybe not. You don't know who you're looking for, so how can I help… my lord?"

"A few days ago, a shipment of rice was delivered to the Lion docks…"

Kitano gave a bark of laughter, followed by a wince. He cradled his bloody hand to his chest. "The poisoned rice."

"You know about it?"

"Everyone knows about it, my lord. It's all over the city."

Shin glanced at Kasami. "And what does the city say?"

"That the Lion are preparing to pick up where they left off, all those years ago. They've declared war, and the governor is too useless to stop it." Kitano hesitated. "Not that I think that, obviously. Loyal to the Hantei, that's me."

"Is that so?"

"It's what the city says," Kitano said. Kasami gave him another light slap on the back of the head, rocking him forward on his knees.

"Mind your tongue, or I'll take it."

"Thank you, Kasami," Shin said. He looked at Kitano. "If you know about the shipment, then you must know who delivered it – or at least where they might be berthed."

"Why would I know that, my lord?" Kitano protested.

"Because a man like you would surely foresee that such knowledge might be worth something to someone at some point." Shin rubbed a finger and thumb together in the universal sign for coin. "I am that someone, and this is some point."

"Yeah, well, today is obviously not my lucky day," Kitano said, harshly, indicating his hand. "Because I don't know anything about it."

Shin gestured sharply as Kasami made to hit their guest again. She grudgingly subsided, blow undelivered. The gambler was pushing his luck. She might well take his head before they'd finished their conversation. "But you could find out."

Kitano was silent for a moment. "I… could. It'll cost you, though." He flinched, as if expecting a blow.

"Of course." Shin gestured to the gambler's hand. "I'll even pay for someone to sew up your injury, just to show that there are no hard feelings."

Kasami snorted, and Kitano gave her a speculative glance. He scratched his unshaven throat and sniffed. "Fine. You want me to find them, my lord? I'll find them. Like I said, it'll cost you."

"How much?"

Kitano named a price that had Kasami reaching for her blade, but Shin waved her aside. "Fine, fine." He looked at Kasami. "Go get it."

The expression on Kasami's face was equal parts horror and astonishment. "What about him?"

"I believe I am capable of looking after our guest for a moment or two." Shin smiled thinly at Kitano, and the gambler looked away. Kasami grunted and made her way inside. When she'd gone, Shin said, "A wise gambler once told me that a man only has so much luck, Kitano. And yours is running a bit thin."

Kitano bowed his head, but didn't reply. Shin continued. "I told you before that I had a use for you. This is it. I am willing to pay for good service, but if you push me, I will find another to run my errands." He leaned forward. "And if you attempt to harm my companion again, I will let her finish what she started. Do we understand one another?"

Kitano swallowed and nodded. "Yes, my lord."

"Good man."

Kasami chose that moment to return with the money. She handed an intricately carved wooden box to Shin, and he opened it and counted out a sum for Kitano. The gambler frowned, and made to speak, but Shin interjected. "Half now, half when you have found what I asked for. That is more than fair, I think."

Kitano stuffed the money into his robes and nodded jerkily. "Most generous, my lord. How do I contact you when I've found it?"

"I trust you will find a way, when the time comes." Still seated, Shin leaned back, every inch the disaffected Crane noble. "You may go now."

Kitano clambered awkwardly to his feet. "I'll- I'll begin tonight."

"See to your wound first," Shin said, magnanimously. He fluttered a hand towards the service entrance. Kasami caught Kitano by the collar of his robes and half-dragged him out of the garden. When she returned, she was frowning.

"Do you think he'll find anything?"

"I believe so. With the proper motivation, even the humblest man might achieve miracles." He retrieved his biwa. "Unfortunately, all we can do now is wait." He gave the strings an idle strum. "I am sorry that he proved obstreperous. I believe he's learned his lesson, however."

"Maybe." Kasami looked around the garden. "What if he doesn't find anything?"

"Then we will look elsewhere." Shin plucked a string and stilled it. "In fact, I already have another path to follow. The actress."

Kasami frowned. "What about her?"

"She's the one who poisoned the rice."

Kasami stared at him. Then she laughed. So loudly and

uproariously that the birds in the trees fell silent. She bent double and braced her hands against her knees, wheezing. Shin waited patiently until she'd regained control of herself. He thought it only fair to allow her a few moments indulgence, given how rarely she laughed.

"Are you quite done?" he asked.

Kasami held up a finger. Shin nodded politely and gave her another moment. When she straightened, he said, "I found certain evidence that pointed in that direction, at least. And her cohorts in the theater confirmed it."

"So where is she?"

"Ah. That is where it gets interesting. She was ambushed."

"By who?"

"I have no idea, but I'm eager to find out. A better question might be who hired her in the first place? For if we find her, we find them."

"If she's still alive."

Shin nodded slowly. "Yes, if she's still alive." He began to play in earnest. "Tomorrow we are going to the shrines to speak to Tonbo Kuma."

"Why? The Dragonfly have nothing to do with this."

"Kaeru Azuma thinks that they might. At least somewhat. He suspects that Tetsua's friendship with Kuma might have weakened his position politically…"

"Which may have motivated someone to attempt to provoke a war," Kasami said.

"Exactly. Also, we will be having guests tonight." He picked up the missive and showed it to her. "The Lion will be coming to call. We had best be prepared."

At that moment, something heavy thumped against the

main entrance. Shin looked at Kasami. "Well. At least they're punctual." He set his biwa aside. "I will meet them in the receiving room. Rouse one of the servants for tea."

He hurried inside, his steps light. If Minami were here, it meant that she wasn't as obstinate as he'd feared. Or that she wished to challenge him in person.

Either way, the next few moments would be interesting.

Okuni's hand was trembling as she pulled her hood back. She was not fully recovered, as Sanemon had so helpfully pointed out. But she was here, nonetheless. It was foolish, she knew. There was every possibility that her client was behind the ambush. And there was every chance that her attackers would be nearby, especially if they had reported their failure to kill her.

But pride held her to her course. She had never failed to collect a payment and would not start now. Especially given the consequences for Sanemon and the rest of the troupe, not to mention herself. Theater brought in precious little money. If they wanted to eat, to travel, it was up to her to provide for them.

Unlike last time, she was prepared. Besides her knives, she was armed with a blowgun of her own, as well as pouches of flash and smoke powder. If her attackers showed themselves, she intended to make as much noise and light as possible.

The alleyway was empty when she arrived. It was much the same as the other, though farther from the theater. She'd thought it best to give her attackers no reason to turn their attentions to Sanemon and the troupe, unless there was no other option.

She'd hidden herself as best she could, among the discarded

barrels and trash. As she sat, she listened to the sounds of the city around her. The streets were full of noise and activity. The city was in an uproar, and many were seeking passage downriver or bringing in extra supplies to weather the coming storm. The streets teemed with mercenary trash, hoping to find a berth with one clan or another and merchants descended on them like scavenger birds. The thought almost made her laugh, and that in turn made her wince.

She touched the bandages beneath her concealing robes, probing the edges of the ache that radiated through her side. The stitches were holding, and the salve helped. Nao had a way with a needle and thread. Even so, she needed time to rest, something she didn't have at the moment. But after this was over, she intended to sleep for a few days, at least.

The smell of the river was strong on the air. A clammy mist crept through the streets, carrying with it the smell of fish. Okuni heard him coming before she saw him. He walked hurriedly, splashing through puddles. Every so often, she caught the clink of coins and knew he had done as he promised, startling as it was. Perhaps he was an honest man after all – but what sort of honest man hired shinobi in the first place? She pushed the thought aside as he came into view.

He paused at the mouth of the alleyway, looking from side to side nervously. Then, slowly he advanced. He was dressed much as he had been before, and once again she was struck by how out of place he looked – how uncomfortable. He was not used to subterfuge. That would come in time. Eventually, you learned – or you died.

"Hello?" he whispered. "Are you there?"

Okuni waited until he'd walked past her, and then rose

swiftly, discarding the ragged cloak that had hidden her huddled form. She caught him from behind, drew one of her knives and placed it against his jugular. "Do not make a sound, or I will end you here and now," she murmured into his ear. "Nod if you understand me."

He nodded fearfully. She relaxed slightly, and reached into his robes. She found the money and extracted it. He swallowed and said, "What is the meaning of this?"

"You tried to kill me," Okuni said, softly, letting her knife play against the man's throat. "Ordinarily, I would not give you a second chance, but I am in a forgiving mood. And you have brought my payment."

"I- I did no such thing!"

"Oh? Is this not my payment?" The knife pressed close, and a thin trickle of blood ran down his neck. "How unfortunate."

"No, no! I didn't try to kill you! Why would I?"

"Who knows why men like you do anything?" she countered, but something about his tone of voice told her he was telling the truth. He was surprised. Not that she had survived, but at her accusation. She flicked the knife out of sight and stepped back, suddenly alert. "Who else knows about this?"

"Just- just that worthless merchant, Saiga," he said, rubbing his throat. "I told no one. We were never supposed to meet, remember?"

"Where is Saiga now?"

He stared at her. "Where he always is, I assume. Why?"

"You might want to warn him. Someone is cleaning up after you, my lord."

He shook his head, puzzled. "What do you mean?"

But she was already moving away, her payment safely secreted within a hidden pocket of her robes. She kept her hand on her knives as she left the alleyway and crossed the street, seeking the safety of the crowd. The wet streets gleamed gold in the lantern light, and noise echoed from every doorway.

She could feel them watching her. They'd followed him, of course. Used him as bait. She'd expected that they might, and had planned accordingly.

A noisy crowd spilled from a nearby puppet theater. She effortlessly joined the jubilant throng, doing her best to avoid having her injured side jostled. As she bathed in the sake fumes, she saw new faces crossing the street, expressions fixed and intent. A true shinobi could kill their target in the open, surrounded by armed guards. The crowd was only a momentary refuge at best. She eased her knives from her belly-sheath and let them dangle by their ring-pommels.

She caught sight of another to her left – Chobei. He smiled slightly, and she knew that he knew he'd been seen. She nodded respectfully, and he returned the gesture. There was no call for incivility, even now.

Chobei joined the throng, slipping towards her as easily as a shark navigated the depths. She turned slightly, keeping him in sight, and began to push towards the front of the crowd. They were singing now, loudly and off-key. She momentarily lost sight of her stalker as someone shoved someone else.

It was only her instincts that saved her. A thin blade darted low through the press of bodies, seeking an artery in her leg. She parried it with a flick of her wrist and kept moving. Another blade darted for the side of her throat, and she bent low, letting it skid over the back of her neck. It stung, but better a little pain than a long death.

They were on all sides of her, boxing her in. No one in the crowd had yet noticed the dance of death occurring in their midst. Two blades slid low, aiming for her kidneys and hamstrings. She blocked both, but almost lost her life to a third, as it jabbed for her eye.

Chobei grinned at her as she artfully stumbled into a singer and spun the man around between herself and her attackers. He bellowed something, but she was already slipping away, threading through the crowd. Her attackers followed.

She had to distract them. She palmed a pouch of flash powder and tossed it underhanded towards a nearby ronin clad in imperial livery. The pop of light and sound had the unwary man reaching for his blade. The crowd scattered in a flurry of surprised shouts and catcalls.

Quickly, she pulled loose a second pouch and spun, hurling it full in the face of Chobei. Instinctively, he cut it from the air, and smoke spewed in all directions. Coughing, he reeled back and she took to her heels. She ran as fast as she could, despite her wound. The pain clawed at her as she caught hold of a low hanging rooftop and shimmied up. She climbed as quickly as possible, seeking the high ground. Shouts echoed behind her, and the soft thump of pursuit.

She didn't stop to look back.

CHAPTER SEVENTEEN
Akodo Minami

Shin poured his guest a cup of tea and smiled. "I am gratified to see you here, Lady Minami. After our last encounter, I did not expect we would speak again."

"If I had any choice in the matter, we would not be," she said, stiffly. Minami sounded tired, but she stood as stiff and as straight as the first time he'd seen her. "But your message implied that it would be inadvisable to ignore your invitation."

The Lion representative had come with a handful of retainers. They were currently in the garden, under the watchful eye of Kasami. He hoped they would all still be alive when Minami and Shin had finished their conversation. "That is not the only reason, I believe," he said. "You do not seem the sort to succumb to oblique blackmail."

Minami sat. "I wish to know what you have discovered."

"About?" He offered her the cup.

"The rice," she growled. She did not take the tea. "It has been several days. Have you learned nothing in that time?"

"Nothing save that no one seems to have done it – or to have reason to do so." Shin took a sip of his own tea and licked his lips. "Tell me Lady Minami, are you a fan of the theater?"

"What?"

"No, I don't suppose you are, are you?" He gave her an insouciant smile, and was rewarded by a visible bristling. She wanted very badly to challenge him, but as yet he hadn't given her sufficient reason. Nor did he intend to.

Minami stared at him for a moment and then looked away. "No."

"Pity. Have you found the boat yet?"

Minami hesitated. "What boat?"

"The one that delivered the poisoned rice." Her hesitation told him he was right – she was searching for it, and probably with more urgency than Shichiro.

"I told you already…" she began. Shin forestalled her with a twitch of his finger.

"I would guess that you have not. And that is because it was never at the Unicorn docks, was it?" It was a guess, and one he'd come to the night before as he pondered the problem. A boat could not simply vanish. It had to be somewhere.

Minami was silent for several moments. "I was mistaken," she said, with obvious reluctance.

"Were you?"

Her eyes narrowed. "Are you accusing me of something?"

"I am merely asking a question. In your place, I might well have obscured the facts in order to buy time for my people to locate the vessel and conduct my own investigation. There is no shame in that."

"Who are you to talk about shame, Crane?" She pointed an

accusing finger at him. "I know all about you, Daidoji Shin. You wouldn't know shame if it pierced your belly and pulled your intestines out."

"What an unpleasant image," Shin said. "But accurate for all that. Shame is something of a foreign country to me, I admit. That is my failing, and I am endeavoring to correct it." He paused. "If you have found it, I would request to see it."

"Why?"

"It may hold answers."

Minami glared at him. "We have not found it. Nor are we looking."

"Because you did not think to – or because it does not matter?"

Minami laughed softly. "I hear contempt in your voice, Crane, though you mask it well. Under all your pretty banter, you are just like all the rest of your clan. You think you are smarter than the rest of us. As if courtesy is any indicator of wisdom."

"Some might say it is."

"Not me."

"No. I suppose not. You have always seen the Dragonfly as your main threat in this city. A fact you have been very open about."

Minami looked at the water. "And so?"

"Why the sudden change of target?"

"The vessel belonged to the Unicorn."

Shin shook his head. "Shichiro insists that it didn't. More to the point, how would you have known?"

"Their papers…" she began, and then trailed off. She realized what she'd just given away. Shin nodded in satisfaction.

"If Shichiro is right, their papers would have shown them to be exactly what they were. Unaffiliated river trash, carrying a shipment of rice that they got – where, exactly?" He paused. "Was it stolen, by chance?"

"Stolen?"

He pressed forward. "Tell me, my lady – how much unlawfully obtained cargo does the Lion have squirreled away in their warehouses?"

"None!"

"You are lying."

Minami's gaze snapped around. "What proof do you have of any of this, Crane?"

"None, of course. It is a theory, nothing more. And if I have given insult, I can but ask for your forgiveness." He wasn't really worried about insulting her, for all that he'd clearly struck a nerve. He was on the right track, and she knew it. "Since neither yourself nor Shichiro seemed to know anything of the ship in question – well, there has to be a reason."

"He claims to know nothing about it?"

"Indeed he does."

"And you believe him."

"As I believe you." Shin looked at her. "Neither of you has reason to lie."

Minami sat back. "You are wrong," she said, after a moment.

"Am I?" He pointed at her. "That is why you prevaricate. You growl and show your fangs, but hesitate to strike. Am I correct?" It was a gamble. He was betting on her pragmatism, betting that she wasn't the sort to simply cut the knot, rather than untangle it.

Minami was silent for several moments. Then, "If you are?"

"I require no admission of guilt, if that's what concerns you. I ask only on behalf of my investigation – to rule you out as a suspect."

Minami snorted. "I admit nothing."

Shin nodded. "That is all the answer I require, thank you."

She was silent for a moment. "I can trace my ancestry back to Akodo himself," she said, finally. "When I first arrived in this city, I thought I had found my battlefield at last. A place to prove myself. I would make a bastion of the city…"

"And now?"

"Now I think I was sent here not to wage war, but to prevent it. My bushi demand action, but my advisors murmur caution. A disruption of trade – any disruption – would be regarded as a failure on my part. And I will not fail."

"That is why you allowed the trade in illicit cargo to continue," Shin said, in sudden understanding. He shook his head. "Your reputation."

Minami nodded. "A little wound to delay a greater one. Though I hoped – hope – to eventually bring it to an end."

"You do not have to explain that decision to me, my lady. I am a Daidoji. I know full well honor's price and what it means to pay it."

She looked at him, and made as if to retort. But instead of an insult, she said, "I think that you do, Crane. And that is why I tell you all of this now. I cannot attack until I know for certain who is to blame."

"There are some who would say you have done due diligence."

She looked at him, her eyes flashing. "I am not some. I will unsheathe my sword when my enemy is before me and not a moment sooner."

"Then help me," Shin said. "I will find your enemy for you, so that you might have justice."

Minami looked away. After a moment she said, "I have discovered that the rice was purchased through a regular contact on the Unicorn docks. I was not aware of this arrangement, obviously."

"Obviously."

Minami stiffened at his tone, but continued. "The contact was a merchant named Saiga. It is he who provided the rice, hired the crew and arranged the entire deal."

"Had you worked with him before?"

"We were not working with him. He was a merchant. He sold goods. We did not ask where those goods came from. Nor were we alone in that. The Unicorn and the Dragonfly both availed themselves of his services."

"Buying stolen cargo, you mean."

She frowned and nodded. "Yes. Ask Shichiro, if you do not believe me."

"I will, the next time I speak with him." Shin took another sip of tea and pondered this revelation. Another name, another link in the chain. He would have to speak to this Saiga as soon as possible. "You knew the rice had been stolen from the Unicorn docks. But why did you assume it was deliberate sabotage?"

"Saiga told us as much when we questioned him."

"Did he now?" Shin leaned forward. "And what else did he say?"

"That the Unicorn had engineered the entire scheme to humiliate us. They intended that we would sell the rice and sicken our customers."

"A mild form of humiliation."

Minami's eyes flashed. "It would have damaged our business for weeks, if not months. No one will buy rice that makes you sick."

"Not intentionally, at least." Shin sat back, his fingers steepled before him. "Why declare war over it, though?"

"This was not the only incident."

Shin raised an eyebrow. "It is the first I have heard of. There have been others?"

"Some. Most of them were simply sabotage of the usual sort. But of late, the number and severity of those incidents have increased. We kept it quiet as we pursued our own investigations, but… there is a pattern."

"Tell me about them."

"We've lost cargo. Stolen or sunk."

"And how do you know the Unicorn was involved… wait." Shin held up a finger. "Saiga told you this as well, under duress."

"Yes."

"How do you know he was telling the truth?"

"What sort of heimin can lie with a blade against his throat?"

Shin nodded. There was a ring of truth to that. "Go on."

"Saiga told us all. It was all the Unicorn. Or so he believed."

"But you doubted him?"

Minami looked uncomfortable. "I was not sure. I believed that he thought it was so, but that does not make it so. I hoped finding the boat would shed more light on the matter."

"But you haven't."

"No. It is not in the city. Or, if it is, it is being hidden where we cannot find it." She sat back. "Now you know all that I know."

"And it is quite helpful, thank you."

She looked at him expectantly. "And what do you know?"

Shin hesitated, wondering how much he ought to share. "The rice was poisoned by a shinobi, though as to who might have employed them to do so, I cannot say. This Saiga, possibly, but there are inconsistencies…"

"Such as?"

"Someone attempted to do away with the shinobi in question. I am not yet certain whether they succeeded in this, or failed." Shin took another swallow of tea. "I will question this Saiga myself tomorrow. You have him under observation, I assume?"

"No. Once we questioned him, I saw no further reason to keep an eye on him."

Shin set his cup down. "That is unfortunate. He might well have left the city in the interim. Still, I have my own agents working to locate the ship. Once we have it, and its crew, I will find Saiga as well. With their testimonies, I should be able to more fully piece together this scheme – and locate its instigator."

"And once you have done so, you will inform me, Crane."

"Of course. We are allies, at least in regards to this matter."

Minami snorted. "I would not go that far."

"I am also obligated to inform Shichiro, you understand."

"Yes. Of course."

Shin looked at her. "What do you know about the Dragonfly shugenja, Tonbo Kuma? I am to meet them later today concerning this matter."

"The Dragonfly have nothing to do with this," she said, bluntly.

"That we know of," he countered. "From where I sit, it is likely that an agitator intended to stir up hostilities between yourself and Shichiro. The Dragonfly would surely benefit from such a conflict…"

Minami shook her head. "That is unlikely. The Dragonfly garrison is minuscule in comparison to mine, or the Unicorn's. They barely have enough men to patrol their own docks. And reinforcements are not within easy reach." Her eyes narrowed. "Unless…"

"Unless they made an alliance with another faction," Shin said. "Whoever they joined with might be able to take the city from the rest of you."

She frowned thoughtfully. "As I said, unlikely."

"But not impossible."

"No."

Shin nodded. "Your hostility to the Dragonfly is well documented. Perhaps this scheme was meant to provoke you into a trap of sorts. Something to consider, perhaps."

"Yes." She paused. "But regardless, you must find who is responsible, or I will not be able to stop what is coming. The Lion will have their due, in honor – or in blood."

Shin met her eyes and gave a solemn nod. "Then let us make sure that it is in the former, and not the latter." He bowed. "I thank you, my lady. I wish you good day."

Minami did not reply. Instead, she rose to her feet. Shin made to rise as well, but she waved him back. "I can show myself out."

Shin settled back, feeling satisfied with himself as he watched her depart. He was certain, now, that neither the Unicorn nor the Lion were behind the poisoned rice. There was a third party involved. But was Saiga the mastermind, or merely another catspaw?

He poured himself another cup of tea and savored it.

CHAPTER EIGHTEEN
Shugenja

"Have you ever met a shugenja before?" Shin asked, shifting in his seat as a near miss with another flatboat caused their pilot to shout at the offending craft and make a sharp gesture. The river was crowded this morning. Above, the sky was all pinks and oranges as Lady Sun began her journey.

"No," Kasami said. She sat opposite him, one hand on her sword and her eyes on the water. In contrast, Shin's eyes were on the shrines that crowded at the intersection of the two rivers. Even at a distance, something about them made him distinctly uncomfortable.

"They are… odd, for lack of a better term. At least I have always found them to be so." He snapped open his fan and gave it a desultory twitch. "Some investigators make use of their abilities to ferret out information, though evidence found in such a way is inadmissible in court. Spirits, it seems, are no more honest than men."

Kasami gave a sharp laugh. "So why bother talking to them, then?"

"Who – the spirits, or the shugenja?"

"Either."

"A good question. And the answer is Kaeru Azuma. He seemed surprised that I had not yet received an invitation to speak to Tonbo Kuma. This made me wonder why that might be – and so, I've decided to ask."

"Do you think they're involved?" Kasami asked.

"I do not know. I am certain a third party is involved. Azuma believes this poisoned rice to be an act against Tetsua's position, rather than against one of the clans. Tetsua himself may hold the same belief, even if he didn't voice it."

"And you?"

"I do not have enough facts to compose an opinion. An investigator must keep an open mind at all times, so that they might assemble a theory free of bias. Only the facts matter." Shin frowned. "That is what Agasha wrote. The key is in finding the facts – and then successfully assembling them into the correct order."

Kasami looked at him. "And what is the correct order?"

Shin began to tick the points off with his fan. "One – someone has been engaged in acts of sabotage against the Lion. Two – someone, possibly the same someone, stole a shipment of rice off the Unicorn wharf. Three – this rice was sold to the Lion by a merchant named Saiga. Four – the rice was delivered by an unknown vessel to the Lion. Five – during the delivery, the rice was poisoned. Six – when the Lion discovered this, they sought out Saiga, who immediately blamed the Unicorn. Seven – someone tried to kill the shinobi who poisoned the rice."

Kasami listened and nodded when he fell silent. "So why aren't we looking for this Saiga?" she asked.

"No need. Ito knows every merchant in the city. I have asked him to come by for lunch – hopefully he will be able to direct us to Saiga. But he is only one link in the chain. We will need all of the links to find the end." He fanned himself furiously, his face set in an expression of discontent. "It's all so… clumsy."

"What do you mean?"

Shin gestured aimlessly. "The whole affair… it's clumsy. Hesitant. The rice, for instance. Clearly a feint, meant to provoke the Lion. All well and good. So why, then, kill the shinobi responsible?"

"Maybe it was just an attempt to cover their tracks," Kasami said.

"Maybe. But something feels off about it." He folded his fan and sighed. "We're here." The flatboat had passed among the shrines now, at the junction of the two rivers. The air was different here – cooler, and quieter save for the incessant frog-song. The noise of the city was muted, as if it were caught in the boughs of the willows that leaned so precariously over the water.

Great reefs of tangled willow root rose from the water, forming small islands. Upon each was a simple stone structure. They resembled nothing so much as the shrines which littered the river banks for miles. But these were larger and sturdier.

The flatboat bumped against a jetty crafted from stone panels and woven roots. A rope rail lined either side of the jetty, stretching back to the abbreviated wharf that encircled the central shrine. Guards clad in the livery of the Dragonfly Clan were waiting. One stepped forward. She was a short woman, stout and round, with a friendly face. She smiled in welcome, and gestured. "Be at peace, Lord Shin. You are expected."

"And here I'd hoped to surprise his lordship," Shin said, gaily. The guard's expression did not falter, and her smile remained fixed as Shin stepped onto the jetty. But as Kasami made to follow him, the guard's hand fell to the hilt of her sword. Kasami paused, and Shin frowned. "Kasami is my companion, and bodyguard. She takes offense if left behind."

"That is not my concern. You – and only you – are allowed to enter the shrine. Lord Kuma made that very clear."

Shin drew himself up. He had expected as much, but saw no reason to accept it gracefully. "Do they fear I mean them harm? I was not aware that I had given them cause to feel thus."

The guard bowed her head. "Lord Kuma fears nothing save the inadvertent pollution of this holy place. One who has shed blood with their own hand is not welcome within. Even we are not allowed to enter."

"And how does Lord Kuma know that I have not?" Shin asked.

The guard looked at him. "Lord Kuma is privy to much that is hidden."

Shin frowned. He looked at Kasami, and she snorted and sat back down. "I'll be here when you're finished," she said, as she leaned back and closed her eyes.

"Very well," Shin murmured. He turned back to the guards. "Now that is settled, please direct me to Lord Kuma."

He was shown into the shrine moments later. It smelled of damp stone and mud. The air was filled with the croaking of frogs. Shin looked around, but saw little save shadows slashed through with shafts of light.

Shrines were the axle of life. Every community, no matter how humble, had its own. Sometimes they were small things –

a single statue, set beside a lonely path – while other times they were mighty complexes of arched rooftops and vast chambers. The shrines of the Three Sides River were of a more primitive construction, built in a time before the kami had shown themselves. Or so the scholars insisted.

They resembled caves made from carefully tumbled stones. The floors were made from willow bark and rough cut timbers, and Shin could feel them twitch with the current. There were stones beneath the wood, but only in certain spots that no doubt had some significance known only to priests.

"Hello?" he called out, and his own voice echoed back at him. The rustle of cloth brought him around. A short, bald man stood a respectful distance away – the shrine keeper, Shin assumed. The man bowed low and, without speaking, gestured towards a crude archway, lit by softly flickering lanterns. Clearly, he was expected.

Shin thanked him with a nod. He'd heard that the priests who maintained the river shrines had taken a vow of silence, though no one was quite sure why. He strode towards the archway, trying to hide the growing unease he felt. It felt strange in here, though he could not say why. As if some miasma were seeping up from the water and tainting the air.

Past the archway was a larger, circular chamber. The walls were covered in primitive pictograms, drawn by some ancient hand. Shin paused just inside the entryway and tried to take it all in. There was a story to the pictures, but it was hard to decipher – shapes of great size and malevolence, moving among a fleeing people. And then – what? A second shape, or shapes, and what might have been a great storm, driving the giants into something he took to be the river – or the river as it had been.

"I have been told that, if one looks too closely, the shapes begin to move," someone said from behind him. Startled, Shin turned to see a slight figure in white standing in the entryway. Shin retreated, and the speaker entered. "I have never seen them move, myself. But then, I know better than to gawp at such things."

Shin bowed. "Lord Kuma. It is a pleasure to meet you at last." The shugenja was a slim, androgynous individual with dark eyes and long hair bound back in a neat knot. They radiated strength. There was a decided firmness to them, beneath the seeming softness of their face and voice, and their gaze pulled at Shin like the river's current.

"Lord Shin," Tonbo Kuma said, in a voice so mild as to be just shy of insulting. "How kind of you to accept my humble invitation. You are quite busy, of late, I am told."

"Busy is as busy does, or so say the sages," Shin said. If Kuma noticed his attempt at humor, they gave no sign. Shin studied them.

Shugenja occupied a rarefied space in society. People of great spiritual potential, whose minds were bent to the gravest of affairs. They could invoke the kami and call up flames or crack the earth. Most of them, at least those of Shin's acquaintance, were quite strange. They saw the world through different eyes.

"Water pervades life," Kuma said. "I was taught to feel its ebb and flow in all things." They raised a hand and the air tensed and rippled about their fingers. Shin watched the gesture, fascinated. To his knowledge, few had the sort of visible control that Kuma displayed. And it was a display – entirely for his benefit.

"I was under the impression that more than just gestures,

however graceful, were required of one seeking to invoke the kami."

Kuma smiled. "You are perceptive."

"I know little, but a little is still an amount."

"A little knowledge can be a dangerous thing."

Shin returned Kuma's smile. "So I'm told."

Kuma looked around. "The pull of the kami is strong here in these temples. They speak loudly, if one but has the wit to hear them." They swept their hand out, and the air rippled like the surface of a pond. "When I came here, the spirit of the river was in turmoil. Too much blood had spilled over the banks, too many bodies glutted the shore."

"It sounds unpleasant."

Kuma nodded. "Things are better now. But, of late, the Lion grows restive, and the Unicorn paws the earth."

"And the Dragon?"

"The Dragon waits."

"The Crane is impatient," Shin said. "Waiting never suited us, save when it did."

"You do not wait for others, you make others wait for you," Kuma said. Shin chuckled appreciatively.

"Yes, exactly. Something we have in common with the Dragon, I think."

"The only thing, perhaps." Kuma looked at him. "Your grandfather is a member of the Daidoji Trading Council, I believe."

Bemused by the abrupt change in subject, Shin nodded. He wondered how Kuma knew that. The identities of the trading council were not common knowledge. "So he is."

"He sent you here to oversee the merchants of the Crane."

"So he did." Another thing they shouldn't have known. Kuma was well informed for a veritable hermit. Perhaps Tetsua had told them, during one of their games.

"But you do not wish to be here."

Shin paused. "Is that a question, or a statement?" Kuma was baiting him with idle conversation. Attempting to lead him down tangents, and off-topic.

"Take it as you wish."

"We'll call it a statement then. And an incorrect one. This city has much to recommend, and I am quite happy to enjoy its largesse."

Kuma nodded. "My apologies."

"No, it is I who should apologize for giving you the impression that I was unhappy with my lot. It could have led to awkwardness, something I am not fond of. Tell me, what else have you heard of me?"

"You made Lonely Shore City too small to hold you," Kuma said. They knelt and extended a hand. A little green frog hopped onto their palm and croaked shrilly. Kuma nodded, as if the frog had said something of substance. "Or so the stories say."

"Hardly so many as all that," Shin protested.

"One story, then. Told many times, by many different mouths." Kuma looked him up and down. They stroked the frog with a gentle finger. "Did you truly leap from the uppermost window of the House of Blue Leaves to escape an angry husband?"

Shin hesitated. "I admit, there is some truth to that one." He smiled widely. "It's really a funny story, if you'd like to hear it…?"

"No, thank you," Kuma said, quickly. They smiled and continued. "Upon your arrival, I took it upon myself to see whom the Crane had sent to replace your predecessor. Imagine my curiosity when I learned of you."

"I have been told that I am fascinating."

Kuma's smile didn't waver. "Yes. Though perhaps not for the reasons you think. You are known for being licentious and self-indulgent. You bring shame to your family by being so unsuitable to bear their name. Where they are dour, you are lazy. Where they speak little, you fear silence. Where they abstain, you engage in all manner of vice."

"You speak as if all Daidoji are stamped from a mould. As if we are tools, hammered and shaped for purpose by an artisan." Shin reached out as if to touch the frog, and Kuma made a slight motion, pulling it out of reach. "Or perhaps you are testing me. Do you wish to know the limits of my tolerance? I assure you, it's quite high."

Kuma was silent for long moments. "We are all tools, in one fashion or another," they said, finally. "We are shaped to serve our families, and our families are shaped to serve the clan. But something went wrong with you." He sank down and let the frog depart.

Shin watched it go. Another insult. And not a subtle one. Kuma was attempting to provoke him now, rather than distract him. "What was it, I wonder?" Kuma continued. "Perhaps you are simply a fledgling struggling to leave the nest."

"Perhaps I simply see no reason to abstain from pleasure. Life is difficult enough, why make it more so?"

Kuma nodded, as if considering this. "Or maybe you are nothing more than a wastrel." Their smile was a sharp slash. "Why are you here, wastrel?"

"To talk."

"We are talking."

"I wish to speak of other matters."

"Such as?"

"Rice."

"Ah, yes. The rice." Kuma looked away. "We had nothing to do with it, of course."

"Of course. The suggestion never crossed my mind."

"Then you are not much of an investigator."

"Or I am an excellent one."

"If our innocence is assured in your mind, why are you here?"

"To see what you know."

"And who says we know anything? A shipment of rice is an innocuous thing. Hundreds of similar shipments arrive and depart daily from the wharfs along the eastern and western banks."

"Tetsua seemed to think that you might be able to help."

At mention of the governor, Kuma paused. "Tetsua is… optimistic. In truth, I do not concern myself with the city or what goes on in it, and thus can be of little help."

"That I find hard to believe," Shin said. "The Dragonfly maintain several wharfs."

"A necessity. Commerce has never been our strength. I leave such matters to those of our clan who are best suited for them." The way Kuma said 'commerce' made it clear how they felt about it. Like many samurai, they regarded it as a necessary evil and a pollutant. To deal in trade was to dirty one's hands and lessen one's spirit. It was no wonder they spent all their time at the shrine. Kuma smiled thinly. "Why does this matter concern you?"

"I'm sure you know the answer to that, at least."

"Tetsua."

"Of course. As you said, I am a wastrel. Much like yourself, I have no interest in the world outside my humble pleasures – my games, my books, my women."

"We are nothing alike," Kuma said. Again, their voice was mild, but Shin nonetheless detected an edge to the words, and felt the temperature drop as Kuma spoke. It was a subtle thing, but Shin had been taught to notice subtle things. "True knowledge comes not from books, but from experience," Kuma continued.

"And what has your experience been, my lord?"

Kuma turned. "You would not understand, I fear. Your perceptions are limited."

The insult was sudden and sharp. Like the jab of a hidden blade. Shin decided to go on the offensive. "You say you have no interest in the city, and yet here you are. One cannot help but assemble a hypothesis. The Dragon have a reputation for strange behavior, and the Dragonfly act as a buffer between them and the rest of the empire. They rarely come down from the mountains, and even then, only with great purpose – though what that purpose might be, they rarely share. That they saw fit to send fifty men – as paltry a number as that might be – is telling. Even more so is the location those men have chosen to garrison…"

Kuma was silent, their gaze betraying nothing. Shin pressed his attack. "And then there is you, Tonbo Kuma. A shugenja of great ability and greater mystery. You are commander of the shrine garrison, the voice of the Dragon in the city, and representative of the Dragonfly. That is a great deal of responsibility. You bear it well."

Kuma sketched the slightest of bows. Shin smiled and went on. "As I said, I have formed a hypothesis. Would you like to hear it?"

"No."

"No?"

Kuma was not smiling now. "No. What you think you know is of little interest to me."

"I am sure it is not," Shin said. He could read annoyance in the shugenja's posture. A tension that had not been there a moment earlier. "My apologies, my lord. Sometimes the reach of my wit exceeds my grasp."

Kuma held his gaze for several seconds before nodding. "It is nothing." They paused. "Are you satisfied, then?"

"Before I even set foot in this holy space, my lord." Shin bowed. "Thank you for seeing me."

"Think nothing of it. I trust a resolution will be swift in coming." Kuma turned away. "I trust you can see yourself out, Lord Shin. I have duties which require my attentions."

Shin bowed low and retreated without argument.

CHAPTER NINETEEN
The Merchants

"Welcome, Ito. Please, sit." Shin gestured to the cushion across from him. The receiving room had been opened to the midday breeze, and the chimes hanging above the doors clinked pleasingly as Ito situated himself.

Shin barely noticed. Something about his talk with Kuma had set his mind to buzzing. Perhaps it was simply due to the shugenja's dismissive attitude. Or maybe it was something else. Something he'd seen or heard, but hadn't yet understood. He dismissed the thought and tried to focus his attentions on his guest.

"I must say, my lord, I was somewhat surprised to receive your invitation." Despite his words, the Crane merchant seemed quite pleased to be invited to his superior's residence. "I thought our business for the week was concluded."

"It was, but I thought you might enjoy lunch." Shin poured his guest a cup of tea, and then one for himself. As he did so, he indicated the bowls of rice and steamed dumplings. It was not common to eat in a receiving room, but Shin preferred it when he mixed business with pleasure. "We so rarely speak outside of our regular meetings."

"I was told you liked your privacy, my lord."

"By whom?" Shin asked as he poked at his rice.

Ito smiled weakly. "We happy vassals do talk about our betters, my lord. Shameful as it might be." A deft sidestep of the question. Humble, apologetic, but containing no real information. Shin decided not to press the issue.

"No matter. Eat, please."

Ito bent obediently and they ate in polite silence. The merchant tossed the occasional nervous glance Shin's way, but said nothing. At last, however, he could restrain himself no longer. Ito set his bowl down, and said, "Why am I here, my lord? Have I offended you in some way?"

Shin paused. "If you had, would I have invited you to lunch?"

Ito's smile was a sad thing. "Some bushi find it amusing to deliver bad news over rice and dumplings."

"I am not them, though I feel I must admit that I did have an ulterior motive." Shin paused. "I have recently come across a matter which you may be able to help me with." As he spoke, he examined the merchant as he had never bothered to do before. Ito was a round man, endeavoring to look soft and succeeding admirably. But it was simply a mask. Beneath it, he was something else entirely.

Ito frowned and sat back. "I will, of course, help you in any way that I might – though I fear that, unless it concerns tariffs, I'm a bit at a loss."

Shin smiled. "Oh, I think your knowledge runs a fair bit deeper than that, Ito. It has seemed to me for some time that you are not quite what you appear to be." He paused. "Am I correct in that assumption?"

Ito frowned. "That depends entirely on what you think me to be, my lord."

Shin smiled. "Let us leave it for now. A question, first – why might one transfer rice from barrels to sacks?"

"Two reasons spring immediately to mind, my lord. Ease of transport is the first. A barrel might be too large or unwieldy for the amount in question. If it is being taken to a temple, or an individual buyer, you might transfer it to a bag or sack. Space in a ship's hold might be at a premium. Sacks take up less room than barrels, in theory."

"And the second?"

Ito smiled thinly. "If you wished to hide the identity of the original owner. Rice barrels are often stamped with the insignia of the clan or trader who produced it. Even the way they're assembled or the materials they're made from can be an identifier. If a shipment is stolen, the first thing a smart thief will do is transfer the rice and destroy the barrels."

Shin nodded in satisfaction. "As I thought. Thank you."

"Is that why you asked me here, my lord?"

"Partially. I am also in need of an introduction to a certain man. A merchant."

"A merchant, my lord?"

"Yes. A fellow by the name of Saiga. Do you know him?"

Ito paused again, as if considering how best to answer. His gregarious expression had shifted into something harder. This was the real Ito, Shin realized. Not the simpering busybody of their last meeting, but someone much more difficult to read. "I… do, my lord. Might I ask why you need to speak to him?"

"Something troubles you, Ito?"

"This Saiga has something of a reputation as a man not concerned with the niceties of ownership, my lord."

"He is a thief, you mean."

Ito frowned. "Though it pains me to say it, theft is common on the waterfront, my lord. Gangs steal whatever they can from one merchant, and sell it on to a competitor. Saiga is rumored to act as a facilitator for these transactions." He looked at Shin, his gaze sharp. "I ask again – why do you need to speak to him?"

"I wish to ask him about a certain shipment of stolen rice."

"He would be the man to ask," Ito said, somewhat hesitantly. He rubbed his chin. "I… may have made use of his service myself, once or twice."

Shin raised an eyebrow. "Really?"

Ito flushed. "Well, sometimes demand outstrips supply, my lord. One must provide regardless. And Saiga was good at providing."

"Is he now?"

"Only when the need was great, I assure you," Ito added quickly. "I would never knowingly bring shame upon the Crane…"

Shin waved his explanations aside. "I understand all too well, Ito. Your secret is safe with me." He paused. "I am to take it, then, that you could introduce me to this man?"

As Ito pushed himself up, a sly look crossed his friendly features. "Am I right, my lord, that this concerns the recent case of sabotage reported on the Lion docks?"

"You heard about that then?" Shin said, feigning surprise.

"Oh indeed, my lord. The city is abuzz with the news. Every

merchant of my acquaintance is battening down the hatches in preparation for the coming conflict."

"Is it deemed a certainty, then?" Shin took a sip of tea.

"As certain as such things can be. It has been brewing for years, and flare-ups are not uncommon. Iuchi Shichiro is old, and Akodo Minami is young and full of wrath. That she should seek to sharpen her claws on the Unicorn's flank is not unexpected. Indeed, there were some – weak men, I assure you – who placed wagers on the likelihood of this very event."

"Really. How much did you win?"

Ito hesitated. Then, with a guilty smile, he said, "Nothing, my lord. The storm has not yet broken, after all."

Shin nodded. "Of course. What do these weak men say of the Dragonfly?"

Ito scratched his chin. "Little enough, and all of it contradictory. They have few men in the city – barely enough to oversee their wharfs and guard the shrine. They take little part in day to day business. Why, we have more of a presence in the city than they do. Tonbo Kuma is not interested in exploiting the Dragonfly's fortune, it seems. They maintain their foothold, but not much else." He took a swallow of tea and added, "Though, given the Lion's belligerence towards them in the past, I have no doubt that they would support the Unicorn in any conflict that arose."

Shin nodded. "That was much my guess as well." He paused, considering his next question carefully. "Lady Minami spoke to me of certain acts of sabotage perpetrated against the Lion of late, of which this business with the rice was but the latest. And I have reason to believe that those acts might be the work of a shinobi…"

Ito paled. "A shinobi, my lord?"

"Or several."

Ito shook his head. "I know of no shinobi in the city, my lord." He hesitated. "Though that does not mean that they are not here." He set his tea down. "You think someone hired them to sabotage the Lion?"

"A working theory," Shin said.

"Someone like Saiga," Ito pressed.

Shin smiled. "Would that surprise you?"

Ito sat back and was silent for several moments. Then, "No. If such folk were in the city, Saiga would be the one to know them." He paused again. "You know of the black market, my lord?"

"I do." A shadow economy existed in the city, though few would admit to it. Stolen or banned goods were bartered and sold in back rooms, or floated down river in the dead of night. Criminal gangs trafficked in opium or black hashish from al-Zawira, and hid it among more innocuous cargoes in order to escape the eyes of the customs agents who prowled the wharfs.

"This city is a haven for smugglers. Mostly petty ones. Saiga is the brain that guides their hands. One of them, at least."

"He is their master?"

"He is their quartermaster," Ito corrected. "And that is far worse. Saiga is a conduit for illicit cargo and sabotage. He arranges things, he buys and sells. Not just goods, but information. I believe he is responsible for the majority of pirate attacks along the rivers. He trades information about a shipment for a cut of the plunder and then sells it back to its original owners for a tidy salvage fee."

"A dangerous man, in his own way," Shin said.

"Yes, which is why I hesitated when you asked to meet him."

Ito shook his head. "He is not the sort of man you should be seen talking to."

"Have no fear, Ito, my reputation is long since buried," Shin said. "Now, can you arrange a meeting with this man? As soon as possible, preferably."

"I can, yes. Though possibly not immediately."

"I will endeavor to show patience," Shin said. "You have my thanks, Ito. You are a useful sort of man to have around."

Ito bowed low, nearly pressing his face to the floor. "I am but a humble feather in your wings, my lord."

Kitano Daichi scratched at the leather cap protecting the stump of his finger, and considered his fortune of late as he threaded through the crowded street. The cap was the best he could afford for the moment. Once he had completed his business with the Crane lord and his vicious retainer, he might be able to procure a prosthetic – one of wood, or perhaps ivory.

Or maybe he'd just spend the money on shōchū and women. That sounded like a much better plan, all things considered. When the Crane had paid him, he'd considered just taking the money and vanishing. There were always ships looking for crew, and places along the river that a man like him could hide.

He doubted the Crane would bother following him. His sort always had more money than they knew what to do with, but the thought of that woman hunting him down wasn't a pleasant one. And she would, too. He knew, it as sure as he knew she'd make his last moments painful ones. He flexed his injured hand, feeling the pull of the wax and honey that had been used to seal the wound.

A lucky escape, all things considered. He'd always had good

luck, even as a riverman. But on the river, you had to win every time and the river only had to win once. Being a gambler was easier, especially if you didn't mind giving luck a nudge every so often. If Daikoku, the Fortune of Wealth, was looking out for you, your opponents were none the wiser, even as they cursed your skill.

But, sometimes, the dice turned against you. He looked at his wounded hand, trying not to think about it. When dice went soft in your hand, you had to pay your debts – but only if you couldn't get out from under them somehow. No shame in that. All part of the game. Every gambler knew that. Luck wasn't just about winning at the table, it was about getting away with it.

Kitano frowned and spat off the wharf. The only way to get away from the Crane's table, it seemed, was to do what he was told. He didn't care for the feeling. Nor did he care for the work. Finding Lun was proving harder than he'd imagined.

He'd spent a night, and most of the day, trawling every waterfront dive and opium den for information on the one-eyed captain and her crew. Lun had a certain reputation, and Kitano had gambled with her bosun, Torun, often enough. The fat bastard was bad at everything but paying his debts. But nothing. It was possible they'd already left the city. He would've, in their place.

His feet took him to the wharfs. Heimin merchants clamored for attention across from the water, shouting about their wares from doorways and stalls. His stomach tightened as he caught the spicy smell drifting from the open doorway of a nearby noodle shop. A wagon, laden with sacks of rice, rattled across his path. When it was gone, he spied the river and the fishermen's wharfs.

The docks were stubby things, barely there at all. Just enough room for the small boats to tie themselves off, and the day's catch to be unloaded onto waiting handcarts or baskets. The fishermen knew everything that went on along the river, more than any merchant or clan sailor. If anyone knew where Lun had gone, it would be them.

Kitano called out to a knot of them sitting on the edge of the wharf and was greeted in kind. He had diced with many of them often enough to be a familiar face. He joined them, and took a swig from the bottle being passed around.

When he mentioned Lun's name, however, the conversation dried up. Kitano pressed, but got no answer, until a familiar voice spoke up. "Why are you looking for her?"

He turned to see a young woman nearby, weaving a fishing net. "Yui," he said, in his friendliest tones. He sidled towards her, putting on his best swagger. He liked Yui, though he'd only rarely had the pleasure of her company. "Last time I saw you, you were as big as a whale."

"Oh, Daichi, you always were the sweet talker." She set her work aside as he sat down. "I heard you got killed by some Crane bushi."

"Almost," Kitano said, showing off his injured hand. "You know me – luckier than most. The kami are on my side."

"You shouldn't boast about such things."

"It's not a boast if it's the truth." Kitano leaned back against a mooring post and looked at her. "Have you seen her, then? Or that fat fool, Torun?"

"Maybe. Why?" Yui asked, archly. "Aren't we good enough?" She tapped Kitano on the chest. He laughed coarsely and patted her cheek.

"For me, oh yes. But I'm looking on behalf of someone else. Someone wealthy." He made to rub his fingers together, but recalled, too late, that one of them was missing. He quickly lowered his hand. Yui frowned.

"Who are you working for, then?"

"What business is it of yours?" he said, playfully. "Looking to improve your circumstances now that I've come into money?" Her husband had been claimed by the river, or so she said. Privately, Kitano thought he'd run off. Yui had a temper, and some men were more fragile than others.

"If I wanted another husband, it wouldn't be a gambler like you, Daichi." Yui smiled as she said it, though. "No, I was just curious." She paused. "I might have heard something."

"Oh?"

Yui tapped her palm meaningfully. Kitano sighed and pulled out a coin – more than she would make in a week – and dropped it into her palm. "Tell me."

"Willow Quay."

"Of course," Kitano said, slapping his head. "Why didn't I think of that?"

"Because you're an idiot?"

"I'll forgive you, but only because you might have saved my life," Kitano said, leaning over and kissing her on the cheek. She laughed and slapped him, though gently.

"Then we'll call the debt paid. Best get going. I don't think she'll be there long." She looked out over the river. "Last I heard, they were preparing to sail tomorrow."

"Excellent," Kitano said. He gave Yui a sly grin. "That gives us enough time for a drink."

CHAPTER TWENTY
Third Party

"There it is, my lord," Ito said. The merchant indicated an ugly little establishment on the other side of Three Finger Street, squeezed between two larger buildings. Ramshackle was the first word that came to Shin's mind as he looked at it. "He works in the back."

"Excellent, Ito." He looked about. The wharfs at the other end of the street were crowded, full of noise and bodies in motion. Fishermen hauled their full nets along creaking jetties as dock workers unloaded shipments of rice, dyes and textiles.

"It smells of fish and sweat," Kasami growled. She stood just behind them, warily keeping watch on their surroundings.

"The smell of the city," Shin said, inhaling the myriad scents of the riverside. "The smell of commerce, of progress."

"I prefer jasmine."

"Truth to tell, so do I." He looked at Ito. "You managed to secure our invitation more quickly than I expected. I thought for certain it might be several days."

"He was quite intrigued by the thought you might wish to see him." Ito pressed a scented rag to his nose, trying to cut the stink of the back streets in late afternoon. Shin didn't mind it, himself. He'd smelled worse in other cities. Even so, he gently stirred the air with his fan, trying to keep it moving about him.

"Intrigued – or suspicious?" Kasami said, watching the street. "This could be a trap."

"It could be, but probably isn't. Not everyone thinks like a bushi from the Uebe marshes, Kasami. Ambushes are rarely of the lethal variety in places like these." Shin gestured to the teahouse. "Lead on, Ito."

Ito led them into the teahouse and made a surreptitious gesture to the proprietor, who directed them to the rear without speaking. The floorboards creaked alarmingly beneath their feet as they proceeded to a back room. Ito tapped at the door, and someone called out from inside. At first glance, Shin took the room to be a storage area, crowded as it was. It was only when he noticed the shelves, and the man sitting before them, that he realized that it was an office, of sorts.

Saiga stood as they entered, and bowed low. "My lord, you honor me with your presence." He glanced at Kasami. "I would ask that your yojimbo waits outside, however. My apologies, but I am a paranoid man."

"You will have to get over it–" Kasami began, but Shin cut her off.

"Wait outside. Make certain we are not disturbed."

She blinked. "What about you?"

"I am certain I will be perfectly safe. After all, I have Ito to defend me."

Kasami snorted and made to argue, but Shin gestured sharply. "Go."

"Fine." She went, and closed the door behind her with a decided lack of gentleness.

"My apologies," Shin said, as he and Ito sat. "Kasami takes her duties seriously."

"You let her berate you openly?" Saiga said, resuming his own seat.

"It is best to let her air her grievances."

"Most nobleman of my acquaintance would not agree."

"I am not most noblemen," Shin said, shifting to a more comfortable position. "I find that the dictates of my status are more in the way of guidelines than laws."

Saiga smiled. "A man of rare wisdom."

"Wisdom is attained with experience, but courage cannot be taught. An old saying among the Daidoji. Are you a courageous man, Saiga?"

"Middling bravery at best. Just enough to take risks, not enough to get caught." Saiga bowed his head. "Shall we dispense with the courtesies, my lord, and get down to business?"

Shin smiled. "A fine idea."

"Ito said you wished to speak to me about something…?"

"I spoke with Lady Minami recently. She made mention of your name, Master Saiga."

"Did she, my lord? I cannot imagine why."

"She recently purchased a shipment of rice from you." Shin waved his fan in front of his face, his gaze straying about the room. "It is the rice we were discussing."

"Ah. The rice."

"Yes. You know the shipment I mean?"

"I would be a fool not to, my lord. It is all anyone is talking about these days."

"So I understand. You told her that you stole it from the Unicorn, yes?"

"Are you accusing me of theft, my lord?" Saiga sounded horrified. Shin snapped his fan closed and leaned forward.

"If I am, there is precious little to be gained by denying it. I could have you arrested now, merchant. But that is a tedious waste of my time. So instead, I ask that you tell me everything, without prevarication or any attempt to dissemble. You stole the rice and transferred it from identifying barrels to more anonymous sacks, before selling it on."

Saiga was silent for a moment. Then, he nodded. "Yes. What of it? Ito has bought stolen cargo from me himself – haven't you, Ito?"

Ito said nothing, but his expression spoke volumes. Shin waved the accusation aside. "We are not here to discuss Ito – only you, and how you knew that the rice had been sabotaged. And by whom."

"It was obvious. The rice was left unguarded. They wanted it stolen."

"But why?"

"Once I learned of what happened, it became clear. The Unicorn have been watching my establishment for some time. They know who I am, and the sort of business I conduct. In retrospect, they have probably been planning this for a while."

"They used you as a catspaw, you mean."

"An unwitting dupe," Ito supplied, softly.

Saiga frowned at the other merchant. "I would not put it in those terms, but yes."

"And when Lady Minami visited you, you told her all of this freely?"

"As freely as I could with a sword to my throat, yes." Saiga shrugged. "I am a humble merchant, my lord. This is a game for bushi, not businessmen. I am well out of it."

Shin sat back on his heels and studied the other man. "Are you indeed?"

"Of course. I sold them the rice, and contracted for its delivery, of course, but I played no more part in it than that."

"The delivery – yes. About the delivery. I have been searching for the boat that made it, with little success. You would not happen to know where they are, would you?"

"Why would you be concerned with them, my lord? Sheerest river trash, I assure you. Of no more help in this matter than myself, if not a good deal less, I'd wager." Saiga waved a thick hand in dismissal. "They are likely long gone, following the wind and current."

"Possibly." Shin fanned himself. "Even so, I have dispatched agents to locate them." He watched Saiga as he said it. It was a calculated slip, and he was rewarded by a momentary tightness in the merchant's expression.

Saiga knew. Shin could read it in his eyes. The merchant was no stranger to wearing a mask over his true thoughts and feelings, but Shin had been trained from birth to read people's faces. And what he read in Saiga's face pleased him. The merchant was involved. He knew something.

"I'm sure you will find them in time, my lord," Saiga said, after a moment. "But as I said, I doubt they will be able to tell you anything. Not trash like that."

"I find that enough money can make the dumb speak and

the blind see." Shin rose smoothly to his feet. "But that is my problem. As you say, you are out of it. I see no reason to take up any more of your, no doubt, valuable time, Master Saiga. I will leave you to the rest of your day." He gestured, and Ito followed suit.

Saiga rose hurriedly. "Of course, my lord. I am happy to be of service, however poor it might have been."

"Not poor at all. You were very helpful." Shin paused at the door and smiled at the merchant. "Yes, very helpful indeed."

When the door had been closed behind them, Ito chuckled. "Oh, well done, my lord. A bit obvious, but he's surely sweating."

"I find that subtlety is often overrated."

"Is that your excuse, then?" Kasami said, as she fell into step with them. She had been waiting in the corridor, decidedly not eavesdropping.

"One of several," Shin said, as he led them out of the teahouse. He was aware of eyes on them as they went, and glanced at Kasami, who gave a terse nod. She'd noticed as well. He signaled Ito to be silent as they left the establishment and crossed the street to the docks.

It was noisy near the water, and crowded. Someone would have to get very close indeed to eavesdrop. And that meant they would be more easily seen. He twitched his fan at Kasami and she nodded, moving a few feet away. While he made himself seen, she would watch. "Well," he said, looking at Ito.

"As I said, my lord. Saiga is not inclined to be helpful." Ito looked at him. "What do you think, my lord? You seemed to come to some conclusion, as we were leaving…"

"He is involved," Shin said.

"Quietly, my lord." Ito tugged discreetly on his earlobe. If he had noticed that Kasami had repositioned herself, he gave no sign. "Anyone might be listening, even here."

"Good. I want them to know." Shin fluttered his fan, watching the light dapple along the river. "Saiga is involved, but I do not think he is alone in that."

"You think there are others?"

"I suspect. Nothing more. Saiga does not profit from war – it is easier to thieve and sell in times of peace. So why, then, instigate conflict?"

"He sees some greater profit to be made?"

"Possibly," Shin said. "If we can locate our missing boat, we might learn more."

"And if it cannot be found?"

Shin snapped his fan closed. "Ito, how difficult would it be to get a record of Saiga's dealings over the past few months? People he's talked to, that sort of thing."

Ito paused. "It might take me some time, my lord."

Shin glanced at him. "But you could get it for me?"

"Almost assuredly, my lord." Ito hesitated. "Though, might I inquire as to why?"

Shin tapped his lips with his fan. "Because, if Saiga does have a partner, that is where we will find them." He glanced at Kasami, and she flashed two fingers in a signal. Two listeners, then. He turned to Ito. "Find me that information, Ito, and you will be well rewarded. You have my word."

"That is all I require, my lord." Ito bowed low and hurried away. Quickly, he lost himself in the crowd. Shin doubted that anyone would be able to follow the little merchant if he didn't wish it.

Kasami joined Shin as he strode along the wharfs, his eyes on the water. "Two of them. I recognized one – they're Shichiro's men."

"Interesting," Shin murmured. "Saiga mentioned that the Unicorn were watching him. I wonder why."

"The stolen rice," Kasami said.

"Possibly." Shin looked at her. And then past her. He pointed his fan at a burly figure, pushing through the crowd towards them. "Is that Kitano?"

Kasami turned, eyes narrowed. "I think so."

The gambler gestured with his injured hand as he approached. "My lord – is that you?" he called out. "I thought I saw you – I was surprised…" He trailed off and bowed low to Shin. "Fortune smiles on me. I have found what you sent me for."

Kasami sniffed. "You smell of fermented sweet potatoes," she said, disapprovingly.

Kitano flinched. "I had to have a drink to get the information."

"It smells like you had more than one."

"Never mind. What did you find out?"

Kitano cleared his throat and glanced around. "The captain's name is Lun. They're anchored downriver, at Willow Quay."

"Of course," Shin said. "I should have thought of that myself." Willow Quay was the largest of the shanty villages outside the city. Like others of its ilk, its crudely constructed wharfs catered to those captains who wanted to avoid exorbitant portage fees or inconvenient questions about the nature of their cargo. According to popular rumor, it was the haunt of smugglers, pirates and mercenaries. Shin felt a thrill of excitement at the thought of finally seeing it for himself. "Well done, Kitano."

The gambler bowed awkwardly. "Thank you, my lord." He'd obviously realized that being deferential was the best way of keeping his remaining fingers. "I'm pleased I was able to be of service."

Kasami snorted. Shin gave her a look and she fell silent. "What's the best way of getting there?" he asked.

"You'll have to take a flatboat," Kitano said. He paused, and added, "I know a man who can rent you one cheap, if you like."

"You mean we'll have to take a flatboat," Shin said. "You'll be accompanying us." He looked at the river, watching the sunlight dance across its surface.

"I will?"

"Naturally. We need you to lead us to the boat, after all."

Kitano swallowed and nodded. "Of- of course, my lord."

"Stout fellow," Shin said. "Go, procure us that flatboat, and we'll set off at once. The sooner we find this boat, and its crew, the better."

CHAPTER TWENTY-ONE
Willow Quay

"You sure this is a good idea, Captain?" Torun asked, passing her the bottle of shōchū. "We won't see half these fools again."

"There are always people looking to ship out, Torun," Lun said, taking a swig. They stood on the deck of her sloop, watching as the last of her crew trudged down the gangplank, carrying their gear. "But things are too hot right now. The Lion are on our trail, and they know what this scow looks like."

"Maybe they don't."

Lun snorted and slapped the bottle into his chest. She turned and leaned over the rail. Below, the muddy waters slapped against the side of the hull. Her reflection was little more than a shadowy blotch on the water's surface, and she was low enough to smell the river.

Torun was still talking. "I'm just saying, there are a lot of boats like ours on the river. And we all look alike to those bastards..."

He continued in that vein, but she wasn't listening. Instead, she was looking around. Taking it all in, one last time. Her sloop wasn't large, but it was sturdy and could survive the roughest of waters without popping a seam. Its single mast loomed high, the patched canvas of the sail rippled noisily in the breeze. It took a crew of five, but could be sailed by one if they knew what they were doing.

She'd saved for years to purchase it, scrimping every coin. And now, here she was, captain of her own vessel, mistress of her own destiny. Or she had been, until this morning. Her hands curled into fists on the rough wood of the rail. She glanced at her bosun. "If you want to take that risk, Torun, you do it without me."

Torun frowned. "No, no. You're right. Still – did you have to pay all of the crew off?"

"Yes."

Torun must have heard the warning in her voice, because he quickly changed the subject. "I don't see why we need to worry, it's not like it was our fault."

"Do you think that matters to them? They'll be looking for scapegoats." Lun thrust a finger beneath the eyepatch that hid her left eye and scratched vigorously at the ruined socket beneath. Though the eye was long gone, she could still feel the phantom pressure of it scraping against the sides of the socket. And when a storm was in the offing, it itched abominably.

She peered up at the cloudless sky in mild annoyance. Usually her ghost eye was as good a barometer as one could find. Only, now, it seemed to be sensing a storm where there was none. Maybe it was just nerves. She hoped so.

She took in the shanty docks and crumbling jetties that spread out in either direction around her sloop. Willow Quay had grown up along the rim of a secluded cove on the Drowned

Merchant River. The cove provided a sort of refuge from the raging current that had claimed so many vessels over the years.

But it wasn't the sort of place anyone with any sense stayed for long. Passing trade was the only sort allowed in Willow Quay. Despite that, the wharfs were crowded. Word had gotten out that trouble was brewing in the City of the Rich Frog. The smell of war was in the wind, and the Lion was on the prowl.

Lun scratched her eye socket again and sighed. If she'd known the rice had been poisoned she'd never have delivered it. Better to toss it over the side and claim there'd been an accident, or that it had been stolen by pirates; something, anything, other than what they'd done. But they'd delivered it, taken their money, and there was nothing for it now.

What she couldn't figure was how it had been done. There'd been no sign of anything amiss when it had been loaded, or on the journey. No dead rats, no smells, nothing to warn them of what they carried. But somehow, it had been poisoned.

"Maybe they did it themselves," she muttered. It wouldn't surprise her. Samurai might pretend that they were better than such things, but they could be as treacherous as any back-alley thug when they wanted to be.

"What?"

"Nothing." She looked at him. "Where are you headed?"

"South, maybe. They're always looking for sailors on the Crane coast. You?"

"Not south." She scratched the inside of her wrist, where the faded tattoo of a crane's feather marked her sun-browned skin. "But first, I need to take care of the boat."

Torun frowned. "Are you sure about this?"

"No, but I'm not letting anyone else have her." She took the bottle from him and took another swig. "Go on, Torun. If the kami are kind, we'll see each other again. If not… you were a decent bosun."

"And you were an adequate captain," Torun said. He paused. "Take care of yourself, Captain." He turned and made for the gangplank. Lun watched him go. When he was out of sight, she sighed and turned back to the river.

She'd known better than to trust Saiga. The merchant was a duplicitous snake. If he had rice to sell, it was almost certainly stolen. She'd known, but the money had been too good. Enough to keep her crew fed and her ship's hull patched for months. She hadn't asked where it had come from, or why he wanted it taken to the Lion.

She should have. She knew that now. Things were getting tense. Best to put some distance between herself and whatever came next. Let the samurai murder each other.

But first, she had to sink her own boat. She took another swallow of shōchū, trying to fortify herself for what was next. She'd unhitch the boat from its mooring and angle it into the current. It was hard with one person, but not impossible. Once she was certain the river had hold of it, she'd swim for shore and collect her things where she'd stashed them. Keepsakes, mostly – and some money. Enough to start over. The next boat would be a smaller one in comparison, but that was enough for her.

It would have to be.

Her eye narrowed. She leaned forward, staring hard at her reflection below. She'd seen something, though she wasn't sure what – a hint of movement? Moments later, a familiar sound scraped across her ears – a sword being drawn from an oiled sheath. Her hand flew to the sharkskin hilt of her own blade and she whirled, drawing the sword even as her attacker plummeted towards her from above.

The man – or woman – was clad in gray, their face hidden behind a cloth mask. They were fast, and sure. Lun parried the first blow, but the second came more quickly. And the third, quicker still. It was all she could do to keep her footing.

Two more gray-clad forms picked their way across the deck, hemming her in on all sides. There was no way out, save possibly over the rail. But she'd be damned if she was going to give up her ship. Not to these bastards.

Lun bared her teeth and set her feet, sword at the ready. "Come on then. One at a time or all at once. But hurry it up."

They obliged her, and soon there was no more time for talk… or anything at all.

Kasami kept one hand on her sword as the flatboat navigated the current. The gambler, Kitano, was at the pole, and seemed competent enough on the water. Shin sat nearby, idly fanning himself.

"What do you know of Willow Quay?" he asked.

Kasami didn't look at him. "It is a slum."

"Not quite. It's an odd sort of place – half-wild and mostly empty, save at certain times of year. A few businesses run year-round; the sake house, the brothel, one or two merchants looking to buy whatever comes their way. I've considered investing in a few of the businesses. With a bit of work, I think something could be made of the place."

Kasami snorted. "Like what? A slightly bigger slum?"

"I'd prefer to call it a free port. Lighter tariffs, less oversight.

One could make a lot of money, building that sort of place."

Kasami turned. "A bushi should be above such things."

"Technically, I am here to oversee our business interests," Shin said. "What do you think, Kitano? A good idea?"

The gambler didn't turn around. "Whatever you say, my lord."

Kasami glared at him. As if sensing her hostility, he hunched forward. The gambler irritated her. This whole affair irritated her, but Kitano especially so. He was disrespectful and untrustworthy. If she'd had her way, he would be dead already. Heimin were untrustworthy as a rule, but men like Kitano especially so. She watched him with suspicion, waiting for him to make a mistake.

Eventually, annoyed by his lack of provocation, she turned her attentions back to the river bank. Buildings became visible amongst the trees, and Kitano slowed the boat. "Why are you slowing down?" she snapped, half-rising to her feet.

"Sentries," Kitano said, quickly. "Keeping a lookout for the magistrates. Better if they get a good look at us. Otherwise they might sound the alarm."

"Wise thinking, Kitano," Shin said.

Kitano bobbed his head in acknowledgement. "Thank you, my lord." He glanced at Kasami and then hurriedly away. Kasami growled wordlessly.

"Something bothering you?" Shin asked.

"How can we trust this fool?" she muttered.

"What does trust have to do with it?" he countered. "We are both armed, and you, at least, are perfectly willing to take his head if he so much as sneezes in my direction." He smiled at her. "I do not have to trust him. I trust you."

Kasami opened her mouth to reply, but could think of no words, so she simply nodded and sat back. Willow Quay spread out around them as they slid into the cove. The wharf itself was a cluttered reef of shanty docks and makeshift jetties springing haphazardly from the curve of a natural inlet. There wasn't much space – only a few vessels at a time could dock in the inlet. The rest had to make do with berths farther down the river.

"Where is it?" Kasami demanded.

"Farther down, I think," Kitano said. "It's a sloop."

"You think?"

"That's what I was told," he clarified, shooting her a nervous glance.

"By whom?" she pressed.

"A fisherwoman of my acquaintance," he said, after a moment's hesitation. "She's never steered me wrong," he added, quickly.

"Let us hope this is not the first time, then," Shin said, mildly. He paused. "Does anyone else see that?"

Kasami followed his gesture. There was a boat some distance ahead. She stood and craned her neck. "It's heading into the current. They might be trying to leave."

"I think we've arrived just in time. Kitano, aim us towards that vessel, please."

"What?" Kitano goggled at Shin. "But–"

"Now," Kasami said. Kitano swallowed and bent to his task. Kasami looked at Shin. "You think that's the one we're looking for?"

"I am not a great believer in coincidence." Shin had an intent look on his face. "Be wary. Keep your hand on your sword."

Kasami nodded. "Gladly."

As they rounded a bend in the river, they saw it – a broken down sloop, drifting away from its dirt berth. A crowd had gathered on shore to watch. "No crew," Kitano said. "At least, no one on deck. She's adrift."

"So it seems." Shin gestured with his fan. "Get us as close as you can. We need to get aboard, and quickly."

"Are you sure that's wise?" Kasami asked, as Kitano poled them towards the drifting boat. "It might be best to let it go."

"It might well hold answers to my questions. And I'm curious, in any event. Aren't you?" He looked at her, a wide grin on his face. For a moment, he looked like an excited child. She'd forgotten how much he enjoyed this sort of thing. His indolence was as much a pose as his foolishness. In truth, he craved stimulation. It was one of the things that reminded her that there was a true bushi beneath that foppish exterior.

"Not even a little bit," she answered, bluntly. "But since you are determined to investigate – I will go first."

"Oh, obviously. You are my bodyguard, after all. That is your duty." Shin sat back. "Rest assured, I have no intention of endangering myself."

"I will hold you to that," she said, as they drew close. She reached down into the bottom of the boat and retrieved a coil of mooring line. "Gambler – look here. Think you can hold this thing steady?"

"Yes, but not for long. Why?"

"I'm going to lasso a bollard. Preferably one of those on the side." She stood and quickly and loosely knotted the line in several places.

"Are you certain you can catch it?" Kitano looked as if he regretted the question, even as he asked it. Kasami grinned as she lashed the other end of the line to the flatboat's mooring ring.

"Do you know how many boats get lost in the marshes?" She tested the line, and nodded in satisfaction. It would hold.

"No?" he said, doubtfully.

"None. Because we know how to catch them. Keep us still." She whirled the rope with a loose, slow spin, not wanting to overshoot the rail. There was an art to boarding a moving boat, and it was one she'd learned as a girl. Ideally, she'd have been attempting it without armor, but one couldn't have everything.

She caught a bollard on the first throw, and pulled the knot tight. The flatboat began to drift along with the larger vessel, and she and Kitano pulled them tight against the hull. It wasn't far to the rail. "How do we get up there?" Kitano asked.

"Give me a boost."

He blinked in confusion. She smacked him on the side of the head. "Bend down." He bent with a muttered oath, which she graciously ignored. She stepped up onto his back and reached for the rail. A moment later, she caught hold and hauled herself up and over.

She took in the deck with a glance. It was a shabby sort of boat. The kind that looked as if it might capsize in a strong wind. There was no one in sight. No sound, save the crackle of unseen flames. The boat was listing slightly. Had someone simply left it to drift?

"Well?" Shin called up.

Kasami hesitated. Then she turned. "Come up. But be careful."

CHAPTER TWENTY-TWO
Ambush

Shin felt uneasy as he clambered up onto the boat. It wasn't just the constant lurching motion that made it hard to focus. It was the noise of the distant crowd, and the creak of the mast. It was as if he'd walked into a room where the occupants had suddenly gone quiet.

"No sign of the crew," Kasami said, as she helped him over the rail.

"Perhaps they abandoned ship."

"Why would they do that?" she said, looking around.

"We can ask them when we find them." The rigging clattered above him, and he tensed. He didn't care for boats at the best of times. And something about this one was making him uneasy. He looked at Kasami, and could tell from her expression that she felt the same way. "Until then, I'll settle for examining the hold."

"Why? What's the point?"

"It's the scene of the crime, obviously. Come along." He

started across the deck, stumbling slightly. Kasami and Kitano followed, the pair of them moving with a sure-footed steadiness that he found somewhat galling.

"This is foolish," Kasami said.

"No one ever said this was going to be easy."

"You're the one making it complicated." Kasami shook her head. "None of this matters. The Lion have already made up their mind."

"No," Shin said. "All appearances to the contrary, I don't believe they have. Otherwise they would have moved against the Unicorn. But instead, they bide their time. Minami, for all her bluster, isn't certain as to the identity of her enemy."

"And you believe her?"

"Of course. She could no more lie than you could. But that doesn't mean she won't. Or that one of the others won't beat her to the punch, if they sense that the Lion is wavering. I expect that, even now, all three clans are extending feelers into the city, testing the mood of the citizenry as well as Tetsua's ronin."

Shin strode across the deck, towards the hatch that led into the hold. "If the governor throws in with a faction, it will all but guarantee victory for that side," he continued. "But, proper bribery takes time and resources that they may not have – or wish to spend without knowing what they're getting in return. If Tetsua is half as smart as I believe him to be, he will be playing them against each other, entertaining offers from each but accepting none."

"He's buying us time," Kasami said.

"Yes. That's all he can do at the moment. The rest is up to us."

"I still don't understand why we're here, though. What does

this ship matter, when you think you already have the man behind it?"

"I would like proof before I ruin a man's livelihood," Shin said. He turned. "I could accuse him, yes. Tetsua would be obliged to take my accusations as fact. Saiga would have no recourse. That is the way the law works – my word against his, and the word of a bushi always outweighs that of a heimin."

"And so?"

"And so, that is not justice."

"It is the law."

Shin shook his head. "The two are not always synonymous. I must have proof before I use the weight of my status against him. And that means we must find this Captain… Kitano, what was her name?"

"Lun, my lord."

"This Captain Lun. Her testimony will be another link in the chain, and it might be that I can use it to force Saiga to talk." Shin gestured to the hatch. It was closed. "Kitano, if you would be so kind?"

Kitano glowered sulkily, but bent to open the hatch. Shin made to go below when he'd gotten it open, but Kasami stopped him. "Me first, remember?"

Shin stepped back reluctantly. "Of course, after you."

He followed her as she descended into the hold. The sunlight streaming down through the hatch banished the gloom. It wasn't a large space, and was fairly empty besides. Kasami stopped. "Wait. Look."

Shin saw the body a moment later. A woman, laying on the floor. He turned. "Kitano, get down here!" He turned back to Kasami. "Is she… ?"

"Unconscious," Kasami said, softly. She tensed, her hand on her sword. "Get back above deck. Now."

Shin was about to reply when he happened to glance up. It was only luck that allowed him to see the figure crouched above him among the wooden beams in the upper reaches of the hold. He spied two more of them a moment later. "Kasami – above us!" he shouted, reaching for his wakizashi.

The closest leapt for him, drawing a blade as he fell. Shin swept his own out, narrowly intercepting the blow. He rocked back on the steps, nearly losing his balance. The shinobi was fast – and intent on his death. It took all of his concentration to keep his opponent's blade from piercing something vital.

Past his attacker, he saw that the other two were busy with Kasami. They'd obviously deemed her the larger threat – a not unfair assumption. He broke away from his opponent and began to back up the steps. If he could draw his attacker out of the hold, he might be able to gain the advantage. Or at least jump over the side, if all else failed.

The shinobi followed him without hesitation, eyes narrowed. As Shin retreated, he studied his opponent, trying to identify some weakness in the man's form that he might be able to exploit. But nothing presented itself. The shinobi was clad in loose-fitting gray clothing, and his head was hidden within a peaked cowl, with only a thin slit for his eyes. He bore no identifying markings, not that Shin had expected any.

"I don't suppose you'd be willing to tell me who hired you?" Shin asked, hopefully. "No? Shame. Still, that this is a bad idea can't have escaped your notice. Killing me won't stop the investigation; in fact, it will only validate it."

The shinobi made no reply. He simply paced after Shin, one

step at a time. Patient and wary. A trained killer, ready to seize the smallest opening. Shin kept his wakizashi between them. He had been trained by some of the finest swordsmen in Rokugan, but he'd rarely held a blade – especially this blade.

He tightened his grip on the hilt. His grandfather had claimed it was a gift but, in truth, it was meant as a reminder to Shin of his familial obligations. The Daidoji were the iron in the blade. Impurities were to be beaten out, as the fire grew hot. Impurities like Shin.

This city – this moment – was the fire. His exile here was to be a tempering, or so his grandfather intended. But Shin had his own ideas – and those ideas did not include being gutted like a fish. As his foot touched the top stair, he began to speed up, forcing the shinobi to move more quickly. He could hear the roaring cascade of the Drowned Merchant River. Soon, the boat would be fully caught by the current.

"No way off, then," he said out loud. "What will you do, I wonder?"

The shinobi hesitated, just for a fraction of an instant – and that was when Shin spied Kitano crouched behind a nearby barrel. The gambler had his knife in his good hand and, as he caught Shin's eye, he rose and sent the blade spinning towards the shinobi.

It bounced off the killer's temple, staggering him. Instinctively, the shinobi whirled, cursing, his short blade whipping out in a savage arc. Kitano threw himself backwards, narrowly avoiding a messy death.

The shinobi realized his mistake as Shin lunged. His wakizashi flashed down, biting into the meat of the shinobi's shoulder, close to his neck. The man gave a strangled groan and twisted away, even as Shin withdrew the blade. He fell, crimson pumping from the wound. Shin flicked blood from his blade.

He leaned forward and used the tip to pull the shinobi's mask off. He studied the man's face for a moment, wondering if he'd perhaps encountered him before, then looked at Kitano. "Well played, Kitano. You continue to prove your usefulness."

"Thank you, my lord," Kitano said, somewhat hesitantly. He stared down at the dying man, his expression unreadable. Both he and Shin turned towards the hold as a shout echoed up. A figure in gray raced onto the deck and paused at the hatch. One of the remaining shinobi – a woman, Shin thought. She hesitated, her gaze flicking from her dying companion, to Shin. Then, without a word, she darted for the rail.

Startled, Shin was slow off the mark pursuing her. By the time he reached the rail, she was gone, lost to the waters below. He turned as Kasami came onto the deck, her sword dripping blood. "Where is she?" she demanded.

Shin indicated the water. "She chose the better part of valor," he said. He didn't ask about the other one. The look on Kasami's face said it all. "I trust the captain is still breathing?"

"As far as I can tell," Kasami said. She looked at Kitano. "And where were you?"

"Providing a timely distraction," Shin interjected. He sheathed his sword. "We need to get her off this boat. Kitano…" Shin paused. Kitano was still staring at the dead man. "What is it?"

"I- I know him."

"How?"

"He is – he was a fisherman." Kitano swallowed. "Why is he here?"

"Why do you think?" Kasami said. "It was an ambush. They were trying to kill us." She stared at Kitano. "The only question is – how did they know we were going to be here?"

"I- I didn't know, I swear," the gambler began. He made to get to his feet, but Kasami pounced on him. She kicked him onto his back and pinned him to the deck with her foot before Shin could speak.

"Kasami…" he began.

"He's lying," she hissed, holding her blade to the trembling man's throat. "He knew they were there. He led us into a trap." It was not the Daidoji way to let traitors live. Treachery had only one reward, and it was not gold but steel. Sweat rolled down the gambler's rough features, and he swallowed.

"I don't believe so," Shin said. Kasami shook her head and tilted the blade so that the edge rested against Kitano's jugular. She let the tip of her blade drift, lightly scoring his flesh. One flick of her wrist, and his neck would be opened to the bone. The gambler closed his eyes, whimpering slightly.

"I didn't…" he began.

"Kitano, be quiet. Kasami, stop threatening him and think – there are easier ways to sink a boat. They could have simply drilled the hull and let it take on water. They set it adrift in order to ensure that we would come aboard – to prick our curiosity. My curiosity," he amended. "They set a trap, yes, but why would Kitano walk into it?"

Kasami paused. "He didn't come willingly."

"But he didn't resist, either." Shin looked down at Kitano. "This fisherman… was he one of the ones you spoke to about Lun?"

"Y- yes," Kitano said, nodding convulsively.

Shin looked down at him, his gaze serene. He stooped and

retrieved Kitano's knife. He weighed it and then sent it into the deck between Kitano's legs, blade-first. It quivered, and Kitano quivered with it. Shin smiled.

A moment later, he dropped the rest of the gambler's payment onto the deck. Kitano cracked an eye, and looked at the coins. Then looked up. "What… ?"

Kasami echoed him, with considerably more invective. "What?"

Shin ignored her. "You are mine now, Kitano. Consider those your wages."

Kitano stared at him in incomprehension. "What?" he said again.

"What?" Kasami echoed. She looked at Shin, but he did not meet her gaze.

"Let him up."

Kasami stepped back, the blade still pressed against Kitano's throat, forcing him to rise. "Are you certain?" she asked.

"Yes. He could have fled, and left us to it. Instead, he threw in his lot with us. That buys him a bit of grace."

She frowned. "Grace? He's a thief, and a fool."

"Yes. I didn't say it bought him much."

"It shouldn't buy him anything."

"No. But mercy can be as keen a cut as any." Shin spoke softly, but firmly. The voice of the Daidoji. Kasami sighed and stepped back, sheathing her katana.

"Fine. But if he bites our hand he's getting a dog's death."

Shin glanced at the gambler. "Good, now that that's settled, we should retrieve our unconscious captain and see about getting this boat back to its berth – Kitano? You were a sailor, yes?"

"Yes," Kitano said, pushing himself to his feet.

"Good. I trust you know how to handle… this sort of thing?" Shin flapped a hand at the sails. "Get us back to shore or something."

"I'll need help, my lord."

Shin looked at Kasami. She rolled her eyes, but nodded. Shin smiled in satisfaction and clasped his hands behind his back. "Excellent. Carry on. And do be quick. I want to be back on dry land before the day is out. I have questions in need of answers."

CHAPTER TWENTY-THREE
Lun

"Are you still alive, Captain?"

Lun cracked her good eye. Her first impression was of a mane of white hair, and a smile that could melt ice. Then she focused on the face – narrow and pretty, in the way some men were. A face that had never been on the wrong end of a boat hook.

"Am I?" she croaked. She tried to sit up, groaned and fell back. "I hurt too much to be dead, so I must be." Her head swam as she tried to focus. "Feels like my skull is cracked." Her hands were bandaged, as was her midsection. The wounds weren't deep, barely more than scratches, but they hurt nonetheless.

"An astute observation. It very nearly was. Lucky for you, they were in a hurry. As it is, I suspect it will be a few days before you feel up to doing more than sitting very still."

She looked at the man more closely, took in the style and hue of his kimono, and her surroundings. There was a woman standing behind him, frowning, clad in armor. Samurai. Her heart seized and her eye flicked away, looking for a way out.

"You are quite safe," the man said. His voice was calm, soothing. She didn't trust it.

"I don't think so," she said.

The woman gave a sharp bark of laughter. "She's smarter than she looks."

Lun bared her teeth. The woman replied in kind. They studied one another for a moment, until the man cleared his throat. "My name is Daidoji Shin. This is Kasami. You are called Lun, I believe. Is that correct?"

Lun nodded slowly, not taking her eye off the other woman. Shin smiled in a friendly fashion. "Excellent, then we have saved the right woman."

"Saved me?" Lun blinked. She remembered the shinobi and rubbed her face to hide her sudden flinch. She'd thought she was dead for certain. "What happened?"

"I was rather hoping you might tell us," Shin said. He caught her wrist, turning it so that he could see her tattoo. "You were in service to the Crane," he said, softly.

"Once." She pulled her wrist back. "I'm my own woman now."

"And so you shall remain." He smoothed his kimono, looking suddenly boyish.

She frowned. "What about the ones who attacked me?"

"Dead," Kasami said. "Save one. They used you as bait."

Lun looked at her. "And you fell for it."

They stared at each other for a moment, until the hint of a smile showed at the corners of Kasami's mouth. She turned away. "I'll check the garden. Just in case we were followed."

Shin waited until she'd left and said, "I am sorry. If we'd gotten there sooner, we might have been able to prevent this." He paused. "We did manage to salvage your boat, however. Though, no sign of your crew..."

"My boat?" Lun frowned. She wasn't sure whether to be happy about that – or disappointed. "Wonderful." She hesitated. "And the crew are fine. I sent them packing."

"Oh? Why?"

"Does it matter?"

"Yes. It implies that you knew something like this might happen." He peered down at her. "Did you, Captain?"

Lun swallowed. "If I did?"

"Then I would very much like to know about it. Not least because I was almost killed today saving your life. A few answers aren't too much to ask, I think."

Lun looked away. Her eyes flicked to the tattoo, then around to the room. It was a simple enough sort of space, but prettily decorated in blues and whites. The Crane did everything prettily. As if he could sense her hesitation, he said, "If you fear repercussions, I can offer my protection."

Lun closed her eye. "You saved me, my lord," she said, slowly. "I owe you what's left of my life, I suppose. Better to owe a Crane. I know what your sort is capable of, at least." She knew her tone verged on the disrespectful, but she didn't care.

Apparently, neither did he. "Excellent. Why were they trying to sink your boat?"

"Were they?" She blinked. If she'd known that, she might have simply let them. But she didn't say it. "Is that why they snuck aboard?"

"I assume so, given that you were adrift in the river's current. Those waters have smashed sturdier vessels, I'm told."

Lun laughed in realization. "That wasn't their doing, my lord. It was mine. I managed to cut the mooring lines before they booted me down into the hold."

Shin paused, digesting this. "Why? Were you trying to escape?"

"Something like that." Lun could see from his expression that he didn't believe her.

"Would the reason have anything to do with why you sent your crew away?"

She fell silent. Part of her – the part that had served onboard a Crane vessel – wanted to tell him. It was a hard thing to shake, that obedience. It was bred into people. But Lun had been her own master for too long to snap to now.

He waited patiently, in no hurry for her reply. One of the worst things about his kind was the way they made other people feel as if time was running out. Finally, she could stand it no more. "Maybe," she said.

He nodded, as if he'd expected that. "And would those two facts be related to a recent shipment of yours?"

"The rice," Lun said, before she could stop herself.

Shin nodded. "Yes. I thought as much. You seem a clever woman, Captain. Once you heard the news, I'm sure you extrapolated the possible consequences with remarkable speed. Is that why you sought refuge in Willow Quay?"

"It was only temporary," Lun said, rubbing her face. "Just until I could pay off the crew and make other arrangements."

"How noble," he said. The worst part was he sounded as if he meant it. She would have preferred an insult. Sincerity was almost too much to bear, coming from one of his kind. She shifted uncomfortably, suddenly overcome with anger. "It is probably the only thing that saved their lives. If not your attackers, then the Lion almost certainly would have caught you – and you would be dead, rather than simply injured."

"I knew it," she growled. "I knew I shouldn't have taken that bastard's money. I knew it would come back to bite me." She pounded her fist into her palm and then winced in pain. Superficial cuts hurt just as badly as the more lethal sort.

"Which bastard might that be?" Shin asked, intently.

Lun frowned and scrubbed at her cheeks with the heels of her palms. "It was a private commission. A merchant looking to offload some rice on the Lion. Their merchants pay well for anything that they can trade for iron and stone."

Shin nodded. "What was this merchant's name?" The way he said it implied he already knew. Lun hesitated, weighing her loyalty to Saiga against her anger.

"Saiga," she said, finally. "Word got around he was looking for a fast ship and a captain who wouldn't ask many questions."

Shin raised an eyebrow. "Is that the usual way?"

"For us," Lun said. "Maybe not for you." She paused. "He works out of a cheap teahouse on Three Finger Street, near the Unicorn docks."

"I am aware. How much do you know about him?"

Lun frowned. "His money was good. That's all I need to know." She sat back. "He set me up, didn't he?"

"Yes. The question is, did he know he was doing so?"

"He did," she said, flatly.

"How can you be sure?"

"Because it's Saiga. And Saiga always knows what he's getting into. He's too canny a bastard not to know. And, I'll tell you what else – he sent those killers after me."

Shin was silent for a moment. "Would you swear to that, before a magistrate?"

Lun hesitated. "In court?"

"Yes."

"Why? You obviously think he's up to something. Handle it yourself… my lord. The way bushi handle things."

"That is not the way I prefer to do things, Captain. Expedience is not justice."

Lun stared at him. "Are you mad?" she said, after a pause.

"I often have the same question," Kasami said as she came back in. "The garden is clear. No sign anyone followed us."

"Kitano?"

"Downstairs, trying to make tea. I thought it best to keep him out of the way for the moment, until we figure out what to do with him." She paused. "He's terrible at it, by the way. I don't think he's ever even drunk anything that wasn't fermented."

"One can't have everything." Shin looked at Lun. "It seems I need to speak to Saiga again. Sooner rather than later."

"Yes. I'll go with you. I want to look that treacherous bastard in the face…" She nearly fell over as she tried to stand. Shin gently forced her back. She resisted the urge to punch him. It might seem ungrateful.

"No need." Shin rose. "You will stay here and rest. No one knows you are here, or that you survived – save perhaps that shinobi who escaped. Nor will they, until I decide it is safe for you to miraculously return to life."

Lun opened her mouth. Closed it. A part of her, the part that recognized the tone of command in his words, wanted to argue. To shout that she was no longer a Crane vassal. But a wiser part told her that she needed rest – and where better than here? Who would think to look for her here, after all? But there was one thing she had to know.

"Why?" Lun said.

Shin hesitated. "Why what?"

"Why are you helping me?"

"Why would I not?" Shin turned away. "Besides, you are helping me as well – and one good turn deserves another. Rest, Captain. You'll be back aboard a ship before you know it, and this will all just be a bad memory."

Lun settled back as they departed. "What's one more?" she murmured.

Okuni ran. Ordinarily, she might have slipped across the rooftops of the city like a shadow. But it was harder when one was injured. As Nao had predicted, her wound was threatening to reopen. She stumbled at the apex of a roof, and the streets swam about her in a blur of lantern light. For a moment, she thought she was falling – but her training saved her, and not for the first time that evening.

Panting, she paused. She cast a look back, searching for any sign of her pursuers. But she saw nothing, save shadows and smoke. That meant little, however. They were close – she could feel them circling, waiting for her guard to slip. A sudden prickle of instinct caused her to fall back and roll down the slope, catching herself at the last moment. A trio of steel darts sprouted from the ridge of the roof moments later. She waited, every sense straining to pierce the din of the city. Only the gleam of flung metal had saved her that time.

She heard the creak of tiles, and turned slightly. A shape slipped through the haze, approaching warily. Man or woman, she could not say. The figure wore no identifying markings, and was masked. But the blade they carried left no doubt as to their intentions. Wincing, Okuni reached into her shirt for one of the small hidden blades sheathed there. The flat leaves of steel were perfectly balanced for throwing.

She drew one, biting back a grunt of pain. She felt the wound in her side pull as she rolled onto her back and whipped the throwing blade towards the approaching shinobi. They swatted the blade aside as they leapt towards her, and she was forced to draw one of her claws. She blocked a blow meant to split her breastbone and swept her legs around, catching her attacker in the ankles. The shinobi gave a grunt of surprise and tumbled from the edge of the roof. Okuni didn't wait to see if they managed to save themselves.

She scrambled up the slope, heading for the far edge of the roof. This part of the city nestled close against the water. Many of the buildings extended out over the river. That was why she'd come this way in the first place. After last time, she'd known she might have to take to the water again, and had thought to wear waterproof wrappings beneath her clothing.

The tiles creaked behind her, and she dove to the side, avoiding a slashing blade. Its wielder chuckled. "Still quick. Very good." The voice was hatefully familiar.

"Chobei," Okuni said, as the shinobi padded towards her across the tiles of the roof. He nodded and smiled.

"You remember me. I am pleased."

"You made quite the impression."

"And you are quite the fool," he said, pointing his sword at her. “I thought you’d escaped for good. Even told my employer as much – what shinobi would be so foolish to hang around after knowing they were marked? But there you were.” He shook his head. “And here you are. Nowhere left to run.”

“You call me a fool,” Okuni said. “A good shinobi knows that there is always somewhere left to run. Even if it doesn’t look that way.”

“Not this time. This is our city. We have you, and we will make your end quick.” He gestured, and she saw two more shinobi appear on nearby rooftops. “Not out of respect, this time, but out of practicality. We have no time left for you. Others require our attentions.”

Okuni looked around. She could hear the others approaching. She had to keep him talking until she could see an opening to get past them. “Like Saiga, you mean.” She was just grabbing at straws – it was just as likely that Saiga had hired them himself.

Chobei smiled gently. “No. Not him. He is no longer a concern.”

She felt a thrill of unease. “Then who? His partner? No. You are protecting him, aren’t you?” She began to back away along the edge of the roof. She could hear the river close by. “Why?”

“Asking questions will not keep you alive,” Chobei said, not unkindly.

“No, but jumping off the roof might.”

Okuni turned and leapt. As she’d hoped – prayed – the water was directly below. She’d folded her arms over her chest and cut the water smoothly as she went in. The shock and cold nearly knocked her senseless, despite her preparations.

She began to swim. A veritable canopy of wharfs and

jetties extended overhead, hiding her from sight. But she knew Chobei would be on her heels in moments. He was smart and deadly. She had to get back to the theater, and quickly. Sanemon and the others had to make ready to leave immediately.

Before Chobei caught up with her for a third time.

CHAPTER TWENTY-FOUR
Saiga

The soft red glow of lanterns lit the path back to Three Finger Street. The Unicorn wharfs were quiet, save for the slap of water and the murmur of night fishermen. The teahouses and sake houses were full, but there was little noise.

"Everyone is scared," Kitano said, when Shin mentioned it. The gambler looked scared himself. "The Lion is mustering their strength, and most people are trying to find ways out of the city. Or preparing for trouble."

"And what about you, Kitano?" Shin asked. He had noticed an increased number of Kaeru ronin on the streets, leading patrols of ashigaru in imperial livery. Tetsua was taking no chances, it seemed.

"I'm with you now, my lord." Kitano didn't look at him as he spoke.

"A gamble on your part."

"A sure thing," Kitano said. He scratched his chin. "Seems to me you're the one who's going to come out on top, my lord. Whatever happens."

"Your confidence is appreciated, Kitano. Tell me, what do you know of our friend, Saiga?" Shin was curious to see if Kitano's information differed from Ito's. He might well know more than the merchant, or at least something different. He was assembling a picture of Saiga, and it was a curious one – it did not seem to fit the facts.

"He deals in stolen goods. Food mostly. It's easier to steal in bulk and sell for a profit. I've done it myself."

"You've worked for him?" Shin asked. He wasn't surprised. Kitano struck him as the sort of man to have many friends in low places.

"Once or twice. He paid well, and on time."

Kasami snorted. "Yes, with someone else's money."

Kitano shrugged. "He might also be a spy."

Shin paused. "A spy?"

"You can't throw a rock in a teahouse without hitting one. Everyone wants to know what's coming in and where it's going. Lot of money to be made if you can get that kind of information."

Disturbing as the thought was, Shin found it unsurprising. Where there was trade, there was information, and where there was information, there were invariably those who would try and profit from it. "Who was Saiga working for?"

Kitano shook his head. "I don't know, my lord, and that's the truth. There were rumors, of course. I heard that he worked for the Scorpion, myself."

Shin snorted. "If every person said to work for the Scorpion did so, half of Rokugan would be employed by them."

"I'm sorry, my lord, but I wouldn't know," Kitano said. He sounded almost sincere.

"No, I don't expect that you would." Shin tapped his lips with his fan, thinking. "Still, perhaps there is something in what you say. It's clear that Saiga has protection. Someone is looking out for him." He stopped, recognizing the front of the teahouse Ito had brought them to. "I'll add it to the list of questions I have for him. Kitano, wait here – keep watch on the street. If you see something…"

"Take care of it," Kitano said, tapping the hilt of his knife.

"Finally, you say something sensible," Kasami said, nodding in approval.

Shin shook his head. "No. Alert us, if possible. Remain out of sight otherwise."

"No worries on that score, my lord."

Shin nodded and started towards the teahouse, Kasami by his side. "I doubt he's here when we get back," she murmured.

"Is that a wager?"

"No."

"Pity. I would have given you good odds."

At this time of night, there was only a handful of patrons in the teahouse when Shin and Kasami arrived. At the sight of Kasami in her armor, that number dwindled still further. Even the staff seemed to have better things to do than to interfere with them. Kasami watched them vanish and snorted. "What if he's not here?"

"Then we take the opportunity for a quick look around. Either way, I have no doubt we will find something of interest." Shin made his way to the back. The boards creaked beneath his feet. There was a light on in Saiga's office. Shin tapped his lips, and Kasami nodded. When no one called out, Shin carefully slid the door open.

Kasami gave a guttural curse as she saw what awaited them.

Shin nodded. "As I feared."

Saiga was dead. He lay folded over on his cushion, hands flung out to either side of him, his head resting on the low writing desk before him. Shin went to him and knelt, palm held just above the bowed head. He noticed a faint, purplish mark on the back of the man's neck, resembling a burn – but it was anything but. Kasami hissed in disgust as he made to examine it more closely. "Do not touch him. What are you thinking?"

"That he's quite cold, and it's a warm night." Shin rose. He looked up, stared at the ceiling for a moment and then pointed. "There. The thatch has been disturbed."

"So? What of it?"

"Give me a boost," he said, gesturing to the floor. Kasami stared at him.

"I will not."

He motioned to the roof. "I need to get up there."

"Why?"

He pointed to the body. "Because whoever killed him did so from up there."

"How do you know?"

Shin pointed upwards again. "Weren't you listening? The thatch has been disturbed. And, of course, the mark on his neck."

"A burn," she said, doubtfully.

"What sort of burn turns the surrounding flesh purple?"

Kasami had no answer for him. "I am still not giving you a boost. Is it poison, then?"

"Yes. A very peculiar sort, derived from a species of scorpion native to al-Zawira. Quite lethal, in a concentrated dose." He leaned over the body, peering at the wound. "I suspect that it was delivered by a sharpened steel wire thrust through the thatch, and into his neck. A prick would have been all it took." He rubbed the back of his own neck. "He probably didn't even notice until his heart stopped." His skin prickled as he considered the ceiling. There might well be more wires waiting. "They would have had to have been fast and quiet."

Kasami dropped a hand to the hilt of her katana. "The same ones we encountered at Willow Quay," she said, softly, as she loosened her blade in its sheath.

"Possibly. The same brotherhood at least."

"They might still be here."

"Doubtful." Shin began to rummage through the scattered papers. "As I said, he's quite cold. And somewhat stiff. That means several hours, at least. They probably killed him before they went after Lun. Following the chain, one link at a time."

"Does that include your actress?"

Shin paused. "Yes, almost certainly. Though I suspect she's managed to avoid Saiga's fate. In fact, I expect that their failure to kill her is what led to this – as well as the attempt on our guest. I – ah. Look here." He showed her a handful of papers. Kasami stared at them blankly. Seeing her expression, he sighed. "Receipts of transaction. I've signed hundreds of these for Ito and the others."

"And that's important why?"

"Saiga dealt in stolen cargo. He would have used these receipts to prove legal ownership, if anyone had asked. I wonder how he got them."

"Clearly they're forged."

"Maybe. Or stolen. But it leads me to wonder what else he

might have." He fell onto all fours and peered at the desk from a low angle. Kasami sighed, no doubt glad that no one was around to see him in so undignified a position.

"My grandfather has a desk like this," Shin continued. "Curious little things. I wonder – ah. There we are." He reached out and touched one of the carved flowers that decorated the sides and back of the desk. There was a soft click, and a drawer in the bottom of the desk fell open.

Kasami gave a grunt of surprise. "What is that?"

"A hidden drawer, obviously." Shin retrieved something and stood. "Sloppy. They didn't think to check. Maybe they weren't told to do so, or didn't have time. In any event, their mistake is our gain." Shin held up what turned out to be a small book. "Look at this. Recognize it?"

"Should I?" Kasami shook her head. "What is it? More receipts?"

"Of a sort. Ito has one of these as well, a patronage book." He flipped it open and scanned the contents. "Saiga was paying someone a percentage of his profits in return for various things – protection, contracts, information." He looked at her. "He wasn't just a merchant – he was a clan vassal." He frowned and turned more pages. "No sign of who his patron might have been, though. Usually these are stamped…"

"If he had a patron, then why is he working out of a place like this?"

"I imagine it served his interests not to be too closely associated with them. And theirs, as well. Not all merchants deal in silk and rice."

"The black market," Kasami said.

Shin nodded and peered at the book. "Precisely. We're not

supposed to acknowledge that such a thing could ever exist, of course. But even the Daidoji make use of it. There are some things it is better to purchase – or sell – in secret. Saiga must have been someone's conduit – and it's likely that someone employed him to hire Lun and Okuni both." He flipped the pages. "It's written in some form of cipher. I can decrypt it, but it will take time." He thrust the book into his kimono, along with the other documents. "We should depart."

"What about the body?"

Shin paused. "Leave it be. No sense alerting our opponents as to our discovery. It will be discovered in time, and we have more important matters to attend to."

"I hope that includes explaining this to me," Iuchi Shichiro said from behind them.

Kasami turned, sword half-drawn. Shichiro stood in the doorway, and the bushi who flanked him had their blades out and ready. Shin took them both in at a glance. Young. Untested. Eager. But skilled. "Kasami?" he asked, softly.

She shook her head. "I can kill one. Probably not both."

Shichiro glanced at his men and smiled. "You heard her. Which of you will it be?" The two warriors looked at one another uneasily, as if uncertain how best to answer.

Shin stepped forward. "Might I humbly suggest that no one has to die at this particular moment – except for the unfortunate Saiga, of course." He indicated the body.

Shichiro chuckled and waved his warriors back. "Leave us. Make sure no one enters this room." The men hesitated. One opened his mouth to speak, but Shichiro silenced him with a glance. "Go."

They went. Kasami let her sword slide back into its sheath.

Shichiro gave her a respectful nod, and she bowed her head in thanks.

Shin watched the interaction with interest. Shichiro might be old, but his authority was unquestionable. He wondered if his sons shared their father's forcefulness. If not, it would be a sad day for the Unicorn when Shichiro took his final ride.

"We have your man outside," Shichiro said.

"You haven't hurt him, I trust," Shin said. He'd expected as much, when Kitano failed to alert them. "I only just paid his retainer."

"He is fine. Whether he stays that way is up to him." Shichiro ambled into the room. "I am not surprised to find you here, little Crane. I heard on the wind that you might have found that boat of yours – down in Willow Quay."

Shin bowed his head. "And I am not surprised that you heard such a thing."

"Is it true?"

"It is."

"And the crew?"

"Nowhere to be found."

Shichiro grunted and stooped to look at the body. "And why are you here?"

"Saiga procured the rice that was sold to the Lion. He commissioned the delivery."

"And where did he procure it from?"

"Your docks."

"Then the mystery is solved," Shichiro said. "Saiga was not one of ours, but I knew of him. He made most of his coin selling stolen cargoes. A bad business, but…"

"Not one you felt like wasting time on."

Shichiro nodded. "You know as well as I that the moment I squashed him, two more would rise up to take his place. Better to have him where I could keep an eye on him, I thought. We even used him on occasion, though I doubt he knew it. He has – had – connections among the local bandit gangs, and was forever looking for information on manifests and the like. At least according to my own spies." He looked at them. "I'd wager he was killed by a dissatisfied client. Men like him never last long."

"I had much the same theory," Shin said.

Kasami barely stopped herself from giving Shin a sharp look. She knew why he was lying, but it was not the proper way of things. Shin ignored her; something he was altogether too skilled at.

Shichiro rose to his feet. "I thought you might." The old man was silent for a moment. "Is that what you will tell Tetsua?"

"I will leave Tetsua to make his own decisions. My task is simply to find the truth. What he does with it is his burden, not mine."

Shichiro nodded. "That is good." He paused. "I am told the Lion came prowling about your home earlier today. What were they looking for?"

"Is this something else the wind whispered to you?"

Shichiro smiled. "If you like." His smile faded. "Answer the question, boy. What did they want?"

"Information."

"Did you give it to them?"

"Of course."

Shichiro frowned. "Why?"

"Because there was no profit in denying it to them," Shin said. "They do not want a war any more than you do."

"So you say. But their actions tell a different story." Shichiro looked down at the merchant's body. "They attacked one of my vessels today."

Shin let no sign of his sudden dismay show on his face. That was bad. If things had progressed to that point, then open conflict wasn't far off. Once the Lion had a taste of blood, they wouldn't rest until they'd eaten their fill. "Was anyone killed?"

"No, thankfully. But that won't last. Things are becoming untenable. If the Lion do not back down we will be forced to match them. Honor demands nothing less."

"And they will not back down until this matter is settled." Shin paused. "Might I ask how you came to find us here?"

Shichiro looked at them. "I suspected Saiga was the one who'd stolen that shipment. I've had him under observation for weeks."

"Then you knew that the Lion had purchased the shipment."

"Suspected," Shichiro corrected. "Only suspected. As I said, Saiga dealt with all sorts. Even your vassals, little Crane. No way of telling which one did him in."

"He seems to have been at the center of a great number of webs. It is a shame your spies did not see who killed him – or who he might have met with before he died."

Shichiro frowned. "Yes. But as I said, it was probably a client of his."

Shin bowed low. "As you say, my lord. With your permission, we shall take our leave. I have a report to prepare for the governor."

Shichiro nodded absently. "Of course." He paused. "You are certain you found nothing of interest?"

"If I had, my lord, I would certainly have told you."

Shichiro turned back to the body. "Very well. Be off with you."

Shin and Kasami bowed deeply and departed. As they reached the street, Shin saw Kitano loitering near the teahouse, looking shamefaced. Kasami gestured curtly, and the gambler hurried to join them. "I am sorry, my lord…" he began.

"Never mind," Shin said. He glanced at Kasami, and saw that she was glowering at him. "Yes, Kasami? Something troubles you?"

"You lied to him," she said.

"I thought it only fair, seeing as he lied to us." Shin glanced over his shoulder at the teahouse. "I would bet that Shichiro knows exactly who we are looking for… but has chosen to say nothing."

"Why would he do that?"

"I don't know. But I intend to find out."

CHAPTER TWENTY-FIVE
Acceptable Solution

The summons to Saibanshoki the next morning was not unexpected. The terseness of the invitation was. Tetsua's ronin were in no mood to bandy words, and Shin saw the futility of arguing with them at once. Leaving Kasami to oversee things, he hurried to the governor's manor as speedily as dignity would allow.

Despite being expected, it was interruption he felt they could ill-afford. Things were moving quickly now, he could feel it. He'd managed to dash off a quick missive to Iuchi Konomi, asking for a moment or two of her time. After that, he'd invited Ito for tea, hoping to get some answers about the papers he'd found in Saiga's offices. One of those two conversations would hold the answers he was in search of, he was certain.

Shin saw no sign of Azuma as he was escorted up to the receiving room. He was either pursuing his own investigation or laying low. Shin would have wagered on either at this point. There had been tense stand-offs reported between the Kaeru and warriors of the Lion, as the latter attempted to fortify certain parts of their district, blocking roads and rousting merchants.

Everywhere there was the growing sense that a storm was on the horizon.

Tetsua was waiting for him on the balcony. The governor looked pensive as Shin was ushered in. He gestured. "Join me, please."

The balcony was cool, and the sounds of river traffic rose to greet him. "There was an incident yesterday," Tetsua said. "The Lion boarded a merchant sloop belonging to the Unicorn. They claimed they were hunting smugglers."

"So I heard."

Tetsua looked at him. "Minami claims that her warriors acted without permission and will be disciplined, and Shichiro has accepted that – for the moment. But it is only a matter of time before another incident occurs. Shichiro might not be so forgiving a second time. What can you tell me?"

"The Lion had good reason to be close-mouthed about that shipment. It was stolen, and they knew it."

"Minami admitted it?"

"Yes," Shin said. "I believe it was bought from a dealer in illicit cargoes named Saiga."

"The one you found dead last night," Tetsua said.

"Yes." Shin didn't ask how he knew. Tetsua wouldn't be much of a governor if he wasn't aware of such things.

Tetsua looked away. "Fine, the rice was stolen," he said. "What of it? Plenty of cargo is stolen and resold. The black market is this city's vibrant shadow."

"That it was stolen was not the issue. Rather, it is who it was stolen from."

Tetsua was silent for a moment. Then, "The Unicorn. Of course."

Shin nodded. "The Lion believe that the Unicorn allowed them to purchase the stolen rice in order to implicate them in a crime. That it was a trick designed to humiliate them."

Tetsua looked at him. "That seems a somewhat complicated way of doing so."

"But it is justification. If the rice had not been discovered – if it had been sold, and someone perished as a result, or, as is more likely, a wave of illness resulted, the Lion's reputation would have suffered."

"As would their profits."

"Exactly. And once an investigation was undertaken, it would soon be discovered that the rice had been bought from a known dealer in stolen cargo, further implicating the Lion in illicit activities. Activities every merchant in this city participates in, but that no one wishes to be connected to."

"Hardly justification for war," Tetsua murmured.

"Good enough for some." Shin looked out over the river. "The Lion are restless. I saw it myself when I visited their district, however briefly. They have more soldiers on their side of the river than any other faction in this city. Bored soldiers, bored bushi. And we both know what that can lead to."

Tetsua paled slightly. The history of Rokugan was full of stories of what happened when a warrior class became too big and had too few enemies to fight. Shin went on. "The Emperor's decision to claim this city as an imperial fiefdom has never sat well with them. And now someone has handed them an excuse to claim what they see as theirs."

"Minami…" Tetsua began.

"She is doing her best to stall, but from what you've said, I fear she is waging a losing battle. There will be more incidents in the coming days."

"Then you must be quicker about finding me a culprit,"

Tetsua said. "We have arrived at the point where guilt and innocence are immaterial. What about this Saiga?"

"As yet, his motives are unclear." Shin decided not to mention the papers he'd found. Not until he knew more, at least. "I am looking into the matter, but it seems he was simply another link in the chain."

"Working for someone, you mean?"

"Yes."

"Who?"

"Also unclear," Shin said. "And there is, of course, the question of who killed him…"

Tetsua gestured sharply. "Irrelevant. Do you have any theories as to the identity of his accomplice – or employer – that I should be aware of?"

"No, my lord." Shin paused. "There is no evidence that he was employed at all, in fact. It is merely an assumption on my part, given the nature of the man."

Tetsua nodded. "So, in theory, he could well have been working alone."

"Yes. Though as to what end, I am at a loss…"

"His motives are unimportant. The question before me is will the clans be satisfied with his death? Will it bring this matter to a close?"

"That is not for me to say, my lord." Shin paused. "But I will say that it does not satisfy me. And it may well not satisfy whoever ended Saiga's life. They will continue their course until they have broken every link in the chain."

"Good," Tetsua said. "The faster this mess is cleaned up, the better for us all." Shin kept his expression carefully neutral, but Tetsua must have seen something in his eyes, for the governor added, "You think me cruel, Daidoji Shin?"

"I think you are the imperial governor," Shin said, carefully. "You must balance the good of some against the good of all. That is no easy thing."

"No. It is not. And if I have been remiss in my duties of late, it has only made such decisions more difficult. But make them I must. This… incident, minor as it might seem, came very close to causing a disaster…"

"And if a few heimin must die so that trade continues uninterrupted, it is a small price to pay," Shin said, without anger or malice. Even so, Tetsua's expression hardened.

"Remember who you speak to, Crane."

Shin bowed wordlessly. "Forgive me, my lord. My emotions have ever had the better of me in matters like these."

Tetsua turned away. "Your grandfather warned me about your lack of respect. I see now I should have listened to him. Perhaps I was wrong to involve you in this matter."

Shin did not reply. Tetsua was silent. Then, finally, he said, "If I commanded you to leave the matter be, would you obey me?"

"I would, my lord."

Tetsua chuckled softly. After a moment, he said, "You have done well. Both the Unicorn and Lion will be satisfied that the matter is settled."

Shin wanted to ask how he could be certain, but suspected that he already knew the answer. Neither side wanted war, and both would be eager for any result that allowed them to save face without showing steel. He bowed low. "Then I am pleased to have been of service, my lord."

Tetsua did not dismiss him as he'd expected, however.

"Our business is not concluded, Daidoji Shin," Tetsua still

did not look at him. "This city is important," he said. "Not just to me, but to the empire as a whole." Shin did not know what to say, so he opted for silence. Tetsua continued. "Here, three clans are forced into an amicable truce. An unwilling one, perhaps, but a truce nonetheless. It is my duty to oversee that truce and the peace it has engendered. I cannot allow that peace to be broken."

"I understand, my lord."

"I do not think that you do. Not fully, at least."

Shin waited as Tetsua gathered his thoughts. "I will do what I must to maintain that peace. Even if it means I must dip my hands in blood and sign away my honor. I will hold that which has been entrusted to me in the most expedient manner which presents itself." Tetsua looked at him. "But you are under no such obligation, Daidoji Shin."

Shin hesitated, unsure if he'd heard correctly. He did not speak, for fear he might say the wrong thing. Tetsua went on. "Until further evidence presents itself, Saiga is the culprit. Do you understand?"

Shin bowed. "I believe so, my lord."

Tetsua smiled again. "Good. You may go." He turned back to the river and said nothing further. Shin backed away, turning Tetsua's words over in his mind.

It wasn't quite permission, but neither was it a denial. A suggestion, then. The sort of thing a Crane lived for. You could do a lot with a suggestion, if you were of a mind to be creative. His steps were light as he returned to the wharf and the craft waiting to take him back to the city. It seemed Tetsua was a man after his own heart after all.

•••

Sanemon hurried across the stage, his mind full to bursting with little problems. Torn costumes, dwindling supplies, arguments between actors – the usual headaches of a man in his position, albeit exacerbated by Okuni's stubbornness.

The woman was a fool. Her pride had blinded her to the realities of their current situation. She thought to brazen it out. Meanwhile, they were running out of everything and the rest of the troupe were getting nervous. He'd tried to tell her, though the day she listened to him was the day he grew wings.

He snorted. Some days he thanked the gods for bringing Nekoma Okuni into his life. She had saved him from drowning in the bottom of a bottle. But other days, he thought she had saved him only to preserve him for a far worse fate. He was dying by increments, drowning in a sea of furious anxiety. One day they'd find him dead, a handful of unpaid bills clutched in one stiff, claw-like hand.

He mopped at his face with a handkerchief. As an ashigaru, he'd thought he'd known fear. But the terrors of the battlefield were nothing next to the manifold horrors of running a minor kabuki troupe.

"She's back," Nao said, falling into step with him as he headed for the dressing rooms. Sanemon glanced at him.

"What?"

"Came in through the back entrance, dressed like a beggar. A wet beggar. I almost had her thrown out."

"You would have regretted that."

"Yes, well, luckily I know a drowned cat when I see one. She's been in the river again, and she is not happy."

"I wouldn't be either. Where is she now?"

"My dressing room. I made sure no one saw her enter."

Sanemon nodded. "Good thinking."

"Well, I do have a reputation to consider."

Sanemon followed Nao back to his dressing room, his heart pounding. When Okuni hadn't returned, he'd feared the worst. But there had been nothing for it but to go on and hope she somehow turned up. Now that she had, he wondered what trouble she'd brought with her this time.

"We must leave," Okuni said, without preamble, as they entered. "Tonight." She looked disheveled and tired, as if she had been running all night.

"Our boat is not scheduled to depart until tomorrow afternoon," Sanemon protested. If it was even going to depart at all. Tensions between the clans had thrown a pall of uncertainty over all river traffic, regardless of where it was heading or what it carried. "And anyway, we still have one last performance to give. Think of our reputation…"

"I'm thinking of our lives," Okuni said, rounding on him. "Someone wants me dead!"

"Not just you," Nao said, from the doorway. Okuni glared at him.

"What are you talking about?"

"Someone killed a merchant a few streets over. No one is really sure how. And I heard from one of the stagehands that there was some sort of massacre elsewhere – the crew of a boat, all killed." He paused. "Or missing. No one is quite sure."

Okuni looked at Sanemon. "You see? They are cleaning up after themselves. I have the money. We must go."

"Where?" Sanemon barked. "And how?" He flailed at the door. "Half of the troupe is getting ready for today's performance, and the other half is already in costume."

Okuni grimaced and looked away. Sanemon read her face and loosed a virulent oath. She blinked and looked at him. "No," he said. "No. We are not abandoning the others. You insisted we stay, and so we did. And now we are here. We will leave tomorrow. For tonight, you will stay hidden – here, in the theater. Do not go back to the house. Nao will collect what you need and bring it to you."

"Will I?" Nao asked, lazily.

Sanemon glared at him. "Yes, or so help me, I will break that skinny arm of yours."

"Brute," Nao said. But he didn't argue. Sanemon turned back to Okuni.

"I learned one thing of value in the army. When the enemy comes, you don't run – you hunker down and hope that you have more bodies than they have arrows. This theater is our palisade. You're safe here if you're safe anywhere."

"And if they followed me?"

"Then I would rather die on stage, like a proper actor, than on some grubby wharf trying to escape." Sanemon turned back to Nao. "Let the others, especially the stage crew, know what's going on – not specifics, but that someone might be looking to cause trouble." Sanemon wished he felt half as confident as he hoped he sounded. "If anyone suspicious starts creeping around, I want to know about it."

Okuni looked at him, a half-smile on her face. "Sometimes I forget that you used to be a soldier."

"Sometimes, so do I." He took a deep breath and let it out, trying to calm his racing nerves. "If these shinobi of yours come calling, we'll give them a performance such as they've never seen."

CHAPTER TWENTY-SIX
Iuchi Konomi

A servant led Shin down a cobbled path to a flat patio of violet stone set beneath a large tree. The garden was larger than his own, and filled with flowers he did not recognize, save from books. It was beautiful, in a wild sort of way.

Iuchi Konomi awaited him on the patio. She sat on one of two low wooden benches, cleverly carved to resemble stampeding horses. A small table sat between the benches. As Shin seated himself on the opposite bench, a pair of servants brought tea and cups. They placed them on the table between the two, and began to prepare the tea.

"Thank you for agreeing to meet with me," Shin began. "I trust it is not an imposition?" He had come straight to the Unicorn quarter from Saibanshoki, hoping to speak to Konomi. Luckily, it seemed that she was inclined to do so, despite Shichiro's prohibition. Then, perhaps she was simply curious about the investigation.

"Not for me," Konomi said, fluttering her fan in front of

her face. "Though my father did not wish us to speak." She waited until the servants had poured the tea, and then waved them away. They bowed low and left. "Perhaps he fears for my virtue."

"I assure you my lady, you are safe with me." Shin smiled. "At least for today."

Konomi giggled politely. Then she lowered her fan. "Your message implied that you wished to ask me something?"

"If you are willing to indulge me," Shin said, with a slight bow.

She smiled slightly. "I have heard you are a man who enjoys his indulgences. They say that is why you are here now."

"Who is they?"

Konomi gestured airily. "The city. Your grandfather sent you here to save you from an honor challenge, I am told. Is it true you kidnapped a daughter of the Scorpion Clan?"

"More of a rescue, really," Shin said. "She was quite cheerful about the whole ordeal. But that is, perhaps, a story for another time."

She took a sip of tea. "Is this about the shipment?"

"Tangentially."

"My father said they had found the culprit."

"Possibly."

"And that he was the one who stole our rice."

"Almost certainly."

"And yet you continue to investigate."

Shin shrugged. "I have a duty and I must see it through. If that means I must risk the anger of men like Iuchi Shichiro, then such is my burden."

"Very noble."

"Thank you, my lady."

"How unlike the man you are reputed to be." Konomi looked at his cup. "You have not touched your tea."

Shin dutifully picked up his tea and tasted it. It was unfamiliar and spicy. Konomi smiled slightly. "Do you like it?"

Shin licked his lips. "It is… unusual. Foreign?"

"In a sense. It is my own blend." She looked at him over the rim of her cup. "My mother taught me the art. It takes patience to do it right."

"I am sure."

"Why did you wish to speak to me?"

"I had heard you were engaged to be married. But the engagement is now… on hold. Is that true?"

"I'm sure my father could have told you that."

"Your father did not wish to speak of it at all."

"And you believe I will?" Konomi paused. "What does the one thing have to do with the other, my lord?"

"It might speak as to the reason your father lied to me last night."

Konomi set her cup down. "That is a grave accusation."

"Nor is it one I make lightly. He has had a watch on the merchant, Saiga, for weeks he claimed. Yet none of Saiga's visitors were known to him."

"And you believe this not to be the case."

Shin nodded. "I do. I believe your father knows something."

"And why does my engagement matter?"

"A conflict between the Lion and the Unicorn would damage the governor's reputation. It might even see him recalled. Fair dues for having interfered in your engagement, as some speculate."

Konomi was silent for a moment. "And how many lives would be lost to achieve such a spiteful end?" She shook her head. "I am not so vain as all that, and my father is no fool. What is done is done, and there is nothing more to it than that."

"What did happen between you three?" Shin asked. It was a discourteous question – rude, in fact. But sometimes rudeness got more answers than politesse.

"It is none of your concern," she said, sharply. It was the first flair of true emotion he'd seen from her, and he seized on it.

"How many engagements does this make now? Four – or five?"

Beneath her mask of powder, her face flushed. He'd struck a nerve. "You are being rude," she said.

"Yes. Forgive me." Shin paused. "I have a number of failed engagements myself. Not the marrying sort, really – a fact which no doubt brings eternal shame to my family. Some people are simply not meant to be married."

"Some people have not found the right person yet," Konomi said. She looked away. Shin set down his cup.

"Is Tonbo Kuma the right person?"

"For someone, certainly."

"But not you."

She sighed. "No. Not me."

"Your father does not agree."

"He is a traditionalist at heart. He wishes to make a strong alliance, and all of my brothers are already married or betrothed. That leaves me. An alliance with the Dragonfly would ensure the Unicorn could maintain their hold on this city, in the face of future aggression from the Lion."

"And what does Tonbo Kuma think of this?"

"Kuma thinks first and only of their clan." She smiled slightly. "There is only a little room for something – someone – in that heart of theirs, and I am not the one it is waiting for."

"Then who?" Shin asked, though he thought he already knew the answer. It would explain a great many things, if it were true. But, if it were not, saying it aloud would lead to great embarrassment for everyone concerned.

She picked up her tea and took a sip. "That is not for me to say."

"Is your father aware of this?"

She frowned. "If he is, he has dismissed it as no more than a blade of grass to be trampled beneath his hooves. He has made overtures to the Tonbo family directly, and to the Dragon as well, to see if they can convince Kuma to move forward with the engagement. He has even harangued the governor on occasion."

"And what was Tetsua's reply?"

She smiled. "Icy, I am told."

Shin peered into his cup, thinking it through. "If your father knew something that might encourage both Kuma and Tetsua to accede to his view, would he use it?"

"My father holds his honor tight, but only so that he might better use it as a club."

Shin nodded. "So I gathered. Thank you, my lady. You have given me much to think on." He made to rise, but she stopped him.

"My father means well, my lord. He sees only the clan, first and foremost."

"I fear that is the problem, my lady. Nor he is the only one to do so." He rose and bowed. "Thank you again. You have been most helpful."

"You will tell me how it turns out, my lord?" she called, as he departed. "I am most interested to know the end of this story."

"As am I, my lady. As am I."

"Where do you think you are going?" Kasami said. Lun turned, her good eye narrowing in obvious consternation. The woman was moving quietly down the steps from the guest room upstairs, heading for the garden. Kasami stood above her, at the top of the steps. At first, she had thought it was Kitano attempting to sneak out again. The gambler was hiding from her somewhere, hoping to avoid another beating.

"I am leaving," Lun said. "The sooner I get out of this city, the better."

"Lord Shin has specified that you are to stay here until he returns."

"Lord Shin can shove it up his–"

Kasami thumbed her katana a few inches from its sheath. Lun fell silent, though it was clearly something of a struggle. "You will not leave."

"Give me one good reason."

"You are injured. And those hunting you are still loose. If you leave, you will be dead in a matter of hours."

"You don't know that."

"I do." Kasami began to descend. Lun backed away. Kasami stopped. She looked down at the woman, studying her with a warrior's eye. Lun was hurt, but not badly. She had regained much of her strength in the past day. She decided to try a different approach. "I saw the tattoo earlier. You are of the Crane."

"I am not," Lun said, harshly. "Not any more."

Kasami frowned. The statement angered her for some reason. Obligation to a clan was not something so easily thrown off. "And who decided that? You?"

Lun grimaced and looked away. Kasami nodded. "Were you an ashigaru? A line soldier?" She stopped again. "No – a marine, perhaps?" Lun had the look of a marine. Kasami had fought beside them once or twice, against pirates. They'd been good soldiers – rough, but brave.

"What does it matter?"

"A good soldier follows orders."

"I'm not a soldier any more. I'm my own woman." Lun bared her teeth and for a moment, Kasami was tempted to let her go. She had courage, of sorts. Not true courage, but a sort of animal valor that was admirable in its way. But Shin would be disappointed if she did that. So instead, she continued to descend.

"What you are, or are not, is of no concern to me. All that matters is that you are here when Lord Shin returns. You can be so of your own free will, or I can force you."

Lun hesitated. Kasami could tell that she was planning on running. She tensed, ready to pursue, when she heard someone cough politely. She looked past Lun to see Shin standing in the garden, looking up at them, a half-smile on his face.

"You look happy. Why do you look happy?" she asked, with no small amount of suspicion. "What did she say?"

"Let us say that she confirmed a suspicion of mine." He looked at Lun. "And how are you today, Captain? Up and out of bed, I see."

"I want to leave."

"Is our hospitality wanting?"

Lun hesitated. "No, my lord. But…"

"You are injured, your crew dispersed, your ship sitting in a berth in Willow Quay, under guard," Kasami began. Lun's eye widened.

"Under guard? By who?"

"Lord Shin hired a handful of bored ronin to make sure no one tampered with it. And if you think they'll let you on board without a bribe, your brains are more rattled than I thought." Kasami paused. "You have nowhere to go. So why not stay here for the time being?"

Lun frowned and scratched at her empty eye socket. "I can take care of myself."

Kasami laughed. "Yes, you've done a fine job of that so far."

Lun narrowed her eye, but knew better than to respond. She had some sense, at least. Kasami looked at Shin.

"That said, as much as it pains me, I agree with her. If the matter is settled…" She trailed off as she saw the look on Shin's face. "It's not settled, is it?"

"Not for me, no. Whoever sent those shinobi to kill Lun, to kill Saiga, and our missing actress as well, is still out there. As are their pet killers. I believe they will not stop until all perceived threats to their anonymity are dealt with. I suspect that includes us, now, given that ambush." Shin smiled. "You should be happy – I know you've been longing for a chance to test your skills against worthy opponents."

"Shinobi are hardly worthy opponents," Kasami said, but he was right. The thought did bring with it a sort of rough satisfaction. Here was a foe she understood and that her training had prepared her for. She tapped the hilt of her sword as she looked around, beginning her mental calculations. The house could be fortified, in a sense, though it would take some effort. The servants would complain, but then they always did. "We should move to a more defensible location – a smaller house, outside the city perhaps..."

"No. We are right where we need to be, I think." Shin started up the steps, his hands folded into his sleeves. "Show Ito up as soon as he gets here. Oh, and–"

Kasami shook her head. "I know, I know. Tea."

Lun snickered and Kasami looked at her. Lun fell silent.

Shin paused and looked down. "I was going to say make sure we are not disturbed, but yes, tea would be nice." He smiled and continued up to the receiving room. Kasami growled softly and slammed her sword back into its sheath.

"This is why I deserted," Lun said, behind her.

Despite herself, Kasami nodded.

CHAPTER TWENTY-SEVEN
Go and Paper

"Have you taken up Go, my lord?" Ito asked with a hint of eagerness as he entered the receiving room and took in the board set up in front of Shin. "A most excellent diversion. I enjoy it myself on occasion."

"I have taken a liking to it of late, yes," Shin said, agreeably. He'd set the board up earlier, and had been studying it when the merchant arrived. "Though, I fear that I did not invite you here to play, Master Ito."

Ito's face fell. "Oh? Then why am I here, if I might ask?"

Shin produced the documents he'd taken from Saiga's office. Ito was taken aback when Shin laid them before him. The merchant seemed nervous, but eager to please. "What is this, my lord?" he asked, looking at them with curiosity.

"Something I hope you might be able to help me with, Ito. Do you recognize these?"

"They look like customs documents, my lord."

"So they do. Tell me what you think of them."

Ito peered closely at the papers and sat back after a moment. "I hesitate to say this, my lord, but it appears this individual was involved in the acquisition and disposal of stolen cargo."

"How can you tell it was stolen?"

Ito tapped the document before him. "These cargoes are very specific – too specific. They match items missing from certain manifests." He frowned. "We – the local merchants, I mean – keep track of such things. We try to inform one another when something turns up where it shouldn't."

"So Saiga was definitely involved, then." Shin paused. "Why was he allowed to continue? Surely the authorities would be aware of his connections…"

"Someone was protecting him." Ito looked at Shin. "Someone powerful."

"A member of one of the Great Clans," Shin said. "But which one?"

"That's harder to determine," Ito said, apologetically. "A man like Saiga might well have more than one master. He was a very useful sort of fellow, loathe as I am to admit it." He studied the documents for several moments, then grunted. "I recognize the markings. They're used by the customs agents of the Dragonfly. Very peculiar, those fellows. They have their own system for these sorts of documents."

"But you can read it?"

"Of course," Ito said, absently. Then, as if realizing what he'd admitted, he hurried to add, "Most of us can, though we pretend otherwise. The Dragonfly enjoy their secrets, and it costs nothing to let them have a few."

Shin nodded. "Can you tell which customs agent might have written these?"

"I recognize the markings, yes. Tonbo Enji. Stiff fellow. Stickler for the rules. We all know him, and dread him."

"Is he so intimidating then?"

"Only if you find boredom intimidating," Ito said. "As I said, he's a stiff sort of fellow. No sense of humor and – well – somewhat touchy on the subject of status."

"Ah. An emperor in miniature."

Ito shook his head. "Not quite that bad, but – yes." He frowned again. "Not the sort I can imagine having dealings with a man like Saiga, frankly."

"And yet here is the proof. Conspiracy makes for strange bedfellows." Shin considered the documents. A thought occurred to him. "Could Saiga have blackmailed this Enji into giving him the documents?"

Ito considered the idea. "It's always possible my lord, but…"

"But?" Shin encouraged.

"Enji is not the sort to be easily blackmailed." Ito hesitated. "He's… well, he's boring, as I said."

"Boring?"

"No vices, my lord. He doesn't drink to excess, he does not like to gamble and has never been seen in the company of a prostitute. More, he has no wife or children to dishonor. He is a lonely man – an island of stolidity."

Shin could not help but show a bit of his amusement. "You sound as if you have investigated this for yourself."

Ito bowed his head. "I might have had an encounter or two with him over the years, my lord. And it is always best to know who is checking your cargo."

"Could Saiga have found something out that even you didn't know?"

"I don't see how, my lord. Unless he… listens to different gossip. Then, maybe. But I think it unlikely." Ito shook his head. "As I said, he is not the sort I could see associating with a man like Saiga – not without good reason."

Shin chewed this over. "I think I may pay a visit to this Tonbo Enji tomorrow and see what he has to say for himself."

"You will need permission, my lord. The Dragonfly are peculiar about such things." Ito paused. "I could put in the request for you. I am somewhat familiar with those channels."

"I have no doubt you are," Shin said. "Please do so, by all means. The sooner I speak to him, the better."

Ito cleared his throat. "And if I might be so bold, my lord – I would advise caution in your dealings with the Dragonfly, and the Tonbo especially. They are not called the 'gatekeepers to the Dragon' for nothing."

"Wise advice, Ito." Shin placed his hand over his heart and bowed his head. "You have my solemn word, I will be on my best behavior."

Ito smiled. "I expect nothing less, my lord." At Shin's nod, he rose to his feet. "If you require my expertise again, please do not hesitate to call upon me, my lord. I am, as ever, at your disposal." He bowed low and saw himself out.

Shin picked up his biwa and plucked at the strings as he turned his attentions back to the Go board. He'd often found that playing a game against himself helped him to think when his mind was otherwise too cluttered to function properly.

He imagined the two sets of stones were the Lion and the Unicorn, arrayed against one another, as in Azuma's history lesson. Of course, for history to repeat itself, a third faction would have to intervene, breaking the stalemate.

He set the biwa aside and began to move the stones idly, first one and then another, not really seeing them. Instead, he saw the city – its wharfs and warehouses, its theaters and alleyways. He saw how easily it could become a battlefield again. Perhaps it had never truly ceased being one.

He paused, his finger atop a stone.

That was it. That was the answer.

"What are you smiling about?" Kasami asked, as she slid the door shut behind her.

"Every crime has a signature. Including this one. I thought it clumsy at first, but it's not. There is a sort of rough precision to it, when viewed from a distance. Not like the stroke of a sword, but like the calculation of weight and cost. They observed the currents of trade and chose a target based on certain criteria…"

"The stolen rice, you mean?"

"Yes. They knew that Saiga would use the origin of the rice as a selling point. Thus, when the Lion discovered the sabotage, they would be quick to blame the Unicorn, seeing it for a trick. Especially when Saiga confirmed it." He indicated the small stack of papers sitting nearby. "Saiga dealt regularly with contacts in all three clans. And, if Ito is correct, he was more than just a procurer of stolen rice – he was a spy, using his position to gather intelligence."

"For who? The Lion?"

"No. For the Dragon."

Kasami blinked. "How do you know that?"

"I don't. Not for certain." He held up the book he'd taken from Saiga's desk. "It is a conclusion based on this cipher. I thought I recognized it that night, and Ito's answers assured me that I was correct. It is archaic – ancient even, from a time just after the Hantei came to power. A form of code prevalent in the mountains of northern Rokugan. A man like Saiga would hardly use such a thing, unless he had good reason."

Kasami shook her head. "How do you know all of this?" she asked in bewilderment.

"All my time reading wasn't entirely wasted, it seems," Shin said, with a shrug. "Still, it is no more than a supposition."

"So, the Dragon are behind it?" she asked.

Shin frowned. "That is the question, isn't it? Because I can see no reason that they would countenance such an act. There is nothing to be gained, given their lack of… hunh." He stopped, thinking about what Ito had said about the customs agent, Enji.

"What? What is it?" Kasami asked.

"The Dragon may gain nothing from this. But, what about the Dragonfly?"

"They do not act without the Dragon's authority behind them," she said.

"Yes, but earlier you were right… what if someone acted without the consent of their superiors? What if someone saw a chance for glory – or perhaps, simply, to increase the influence of the Dragonfly in the city?" Shin hunched forward, staring at the board. "Perhaps they thought that, in the event of a clash between the clans, Tetsua would be forced to turn to them for aid – thus assuring that the Dragonfly were given pre-eminence in all future affairs of the city."

"Why would they think that?"

Shin gave her a pitying look. "This is why you should learn to listen to gossip. Tetsua is close – some say to an unfortunate degree – with Tonbo Kuma."

"Is this your long-winded way of saying Kuma is behind it?" Kasami asked.

"No. At least, not without more proof." Shin relaxed. "Tetsua is… biased when it comes to the shugenja. Accusing them without solid proof would be a mistake."

"And how are you planning to get this proof?"

Shin picked up a stone and bounced it on his palm. "I have no idea. But I'm sure something will occur to me before long."

CHAPTER TWENTY-EIGHT
A Visitor

Kasami prowled the edges of the moonlit garden, her eyes sweeping across the walls and doorways that separated them from the rest of the city. The house was dark, save for the lantern in Shin's room. The servants had gone to bed, and Kitano as well.

The gambler had claimed a spot in the kitchen, near the stove. He seemed happy enough, though she expected him to make a break for it any day now. Street curs could not be tamed, no matter how much you fed them.

Lun was asleep as well. Despite her bravado, she was still weak from her near-miss. Kasami did not like having either of them here. Kitano had proven susceptible to bribery, and was a criminal. Lun was probably a pirate, and a target. But Shin insisted, so Kasami abided. She was not mistress here, only a companion.

A noise caught her attention. Something – someone – had disturbed one of the gourds hanging from the trees. She turned slowly, one hand on her sword. She doubted that the shinobi would try anything here. There was a large difference between attacking an unknown heimin captain, and a member of a Great Clan. But even so, they might well be watching the house, especially given the fact that Shin hadn't kept an especially low profile.

She peered into the shadows of the garden, listening for the slightest hint of movement. She heard the knocking of the bamboo tubes in the garden's fountain. Then, a rustle of grass. She drew her sword and pressed it to the neck of the man hiding behind her. "I thought you were asleep," she said, not looking at him.

"I heard something," Kitano said, hesitantly.

"Did you now? And what might you have heard, gambler?"

"Someone talking – or maybe praying?" He stepped back as she turned. He had his hand on his knife. Perhaps he was telling the truth. "I was just about to fall asleep when I heard it and I came out to see and… and…"

"And what?"

"I thought I saw someone. Standing near the fountain."

"Who?"

"I didn't recognize them." His face was pale in the light of the moon. "I swear, I don't…" He trailed off. "What's that?"

Kasami turned in the direction of the fountain. She heard it now. A soft, wet rustling. Like footsteps, but there was a strange lack of weight to them. It reminded her of the patter of heavy rain. Something glistened in the moonlight between the trees. Kitano gave a strangled yelp as the intruder turned towards them.

It had no face. Or rather, its face was a shimmering, shifting ovoid of water. A man of water, standing before them. She froze, just for an instant. She had never seen such a thing before, though she had heard of them. Every body of water had its kami, large or small. A shugenja could call them up with the proper rites, if they were of a mind to do so. But once summoned, there was no telling what the spirits might do – especially if they were provoked. She tried to remember whether they had propitiated the spirit of the fountain lately, and found her mind drawing a blank. The thing tilted the mass that passed for a head.

"What do we do?" Kitano muttered.

"Don't do anything. Just… stand… still."

Kitano took a step back, and the grass rustled beneath his feet. The watery shape seemed to bristle. It reminded Kasami of the wind rushing across the surface of a lake. She tossed a glare at Kitano. "Idiot."

The watery shape took a wet step towards them. It had limbs, but no hands or feet. Rather, there were sprays of liquid that spurted and coalesced into an approximation of fingers and toes. There was a gurgling sound that might have been words – a challenge, perhaps, or an imprecation. Either way, she judged its intentions hostile.

"Get behind me," she said. As Kitano hastened to obey, the watery shape took another step. Then another, and another, until it was darting towards them as fast as a rolling wave crashing towards shore. Kasami lunged to meet it, and her blade smoothly bisected the shape as it made to envelop her. It splashed down around her, soaking her clothes and armor.

Kitano yelped as the resulting puddles surged upwards almost immediately, becoming smaller copies of the shape she had just destroyed. The shapes scattered and Kasami flung out a hand to Kitano. "Rouse the servants! We have to catch them! Quick!"

"What? Why?"

She reached him in two strides and buffeted him about the ear. "Someone summoned them for a reason other than just scaring you, fool. Now go – quickly!"

Shin sat in his room, strumming his biwa as he turned the problem over in his mind. From different angles, it took on new permutations. New possibilities arose and were discarded as sheerest fancy.

On its face, the problem was simple. The poisoned rice was a tool, nothing more. Someone had put it into place in order to exacerbate the tensions between the clans. It had not been intended to harm anyone, of that he was certain. Whoever had devised the scheme had done so knowing that the rice would be discovered before it reached anyone's bowl.

But why play such a devilish prank? What gain was there to be had, save war? And if that was the desired outcome – why use such an oblique method? There were simpler means, if bloodier. He was missing something. He could feel it, just at the edge of his perceptions, but could not see it. Not yet. It would come in time, he was certain. But, by then, it might well be too late.

He heard the stairs outside his room creak. He stilled the biwa's strings and listened. He could hear soft rustlings, as if someone were endeavoring to be quiet. The servants had been given the evening off, and Kasami wouldn't have bothered. His heart sped up as he waited to see what would happen.

Someone knocked on the door.

"Enter," Shin said, with as much calm as he could muster.

The door slid back, and a familiar face beamed at him. Tonbo Kuma bowed slightly, as they entered. "My apologies, my lord. I am here without invitation, but I wished to speak with you in private."

"And my bodyguard did not protest?"

Kuma smiled. "She is otherwise occupied."

Shin kept his expression neutral. "Is she alive?"

"Of course! What sort of person do you take me for?"

"That is a good question," Shin said. "Thus far, I do not have a satisfactory answer."

Kuma laughed softly, and Shin felt a twinge of irritation. As he had during their first meeting, he had the feeling that the shugenja was mocking him. "What did you want to speak to me about?" he asked, letting some of the annoyance he felt creep into his voice. If Kuma noticed, they gave no sign.

The shugenja did not reply. Instead, they began to wander about his rooms, picking up objects and putting them down. It was as if they were trying to get a feel for him – Shin had done much the same himself on other occasions.

Kuma paused beside a shelf, and pulled down a flimsy book. "The Cost of Grace," they said, holding it up. "I was under the impression that this particular treatise was banned."

"Is it? I rarely pay attention to such things."

The shugenja smiled. "That is a lie, I think. I think there is little that escapes your attention, Daidoji Shin."

Shin strummed his biwa, trying to hide the growing uneasiness he felt. Why had the shugenja come? And what had happened to Kasami? "Again, I ask, to what do I owe this visit? It comes as something of a surprise. If I had known that you were coming..."

"You would have laid out a proper welcome?" Kuma chuckled softly and set the book aside. "The fewer eyes that witness our interaction, the better."

"You make it sound as if we are up to something illicit." Shin watched the shugenja as they made a slow circuit of his room.

"Are we not?" Kuma paused at the balcony, looking out over the city. "We stand here, the fate of a city in our hands. Some might view that as a conspiracy of sorts."

"Then let us make it a successful one." Shin stilled the strings of his biwa. "You want to know what I have learned."

"Yes."

"Why not ask Tetsua?"

Kuma turned. "I have inconvenienced him enough, don't you think?"

"That is not for me to say." Unable to contain his curiosity, he added, "I heard that you were engaged to be married. Is that still the case?"

"What does that have to do with the matter at hand?"

"Perhaps nothing. Perhaps something." Shin set his biwa aside and rose. "Such a thing might be construed as motive." He heard shouts from below, and the sound of running feet. Kuma's distraction, he assumed.

"And do you think that is the case?"

"What I think, and what I know, are two separate things." Shin stepped onto the balcony and looked out over the city.

"A wise distinction." Kuma joined him on the balcony. "Have you asked yourself why he did not summon an Emerald Magistrate to deal with this situation?"

"Presumably because he's hoping to handle it quietly. Or, else, because he fears that the presence of an Emerald Magistrate would invariably lead to a number of unfortunate revelations." Shin looked pointedly at the shugenja.

Kuma nodded without looking at him. "Tetsua is in a bad position. He is who he is because the city is divided. If one clan supersedes the others, control of the city might well be turned over to them. Tetsua would lose his position."

"He would find another."

"Would he?" Kuma smiled enigmatically. "You have strayed far from court. You do not hear the whispers."

"I do not listen to the whispers," Shin said. "I am not a spymaster or a gossipmonger. I am a disappointment, and I am content."

"Contentment is stagnation."

Shin frowned. "Now you're quoting The Cost of Grace at me. Is there a point? If so, do me the courtesy of coming to it sooner rather than later."

Kuma laughed throatily. "You are impatient."

"Forgive me, I am tired. You wished me to know that Tetsua has as much to gain – or lose – from this matter as anyone. Very well. I had already considered that angle and discarded it. If the situation served his purposes, why involve me?"

"Because he believes that you will fail – or worse, exacerbate the situation."

Shin hesitated. "Even if that is the case, it is a needless complication. And Tetsua does not strike me as a man given to complications – at least, not in this area." He saw Kuma's cheek twitch – a barely perceptible sign that he'd scored a point. "Then, perhaps, someone else suggested it. I'm told he holds you in high esteem."

It was Kuma's turn to hesitate. "And who told you this?"

"Whispers. Just whispers."

"I thought you did not listen to whispers."

Shin shrugged. "Sometimes one cannot help what one hears."

"True enough. But one ought to be careful about such things." Kuma's gaze was steady. "A word can be as deadly as a poison, if spoken into the wrong ear."

"I shall keep that in mind for the future."

Kuma's smile was sharp and thin. "Tetsua is not the only one to gain by this, of course. There are others. Individuals you might not have considered."

"You mean besides yourself?"

"Yes. Though the city is divided into three parts, it could be divided still further – or those divisions could fall under the purview of new masters. The Crane are not the only clan with warehouses in the city. The Phoenix, too, have their wharfs, farther down the river. And the Scorpion. Even the imperial families are not exempt… it is said that Tetsua's promotion to governor was not looked on kindly by some among the Miya." Kuma spread their hands as if in apology. "So you see, it is not perhaps so simple a problem as you consider it."

"Have you been speaking to Kaeru Azuma, then?"

Kuma frowned. "No."

"Ah, well. Never mind." Then, with a hard smile, Shin said, "You have given me much to think about, my lord. Rest assured, I shall pursue every avenue of inquiry to my own satisfaction and, I hope, yours."

Kuma nodded. "Good. An open mind is a productive one." They turned as if to go, but stopped, as if a sudden thought had occurred to them. "One of your people made a request to speak to a customs agent named Enji… might I inquire as to why?"

"He may have information pertinent to my investigation."

"Highly doubtful."

"Then there is no harm in letting me speak to him." Shin turned. "Of course, if you do not wish me to speak to him, I have little recourse. I will have to inform Tetsua of your refusal, but I'm certain he will understand."

Kuma gave another nod and made to leave. Shin cleared his throat. "Though, I fear the Lion and the Unicorn might not be so considerate."

Kuma stopped. Without turning, they said, "Is that a threat?"

"Well – yes," Shin said. "I thought that was obvious."

The night air, cool with a hint of river damp, suddenly turned cold. Shin felt beads of moisture prickle on his arms and neck. Kuma's form, half in shadow, seemed to waver as if they were underwater. Shin's hand fell to his wakizashi.

"I am not the sort to take threats lightly, Crane."

"I am not the sort to make them without good reason." Shin stared at him. "And ask yourself this, shugenja – will it serve your cause to drown me here, on my balcony? Because if not, I would ask that you restrain yourself and cease this display."

Kuma made a soft exhalation – not quite a sigh – and the moisture faded from the air, and Shin's skin, as if it had never been there at all. "Thank you," Shin said. "Now you may show yourself out the same way you came in."

"You are quite the riddle, Crane," Kuma said, as they departed. "I shall look forward to finding the answer to you."

Shin relaxed, releasing a shaky breath once he was sure Kuma had gone. A moment later, Kasami burst into the room. "Are you all right?" she nearly shouted. Her clothes and armor were soaking wet, and she left a trail of water behind her as she stalked into his room.

"Yes, no thanks to you. Where were you?"

"Chasing shadows," she snapped. "Literally. They let me see them, but I didn't realize why until I saw Kuma leaving through the garden."

"Lun?"

"Sleeping," Kasami said. "She can apparently sleep through anything. Kitano is rousing the servants…"

"No. No, leave them. Kuma has delivered their message and gone. There will be no more trouble tonight, I expect."

"What did the shugenja want?"

"To threaten me, I think. Or perhaps warn me. Either way, the message was the same – full of nonsense about unknown parties being involved." Shin shook his head. "Kuma is trying to muddy the waters, but I don't know why."

"Maybe they're right," Kasami said. "Maybe it is someone we haven't considered."

"Or maybe it's someone I've already dismissed. But it's not." Shin pinched the bridge of his nose. He was beginning to get a headache. He looked at his books, and saw with some annoyance that Kuma had rearranged them. Another message – or perhaps just idle amusement. He went to the shelves and began to put the books back into their proper places. "If Kitano is awake, let him know I have a task for him. I want him to watch the kabuki theater for me."

"Why?"

"If Okuni is still alive, then she is likely hiding with her troupe. If I were her, I would not attempt to move until it was time for me and my companions to depart."

"You think she's in the theater?"

"As safe a place as any. There are places to hide, plenty of people going in and out, and a number of exits. It is also familiar ground for her – the only familiar ground in the city." He paused. "If she is alive, that is where she will be."

"And if she's dead?"

"Then it won't matter, and only Kitano's time will have been wasted." He paused in his reorganization when he got to Kakita's treatise on swordplay. It was a perennial favorite. There was much wisdom to be had in its pages, especially given its subject matter. As was his habit, he flipped open the text to a random page. "Defeat comes from the single imperfection in the opponent's soul."

He turned the words over in his mind for a moment, trying to find some connection to his current situation. Several came to mind, none immediately helpful. Frowning, he put the treatise back in its place on the shelf. He paused.

Then, softly, he laughed.

CHAPTER TWENTY-NINE
Tonbo Enji

The customs and tariffs offices of the Dragonfly were located in a neat row along the north side of the Drowned Merchant River. Eleven modest wharfs of stone and wood ringed the sides of an artificial basin, gouged into the bank long ago. The basin was shaped into a rough dodecagon. The twelfth facet was occupied, not by a wharf, but by a sturdy river gate that arched over a wide opening, allowing the passage of vessels.

It was late in the morning, and Shin had barely slept the night before. Kuma's visit had raised too many questions, and his mind refused to settle itself. As their flatboat passed beneath the arch of the gate, he noted the presence of archers and spearmen moving to and fro across the wooden parapet above. "Quite a few of them," he murmured, so that the woman poling the boat couldn't hear.

Kasami didn't look up. "They're nervous. The Lion has been growling at them from the other side of the river for as long as anyone can remember. Just because it's turned away for the moment doesn't mean it's forgotten them."

Shin turned his attentions to the shore, where great statues in the shape of animals glared out at new arrivals. The beasts crouched one to a wharf, and corresponded to the months of the year – Hare, Dragon, Horse, Goat, Monkey and all the rest. Dragon had pride of place, of course, coiled about the archway of the gate. The rest had to make do with humble stone plinths. So was the world reminded of its place.

"You're frowning," Kasami said.

"I am angry."

"Because Kuma threatened you."

"Yes. It is impolite, as well as clumsy. Shugenja are unworldly, so I forgive the latter but not the former."

"How do you know it was a threat?"

"Because of the way in which it was delivered." He looked at her. "Kuma has been involved in this from the start, though only peripherally. But last night they thrust themselves into the light. Perhaps they did so out of desperation – or perhaps arrogance. Regardless, I believe that it was our request to see this customs officer that prompted it."

"Seems unlikely."

"It does, until you take a step back and realize that we are not following one chain – but two." He held up two fingers for emphasis. "The first is the rice. The second, the deaths of those involved in the first."

"What do you mean?"

"After Kuma's visit last night, I recalled the way they'd prowled about my rooms. I realized, a touch belatedly, that they were looking for something."

"The papers you found in Saiga's office," Kasami said.

Shin nodded. "I am glad to see that you have been paying

attention. Yes – the papers. Why? Because they realized that the shinobi missed them when they killed Saiga."

"Why would they care?" she asked.

"Because among those papers, was this." Shin produced a folded missive. "I didn't notice it at first. It seemed nothing more than another Dragonfly shipping invoice, until I took a closer look and realized that it was a coded message, pertaining to a certain school of shinobi residing in the city."

Kasami frowned. "Saiga was hiring shinobi?"

"No, but he was putting his employer in contact with them." Shin thrust the note back into his kimono. "Do you see? Saiga may well have acted as a go-between for the very individuals who likely killed him." He shook his head. "Now why should they do that, I wonder?"

"They were cleaning up after themselves," she said.

"Exactly. But why? What provoked it?" He shook his head. "Why seek to kill Okuni, if she's already planning on leaving the city? Why kill Lun and her crew? Why kill Saiga? It made no sense, when I thought it all of one piece – but what if someone – say Kuma – discovered that someone else had engineered all of this. And what if somehow, in some way, they feared that the crime would be discovered?"

"But why hire mercenary shinobi? The Dragonfly employ their own killers, surely."

"For the same reason Okuni was hired – a further level of deniability." He looked at her. "Shinobi are the dirty secret of the clans. We all know that we employ them, but they are outlawed for good reason. They do what samurai cannot."

"They do what we will not," Kasami said, stiffly.

Shin didn't argue the point. "Regardless, someone hired

them to clean up a mess. I do not know who. But I bet that this Tonbo Enji does."

The boat bumped against a mooring post, ending their conversation. Shin was up onto the jetty a moment later, Kasami following in his wake. A quick interrogation of a nearby dockworker directed them to the offices of the head customs official.

Shin waved Kasami back before he entered. "Stay here."

She gave him a doubtful look. "Are you certain?"

"You are quite intimidating, and if I am right, he already has enough reason to be nervous. No sense scaring him – not yet, at any rate."

"Very well. But if he makes a move…"

"Then I expect you to make him regret it." Shin went inside and closed the door behind him. The office was spacious, but spartan in its décor. Empty of sentiment or distraction. A large writing desk occupied the center of the room, and heavy shelves, neatly crammed with scrolls and ledgers, filled the wall behind it. There were benches placed against the walls for visitors.

Shin ignored these and went up to the desk, and the man sitting there. The latter was hunched over, writing in a ledger. He did not look up as Shin entered. "Take a seat and I will be with you in a moment."

"I have an appointment, I believe."

"And I believe that I said take a seat…" Tonbo Enji looked up, a scowl on his face. It melted away into a look of nervous regret as he took in Shin's garments and poise. "My- my lord. I thought – I assumed I would be speaking with your representative today, not- not a personage such as yourself."

"May I sit?" Shin asked.

"Of course, my lord, forgive my rudeness!" Enji leapt to his feet and snatched a small stool from beside the shelves, bringing it around for Shin. He set it down and hurried back to his own. "Forgive me, my lord, my furnishings are, as you can see, quite humble. Not what you are used to at all, I am sure."

"I have endured worse, I assure you. Be at ease." Shin sat. "You are Tonbo Enji," he said, straightening his kimono.

"I am, my lord." Enji was a thin man, ascetic and spare. He put Shin in mind of a piece of fruit, emptied of its juices.

"You are the chief customs officer."

Enji preened slightly. "I have that privilege, my lord."

"You spoke to a merchant named Ito yesterday. A representative of the Crane."

Enji nodded again, somewhat puzzled. "Yes, he said he wished to discuss a certain matter of import fees – though, I admit that I can find no record of the fees in question."

Shin waved the matter aside. "A harmless subterfuge on my behalf. In reality, I wished to speak to you in private, and this seemed the most efficient manner of doing so."

Enji hesitated. "Me, my lord?"

"Yes. Is it so strange?"

"I – no? But what could we have to discuss?"

"Many things. For instance…" Shin leaned forward and tapped the desk with his fan. There was a rough hole, newly sanded but not yet filled. "It appears as though someone has stabbed your desk." He felt at the edges of the hole.

"An angry captain," Enji said, quickly.

"It was a thin blade, I imagine – not a sailor's knife." There was a scrap of something in the hole – paper? Before he could extract it, Enji cleared his throat.

"A minor disagreement. I do apologize, my lord, but I am very busy. If you have some business to discuss…"

Shin fixed him with a cold stare. "You know who I am, do you not?"

Enji hesitated again, and then nodded. "I do."

"Then you might have guessed why I am here."

Enji shook his head. "I find myself at a loss, my lord."

"Then allow me to illuminate you. Do these look familiar?" Shin produced one of the documents he'd found in Saiga's offices. "I happened across them, and thought I ought to make some effort to return them to their rightful owner."

Enji froze for a moment. His eyes widened and his gaze flicked up. Shin smiled. "Ah, you do recognize them, then. I thought as much. This is your seal, I believe."

Enji shook his head. "No…"

"But it is," Shin said. He indicated the bills of import on Enji's desk. "I see it there."

"The- the cipher…"

"Oh, it took some time to decode, I admit. But, well, time is something I have an abundance of. It might interest you to know that I found these in the offices of a merchant named Saiga. Do you recognize the name?"

"N- no."

"How curious. I wonder how he came by these?"

"Stolen, I suspect," Enji said, in a hollow tone. "Where is he now?"

"Dead, sadly."

Another hesitation. Enji was surprised – more, he was frightened. "What?"

"Yes. He was murdered in his office."

Enji looked away, out the window. He was silent for a long moment. Shin could almost hear the mechanisms of his mind chewing away at the problem. He almost felt pity for the man. Enji was clearly clever, but not especially cunning. He was the sort of gray little man without whom the machinery of an empire would not run, but who would never truly enjoy the fruits of his labor. His honor was a brittle sort, and one misstep might see him reaching for a blade to open his belly.

Finally, he looked back at Shin. His gaze was almost forlorn. "Thank you for returning them," he said, softly. "I am in your debt."

"There is no debt. Though I would like to ask you a few questions, if I might."

Enji took a deep breath and nodded.

"You say this man, Saiga, must have stolen these… how might he have done so, and why? Though I am not a merchant myself, I did have one look over these documents, and he informed me that they were authorization forms for the sale of certain goods…"

Enji stood quickly. "Forgive me, I have just remembered an urgent appointment. I must cut our discussion short…"

Shin did not move. "These goods," he continued, remorselessly, "were stolen prior to being sold. Both the theft and the sale were seemingly done on your authority."

"A lie," Enji croaked.

Shin frowned. "Was that an accusation?"

Enji started, and shook his head. "No, no. Forgive me, my lord. It was – I believe you have made a mistake. Such documents might easily be forged by a clever criminal."

"And was Saiga a clever criminal?"

"I- I do not – as I said, I do not know him. Did not know him." Enji had no skill as a dissembler. Shin could read the lie in his eyes, in his body language. As Ito had said, he was stiff. A stickler, now being forced to face his mistakes.

"Why might such a man forge these documents?"

Enji swallowed. "Perhaps… perhaps he wished to implicate me in some wrongdoing." He was scrambling now, trying to find the lie that would save him.

"Do you have many enemies, then?"

Enji stiffened. "I – well, no." He laughed, softly. "Enemies are for the powerful and the important, are they not, my lord?"

"A man's quality is often judged by the number of people who want him dead," Shin said, coopting one of his grandfather's favorite sayings.

"Then my quality is lacking, for I am of no importance to anyone at all." Enji paused. "I am nothing and no one, save what I am. And that is all I will ever be."

"There is no room for advancement here, then?"

"Not for me, my lord." Enji straightened. "But I am content to serve. I am where the clan needs me most, and that is enough for any man."

"Yet, those who fail to achieve excellence can only fall to obscurity," Shin said. Another saying his grandfather was fond of.

Enji hesitated, and then nodded. "Yes," he said, in his thin voice. "That is it exactly, my lord." He shook himself and stood. "I apologize again. I do not believe I can help you any further, my lord."

"No, you have helped me quite enough," Shin said. He rose, but paused at the door. "One more thing, if I might…"

"Yes, my lord?"

"Are you a patron of the theater, by chance?"

"No. I do not think it fitting for a man of status to indulge in such useless entertainments."

"I thought you might say that," Shin said. He departed, feeling Enji's eyes on him the entire way. Kasami fell into step with him as he left the building.

"Well?"

"Not here," Shin said, softly. Kasami nodded.

He did not speak again until they'd reached their boat and were once more crossing the river. "It was him," he said, looking out over the water. Kasami glanced back the way they'd come. She reached for her sword, but Shin made a surreptitious gesture, stopping her.

"Are you certain?"

"No. But it was him even so." Shin frowned. "He became nervous when I mentioned Saiga – but he was startled when I told him the merchant was dead."

"He didn't know," Kasami said.

"It seems not." He looked at the sun and nodded to himself. "I think it is time we paid one last visit to the theater."

"Aren't they leaving today?"

"That is why it is the perfect time."

Chobei sat on the rooftop and studied the kabuki theater with a calculating eye. He frowned and shifted his weight ever so slightly. His body ached from holding his vigil for so long. Or maybe it was just age catching up with him. He flexed his hands, stretching the tendons and cracking his knuckles.

"She's in there," someone said from behind him. Chobei didn't turn.

"You've confirmed it?"

"One of the stage crew saw someone of her description backstage."

"You're certain the information can be trusted, Yui?"

The other shinobi shrugged. "You know what these people are like," she said. "He might have only told me what I wanted to know, hoping to get a few extra coins."

Chobei nodded. He did know. He had dealt with the worst the city had to offer often enough in his life. "That is a risk we will have to take," he said, after a moment. "If she is in there, she must be silenced."

"What if she escapes again?"

"She will not." Chobei turned. "What about the pirate?"

Yui's face was mostly hidden within her cowl, but her eyes narrowed. "The Crane has her stashed at his manor. Seka is keeping an eye on them."

"From a safe distance, I hope. Remember what happened to Kino and Riku."

"Hard to forget," Yui said.

Chobei grunted and turned back to the theater. He could feel the anger emanating from her. "You acted rashly, and your brothers paid with their lives. Choosing to fight a fully armored samurai is not something one should undertake, unless absolutely necessary. Not to mention that samurai's master…"

"I thought that by killing him–" she began.

Chobei cut her off. "You made a mistake. You took the initiative. That is not our path – we are blades in the hands of others. We do not wield ourselves." He didn't look at her as he spoke. "Kino and Riku paid the price for your foolishness. I would hope that you have learned your lesson."

"My apologies, Master."

"Do not apologize. Learn." He turned. She had her head bowed in an attitude of contrition. He nodded, pleased by this show of deference. Yui was not the first student to get her fellows killed in a moment of foolishness, nor would she be the last. Such was the nature of students. And all of them understood that a shinobi's ultimate lot was to die by the sword – whether wielded by an enemy, or their master. "Do you understand?"

"Yes, Master," Yui said, head still bowed.

Hearing her tone, Chobei snorted. "Sarcasm is also a choice not to be made lightly."

Yui settled back on her haunches. "What now?"

"We wait."

"Why not go in there after her?"

"Too many exits, too many places to hide." Chobei looked at her. "We wait until they leave, follow them home, and strike there."

"What if she doesn't go with them?"

"Then we will wait until she emerges."

Yui fell silent. They were not often employed to kill. Mostly, they were saboteurs and spies. Murder was something else again – there was more risk, for one thing. But it also brought more rewards. Saiga's death had been unfortunate, but necessary. He could have identified his partner, something Chobei's employer was desperate to prevent.

He wondered if Saiga had known what was coming. If he had known that his life, too, would be forfeit, even as he oversaw the elimination of the other loose ends. Chobei liked to think so. It pleased him to think of Saiga as something other than the reprobate he had presented himself as.

"Maybe we should just burn the place," Yui said, interrupting his train of thought. "Set it aflame, kill whoever comes out."

Chobei peered at her. "Our employer would be most unhappy with that." Not because of the loss of life, necessarily, but because of the attention it would draw.

"Maybe not. These sorts of places burn down all the time. Flea traps, the lot of them."

Chobei sighed. He wished it were simpler. Easier. Okuni had skirted death twice. He could not allow her to get away a third time. A shinobi's honor was not that of a samurai, but they had it nonetheless, and Chobei held his as sacred as any bushi. "No," he said. "We are not here to murder actors."

"She might have told them something."

"Would you?"

Yui hesitated. "She is not like us." There was disdain in her voice. Some of that was due to frustration. The rest – simple bias. Their quarry was of another school, and therefore not worth thinking about.

He fixed her with a steady look. "She is. That is why we show her this respect. Samurai might cut us down like dogs, but we are not dogs, and we have as much honor as they do, though it is a thing of shadows and smoke rather than steel. She will not have told them enough to warrant their deaths. So we will wait."

"And what about the Crane?"

Chobei was silent. In truth, it was a question he had no answer for. The Crane was outside their remit, unless their employer decided otherwise. Alone, the pirate was no danger. She had likely already told the Crane everything she knew. Otherwise he would not have found Saiga's body so quickly.

But the trail ended there, provided they could silence Okuni before she fled the city – or fell into the hands of the Crane.

Killing the Crane would be sensible. But he was bushi. Noble. His death would draw attention and not the sort their school could easily weather. Chobei wanted to avoid such an outcome, if at all possible. "We watch and wait," he said, finally.

"The deaths of my brothers demand restitution," Yui said, softly.

Chobei silenced her with a gesture.

"We watch and wait," he said again."And if it comes to it, we will strike quick and clean, Crane or no Crane."

CHAPTER THIRTY
Claws of the Cat

Sanemon looked out over the empty theater and sighed softly. One last check to make sure everything had been properly removed, and then he would join the others outside. He had hired several wagons to transport their props, costumes and backdrops to the wharf where their ship was waiting. There was only one thing left to do.

He started across the stage, taking it all in. He always felt a bit sad, leaving a theater. They became home so quickly. Or maybe that was just him. He approached the trap door set into the center of the stage and gave it a polite thump with his heel.

Somewhere below, Okuni would be waiting – impatiently, most likely. She was eager to be out of the city, and he didn't blame her. It wasn't the first time someone had tried to kill her, but it was the first time they'd come so close – and not once, but twice.

She would need time to heal. That meant they might not have to endure another episode like this for a good long while.

He hoped so. He was getting tired of fleeing with angry killers in pursuit. It did bad things to his digestion.

"Is the knocking the signal?" a mild voice asked.

Sanemon jolted, looking around in surprise. He thought he'd been alone in the theater. He spied a familiar figure standing just offstage, obviously pretending to study the backdrop. Sanemon, flustered, babbled inanely, but the intruder continued without missing a beat. "Hello, Master Sanemon. I thought I might visit and see if you had heard anything concerning the whereabouts of your missing actress."

"Ah – yes. About that…"

"I was concerned that I had not heard from you," Shin said, still looking at the backdrop. Sanemon felt like a mouse with his tail between the cat's claws. Escape was possible, but unlikely. "You can see why I might be, can't you?"

"Yes. Yes, of course."

"And?" Shin turned, fixing Sanemon with his cool, calculating gaze. The man had a gaze like water – placid one moment, raging the next. And all of it terribly calculated. That was the worst of it, Sanemon thought. Okuni was mercurial, sometimes arrogant. But this man was a better actor than most. His arrogance was a mask, hiding a sharp mind.

Sanemon defaulted to inane courtesies. "I am sorry, my lord. You must forgive me. Things have been ever so hectic of late – you understand, of course…"

"Indeed. Losing your lead actress must be quite a blow."

"Oh indeed, sir, indeed." Sanemon nodded quickly. "Sadly, we are preparing to depart this fine city – we must seek to put this tragedy behind us…"

"No doubt. And what of Okuni?"

"She – she is on her own," Sanemon said, scrambling for the words. "There is no need to trouble yourself on her account further. I thank you for your kindness in this matter, my lord. I – we – are unworthy of such consideration."

Shin stared at him. "This is… most unexpected," he said, finally. "And somewhat disheartening. It pains me to see you abandon a member of your troupe, Master Sanemon. Is there no charity in you?"

Sanemon looked away, feeling his gut clench. "I can afford none, my lord. A troupe lives or dies by its actors. If she cannot be counted on, she must be cut loose. Such are the hardships we face…"

"Did you know she was a shinobi?"

Sanemon froze. He had dreaded this question for as long as he had known Okuni. He'd known that someone, somewhere, was bound to ask it – and when they did, things would only get worse.

"I – what?" He tried to look innocent, but feared he was sweating too much. "No!"

"I fear you are lying. I can think of only two reasons that such might be the case, Master Sanemon. And that is because Okuni has turned up dead, which I would have heard about, or she has returned. Which is it?" He swept forward, eyes on the trapdoor. "Is she under there, perhaps? Listening to us?"

"My lord, I do not know what you are talking about."

Shin paused. "Your loyalty does you credit. But it is unfortunate in this instance. And it may well get you killed."

Sanemon frowned. "Is that a threat, my lord?"

"No. It is a warning. Even now, I believe that a number of shinobi are watching this theater. Waiting to strike the moment

Okuni sticks her head into the open. I assume she has thought of this – but even so, the risk will be great. Not just to her, but to the rest of you as well. You know this."

Sanemon looked away. He wondered how Shin knew they were being watched, but didn't question. He'd expected this day for some time. "If that is the case – we will handle it. We have been in tight spots before…" He paused, realizing what he'd just admitted. He cleared his throat and looked at Shin. "Thank you for your concern, my lord, but it is unnecessary."

Shin had not moved. Instead, he watched the stage, head slightly tilted. Sanemon realized that the other man wasn't listening to him – rather, he was listening to something else. "Do you hear that?" Shin said. "The scuff of soft footwear against wood. I heard a similar sound onboard a boat recently. Master Sanemon, I must apologize. I may have inadvertently provoked a reaction from someone…"

Sanemon's eyes widened as he heard the hiss of drawn steel. "Okuni – no!"

Sanemon's cry was all that saved Shin from a nasty end. He twisted aside as the curved blade cut the air where his head had been. He reached for his wakizashi, but found himself falling backwards as a foot connected solidly with his chest. He tumbled against the side of the stage and slid down, wheezing.

Okuni stepped lightly towards him before he could get to his feet, knives in her hands. She was shorter than he'd imagined, and moved with a dancer's grace. She was dressed simply in a dark tunic and trousers, her hair short. "I heard you were looking for me," she said, her blade a whisper's breadth from Shin's throat. "Why? Explain quickly."

Shin swallowed, and cursed himself for insisting that Kasami stay outside. He'd hoped to avoid any unpleasantness, and the presence of an armed samurai might be seen as a provocation. "Nekoma Okuni, I presume. At least I hope so."

"Okuni is my stage name."

"And your real one?"

"Okuni will do. Who are you? Why are you looking for me?" Her voice was ragged with exhaustion and pain. Shin could smell blood. She was hurt. The pale rose stain on her side told him where.

"I want to help you."

"Why?"

"I am a great admirer of the performing arts."

Okuni frowned. Her blade twitched, and he could feel the edge resting just against the hollow of his throat. "Wait, wait," Shin said, quickly. "I need you. I need what you know."

"The rice," she said.

"Exactly."

"I told you," Sanemon said. "I told you it was a bad idea!"

"Quiet, Sanemon," Okuni said. "Why do you care?"

"A man was murdered."

"Men are murdered every day."

"That does not make it right. That does not mean someone should not answer for those crimes." Shin made to rise, and she tensed. He stopped moving.

"And you will do that, will you?" She smiled, despite the obvious pain she was in.

"Someone must." Shin paused. "I can protect you, if you let me. I will protect you."

"And what must I do in return?" she asked, her expression

speculative. It wasn't clear whether she believed him or not, but he pressed ahead on the assumption that she did.

"Tell me all you know."

Okuni hesitated. Shin hoped she was weighing his words. It would be embarrassing to die here and now, so close to having all of the pieces at last. "About the rice?"

"About everything." Carefully, he reached up and pushed aside the edge of her blade as he stood. "I want to know who hired you. In return, I will give you sanctuary and see that you do not come to harm."

"A bit late for that," she said, with a pained grin. She stepped back.

"Further harm," he amended, without hesitation. "You may as well trust me. After all, what have you got to lose at this point?"

"You are a strange sort of Crane."

"I will take that as a compliment." As he spoke, he caught a flash of metal out of the corner of his eye. Acting on instinct, he lunged forward, whirling Okuni back against the wall and shielding her with his body. Something sharp thudded into the stage behind him – shuriken. Similar to those he had found in Three Duck Street.

Shin looked at Okuni. She was pale, eyes wide. He glanced down and saw that her blade had almost pierced his stomach – if she had not twisted aside at the last moment, his rash lunge would've ended quite badly. "You saved me," she said.

"And you spared me. We'll call it even. For now, however, it might be best if we departed." He turned and saw Sanemon staring at them in shock.

"What–?" he began.

"Run, Sanemon," Okuni barked. "Find the others and get out of here."

"What about you?" he demanded.

"They won't bother with you if they know I'm still here."

"A good theory," Shin said, as he straightened his clothes. He looked up towards the catwalks that ran above the stage. He could see something moving up there. Why weren't they attacking? What were they waiting for? "I would do as she says, Sanemon," he said, loudly. "And quickly."

"I won't leave without you," Sanemon said, ignoring Shin. "We can hide you in the wagons – on the boat…"

"They'll burn the wagons and sink the boats." Okuni looked at him, and Shin saw her face soften. Then her eyes flicked upwards, as his had done and he knew her words were as much for their unseen watchers as for Sanemon. "I'll catch up to you. And if I don't… consider finding a new lead actress."

Sanemon opened his mouth. Closed it. Then, without another word, he turned and ran offstage. Shin looked at Okuni. "Can you run?"

"If I must."

"You must. Come." Shin took her hand and started towards the exit. He could hear movement above them and around them. He wondered if they had been waiting for Sanemon to leave. Okuni pulled her hand free.

"No. This way." She gestured to the trapdoor.

"We'll be trapped down there."

She shook her head. "And you seemed so smart." She opened the trapdoor and dropped below the stage. With little choice, Shin followed. It was dark beneath the stage, and smelled faintly of earth. A labyrinth of paper walls stretched out around him. “Come on,” Okuni said. “Follow me.”

“It would be wise to get out of this place as fast as possible.”

“I would prefer to get out alive, myself.” She glanced at him, her face a pale oval in the gloom beneath the stage. “We need to give Sanemon time to escape. Then we will go out through the – wait.” She paused.

Shin sniffed the air. “Smoke. They’ve set the building on fire.” He looked up. “No wonder they didn’t pursue us. They just wanted to occupy us until they could set the theater ablaze.”

“They’re mad,” Okuni said, in disbelief.

“Or desperate. You are the last piece of the puzzle.” Shin looked around. “Tell me, can you access the city’s drainage tunnels from here?”

She frowned. “What?”

“Drainage tunnels. The stone culverts that drain off the excess water when the river floods, or carry it to the wells. Under the city.” He pointed down for emphasis.

“I know what they are,” she snapped, “and yes. Come. This way.” She turned and hurried away. Shin followed quickly. Soon, the smoke became visible, weaving in and out of the corridors. He could hear the crackle of flames from above, and the sound of paper walls crumbling in the heat. The smoke became so thick that Shin was forced to hold onto Okuni’s tunic and pray that she could find what she was looking for, for he could see nothing at all.

Finally, she brought him to a room of damp wood with a stone cistern at its heart. “Here,” she coughed. “They bring water up from here for the baths.”

Shin covered his mouth and his nose with his sleeve. “I suppose they also dump the waste here as well,” he wheezed, peering into the dark of the cistern with smoke-stung eyes.

"Feel free to burn to death," she said, as she climbed over the edge of the cistern and dropped down into the dark. Shin heard a splash a moment later, and judged the distance to be only a few feet. Awkwardly, he lowered himself into the cistern, nearly losing his grip on the slimy stones more than once. Finally, with a quiet prayer, he let go and dropped into the icy water. It slopped up around him, slapping against his belly.

The tunnel was not large. The wooden floor of the theater's lower levels stretched along a handbreadth above his head. The walls were made from irregular stone and the sloped floor was precariously narrow and slippery beneath his sandals. Yielding to practicality, he kicked his sandals off and followed Okuni on bare feet. The water moved slowly about them, swirling and splashing against the walls, but not so swiftly that it threatened to yank them off of their feet. "Where will this take us?" he asked.

"Not far. There's a well near here. I used to get back into the theater that way."

Shin caught her arm. "They might be waiting for us. In fact, I am certain they will be. The shuriken – the fire – it was all meant to herd you – to herd us – in a direction of their choosing. They wanted you to come this way."

She shook her arm free and looked at him. "There is no other option. I do not intend to stay here." She showed him her knife. "If they try to stop me, then I shall show them my claws."

Shin stared at her. Then, slowly, he smiled.

"Or, we could be clever about it. Your choice."

CHAPTER THIRTY-ONE
Last Piece of the Puzzle

Shin clambered out of the well, kimono dripping, and fell heavily onto the street. Coughing, he made to haul himself up – and stopped. The flat of a sword tapped him on the cheek. "Where is she?" a woman's voice asked.

"Who?" Shin replied.

The sword sliced across his cheek, and he hissed in pain. "Where is she?" the shinobi asked again. Shin looked up at her and touched his cheek.

"Do you know who I am?"

"A fool courting death."

"Besides that." Shin gave a thin smile. He recognized her now. She was the survivor from the ambush. No wonder she sounded annoyed. "I am Lord Daidoji Shin. I assume you've heard of me?"

The shinobi hesitated. Shin slowly pushed himself to his feet, and the shinobi backed away, as if uncertain as to how to proceed. Even as he had hoped. "I see that you have." He looked down at his kimono in disgust. It was ruined. "I wonder – has your employer given you instructions on how to deal with me?"

Something pricked him, just above the kidney. He froze. Behind him, someone chuckled. "Quite a gamble, my lord." The voice was mild, but held a hint of steel. "Then, I had heard that about you."

"I am flattered," Shin said. He turned. A second shinobi stood close behind him. A man, older, with one eye. He held a dagger in one hand. "And I suppose I must put the same question to you," Shin continued. "For if you kill me, your school may well follow me into death. The governor cannot allow such an act to go unpunished, and you know it."

The one-eyed shinobi nodded. "A pretty conundrum, my lord." His gaze flicked to the woman. "You see? I warned you. Mistakes double in weight."

The other shinobi hesitated, and Shin nodded. "Ah. I see." He decided to seize the opening. "Was the ambush another such mistake?"

Now it was the one-eyed man's turn to hesitate. Shin allowed himself a chuckle. "Yes. Good help is hard to find, isn't it?"

"Shut up," the woman began.

"Quiet." The one-eyed man leaned forward, and Shin was suddenly aware of the pressure on the knife. "What do you propose?" he asked.

"Let me go. Neither of us gains anything by my death." Shin gestured carelessly. "Take all the time you need. I am in no rush."

The one-eyed shinobi chuckled again and bowed his head. "Thank you, my lord. Very considerate of you." He fell silent for a few moments. Then he looked past Shin. "Go."

"But…" the woman began.

"He is right. Go. We cannot commit to such an act – not without permission. I will not compound your errors." The one-eyed man turned his gaze back to Shin. "Your gamble has paid off, my lord. But do not press your luck. Next time – step aside."

"I might say the same to you," Shin murmured, as the shinobi turned away. They were gone in moments. He touched his cheek and looked at the blood. "Bit of a close shave, that." He laughed weakly and looked down into the well. "You haven't drowned, have you?"

"No," Okuni said, weakly. "But I would like to get out now."

Shin leaned over and reached down a hand. Okuni caught it, and he hauled her up. As she leaned against him, coughing, he heard the sound of running feet and looked up to see Kasami and Kitano racing into the alleyway. "The theater…" Kasami began. She looked perturbed. Angry, even. Her face was pale, eyes wide.

"On fire, yes. Did everyone else get out?"

"I wasn't worrying about them." For a moment, Kasami looked as if she might punch him. But instead, she turned to Okuni. "Is this her?"

"I'm me," Okuni said. She pressed a hand to her side and bent nearly double. "I would like to sit down now, please."

"Not here, I'm afraid. Your playmates won't have gone far. We need to get somewhere safe." Shin looked at Kitano. "Help me with her. Kasami, keep an eye out. There're at least two shinobi prowling about, and probably more that I haven't seen."

"Shinobi?" Kitano said, eyes bulging.

"Shut up," Kasami said, without rancor. She gripped her sword. "Back to the house?"

"Where else?"

"Outside the city, for a start."

Shin shook his head. "The house is safe enough. Let's go."

It took them longer than he liked to return to the house. He could feel someone shadowing them the entire way. A black pall of smoke hung over the streets, and he could hear the sounds of rival fire-fighting gangs scuffling for the right to extinguish the blaze consuming the theater. There was no telling whether a winner would be recognized before the fire spread to the surrounding buildings.

Crowds began to fill the streets as they reached the front gate. People wanted to know what was going on. "Lock the gates, and the service entrance as well," he said.

"They can get over the walls. I know I could," Okuni said, as Kitano helped her up the garden path. Shin nodded.

"I doubt there is any way to stop them, if they wish to get in here."

"There's one way," Kasami said, flatly.

Shin didn't reply as he followed Kitano and Okuni up the stairs to his rooms. A moment later, there was a startled yelp and Shin nearly ran into them.

Lun stood before them. The flat tip of her knife rested against Okuni's breastbone. Shin nudged the blade aside. "No need for violence, all is well."

"Who's she?"

"Someone being hunted by the same people who want you dead," Shin said. He stooped and retrieved his biwa. Music might ease the tension.

"An injured pirate and an injured actress. You have quite the collection of wounded birds," Okuni said, a slight smile on her face. She stepped back, out of reach of Lun's knife.

"I'm not a pirate," Lun said, before Shin could reply. "I'm an honest trader."

"And when no one is looking?"

Lun smirked. "That's different, ain't it?"

Shin strummed his biwa, interrupting them. "Neither of you is entirely what you appear to be, but at the moment that is not important. You are both witnesses to a crime, and therefore important to my investigation."

Lun's good eye narrowed. "You look familiar."

"I doubt that," Okuni said.

"She poisoned the rice you delivered to the Lion," Kasami said, from the doorway.

"Why would you say that?" Shin sighed, as Lun's knife came back up.

"My apologies," Kasami said, obviously not meaning a word of it.

Shin pushed Lun's knife aside for a second time. She didn't resist, but he could tell that it was only because she'd considered it and thought better of it. "What's done is done. You both worked for the same man." He pointed at Lun. "He hired you to deliver a shipment of rice…" He swung his finger towards Okuni. "And you to poison said shipment."

The two women looked at one another, and then at him. "And you know this how?" Okuni asked. Lun frowned, but said nothing.

"I don't," Shin said. "I suspect, but I don't know for certain. Not until we identify him." He turned to Okuni. "And that means you need to tell me everything."

Okuni frowned. Then she sighed and sagged. Kitano grunted

as her weight settled against him. "She's bleeding," he said.

"Quickly, get her to the bed," Shin said. Between them, he and Kitano managed to get her lying down. He waved Kitano back and carefully rearranged Okuni's tunic to expose her wound. It had come unbound during their flight, and she'd torn a number of stitches. Shin cursed softly. Lun looked over his shoulder and then nudged Kitano.

"Fetch a needle and thread. And some hot water."

Shin looked at her. "You can sew wounds?"

"Learned when I was a soldier. Better to do it yourself than leave it up to some battlefield leech who might cut off the wrong bit." Kitano returned a few moments later, and Lun went to work. Shin hovered over her, watching with interest.

Okuni hissed and winced as Lun extracted the broken stitches and threaded in new ones. "If you want to – ah! – talk, now is the time," she said.

Shin pulled a stool over and sat. "You are a shinobi."

"That is obvious."

"Nekoma… you are of the Cat Clan."

"Also obvious."

"I know a little about the ways of your folk. A humble clan. Actors and acrobats. When they travel in troupes, they do so with kith and kin. And yet you are alone…"

Okuni was silent for a moment. Then, "Sometimes, we make our own family."

Shin accepted this with a nod. "You are a very good actress."

Okuni smiled. "And you are a discerning man."

"So I have been told," he said. "You were hired by Saiga to poison the rice shipment. How did you do it?"

"I stowed away, and slipped over the side when I was done."

Shin glanced back at Kasami, who still stood in the doorway. She shook her head and turned away. Satisfied, he turned back to Okuni. "Why did he want it poisoned?"

"I didn't ask."

Shin frowned. "Did you kill Saiga?"

Okuni hesitated. "He's dead?" She shook her head. "Of course he is. No. Though I might have, if I'd been given the opportunity. He's the reason I'm in this mess in the first place." She looked at him. "He's the one who hired me, you know."

"Yes. As I know that he was a vassal for one of the clans."

Okuni smirked. "Ah. Well, there I can be of help. I know who he worked with."

Shin gave her a sharp look. "Who?"

"What do I get out of it?"

"I did save your life," he said. She tossed her head.

"I could have saved myself, thank you."

"What about Sanemon and the others? Could you have saved them as well?"

She froze, just for an instant, and he knew that he'd struck a nerve. Though she might play the heartless shinobi, Okuni was anything but. One could not live and work with people for so long without growing to either love or hate them – or both. She bowed her head.

"You have my eternal gratitude for that," she said, softly, all trace of evasiveness gone. "Very well. Saiga was a vassal of the Dragon Clan. I know this because I made it my business to seek out his partner and blackmail him."

Shin blinked. "Why?"

"Saiga chose not to pay me." She shook her head. "Now, I begin to wonder if he was ordered to do so."

"By his partner?"

"No. By his master's master."

"Tonbo Kuma."

It was her turn to pause. "Yes." She peered at him suspiciously. "You already knew."

"I suspected. But it makes sense. Whoever hired you isn't the same person trying to kill you. Rather, I believe that whoever hired those other shinobi is looking to clean up the first conspirator's mess. We are not dealing with one conspiracy, but two." He peered at her. "This partner of Saiga's... was his name Tonbo Enji?"

Okuni nodded slowly. "Yes."

Shin sat back. "If I could bring him here, would you identify him?" He looked at Kasami. "Before myself and Kasami. That way we can vouch for it in court." While the word of a shinobi would not be accepted by a magistrate, the word of two high-ranking bushi would carry more than enough weight to see justice done.

Okuni frowned. "For a price."

"Name it."

"Protection."

"I thought that is what I was doing," Shin said.

"Not for me. For my troupe. They are innocent." Okuni smiled. "And – well – we are in need of a patron."

Shin stared at her. "My own... kabuki troupe?" Kasami made a strangled cough. Slowly, he smiled. "How delightful. But what will Sanemon say?"

"Whatever I tell him to say." Okuni winced as Lun finished up and began to re-wrap the bandage. Shin looked at the captain.

"Well?"

"She'll live, if she doesn't strain herself." Lun washed her hands in the hot water. "Can't speak for the rest of us, if you go through with this, though."

"I agree with the pirate," Kasami said. "You are testing fate at this point. Why not let the matter die, as Tetsua wishes?"

Shin paused. "Because there are some things that cannot be excused. People are dead. More may die, before the end." He looked at Kasami. "If you stood between me and an arrow, would you intercept it?"

"Yes, of course. That is my duty."

"And this is mine. I will not fail." He looked at Okuni. "Very well. I will take Sanemon and the others under my wing – provided you identify our conspirator."

Okuni sat back. "If you can get him here, I'll be happy to. He deserves nothing less than to be revealed for the petty fool he is."

"Easily accomplished," Shin said. "In fact, I've already made arrangements."

"Confident sort, aren't you?"

"With good reason. I had a servant carry a message to him before I confronted Sanemon at the theater. No doubt it will provoke some form of climactic reaction from Kuma and their shinobi associates, so we must be ready. But that is for tomorrow. For tonight, I wish to discuss more entertaining topics. And, perhaps, have a meal and a bath." He glanced down at his kimono in disgust, before turning his attentions back to Okuni. "Now, tell me more about this troupe of yours. How extensive is your catalogue of plays?"

Okuni blinked and looked at the others. "Our… plays?"

"Yes. Because I have some suggestions…"

CHAPTER THIRTY-TWO
Customs of Honor

As the morning light spread across the rooftops, Shin breakfasted on his balcony. Kasami stood behind him, looking out over the city. He could feel the tension in her body as he ate, but he didn't speak until he'd finished. "What's wrong?"

"Nothing."

He sighed and turned without rising. "That is clearly a lie. What is wrong?" That she hadn't slept was obvious. Neither had he, for that matter. "Do you still think my plan is foolish?"

"Obviously."

"But that isn't it, is it?" He peered at her. "You're angry about something else."

"I thought you were dead," Kasami said, after a moment. "I thought I had failed."

"I am not, and you didn't."

"But I might have." She looked at him. "Do you understand what that means?"

Shin did, and looked away without answering. A bodyguard

who failed in their duty was expected to take their own life in recompense. To erase the stain of their failure. It was something he'd rarely thought about. He'd never considered that Kasami might go through with it, even as part of him knew that she could not do otherwise.

Finally, he said, "I apologize. I should not have left you outside."

"No, you shouldn't have. And I shouldn't have let you leave me outside."

"Can we agree that we're both somewhat at fault, and leave it at that?"

Her eyes narrowed. "Fine. But never again."

He raised his hand in a mock-pledge. "I solemnly promise to never leave you behind again." He paused. "Unless absolutely necessary."

She grunted in satisfaction. Another moment passed, and she said, "And your plan is still foolish. Do you truly think that they won't follow him?"

"No. In fact, I am counting on it."

"That is why it is foolish." She tapped the hilt of her sword. "I do not like this. We have made ourselves bait in a trap."

"The alternative is to let them do as they will, and erase all evidence of their crime." Shin stood. "I will not allow that. That is not justice, but expedience."

"All this, because they killed a man unworthy of your concern?"

Shin looked at her. "They tried to kill Lun, as well. And Okuni. As they will undoubtedly try to kill our guest when he arrives." He scratched his chin and looked out over the city. "Saiga was not unworthy. I have made a thorough study of his papers. He knew that reporting Enji's foolishness to his masters would likely mean his own death. But he did it regardless. Out of loyalty. He did not deserve to die like a dog in order to spare the embarrassment of another. No man does."

"Pretty words, my lord," Lun said. She stood in the doorway, hair tousled from sleep and a bowl of rice in her hand. She spoke as she ate. "And ones I've never heard from a Crane before. I thought your sort thought embarrassment worse than death."

"And I thought your sort knew better than to speak so bluntly to your superior. Yet, here we are." Shin smiled. "I find I prefer it this way, don't you?"

Lun snorted and took another bite. "Someone's at the service entrance, by the way."

Shin looked at Kasami. "It seems he's punctual, as well as guilty. I'll meet him in the receiving room. Have Kitano prepare tea."

"It'll be awful."

"I doubt we'll get the chance to drink it, and he needs the practice." Shin smoothed his kimono. "Well, let's get to it, shall we?"

Tonbo Enji looked nervous. Bedraggled, even. His clothes were rumpled, as if he'd slept in them, and his hands clenched repeatedly on empty air. A guilty conscience perhaps. He bowed jerkily as Kasami showed him into Shin's receiving room. "My lord," he said, softly.

"Welcome. Sit. Please." Shin gestured to the seat opposite him. Enji sat. He made for a hunched, forlorn figure. A broken man. Shin realized that their earlier confrontation had done more than simply shaken Enji's resolve – it had undone him utterly. He felt a cold sort of pity for the little man, but more than that, he felt satisfaction. Here was the tip of the chain, at last. The mystery solved. "Tea?"

"No, thank you, my lord."

Shin poured himself a cup. "Are you certain? I find a good cup of tea is quite the restorative. Something you look to be in need of."

"Why did you invite me here?" Enji spoke hoarsely, without the barest hint of politesse. "Not for tea, I think."

"No. Not for tea." Shin paused. "You were lying, earlier."

Enji said nothing. Shin went on. "You claimed not to know the merchant, Saiga. In fact, you did know him – and quite well, I think."

"I did not lie," Enji said, softly. But he did not meet Shin's gaze.

"Another lie. You should stick to the truth, Tonbo Enji. You are bad at deception."

Enji flinched, as if he wanted to argue but had thought better of it. His hands gripped his knees like talons, the knuckles gone white. Shin did not relent. "Earlier, you implied Saiga must have stolen the documents I showed you. The ones he used to forge a bill of sale for the stolen Unicorn rice, so that the Lion could buy it without risk. You remember?"

Again, no reply. Shin had not expected one. "I wondered how he might have done so. A simple theft would have surely been reported. Someone must have given them to him. And since they bore your cipher, you were the obvious culprit. I then wondered why you might have done so. Blackmail was my first thought."

Enji looked up. "Yes. Yes, he blackmailed me. That is what happened."

Shin held up a warning finger. "That is your third and final lie. Unless you intend to speak the truth, remain silent." He took a sip of tea. "I have it on good authority that he did not blackmail you. Rather, it was you who involved him."

"And why would I have done that? How would I know such a man?"

"Because you were both loyal to the same masters – albeit at a substantial remove. Saiga was a spy, but not a mercenary – he was a vassal of the Dragon. And a loyal one, by all accounts. It took some effort, but I uncovered much of what he'd been up to of late – Saiga was well-placed to observe, and perhaps even control, the city's criminal element. Indeed, I believe that was his main function… rather than wait for such a figure to spring up, someone invented one. As to why, I can but guess – perhaps controlling the underworld keeps the city stable in some way. I suspect it has something to do with those curious shrines your kinsman stands sentinel over. In any event, it no longer matters. What does matter is that Saiga was loyal, and you played on that loyalty."

Enji hunched into himself, as if trying to shrink out of sight. Shin continued, remorselessly. "Like you, he might have felt unappreciated – unseen. Possibly you used that to rope him into your scheme. Whatever occurred between you, you managed to concoct a plan you hoped would throw the Dragon's rivals into open war."

Enji bowed his head and didn't reply. Shin was silent for a moment, and then pressed on. "And it might well have worked, if cooler heads hadn't prevailed. Tell me – what did you think would happen? Did you believe that Tetsua would stand idly by while his city tore itself apart?"

Enji's hands clenched. "Kuma…" he began, and then fell silent.

"Kuma. Of course. You thought Kuma's relationship with Tetsua would serve to hold the imperial authorities at bay while the Lion and the Unicorn savaged each other. Or maybe, even, that Tetsua would declare for the Dragon, and hand the city over to the Dragonfly in order to bring the chaos to an end."

"Is that so wrong?" Enji said, suddenly. He looked up. "The city is ours by right. It is our duty to guard this place. Our responsibility… ours…" He trailed off. "You don't understand. Even Saiga didn't understand."

"Then why did he help you?"

"Glory. He thought we would be rewarded for our efforts."

"And wouldn't you have been?"

Enji shook his head. "It was never about that. Not for me. I saw an opportunity – and I seized it. A chance to right an old wrong. If all had gone well, no one would even have known we were involved." His expression turned plaintive. "It would have been for the best. There's so much at stake…"

Shin leaned forward. "What is at stake? What do you know of it?"

Enji fell silent. Shin resisted the urge to give him a violent shake. Instead, he refilled his cup and waited. Now that he had been discovered, Enji wanted to unburden himself. Finally, Enji said, "I know only what Saiga told me."

"And what did he tell you?"

"This city, this place, it is important. Too important to leave in unworthy hands. And I believed him."

"Because you wanted to," Shin said, setting his cup down. "And together, you tried to start a war. Now he and many others are dead."

"I am not responsible for any of that!"

"Then who is?" Shin pinned him in place with a glare. "Who is trying to clean up your mess, Tonbo Enji?" He already knew the answer, but he wanted spoken confirmation. One beyond reproach. Proof – something he could take to Tetsua, or, at the very least, use to bargain with. "You'd best tell me quickly, else they might well come after you next."

Almost as if to prove his point, there was a soft thump from the hall. Shin held up a hand, silencing Enji. He stood. "Kasami?"

Silence.

Then the door slid open and a figure in gray stepped through. "Ah," Shin said. "I wondered if they might send you. A desperate gamble on their part."

"A sign of the matter's importance, my lord," the one-eyed shinobi said. "Will you stand aside this time? I humbly request that you give it a moment's consideration, at least."

Shin stood, putting himself between the newcomer and Enji. "Get up," he said, as he drew his wakizashi. Enji gawped for a moment, and then hurriedly stood. "When you see an opening, I want you to run. Don't stop. Don't look back. Just run."

"What – what is this?"

"They are here to kill you," Shin said.

The one-eyed man shrugged. "Him and anyone who tries to stop us. That includes you, my lord. One last time – will you step aside?"

Shin sighed. It wasn't quite the answer he had hoped for, but it was enough to convince Enji, who made a sound that might have been a moan low in his throat. "No, I'm afraid that I can't let you do that. I need him in one piece, you see."

Shin raised his sword. The one-eyed man was armed with a kodachi, and was likely quite skillful in its use. He wondered what had happened to Kasami and the others, but only for a moment – he could hear the ring of steel and knew she was otherwise occupied. There would be time to worry later, if he survived the next few moments.

"You came in force," he said, trying to buy a bit more time.

"It has been said that a samurai's home is his castle," the shinobi said. "I thought it best to bring an army." He looked around. "Where is she? I know you brought her here afterwards."

"Who?"

The shinobi's good eye narrowed. "It doesn't matter I suppose. So long as she is gone, our employer will be pleased. And if not, we will find her and kill her. But first…" The one-eyed man darted forward, kodachi held low.

As he did so, Shin heard Enji shout, and narrowly avoided a blow that might have split his skull. A second killer – the woman from the alleyway, he thought – had entered the room from the other door, and had used his distraction to creep close. Shin spun back, parrying the one-eyed man's thrust.

Out of the corner of his eye he saw Enji run for the door. The two shinobi were more concerned with Shin than with the escaping customs agent. Perhaps they had people waiting. Regardless, he couldn't worry about it now. Not when the trap was about to slam shut. "Any time, Okuni," he shouted.

The shinobi stepped back, eyes widening slightly. But to his credit, the assassin reacted swiftly, striking again, this time at Shin. Shin found himself driven back by his opponent's ferocity. As he fell back, he realized he would not be able to counter the next blow. Thankfully, someone was there to do it for him.

"Hello, Chobei," Okuni said as she lunged into view and parried the one-eyed man's blade. "You are most determined, I must commend you." She glanced at Shin as she went back-to-back with him, facing the other shinobi. "I heard everything. It was him."

"Of course it was. They wouldn't be here otherwise."

"That closet was very cramped, by the way."

"Is that why it took you so long to appear?"

"I like to make an entrance."

"Enough. This is not a stage." Chobei raised his sword. "I thought you might have fled. It would have been the wise thing to do."

"And miss this?" Okuni inclined her head. "I am afraid our dance ends here, however." She extended one of her knives. "If you depart now, I will not seek vengeance."

The other shinobi laughed. "You cannot seriously..." she began.

"Quiet," Chobei said. He kept his eye on Shin. "And what about your friend?"

"I have no interest in you," Shin said, quickly.

Chobei paused. Then, he gave another shrug. "Unfortunately, we have our reputation to consider. My apologies." He darted forward, more quickly than Shin expected. It was all he could do to parry the blow. Okuni had leapt to meet the other shinobi, and he quickly lost sight of them as Chobei occupied all of his attentions.

Shin was not a warrior by inclination or nature. But every Daidoji learned how to wield a blade from an early age. Shin found those lessons flooding back to him as he and the shinobi began to circle each other. Now that the advantage of surprise was gone, Chobei had decided to refrain from hacking at him. Instead, they faced one another across a sword's length. "You are skilled, my lord," Chobei said.

"As are you," Shin said. Chobei inclined his head. Shin studied him, noting his stance, the tension in his limbs. Time seemed to slow. He could hear nothing but the hammering of his own heart. He relaxed slightly, recalling his lessons. Recalling the words of his grandfather. Know the length of your steel.

When Chobei moved, Shin was ready. Steel rose in a spray of red. Chobei fell as Shin stepped past him, avoiding the blood that fell across the floor like rain. He paused, panting slightly as the buzz of adrenaline began to fade.

He turned and saw Okuni and her opponent watching him. "You… he…" Okuni began. Shin turned. Chobei lay gasping on the floor, clutching the stump of his wrist. His sword – and the hand that still gripped its hilt – lay some distance away. The shinobi looked up at him with pain-filled eyes.

"You had me," he said, flatly.

"I still have you." Shin lifted his sword and studied the bloody edge. "I have been responsible for the deaths of two of your number. I would not have any more lives on my head. Unlike some, I have no taste for it." He flicked Chobei's blood from his wakizashi and sheathed it. "I will give you your life, in return for mine – and the lives of those under my protection."

Chobei grunted and tore a strip from his tunic to fashion into a makeshift tourniquet. Shin did not offer to help. Chobei did not seem the sort to appreciate such a gesture. The shinobi glanced at his companion, and she hurried to his side to aid him in tying the bandage. Shin said nothing, aware of how much rested on his silence. Chobei could not be bullied. Shinobi had their own code, even if it wasn't one Shin was overly familiar with. So he waited. And hoped.

Kasami entered the room, and all eyes turned towards her. There was blood on her armor and face. None of it hers, from the look of it. If she was surprised by the sight that greeted her, she didn't show it. "Three of them tried to get in through the service entrance," she said, as if it were no more a concern than the weather.

"And?" Shin asked.

"I expressed my displeasure." She ran a handful of silk along her blade, freeing it of blood, and sheathed the weapon. "Two survived, one did not. There may be others. The servants are lighting lanterns."

"Lun and Kitano?"

"Both still alive," Kasami said. "I left the pirate in the gambler's care." She looked at Chobei for the first time. "Should I send someone for the magistrate – or the governor?"

"That is up to our guest." Shin turned back to Chobei. "I would guess that your cadre was not large. A dozen, maybe less. Am I right?"

Chobei said nothing. Shin went on, regardless. "Three dead, in as many days, is a blow both to your reputation and your capabilities. You are injured, and if I wish it, you will die here, as will your companion. What will happen then?"

Chobei glanced at his companion. Shin read something in his expression – fear, maybe, or worry. "I cannot cancel a contract once it is undertaken," Chobei began.

"Yes. But you can retreat. And give me a day to speak to the one who hired you."

"He is dead," the woman spat. "We killed him." She still looked ready for a fight, but Chobei wasn't. The older shinobi knew he was beaten. Shin just had to get him to admit it.

He decided to seize the opening he'd been given. "Saiga, you mean?"

Chobei nodded after a moment's hesitation, and something that might have been regret passed through his eyes. Shin nodded. "Then I will speak to his master. The one responsible for all of this. Give me a day. If I fail, feel free to return for another try."

Chobei laughed hoarsely as his companion helped him to his feet. "You have me at your mercy, but act as if I am the one with the advantage. How like a Crane."

Shin accepted the compliment with a nod, but said nothing. Chobei seemed to take his silence as some sign, and said, "Very well." His companion made to protest, but he silenced her with a shake of his head. "Would you make your child an orphan? We are leaving."

Kasami stepped aside to let them pass. Chobei stopped at the door and turned. His face was pale, and his mangled wrist was pressed tight to his chest. "I wish you luck, Crane. For both our sakes." Then he was gone. Even injured, he moved quietly. His companion followed more slowly, with several lingering looks.

"That one might be trouble," Okuni said.

"But that is for tomorrow. Today, we have other concerns." He took a deep breath. "It is time to face the cause of all of this. Let us pray they are in the mood to talk. Otherwise, we may well wish we'd let the shinobi kill us."

CHAPTER THIRTY-THREE
The Truth of Water

Shin stepped onto the dock of the shrine as Kitano tied the flatboat off. Kuma's guards were there to meet them, as he had expected. Kasami stepped forward, one hand on her sword. He waved her back. Neither had bothered to change, or cleanse themselves. A calculated insult – and a message. He studied them in silence.

The night was quiet, save the sound of the river and the distant bells of the boats making for their berths. "Expecting us?" Shin asked, finally. There were five of them, all in Dragonfly heraldry and all looking distinctly nervous. Then, if he'd been tasked with stopping a lunatic nobleman, covered in blood, he might be nervous as well.

The guards shared a look, and one cleared his throat. "You may not enter, my lord."

"And how are you going to stop me?" Shin asked, taking a step towards them. "Will you draw your swords and put yourselves in my path? Why? All I wish to do is speak to your master on a matter of great import to us both."

Another look passed between them. Kasami loosened her sword in its sheath. Shin gestured, and she subsided, if grudgingly. "Tell them I am here," he said, firmly. "Tell them now. I will wait here until you return. But I warn you, my patience is not limitless – and I do not intend to leave until I have spoken to them." He settled himself to wait as one of the guards vanished into the shrine. As he'd suspected, at least some of them were unblooded, otherwise they'd have never been allowed inside.

"You were right," Kasami said, before he could speak.

"Yes."

They stood in silence for a time, before she said, "Are you certain that this is the best course of action? They might decide to kill you themselves."

"Then I expect you will fulfil your duty and take vengeance on my behalf."

"They might kill me too."

"That is a risk I am willing to take," Shin said. He smiled as he felt Kasami's glare boring into him. "If it comes to it, shugenja die as easily as other men, or so I have been told. You might have less difficulty than you imagine."

"I'd rather not find out, if it's all the same to you."

Shin looked at her. "Neither would I, come to that."

After a few moments of silence, Kasami asked, "How long do you think they'll make us wait out here?"

As if in answer to her question, the guard returned. "Lord Kuma asks that you meet them down near the water's edge." He cleared his throat. "For obvious reasons, you cannot be allowed inside, my lord."

Shin looked at Kasami. "Wait here."

"I thought we weren't doing that any more."

He hesitated. "I said unless it was absolutely necessary. Which, in this case, it seems to be. So, wait here."

"What if you don't come back?"

"Then do as you see fit."

She eyed the guards speculatively and tapped the hilt of her sword. "Right."

Kuma was waiting for him down by the water's edge, where stone gave way to mud and roots. The shugenja looked as composed as ever, but there was a harried light in their eyes. The look they gave him was challenging. "I have always thought there is a truth in water," they said, as they crouched atop a curve of root. They were washing their hands with unhurried precision. "It washes away all falsehood, revealing what lies beneath. But it also protects. Keeping the lies at bay."

"Not in this case, I think."

Kuma frowned and stood. "You forget yourself."

"Or maybe it is you who forget yourself," Shin said. "So many deaths – why?"

"They were necessary."

"Another lie."

Kuma stared at him. Then looked out over the river. "What do you want here, Lord Shin?"

"Where is Tonbo Enji?"

Kuma hesitated. "Safe."

Shin nodded. After Enji had fled, Shin had deduced that there was only one place he could go – or would go. Had he gone to confess, or maybe to beg for his life? Either way, it would have had the same result. "You sent the shinobi to silence him because you could not do it yourself. Not because you lacked the courage to do so, but because you must remain pure in order to guard this place."

"Is that a question?"

"It is a theory. And one you do not seem in a rush to deny." Shin looked around. "Is he here, taking sanctuary?"

"No."

Shin nodded. "That is probably for the best." He straightened. Shin sighed. "Oh you have created a pretty problem for yourself here. You should really keep a closer eye on your subordinates. How did a mere scribe like Enji manage all this, right under your nose?"

That did it. Kuma's mask slipped for the first time. "There is no proof," they said, harshly. "Only the word of a shinobi."

Shin smiled. "Then why did you send someone to kill her?"

Kuma stiffened, just for an instant. But it was enough to tell Shin that he'd hit the target dead center. He gave the shugenja no time to recover their equilibrium. "At first, I thought it was simply Enji cleaning up after himself. But when I confronted him, he was startled. I knew then he wasn't responsible – at least not for that part of it."

Kuma stared at him. The air felt heavy and wet. Shin fancied that the sound of the river was louder than it had been, as if it were growing angry. Despite a sudden flicker of fear, he pressed on. "You must have figured it out not long after our first meeting. Perhaps even before then, eh? Perhaps you knew the entire time – maybe it was Saiga who told you, once Okuni blackmailed Enji. I wonder if he expected the reward you gave him."

Shin was speaking quickly now, his words practically tripping over one another. "Maybe you hoped to settle the matter before anyone realized what had happened. But then, complications – one after the next. The shinobi, the captain of the delivery vessel, Saiga… and then Enji himself."

"You are forgetting someone," Kuma said, softly.

"Yes. Myself." Shin paused, and then launched his next volley. "Shichiro is aware of your involvement."

Kuma paused. "How do you know this?"

"Does it matter?" Shin was speaking quickly now. "Shichiro knows."

Kuma blinked, clearly at a loss. Shin kept going. That was the Daidoji way – when in doubt, charge. "So, you see, not so simple now. You could kill me. There would be questions, but not many. But Shichiro is another matter. You stand on the edge of a precipice."

"And you intend to tip me over."

"On the contrary, I am offering you my hand. But first you must tell me what happened. All of it. I must know the truth if I am to help us both."

Kuma was silent for several moments. Then, with a sigh like falling rain, they said, "Saiga wrote to me, even as you said. He insisted that I speak with him. I could not risk meeting him here. Shichiro already suspected that Saiga was not the criminal he appeared to be. The old man is cannier than he lets on."

"It is a mistake to confuse crudity with stupidity, and one the enemies of the Unicorn often make, to their detriment."

Kuma nodded grudgingly. "I met with Saiga and he confessed to everything. And I knew then what the result would be, should it come to light."

"The Dragonfly might find themselves alone, against the Lion and the Unicorn."

"A fight we could not win, but could not afford to lose." Kuma gestured to the walls. "This place needs a guardian. Fate has chosen me. I could not risk losing control of these shrines."

"Which is almost certainly what would have happened. The Unicorn might not have raised the issue, but your presence here has never sat well with the Lion. They might have claimed these shrines as recompense, and brought in their own shugenja."

"Lesser shugenja," Kuma said.

Shin let it go. "So, you decided to act for the good of your clan. Saiga had ties to a school of mercenary shinobi in the city – the perfect tools for the job."

Kuma nodded again. "Yes. Though perhaps not so perfect in retrospect."

Shin allowed himself a smile. "They came close. But there were too many factors, too many complications. Okuni escaping not once but several times, Lun's survival… the kami were against you from the start."

"That is my fear." Kuma looked at the paintings on the walls. "There are more shinobi. The contract still stands. They will come for you again and again, until they are all dead – or you are."

"It might be simpler to kill me now."

"I considered it." The way Kuma said it sent a chill through Shin. "I thought about asking the spirits of the river to drown you as you made your way here. To pull you under and send your bodies far downstream, where none would ever discover them." Kuma gestured. "I could do so even now. You stand but a hairsbreadth from the water, and it would be so easy to simply… wash you away."

"But you thought better of it, clearly."

"I cannot shed blood. Not with these hands. To invoke the kami for such a deed would be the same as thrusting a sword into your belly."

"But hiring shinobi was allowed, was it?"

"Saiga hired them."

"And I suppose he allowed them to kill him as well? How considerate of him." Shin saw the expression on Kuma's face and knew he'd scored another point. "That is what he did, isn't it? I suspect he was well aware of the possibility, at least…"

"He was loyal to the Dragon. If he had been caught, he might well have been forced to spill his secrets. There was only one option." Kuma looked away. "I argued against it."

"But not too forcefully, I imagine."

"No. We both knew it was the only way."

Shin restrained a sudden urge to strike the shugenja. It would solve nothing. Kuma was convinced of their righteousness, and Shin could not say they were wrong. Instead, he said, "And for a few moments, it was enough. Saiga was the perfect scapegoat. A known criminal, with no known connection to any clan."

"Yes," Kuma said. Shin felt the air quiver about him, and the stink of the river bottom was suddenly thick in his nose. He tensed. "Why could you not just leave it be? I gave you a chance, Crane…"

"No. You gave yourself away. And maybe intentionally."

Kuma jolted, as if struck. Shin decided to press his advantage while he had it. "You felt guilt – remorse for what you'd engineered, even as you saw the necessity. You wanted me to find out. To uncover the truth, even as Tetsua did. Even as poor, misguided Enji did, when he came to you to confess." Shin could see that his words had pierced Kuma's composure at last. The shugenja had a weakness after all, and had willingly revealed it.

"What was it you said earlier, about water and truth?" Shin continued. "You wanted me to wash away the lies. To cleanse you of your sin. But I can't absolve you, Tonbo Kuma. I am as imperfect a vessel as you are."

Kuma was silent for a long moment. Then, they sighed, softly. "Yes." As they spoke, the pressure in the air lessened and the presence of the river seemed to retreat. Shin relaxed and released a breath he hadn't realized he'd been holding. "But the matter is settled, whatever my feelings on it. Or yours."

"No. It is not. As I said, Shichiro knows."

"What does he know? Nothing."

"He knows enough. And he is ambitious in the way of all patriarchs, eager to cement his legacy in blood – spilled or mingled."

Kuma frowned, not following the logic. "I don't…" Then, the light of understanding filled their eyes. "Konomi."

"Yes. Shichiro hid what he knew because he did not want war. But now that the threat of violence has receded, he will use that information to get what he wants. You were so worried about the obvious threat of the Lion that you ignored a subtler one. Shichiro will tell Tetsua, likely in the next few days. Tetsua will have a choice – accede to Shichiro's demands, or risk yet more upheaval."

"And all that we have sacrificed for will be undone, because of one old man's stubborn refusal to see the obvious."

Shin could hear the bitterness in the shugenja's words and

he shook his head. "You think you are the only one with a duty to their clan? Minami was willing to go to war for hers, even at the risk of imperial censure. You were willing to abet murder for yours. Why, then, should Shichiro be any different?" Shin chuckled. "Enji was more accurate than he knew. He created an opportunity. He simply did not foresee that others would take advantage of it. A failure of logic. Or perhaps a misunderstanding of human nature."

Kuma looked at him. "And you? You understand human nature, do you?"

"Better than most. Enough to see the solution. I expect it has already occurred to you." He paused. "And to Enji."

Kuma stiffened. "Has there not been enough death?"

"A funny question, coming from you." Shin sighed. "But no – one more should do it." He spoke flatly, the words bitter in his mouth. He felt sick, but he met Kuma's dark gaze and they looked away first.

"He is loyal," they said. "What he did, he did out of loyalty."

"So did Saiga."

"Even so, it is a heavy price you ask."

"Is it?" Shin gave a sour chuckle. "We would not be having this conversation if you had not already considered this very option. It is the only door that does not hide a hungry tiger." He bowed his head. "Enji will no doubt agree, given that it was his foolishness that started this whole affair."

"And then what?"

"And then we make a gift of it to Tetsua. We will say that you had no part in the affair and were, in fact, conducting your own investigation. That is why you visited Saiga. Tetsua will know that it is not the whole story, but it will be one he can accept. Saiga is still the mastermind, but Enji will share responsibility."

"What of the others?"

Shin looked at them. "Captain Lun is under my protection henceforth. Should she come to harm, I will take it amiss. The same goes for Okuni and her troupe. As far as they are concerned, the matter is settled. And that is where we will leave it."

Kuma smiled, but it did not reach their eyes. "You truly are an Iron Crane, Daidoji Shin." They bowed deeply. "I will cancel the contract."

"You have my thanks, my lord."

As Kuma straightened, they said, "There is, of course, something you have not considered."

Shin, wary now, said, "Oh?"

Kuma paused. "Enji is not an imaginative man, you know. Even as a boy, he was clever, but not cunning." They looked at Shin. "If he conceived of such a stratagem, I am certain that he did not do so alone – or of his own initiative. Do you understand?"

Shin did, and the thought was not a pleasant one. If Saiga had not been the one to suggest it, as Enji had said, then – who had? Kuma studied him for a moment, and then shrugged. "But sadly, by the time you seek to put that question to him, Enji will no longer be able to answer any questions you might have. He will have acted as honor dictated, and committed the ultimate act of repentance."

"Something this hypothetical partner would know," Shin said. Kuma smiled.

"Yes. And expect."

Shin nodded slowly, digesting this. "What do you intend to do about it?"

Kuma shrugged. "I will do as I have always done." They smiled. "And you, I expect, will do as you have done. Such is the will of the gods."

CHAPTER THIRTY-FOUR
Resolutions

After that, all that was left was the waiting.

Two days after his last confrontation with Kuma, Shin sat on his balcony, his biwa on his lap. Life in the city had resumed its normal rhythms as the tensions – so close to boiling over – abated. River birds circled overhead, their shrill cries mingling with those of the merchants and sailors on the nearby wharfs.

"You are tense," Kasami said from behind him.

"Not tense. Prepared." Shin plucked half-heartedly at his biwa and looked up, watching the birds. "Shichiro will be making his move soon. I must be ready to depart at a moment's notice, if I am to hold up my end of the bargain …"

Kasami gave a grunt of disapproval. Shin paused and looked at her. "Yes?"

"So that's it then? Kuma just goes on, without any sort of punishment?"

"And what sort of punishment would you inflict? What is justice, in this case?" Shin shook his head. "There is nothing to connect them to the death of Saiga, or the rice. Just a supposition on my part – with no proof nothing can be done." If it came to it, Kuma's testimony would carry far more weight than that of either Lun or Okuni – perhaps even himself, come to that. Such was the nature of justice.

Kasami nodded reluctantly. "They tried to kill us."

"No. The killers they hired to eliminate witnesses tried to kill us. Kuma did not order it, nor did they condone it. Or so I hope."

"They didn't stop it either."

"No." Shin looked up. Birds swooped and danced, chasing one another through the sky. "They did apologize, if it helps."

"It doesn't." Kasami frowned. "All that effort, and for what?"

"We stopped a war," Shin said. "Surely that's enough for you?"

She looked at him speculatively. "And what about you?"

"Meaning what?"

"These last few days you have seemed more alive than ever I can recall," she said. "You have thought about something other than wasting money or lazing about." She frowned thoughtfully. "It was … good."

Shin nodded. "It was, wasn't it?" He scratched his chin. "A worthy exercise of my myriad talents. It was more entertaining than overseeing merchants, at any rate."

"Yes," she said, if somewhat grudgingly he thought.

"Still, it is done now. And such opportunities do not come around with any regularity." He paused. A slow smile crept across his features. "Then again, perhaps it's simply a matter of knowing where to look."

"What about the others?" Kasami asked, interrupting his idle speculation.

Shin sat back. "Is this about Kitano? I told you – he's staying here. He seems happy enough with our arrangement." It was obvious that the gambler would never be a proper house servant, but Shin already had three of those. Kitano had skills other than making tea, and Shin intended to make full use of them in the future.

"No. I have resigned myself to his presence. I meant the others."

"Ah." Shin looked away. Okuni had been gone before dawn. Her troupe had already left the city. He suspected that she'd gone to meet them, and perhaps inform them that they had a new patron. He'd already begun outlining plans to rebuild the theater Chobei and his shinobi had burned. Something grand, he thought. A true monument to art. He smiled at the thought and said, "I have no doubt Okuni intends to make herself hard to find until this blows over. Though I'm certain we haven't heard the last of them."

"Especially since you're now funding their tour."

Shin ignored the disapproval in her tone. "Everyone needs a hobby."

"What about the pirate?"

"Yes, what about me?" Lun asked, from behind them. She leaned against the doorframe, eating a piece of fruit. "Going to clap me in irons? Turn me over to the governor?"

Shin turned. Lun was looking somewhat better for a few days' rest. She wasn't fully healed, but she was in one piece. "No," he said. "You are free to go. The Lion have no idea who you are, and the Dragonfly are no longer interested in you."

"And where am I supposed to go?" Lun asked, still focused on her fruit. "I've got no ship, no crew and no prospects."

"About that," Shin said. "I wrote to my grandfather earlier, explaining the situation. Not in depth, but the pertinent details … at any rate, I requested that you be offered a patronage. The Crane can always use a good captain, and our operations in this city are long overdue for expansion, in my opinion."

Lun stared at him. Then, she nodded. "Least you could do."

"Indeed, my words exactly." Shin smiled. "Your ship is where you left it, and I have no doubt you can find your crew in time."

"Maybe," she said.

"Excellent. You accept then?"

"I'll think about it." Lun straightened and tossed the rest of her fruit to Kasami, who caught it instinctively. "I'll let you know what I decide." She turned and left. Shin didn't try to stop her. He looked at Kasami, who was wiping her hands on her armor.

"I like her," he said.

"You would."

"It's the eyepatch. Rather rakish, I think."

Kasami looked at him. "Stop."

"Makes her look like a pirate."

"Stop, please." She frowned. "And she is a pirate."

"Allegedly." Shin turned back to the city. "One never knows when one might require the services of such a person. Especially in matters of trade." He paused as Kitano appeared in the doorway. "Yes, Kitano?"

"A message, my lord," the gambler said, diffidently. Kasami took it from him and passed it to Shin, who unfolded it – and shot to his feet, startling both of them.

"It is time," he said, excitedly. "Shichiro is making his move! Come on!"

"Where?" Kasami asked, hurrying after him.

"Where else? Saibanshoki!"

Compared to his recent trips, it seemed to take forever to reach Saibanshoki this time. The whole way, he silently went over what he knew, and how the situation might unfold. His plan rested wholly on the stubbornness of one old man, and he prayed Shichiro was as determined as he suspected.

Kaeru Azuma was waiting for him on the docks when he arrived. "I worried you might not come," Azuma said, helping him out of the boat. "I received Kuma's letter yesterday."

"Good. You read it?" Shin gestured for Kitano to stay with the boat. Kasami followed him and Azuma in silence.

"I did. It is the truth?"

"Insofar as I can determine."

"Why did you not let me tell Tetsua immediately?" Azuma asked, as they hurried up the steps. "We could have headed this moment off, and–"

"Saved Shichiro some embarrassment?" Shin interjected. "Why? The best way to counter an opponent is to let them overextend themselves. And that is what we are doing."

At the top of the landing, two Kaeru samurai and a quintet of Unicorn ashigaru stood in tense harmony. The Kaeru bowed as Azuma appeared, and the Unicorn shuffled nervously, uncertain as to what to make of the newcomers – especially Kasami, who took up position across from them, her face a hardened mask. None of them protested as Azuma led Shin into the manor's receiving room.

Shichiro and Tetsua turned as they entered. The two men stood not quite face-to-face, tension evident in their postures.

Shin wasn't surprised that Shichiro had managed to provoke Tetsua, but he was somewhat annoyed that the old man had chosen to do so.

"What are you doing here, little Crane?" Shichiro asked.

"I might put the same question to you, Lord Shichiro," Shin said. "Perhaps you are informing the governor of what your spies saw that night in Three Finger Street? Or perhaps what they saw a few days before that, even?"

"Are you accusing me of something?" Shichiro asked, after a moment's hesitation.

"Regrettably, I must."

"Azuma, what is the meaning of this?" Tetsua asked, before Shichiro could reply. Shin could hear the hope in his voice. Azuma was about to reply when Shichiro cut him off.

"Indeed. I was promised a private audience."

Shin nodded. "I imagine you were, given what you know."

Shichiro frowned. "That is the second time you have made that vague accusation. What are you talking about?"

"Yes, please explain," Tetsua said. Shichiro frowned, as if realizing that he'd possibly miscalculated. Shin bowed and cleared his throat.

"Gladly, my lord. It is simply thus – I have solved the mystery of the poison rice shipment."

"It was already solved," Shichiro growled. "It was that merchant, Saiga."

"Yes – and no," Shin said. "If you will let me continue?"

"I insist," Tetsua said, with a warning glance at Shichiro. "Was Saiga innocent?"

"No, my lord. But he did not act alone. Others were involved."

"Yes, even as I have said," Shichiro interjected. He gave Shin a triumphant look. "The Crane will no doubt back my statement, Tetsua."

"It was Kuma, then." Tetsua's voice had a hollow quality to it.

Shin shook his head. "No, they were not the instigator, if that is what you are asking." Shin took a deep breath. "The scheme was concocted by a minor functionary, named Enji, who saw an opportunity for advancement. Through Saiga, this individual sold the Lion a shipment of rice, hired a crew to deliver it, and a shinobi to poison it in transit."

"And then?" Tetsua glanced at Shichiro, who was frowning. "There is more to the story than that, I think."

"From the moment my investigation began, I felt I was being watched. My every move was shadowed. Someone was conducting their own investigation off the back of mine."

"Kuma," Tetsua said.

"Yes, though we would be hard pressed to find proof." Shin smiled, but there was no mirth to it. The lie stuck in his craw, but there was nothing for it. What was one more falsehood, after all? "The shugenja is adept at covering their tracks. I must admit, they put it together first, though they had the advantage, I think. They recognized the pieces for what they were, whereas I had to figure them out for myself."

"Yes, yes, you were very clever," Shichiro said, impatiently.

He subsided at a look from Tetsua. The governor motioned apologetically. "Continue, please, Lord Shin."

Shin nodded. "Kuma was working from the opposite end of the problem. They knew the perpetrator, and knew that their actions – whatever the reason behind them – would bring shame upon the Dragonfly, and perhaps the Dragon. There's an old saying, 'feeding a lion raw meat only makes it hungrier.'"

"A Crane saying?"

"I'm happy to claim it on our behalf," Shin said. "Kuma decided to clean up after their subordinate, but knew that to use clan resources to do so would leave a trail. To that end, they hired a group of mercenary shinobi to deal with any potential links between the Dragonfly and the poison rice."

Tetsua made a sound that might have been a sigh, or a groan. Shin pretended not to notice. Tetsua's dismay was understandable and, in his opinion, forgivable. Shin continued. "I managed to intercept these assassins on two occasions, nearly losing my life both times. But I managed to preserve the life – and testimony – of two witnesses, both of whom are willing to attest to the identity of the individual who hired them."

"These witnesses – who are they?" Shichiro demanded.

"The captain of the vessel that delivered the rice, and the shinobi who poisoned it."

Tetsua's intake of breath was audible. Shin paused. Now they had come to it – would Tetsua use his influence to finish what Kuma had started, and ensure their names were free of any possible shame? If Tetsua demanded their names, or to take custody of them, Shin would have no recourse. He could stall, but not for long. And if Okuni and Lun were taken into custody, their chances of survival would drop precipitously. He waited for Tetsua to come to a decision, careful to keep the anxiety he felt hidden.

Finally, Tetsua relaxed. "And have they confirmed your theory?"

"Yes."

Another pause. "You realize that their testimony will be worthless in court."

"Unless I am greatly mistaken, my lord, this will not go to court." Shin looked at Shichiro. "No doubt Lord Shichiro has come with tales of Kuma's involvement in the plot. What he has failed to mention is that he has no proof, save the accounts of his own men. Men who would gladly lie for their lord."

"Careful, little Crane," Shichiro said, warningly.

"It is you who should be careful, my lord. You walk a thin ledge." Shin gazed at him steadily. "You knew Kuma was involved, but it suited you to say nothing."

Shichiro frowned but did not argue. Shin pressed on. "I believe that you did this out of a misguided desire to protect your daughter's intended. You told me yourself that you believed the engagement to still be on – though Konomi believes otherwise."

"You spoke to her?" Shichiro demanded. "Without my permission?"

Shin nodded. "And I apologize for doing so. But by hiding what you knew, you immediately cast suspicion on yourself. You obviously trusted that Tetsua would do the pragmatic thing and rule the matter closed."

"Which I did," Tetsua said.

"And yet here he is, flapping his wings," Shichiro growled.

"Unofficially, I assure you. What I am about to say will not leave this room." Shin looked at Tetsua. "In a way, Lord Shichiro is to be commended. It is he who set me on the right track, however unintentionally." Shin bowed to the old man, eliciting another growl of anger. He smiled and continued.

"Of course, if Kuma refused, you could always use the information to your advantage in other ways. Such a revelation would no doubt stoke the fires of the Lion's rage anew. And this time, Minami would likely not be able to rein her followers in. The Lion would lash out at the Dragonfly, and the Unicorn would be there to aid them – provided Tonbo Kuma agreed to marry your daughter, Konomi." Shin looked at Tetsua. "Conversely, it is possible that you decided that she might have better prospects than a humble shugenja…"

"I did no such thing," Shichiro burst out. "To Kuma she is promised, and it is Kuma she shall marry! I merely came here to ensure that the agreement would be enforced." He faltered, realizing that he'd been shouting. He looked away.

Shin shook his head. "Trusting in alliances built on blackmail is rather like riding an unbroken horse. The question isn't if the beast will throw you – but when."

Shichiro frowned and looked at Tetsua. He made to speak, but the governor silenced him with a gesture. "If what you say is true, Lord Shin, then it seems that I have little choice. For the good of the city, I must acquiesce."

"I think not." Shin motioned to Azuma, who produced Kuma's letter. "Earlier today, Tonbo Kuma sent Azuma a letter detailing his investigation into Enji's activities. That investigation is what took him to Saiga's place of business – not anything illicit. In fact, it was Enji who was working with Saiga."

"And where is this Enji now?" Shichiro asked.

"Dead," Azuma said. "He confessed his crimes to Lord Kuma and committed ritual disembowelment early this morning. Upon witnessing the act, Kuma immediately wrote the letter and sent it to me."

"A likely story," Shichiro said.

Shin nodded. "But a true one, as Kuma, Azuma and I will all attest to."

Shichiro grunted and looked at Tetsua. "My word against theirs. Not good odds, I admit." He sighed and shook his head. "Very well. I am no Lion, to batter myself against an impregnable gate. I know when to sound a tactical withdrawal." He looked at Shin. "Very clever, little Crane. There's something of your grandfather in you after all." He paused. "So, what now? Pretend it never happened?"

"That is up to you both," Shin said. "Kuma's actions were those of any samurai faced with such a situation. It is their duty to defend the shrines from all threats. Enji's actions, however well-intentioned, would have opened the Dragonfly up to reprisal – perhaps even censure." As he spoke, both Shichiro and Tetsua nodded. They both understood, even as Shin himself did. That did not mean they had to like it.

"I believe," he went on, "that Kuma regrets what they have been forced to do. It does not make up for the lives lost, but further censure is unnecessary. And it might well make the Lion suspicious. As far as they are concerned, the matter is settled."

"And so it is," Tetsua said, with the air of a proclamation. Shichiro and Shin both bowed. "What has been spoken of here will not leave this room. It is forgotten. Is that clear?"

"As crystal, my lord," Shin said. He glanced at Shichiro. "For what it's worth, Konomi seems to have no desire to actually marry Kuma. Nor do they appear to have any interest in her. I should think about seeking a more suitable match for her going forward."

Shichiro nodded reluctantly. "I will consider your words." He gave Shin a calculating look. "You're not married are you, little Crane?"

"Enough," Tetsua said. "Lord Shichiro, if you would please

leave us … ? Azuma, show him out. I would like to talk to Lord Shin alone."

Shichiro bowed and left the room without complaint, Azuma following. Shin relaxed. Whatever else, the old man took defeat gracefully. "My thanks, my lord."

Tetsua made a gesture of dismissal. "You have already spoken to Kuma then." It was not a question.

"Yes."

"And?" Tetsua asked, softly.

Shin hesitated. How to explain? Even he wasn't sure what Kuma intended to do. He cleared his throat. "We crossed swords, if only figuratively, and decided there was nothing to be gained by continuing the duel."

"Ah." Tetsua nodded in understanding. "Good. Then the matter is truly settled." His face might have been a wooden mask. "You have my thanks for your efforts, Daidoji Shin. I will not soon forget what you have done for me – and for the city."

Shin bowed. "I am at your service, now and always, Governor Tetsua."

Tetsua cracked a small smile. "That is good to hear. But let us hope that I do not have reason to ever call upon your particular talents again."

Shin laughed. "Yes. I can only imagine how my reputation would suffer!" Having been dismissed, he turned to go, but Tetsua stopped him with a gesture.

"Your grandfather would be proud, I think."

Shin nodded. "Perhaps. Even so, let's keep it between us, shall we?"

Outside, Kasami fell into step beside him as he went down the steps back towards the waiting boat. "Well?"

"Well what?"

"Did it work?"

"Did you doubt that it would?"

Kasami snorted in derision. Shin decided to overlook it. "It worked. Shichiro is placated, Kuma's reputation is safe and Enji is…"

"Dead," Kasami said, softly.

Shin nodded. He stopped at the bottom of the steps and looked out over the water. "Toscho many people are dead because of this foolishness. But more would have died if we hadn't intervened. Small comfort, but comfort nonetheless."

Kasami bowed her head. "Of course. What now?"

"Now?" Shin smiled. "I've heard that there's a new kabuki troupe in town. They're supposed to be quite good. I was thinking we might take in a performance, check out the competition, that sort of thing."

Kasami stifled a groan and Shin laughed.

"And after that, well, who knows where the day might take us?"

DAIDOJI SHIN WILL RETURN
IN

Death's Kiss

CHARACTERS IN ORDER OF APPEARANCE

Daidoji Shin	*Crane nobleman*
Hiramori Kasami	*Crane yojimbo in service to Daidoji Shin*
Kitano Daichi	*Gambler*
Lun	*Free captain and occasional pirate*
Torun	*Lun's bosun*
Saiga Eito	*Merchant and spy in service to a secret master*
Wada Sanemon	*Master of the Three Flower Kabuki Troupe*
Nao	*Actor of the Three Flower Kabuki Troupe and annoyance*
Nekoma Okuni	*Actress of the Three Flower Kabuki Troupe and shinobi*
Kaeru Azuma	*Ronin and advisor to the governor*
Miya Tetsua	*Governor and Go enthusiast*
Ito	*Merchant and Crane vassal*
Chobei	*Shinobi*
Akodo Minami	*Lion representative*
Yui	*Shinobi of Chobei's cadre*
Iuchi Shichiro	*Unicorn representative*
Iuchi Konomi	*Daughter of Iuchi Shichiro*
Tonbo Kuma	*Dragonfly representative and shugenja*
Tonbo Enji	*Tariff agent*

ABOUT THE AUTHOR

JOSH REYNOLDS is a writer, editor and semi-professional monster movie enthusiast. He has been a professional author since 2007, writing over thirty novels and numerous short stories, including *Arkham Horror, Warhammer: Age of Sigmar, Warhammer 40,000,* and the occasional audio script. He grew up in South Carolina and now lives in Sheffield, UK.

joshuamreynolds.co.uk
twitter.com/jmreynolds

Explore the Emerald Empire

The mountainous border dividing the empire of Rokugan from the dark Shadowlands is perilous. Discovering a mythical city amid the blizzard-swept peaks offers heroes an opportunity to prove their honor, but risks exposing the empire to demonic invasion.

Chaos has broken out in the isolated Dragon Clan settlement of Seibo Mura. During the full moon, horrifying creatures rampage through the village, unleashing havoc and death, but it will take more than one clan to resolve this lethal supernatural mystery.